About the Author

Nina Whyle is a writing [illegible] ina
Bowden and Clare Whyl [illegible] ub-
lish their first book tog [illegible] oon
became a bestseller, reac [illegible] rts,
and in the following years [illegible] oes
Pop! were also published. My DisOrganised Life is their fourth book together, published under the dynamic wings of So Vain Books. Nina lives in Devon and Clare lives in Berkshire, but they used to write via London to Copenhagen, where a lot of their inspiration came from the city buzz. Now they enjoy putting those stories together in a calmer setting of the countryside.

Visit the website: www.ninawhyle.blogspot.co.uk

My ~~Dis~~Organised Life

Sometimes things have to go really wrong
before they can go right!

Nina Whyle

It's a So Vain Book

Published in Great Britain in 2015 by:
SO VAIN BOOKS Ltd
75 London Road
Oxford OX3 9BB

www.sovainbooks.co.uk
Email: info@sovainbooks.co.uk

A catalogue record from this book is available from the British Library

ISBN: 978-1-910869-09-3

Printed and Bound in Great Britain by PrintOnDemand, Worldwide

FSC
www.fsc.org
MIX
Paper from responsible sources
FSC® C004959

To the women in our lives who have been with us through the highs and lows. You are the best, the sun in our universe. Thank you all.

Foolish and slightly dangerous not to mention our phenomenal mothers, who inspired us to always dream big.

To Jessica,

Love you lots

enjoy the read.

xx

Glazomania: a passion for listmaking

Death by Tequila

Prologue

Two years ago my life was unravelling at the speed of a hopeless homemade jumper.

No. Worse. It had shredded all over the floor in one giant frayed ball of yarn, and I was sat in the middle of it, vomit-stained, violently shaking, and a headache that felt like a faulty ticking bomb on a thunderous loop.

But making a monumental spectacle of oneself at least once in your life is a rite of passage, isn't it?

My god-fearing parents didn't seem to think so. They had to drive up to Manchester to bail me out. Oh, they had a biblical field day when they saw me. Spouting the evils of my wayward life, the perils of drink… basically the devil had taken hold and God had put his boots on and this scenario was for pure contemplation. Having religious parents somehow equates to a constant recall of all your growing pains – aka *fuck ups* – at any given moment. I wonder if that's to do with all that verse and chapter learning? After that accident my parents told me to repent and seek forgiveness, but no way was I apologising to Ben or Tara Mc*Fucking*Auley.

Ben was my boyfriend at the time, and seeing that I'm

sharing, he was also the man who popped my cherry. It wasn't like I was saving myself for my wedding day or anything, but it was still a big deal to me. So to find out he was also shagging Tara McAuley behind my back… well, let's just say I was gutted. And the reason he cheated – oh this is hilarious – was because I was a "shitty lay". That was his parting shot. So what did I do? I gorged my way through an entire bucket of bargain basement chocolate and washed it down with a bottle of Tequila (that was my friend Lucy's idea). A very bad idea, as it happens. She said the Tequila would help me relax into a more laid-back Mexican version of myself.

It didn't.

What it actually did was make me a crazy and felonious Mexican version of myself.

We were in the pub doing – yes you guessed it – Tequila shots, when Ben walked in with HER, Tara Mc*Fucking*Auley. I thought it would be a good idea to confront him and ask him what he meant by a shitty lay. Lucy tried to stop me but I shrugged her away and sashayed (as in I wobbled, staggered) over to the smug pair.

I know, I know… if I could go back in time I would have dragged my silly self away before it was too late. I really don't know what possessed me. Oh yes I do, Tequila definitely possessed me.

Ben said, and I am quoting, "*You lay there like a dead fish and lack creativity.*" Then Tara opened her mouth and said, "*You should try being more enthusiastic.*" Like she was doing me a favour, giving me tips. "*Doggy style is appreciated,*" she said. "*And blowjobs are a no-brainer.*" I have never hit anything or anyone in my entire life (although I once hit the family cat with the *Wii* during baseball practice, but that was totally an accident), but with Tara*McFucking*Auley standing in front of me looking all smug and sexually pious I couldn't help myself. I slapped her in the face and kicked him in the balls, swiftly followed with a serving of jumbo tapas of lewd profanities, building volume and ferocity with each and every slurred syllable. I had discovered my Defcon 1.

My line of defence didn't wash with the old bill either; apparently *my* decorum was in question, but it was those two-faced hypocrites who were the real culprits. It just wasn't fair! Why couldn't the police see that disturbances to the peace charges are definitely trumped by the actions of the humiliated? Where's the consideration to the woman who was cuckolded?

Then 'Bitch Better Have my Money' by Rihanna came blasting out the pub speakers, and I thought I could flirt myself out of an arrest with some sexy hip-hop dance moves. However, I'm not much of a raunchy Rihanna type, and my sexy come-hither attempt is more akin to ramblers who have lost their footing, but with half of Mexico's Tequila production inside me, my emulation was painfully dire. I bent over and stuck my bum in the air, wiggling it suggestively as I pushed myself up against the officer. My balance might have been questionable, but I wasn't about to be trumped by a tart with no morals or regard for others. Especially one who thought blowjobs were the root of all successful pairings, who said I couldn't be sexy!

The pub crowd went wild and I basked in this rare adoration by leaping onto the table bumping and grinding in front of my newly found audience. Only this time, when I bent over, the blood rushed to my head, my stomach heaved, and the next thing I knew I was airborne. I crash-landed onto the floor; my knickers introducing themselves to all flying aircrafts in the sky and the Pope. At this point the policeman promptly handcuffed me, dragged me out of the pub to raucous catcalls and a round of applause. But the crescendo to my performance was yet to come.

Let's just say, projectile vomit is difficult to aim at the best of times, but even more so when you're being manhandled across a pub. The arresting cop had a tsunami of what I can only describe as winter vegetable soup gone rancid; carrots and Tequila – a speedy fermentation Heston would be proud of.

And it gets worse. A clip of all this appeared on YouTube the next morning and went viral across the university.

I think it was used as an anti-binge drinking piss-take. I still can't listen to 'Rude Boy' without cringing. Hasten to add the rest of my semester was… just… well… AWFUL.

I couldn't face anyone. I was a rubbish drunk and a crap lay, people backed away when I approached, the projectile vomit incident had its own flipping Facebook page with 3,000 likes just from campus and growing daily. I stayed in my room, I cut my hair, then dyed it, then cut it some more – very badly, I might add – imagining myself in *Bourne Identity* with the same crappy sink to do it in. I wouldn't stray from my room, not even to go to the bathroom unless it was after dark. If it were for me, I would have stayed in there forever, but Lucy dragged me kicking and screaming to lessons every day. I knew people were talking and laughing about me, they didn't even have the decency to do it behind my back.

There I thought I had the beginnings of a fantastic love story and all the while he was shagging someone else because I knew nothing about sex and its mysterious workings, and my first encounter was blemished forever. There really should be proper pointers for newbie sex doers. Pointers that don't involve talking about it. Maybe instruction flip-cards that you can refer to.

When university finished I hightailed it back home to my parents (aka The Goading Gospel of Jeremiah and Dippy Delilah). My sister and I have often been referred to as fallen Babylonians. Actually it was a reassuring praise in a house of sanctimonious silliness. To give my parents credit, they never gave up on us. However, I swear the cat Tabitha always held more esteem in our household than either of us daughters. The egocentric vicious devil can do no wrong. The name came to my mother in an epiphany, and the meaning of Tabitha is good, charitable, one who helps those less fortunate than themselves, which is somewhat ironic for the *'Damien Omen'* of feline pests.

The thing is, I felt utterly lost. I felt as if my life was over before it had really begun. I didn't want to go back to living with "sermon on the mount" for breakfast, lunch and dinner, but I had no where else to go. I had no come back strategy, nothing left to redeem. I kept thinking about Ben's betrayal and my whole drunken, excruciatingly public performance. It played over and over in my head a million times a day. However, it's amazing how time flies when you are doing absolutely nothing but watching daytime TV, forcefully cohabiting with your parents and generally feeling sorry for yourself. Living back in the land of Lazarus was an all-consuming nightmare and my temper made frequent trips back to Defcon 1.

Move on six months and I still didn't know what I was doing with my life. I was no longer on Prozac and I wasn't wandering aimlessly about the house in my disgustingly smelly threadbare flannel pyjamas. But it was New Year's Eve, and I knew I couldn't go on like this. Lucy had given up asking if I wanted to join her on a night out, and my sister Nell (not in a nun way, my fellow Babylonian) was singing at The Stooges Club in London on that night. As for me, I was watching some religious nut with greased black hair and a name beginning with Z with my parents. A showman more appropriate in the cast of a Superman movie, with a beard not dissimilar to General Zod.

New Year's Eve is supposed to be a time of reflection but all I wanted to do was forget. Forget about everything. Weird thing is that underneath my depression I could still see that the programme on the TV was a tiny bit humorous. I mean a Messiah who clearly uses boot polish as hair dye, oh come on! Honestly, my pious parents getting cable was such a bad idea. They now sat glued to evangelical broadcasts from the States until late evening. When they did finally go to bed I began flicking through the channels and got drawn in by a Liz Taylor film, *Butterfield 8*. I quite like the old classic movies and I started thinking. Miss Taylor was definitely a strong, independent woman, and I bet she wouldn't let a break-up ruin her life. And then the most peculiar thing happened, Elizabeth Taylor started talking to me, as if she were right there in the room.

Now I truly had lost the plot.

"You just do it. You force yourself to get up. You force yourself to put one foot before the other, and God damn it you refuse to let it get to you. You fight. You cry. You curse. Then you go about the business of living. That's how I've done it. There's no other way. So have one failed marriage, try another, then another, for Christ's sake look at my diamonds!"

That was my epiphany! Feeling galvanized for the first time in ages, I rushed to find a pen and paper - rising like a phoenix from the ashtray of drunken remorse and colossal fuck-ups, and I suddenly knew what I had to do. I had my own life to lead and I had to lead that life. No more hiding. I didn't need Ben. I didn't need any man.

I started writing three things down that would change my life for the better:

1. Become a TV producer
2. Move out of my parents' house. Pronto.
3. Invest in matching bra and knickers in case of unforeseen circumstances whether that is A&E or a lucky night out.

It was now way past midnight and suddenly I was actually looking forward to the year ahead. However, this list wasn't my New Year's resolution, oh no, this was much more important than that, because everyone knows that most New Year's resolutions don't actually get any resolute in the light of day. This was rather my vision for my future, my *Things to do while I'm still twenty-something*

And I, Eve Poots, did it, I put one foot in front of the other and I moved forward. I stopped obsessing over things I couldn't change and faced the world again. My life wasn't over. And even though I still wished I could go back in time, it was like Liz T said, "you just have to refuse to let it get to you." So I denied access and buried the burden of humiliation in a deep dark place of no return – at least the Facebook page had dried up and the video seems to have vanished. It was high time I moved on, too.

CHAPTER ONE

Six months later

My list has somewhat grown since its humble beginnings. I certainly worry less about my future now that I have my goals set, even if they are a little random.

1. Become a successful TV/film producer .

Five months ago I started working at Lookback TV. I'm only an assistant for the moment, but it's a proper paid job in the TV & Film industry, so it's kind of a big deal.

2. ~~Move out of parents' house. Pronto.~~

I moved in with my boyfriend five months ago. More about him in a second.

3. ~~Always wear matching bra and knickers in case of unforeseen circumstances, whether that is A&E or a lucky night out!~~

That's how I met Adam, my new boyfriend. I really did end up in A&E, a mere miscalculation of sticking the heel of my stilettos with a glue stick. Adam was the doctor who attended to my twisted ankle (he's actually a junior doctor). He didn't get to see my matching bra and knickers that night but he did ask me out on a date. And two weeks later I moved in with him. It was all very whirlwind, but isn't that the way of true love? And no more listening to my parent's dodgy TV choices is definitely a bonus.

4. Learn Spanish or French. (Well a bit of some other language to vaguely converse with).
5. Conveniently lose family cat to a farm needing a willing murderer for vermin!
6. Have lots of sex. More than that, have "the" Orgasm with a capital O when having sex. Still haven't felt the earth shake but it's early days. Adam and I are still getting to know each other so it's bound to be awkward.
7. Re-read books from college. (The ones that you don't really read properly, or grasp their profundity first time round because the duress to finish a paper that was due in two weeks ago meddles with your concentration i.e. Brave New World, Lord of the Flies, The Plague, The Grapes of Wrath, Heart of Darkness (they all sound rather depressing if you ask me), and other such literary giants like Woolf, Proust etc.... in other words an entire library full of Magnus opus selected by culture. I've been reading – let me correct that – falling asleep to War and Peace for years and totally miss the tragedy of the Greeks. James Joyce fairs better with my gnats attention span somehow.

8. Sleep under the stars.
9. Have lots of 'ORGASMIC' sex (I didn't think I made that clear enough in point 6).
10. Go to Vegas, and have a moment of "what goes on in Vegas stays in Vegas."
11. Drink responsibly on nights out (well, try to). Perhaps have the right intentions pre-third cocktail at least! And stop drinking tequila. I say this every morning when I wake up with a vicious hangover due to that poisonous Mexican drink. Did I learn nothing at university?
12. Kiss on top of the Eiffel Tower.
13. Master a one-handed cartwheel.
14. Own a pair of Jimmy Choo's or Manolo's or both if I'm lucky.
15. Girls-only clubbing holiday.
16. Take a road trip without planning every detail.
17. Learn to bake (ok, cook in general)
18. Learn to spell without auto-correction on.
19. Treat my sister to a session at a recording studio.
20. Learn how to fold clothes nicely so everything doesn't look like it's made out of crepe paper.
21. Marry someone. (Marry Adam!)
22. Buy an apartment.
23. Listen to my own voice and not others (and ignore A-holes like Brian).
24. Get brave and tell my parents I'm an atheist.
25. Get a hobby. (Refer to independent hobby list.)

26. Remember unlisted things and save time by not writing so many lists, it's getting a bit OCD.
27. Try something new. Hmm... maybe that should be learn how to iron, which would also help out No.20

Ok that last point is not really on the list yet, but as I look at Adam's creased shirt hanging up over the wardrobe's door it probably should be, I let out a frustrated sigh. There must be a lesson on how to iron shirts on YouTube!

I take a pink post-it note from the bedside table (I always have them close by). I write, "*YouTube. Ironing.*" and stuff it into the pocket of my jeans.

I've become somewhat big on lists (you may have guessed), and some might say I'm a little too obsessed. I have my normal everyday to-do list then there's my not-really-urgent-but-got-to-be-done list (such as go to dentist, sort out boxes of old clothes, print off photos), a list for work, a list for the week, a list for the weekend, and a list for shopping. I've also moved onto advanced listing of the lists and operate a post-it note system on the kitchen cupboards, colour coded of course into categories of the initial lists. Sounds scarily menta-*list*!

Sometimes I think I might combust under the sheer weight of trying to remember what was on the list to begin with. The cross referencing is becoming laboriously time-consuming, but the satisfaction of crossing something out… oh there's nothing like it, it's … well it's incredibly… *satisfying?* And darn right motivating.

I wouldn't be where I am today without my lists.

I bend over and plant a kiss on my boyfriend's lips. 'Adam!

It's 7.30am. You've got to get up.'

He grunts and rolls away.

Adam is not much of a morning person. He could quite happily sleep through Armageddon, grumbling that good and evil should keep the noise down until a more civilised time. I, on the other hand, want to be up and out, seizing the day.

When he becomes a fully-fledged specialist Doctor I'm sure he'll be full of morning joy. I'm certainly not going to shake him; last time I did that he head-butted me in the nose. Fortunately a simple nosebleed isn't the most perplexing injury for a medic.

I pad out of the bedroom, slope into the kitchen and grab the slightly incinerated square-looking object that has popped out the toaster. I promptly unscrew the marmite, spreading it quickly as well as thickly before the toast disintegrates, all in tandem with slurping coffee. There's no room for table manners at breakfast. My mind starts kicking in and I get a flash reminder: dad asked for grass trimmers. I dig out the post-it note from my pocket and write, *"Bosch Qualcast Art 23 trimmers."* I also add, *"book-rest bathtub for mum."* Adam and I are going to my parents on Saturday for lunch, and neither approve or know how to purchase anything from the Internet, fearing Lucifer might leave cookies in their mailbox. Ironically they don't mind pledging dollars to a fake messiah in a TV studio on a premium number.

'Morning!'

I look up as Ali, our flatmate, walks into the kitchen, flaxen hair sweeping across her brow.

'Morning Ali,' I take another bite of my crunchy gooey toast.

Alison is a music teacher in a rough inner-city school for problematic boys. She is brilliantly dedicated. She has to deal with the upcoming juvenile delinquents and underprivileged boys where the odds are stacked against them higher than the high rises they live in. Mostly, she spends her time fighting the biases that society has branded them with. She's a firm believer that the opportunity of education is key to their development. She introduces them to the works of Mozart, Bach, Beethoven, Tchaikovsky, Strauss, Vivaldi, Chopin, Handel, and Debussy to name a meagre few. She's riddled my brain with composers over morning coffees. She loves seeing the tough melt at the tones of *Clair de Lune.* Equally the stories she's told me make my hair stand on end. A kid once knifed her harp strings as she was playing trills. Even after this incident she still maintains the sound of a harp brings angels out from the darkness. Pity on that day a male Harpy-demon came out of double geography equipped for combat. But somehow she connects with these kids with her unwavering conviction that art can release the mind.

I watch Ali shuffle across the vinyl flooring, blearily navigating the kitchen chairs. She's as blind as a bat without her contacts in.

I remember Adam wants a cycling cap to go under his helmet so I add that to my list. Adam's a bit of a keen cyclist, actually that's like saying I'm a bit keen on lists. Adam is as obsessed with his bike as I am with my lists. He says cycling clears his head. He has asked me to join him several times before, but I'm really not good on wheels, and not to mention helmet hair.

Anyway, I think it's healthy in a relationship to have separate hobbies. Although I haven't really got a hobby at the moment, but I do have a list of hobbies that I definitely will get around to starting. Maybe I should add cycling to it? He's always so busy with studying then working, then working then studying, and when he's not studying and working or working and studying, he's out on his bike.

It's a well-known fact that junior doctors are not renowned for their ample free time. There are some really, really tough exams, all the while having to go to the hospital every day and don't get me started on the night shifts. He has to be unbelievably knowledgeable about, well, everything to do with the… erm… human body. He doesn't like to be wrong, and every theory has to have a scientific fact, and if he thinks he's right, which is most of the time, he'll argue like a noble prize depended upon it. I suppose you could call him a know-it-all, although I would never say so to his face. But that's what I love about him: he's so smart. I have on occasions made preposterous statements just to see how far he'll go to prove me wrong. Basing anything on feelings or whims is really playing devils advocate, and he'll bring it all down to molecular levels of chemistry. Case in point, he said that women's intuition is poppycock and men are equally intuitive and aren't ruled by hormonal swings, whereas I later read an article that studied the female brain's reaction to facial expressions and a whole area was firing up more than males. Therefore, there was no doubt a woman's perception was hugely different, an electrical storm in comparison to the sleepy male brain. Women's brains work differently because we are the ones (generally) raising the infant (initially). Medical science hasn't rearranged the womb to be portable – yet. Having to understand a noisy, squishy, small being who is unable to communicate what's wrong with them really develops your brain power in a way. So women's intuition is basically a survival trait, a pure protective instinct. Women also shy away from conflict and danger so reading a situation without fully knowing what's going on is again naturally programmed in us. But men have a better stress function and can process high stress far better; it is not merely due to estrogen's and progesterone's onward surge and battle war cries. My facts are scientifically proven, but Adam feels a little authoritative on all matters of medical research. When we get married I will have to slip that into a conversation with the article up my sleeve.

Not that he's proposed. I know, we haven't been together long, but the other weekend we were passing a jewellery boutique and there was a beautiful diamond ring and Adam walked into the shop uncomplaining. This is not his usual position on frivolous window-shopping – far from it, as he's not what you would call a natural shopper. He even shies away from online grocery decisions, saying all shampoo is the same, it does the same function chemically whether it's cheap or been heavenly produced by hair fairies in meadows of floral rhapsody, sailing on argan oil lakes churning out bottles to save your split-ends of doom. That was quite funny for him. But the other day he mentioned that after his end-of-year exams we should go away for a short break, somewhere like Paris. He knows I think Paris is the most romantic city in the world, or at least he should do, as I've hinted enough times.

Realising I'm humming *Here Comes The Bride,* I stop and quickly rinse out my cup chucking it on the draining board as if it never happened. I give the kitchen counter a quick once over with the dishcloth then head back to the bedroom.

Adam is now lying in the foetal position with his hands covering his ears like he's trying to ignore time.

'Adam! ' I give him a gentle prod. 'You're going to be late.'

It's a funny thing when you've been left heartbroken you never ever think you can love again, and yet Adam came along all chirpy with solemn earnest and my parents approved, which is by itself a miracle (although you have to be careful using that type of language in front of my family). Him being a doctor is a bonus. It's one of those trusted professions that causes ceremonial nods of approvals and inevitable coo's from the elders in the family (or is that just mine?)

No one in my family understands what it is I actually do. When anyone mentions that I am a Producer's Assistant (basically I am a personal assistant to the producer) I just get an audible grunt from concurring armchairs. You would think I was trying to explain the finer workings of Twitter to my great, great grandparents. It's as if my job is thin air or just exists in my own head. It might change when I get promoted to Associate Producer and produce my own TV show. I can go home and casually say, *"Oh my TV Show is airing tonight."* And my parents will be bound by the almighty to mention me when sermon spouting, *"Yes my parishioners, belief is the essence of our sermon today. Our Lord gives hope where belief has abandoned the soul, our lord fights for our beliefs, so believe in him as he believes in you."*

Good grief! I probably should watch what I say to them, it's not good to encourage the bonkers-bible wagon any further. They'll drag me out under false pretences to someone's random coffee morning saying, *"would you like to speak about your success"* and low and behold we'll have the prison episode all over again, *"God looked down and took pity on my daughter in her darkest moment. Subterfuge with drink on a prison floor and showed her the way."* Sensible biscuits have a designated cupboard in my mother's kitchen, just in case she meets more than three people on her morning walk, and this constitutes more than enough reason to break out the rich tea biscuits and collude them into sharing a cuppa. Why they have coffee with something that's designed for tea is a question only their God can answer.

During that time when I refused to come out of my room, my parents bundled me off (forcefully on sedatives) in my pyjamas to their good friend, Pastor Pickles. Nell and I call him "Past the Pickles" under our breath, but he never catches on, so in love with the sound of his own voice. If we say "Past the Pickles" in a natural conversation more than five times we owe the other a bottle of wine. When we did this as kids it was for a can of pop, the secret pocket money swag that was sacrilege contraband in our house.

"Belief is all you need and belief is what our lord blesses us with." - that and dodgy haircuts. Our family is the very definition of dodgy haircuts. We are the chosen ones, our Lord chooses us for different roles and our role is to support bad hairdressing salons across rural Berkshire, giving those less fortunate with scissors their moment of belief.

I knew I shouldn't have let my mother's hairdresser loose with my hair the other night. She cuts hair like farmers harvest wheat: quickly and to the ground. Before you've had the chance to look, massive chunks lay miserably on the floor, severed, limp and banished forever from your crown of glory and it's too late to change your mind as half your head is sheered beyond saving. Adam said I looked like a child from *Village of the Damned*. On the other hand, Adam sports a ginger military buzz-cut, but neither of us graces the realms of Vidal Sassoon's award winning style of the century; even sheep tend to have better cuts. Oh, yes, my wonderful loving boyfriend is a redhead. He doesn't have the pale freckly skin that one mostly associates with red hair. However, he has really muscular legs (from all that cycling I guess), with quite a toned upper body sitting on top of them. Actually it looks a bit odd, like his legs are too big for his frame, but it doesn't matter at all because the best bit about him are his gorgeous brown eyes, which are slightly hooded, puppy-dog eyes.

'Adam!' I try one last time, listening for a stir, a grunt, anything...

Well he can't say I didn't try.

It takes me less than ten minutes to walk to Vauxhall tube station, and with a copy of *The Metro* I grab a seat. The first page I open is a section on "The Hottest Haircuts." As if I need anymore reminding that I have the world's worst haircut. I look around and even the carriage is full of cool coiffures. Surely there must be a dodgy haircut amongst them? Oh wait, that would be me.

By the time I reach Oxford Circus I'm lost in a fantasy in which I've given myself long, wispy bangs and flowing locks that a Hassleblad would have difficulty capturing. Only when I step out of the tube do I make the mistake of looking in a shop window and come crashing back to reality.

'It will grow out,' I tell myself as I walk to work. 'And until it does I won't look in any mirror. Aren't hairdressers always saying if you cut your hair frequently it will grow faster, longer and healthier?' I savour this thought.

I love my walk into work, passing the bleary-eyed delivery people, confused waifs and strays from the night before. The street is still dirty, and the road cleaner turns back to his magical sweeping machine as if his Lord's cricket ground is ready for its debut. Fresh air mingles with the smell of last night's activities; the sun shining in its nonchalant, casual London way, threatening to disappear when you turn the next corner. My lovely Soho brimming with all my favourite restaurants and drinking haunts. Lucy and I always meet at *Cocteau Bar* on a Friday for a quick 'after work' G&T, but we never manage to make it quick or the one! I religiously buy my sandwiches (when I've forgotten to grab the pathetic soggy cling-filmed package from the fridge) from *Garibaldi's Deli* and my coffee from *Akarsu's*, which is as far as my devout following practices go. And of course, when I'm looking for that *"all important"* outfit for a night out I head over to *Topshop*.

I'm in the dream location and my dream job. Well, it would be if Brian didn't work there. Alastair is my boss so he's all that matters and he's lovely. When I first got the job I did worry that perhaps I might not be fashionable enough or fast thinking enough. These media Soho types always look so cool. Most of the time I feel as cool as the forgotten lettuce in my quite possibly deliberately forgotten tepid sandwiches squished at the bottom of my wreck of a bag. Like a lot of women, my handbag, is full of the most unnecessary items, which could be handy because you once used it two years ago. I think I'm more Magoo than Mui Mui. But working with Alastair you quickly come to realise that being fashionable is not important. He expects me to work hard and care about what I'm doing and not about what I'm wearing. But I'm still dedicated to fashion and with temptation everywhere around me I'm locking up my credit card under last week's soggy lunch. If it's not at hand it's not in danger - the feminine warzone that is chip and pin.

I let myself in the front door and take the steps two at a

time. That's my quick burst of exercise done for the day.

'Eve! Eve! Is that you,' shouts a male voice.

I plonk my bag on my desk. 'Morning Alastair,' I say, cheerily.

Alastair charges into the office. He lives in the apartment upstairs. In fact he owns the whole building and rents the ground floor spaces out. He only has to open his front door, step down a flight of stairs and voilà - he's here.

'Would you be a darling and get me a triple espresso. Sweet Eve, you little morning star! And give Misery-Guts my love. Not like we don't prop up his morning trade. He must put grumpy sprinkles on his morning porridge!'

My eyes crease as a broad smile ripples up my face imagining Mr Akarsu searching for his grumpy sprinkles in chequered pyjamas, getting really cross and swearing loudly in Turkish when he can't find them. He can never find anything in his café, always asking his staff to do everything. A simple request becomes more stressful than competing in Ironman. Most are confused and none are happy to help. His deportment is a bit on the sour side, but he always seems to have a smile for me. And I really don't mind getting the coffees in the morning. When Alastair asks for anything, no matter how mundane, it always sounds like a mini adventure, an errand with colourful dialogue – he evokes a world most people would blink past.

'How did last night go?' I ask whilst I walk towards the door. I know he was wining and dining some hotshot French producer, François Deville, which was kind of a big deal.

'Not too shabby at all Eve,' he says, giving nothing away.

Alastair is a giant of a man with a brilliant mind and a wicked sense of humour. He's in his late fifties, had a great career in his mid-twenties then hit his forties and… well I don't know what happened but something happened. Apparently he ended up in rehab for a year, or so says Sue, the accountant. I've never had the nerve to ask why. If no one naturally expands on the story then you shouldn't pry. It hasn't stopped me speculating though; I can be rather dramatic in my mind. Not in life though, I prefer things steady and manageable. I don't like feeling out of control. Well, you might have guessed that from all my lists. One's first incarceration does put a dampener on the next day.

Back to Alastair and the present, today he is wearing reddish coloured cords and an oddly-patterned waistcoat, accompanied by his treasured fob watch; his variety of dickie-bows is unsurpassed. I haven't seen the same one twice since I started here. He always has an unlit cigar in his mouth and wears tiny heavy framed glasses, those round fashionable ones, which look uncannily cartoonish. He's a bit of a scruff but it works, in that English eccentric way.

I take out my purse to check if I have enough money. Alastair never has money on him, says it ruins how his extensive wardrobe hangs. He does make quite a joke of his predictable style. When I first started working here I was spending fifty per cent of my own money buying coffees. I was too shy to say anything, thinking I'd douse my chance to get into the film industry, until Sue the accountant realised what was happening and reimbursed me. Now she gives me a weekly allowance. All I need to do is keep the receipts and give them to her on a Friday morning. I've been trying to get Alastair to save money and drink instant coffee or the ground coffee I buy for the carafe we have in the little kitchenette, but he just mutters something like "a man of fifty can afford a little luxury in a cup now and then". He's fussy like that.

'And you can get me a tall skinny mocha latte.'

A violent shiver slides down my spine.

I turn around just as Brian comes out of the toilet. I hope he washed his hands.

Brian is tall and skinny (much like the coffee he orders!) but with a pot belly that makes him look pregnant. He dresses like he is trying to audition for *Strictly Come Dancing*: open shiny shirt, tight trousers and always a hint of tawdry jewellery. He doesn't walk into a room, he rather enters like a puffed up alligator and always with a whiff of pickling vinegar. I don't know what that's about. Up close, his cologne is quite overpowering, but I could forgive his fashion sense and how he smells if he wasn't such a loathsome individual and sexist pig, prone to saying things like, *"I hear Harley Street are doing an offer on silicon this week. Worth a thought, if you can conjure one up today!"* He's not funny. He's a jerk.

But him and Alastair go way back (I think they went to boarding school together), so I just try to ignore him.

'And make it snappy, Barbie.'

See. Jerk!

I have no idea why he's started calling me Barbie, there's nothing remotely fake about me. I never wear pink, I obviously don't have triple D cups and we know I don't have flawless tresses.

Brian's actually made me cry a few times, but never in front of him, I go and hide in the toilet to let it all out. I keep telling myself if I want to become a hotshot producer then I am going to have to toughen up and rise above his obvious contempt. I just wish I knew how exactly to do that? If only I possessed an ounce of fierceness like my sister Nell or even my friend Lucy.

I bound down the stairs and, talk of the devil, Lucy is

balancing a coffee in one hand and an oversized bag in another, simultaneously shoving the keys in the door and gripping a take-away bag in her teeth.

'Need a hand?'

'Noimfine!' she mumbles through gritted teeth.

Lucy never needs a hand, she forges ahead in work and life and nothing gets in her way. She's the most self-assured, most put-together person I know. And we've known each other forever. To quantify, ever since she asked me to pinky-promise that we would be best friends. Neither of us could read nor write proficiently at the time; motor skills of apes. Two four year olds sitting on the naughty stone again after chasing horses in the muddy field, solemnly promising with their little fingers entwined "*To protect each other (especially from parents), fight for one another and have secrets that are top secret. Really top secret.*" The pact on the stone has stuck with us all these years.

Our parents never succumbed to our constant whining to have horse riding lessons. From that point on we were united. That year's village fete was our saviour. We put our pathetic pocket money together and bought a box of second hand toys, that box had all the hooves we so desired. If her or *My Little Pony* could talk we'd have to come to some sort of out of court settlement with their wealth of golden nuggets. When we started school, the naughty stone changed to the naughty mat.

"No your honour we did not knowingly deplete the rollerball pens from the stock cupboard with intent to supply. We were five and had no concept that charging 10p a pen was fraudulent profiteering.

We only wanted to give hope to all those inept hand-writers who were never going to get promoted to pen. So tell me this, was it wrong to encourage hope to the messy?"

"That's not what Twilight Sparkle indicated with her rainbow hair hoofs!"

"Twilight Sparkle you eat grass. Keep quiet!"

"So what happened to the funds?"

"We invested in the mini cookie trade to share... um... sometimes. More of a conscientious Robin Hood than international embezzlement."

"Twilight Sparkle mentioned some white stuff, which may have been contraband, highly illegal."

"White stuff? What white stuff?"

"The type that hangs beneath your nose."

"What's Twilight Sparkle's evidence backed up with?"

"Empty Colombian milk bottles from the teachers staffroom, a putrid smelling mane and white moustaches Miss Poots and Miss Fraser!"

"You're going down Twilight Sparkle, we can get to you even if we're in detention. We've got psycho Sylvanian families waiting on our orders. Liked the show-jumping ring we built you; there'll be no more show jumping in daisies for you pink princess! And don't you look so innocent Penelope Glitter with all your purple eyelashes."

Our mothers used to call us the conjoined twins of mischief. My own mother tried to convince Lucy's mother to let Lucy go along to Sunday school with me, as I used to kick up such a fuss on a Sunday morning. Once I even hid every bit of decent clothing and all my shoes in the garden, and not in pairs, but scattered along bushes, up in tree branches, and underneath hedges. I thought my mother would deem them too dirty, and she wouldn't possibly let me go to Church like that, but she made me wear old clothes from the attic that fit about two years previous to teach me a lesson. I spent the whole morning being subjected to nasty comments from Peter Willis and his big fat head.

Social embarrassment should be my middle name.

Back to the present day, the adult Lucy is very impressive. She boasts dark flowing locks, a beautifully made-up face with pillar-box red lipstick, but that's as far as her femininity goes, as the rest is clad in the darkness of grunge, black leather jacket, black jeans and black chunky boots. She works for an independent, young and sparky social-media type of… um… ad agency? (Not really quite sure of the correct titles) She is in the offices directly below us and it's really Lucy I have to thank for my job. She was talking to Alastair one day when he mentioned his PA had just quit and he was desperate. Lucy talked about my brilliant organisational skills and love for TV and films and – hey presto – I'm having an interview in *The Groucho Club*. Alastair and I bonded over a bottle of wine putting the world to rights. Midway through the second bottle, I took a trip to the loo not realising the ribbon of my right shoe somehow became entangled with the left and ended up walking towards the ladies a bit like a manic mouse in foxtrot lessons. Being the gentleman, Alastair pretended not to notice. After some nibbley tapas he offers me the job and a pair of Velcro trainers.

'Haveyoudonesomethingtoyourhair?' Lucy asks.

I change the subject. 'Are we still meeting up tomorrow night?'

She gives the door a shove with her bum and she's in. She takes the takeaway bag from her mouth, 'Hell yeah! They have that Troxler playing.'

'Who?'

'You really should come out with the young whippersnappers more often Eve. I do believe he's a DJ of what they call popular music.'

'Shut up.' I say, as she closes the door behind her sticking out her tongue at me. Our Friday nights at *Cocteau* have become a bit of ritual, but Lucy is always complaining that I don't go out that much anymore.

Trying not to worry about my head-turning abomination of a haircut, I dash across to Akarsu's café. It really serves the best coffee in the area, so there's already a queue forming, but it's worth the wait. When it finally gets to me they know exactly what I want without me having to go through the whole "triple espresso, tall skinny mocha latte but with a bit more milk" thing, and a regular latte for me.

'The usual?'

'Yes please.'

Mr Akarsu gets to work for about ten seconds before calling his daughter over who's laden with plates, clothes and receipts so she can also make the coffee as he just takes the money.

'Thank you.'

'A most pleasure for me,' he says, with a wink.

By the time I get back, Sue the accountant is sitting at her desk, nose deep in… accounts and accountancy stuff I guess, and some of the crew for the new Reality TV Game Show are here.

Jake Richards, the Director, is chatting away to Alastair and Brian. Then there's Mel, the new researcher. I like Mel a lot. We're the same age and she's an incessant list maker, too.

Naturally, we hit it off straight away. I'm not too sure about the director though; he acts a bit smug and he never even acknowledges the little people, i.e. me! Although, I do like his editor, he is much more easy-going. Stefan, the editor, has been set up in an office, which used to be Brian's room, and needless to say, Brian was none too pleased about it. I'm not too thrilled either, because now I have to watch him swagger around the office, and all ears are assaulted with his, *"listen to me everyone, for what I do is far more important than you cretins trying to concentrate."* So the office is now subjected to an egomaniac who is gratuitously loud and obnoxious for no reason, apart from his rancid excuse for a personality. Ooh, that's the fighting spirit! I must channel some of that next time he's says something mean.

I've met some other crewmembers but there's many more to come, as the line producer Pete is crewing up more people than Ikea stocks tea-lights. I've been trying to remember names, and I'm using fruit as a memory tool; Paul is Pineapple, Brad is banana, Cherry is… well Cherry, Tom is Tomato. It is a fruit isn't it?

'What took you so long?'

'The queue…' I trail off, as Brian snatches his coffee out of my hand and turns his back on me.

Alastair smiles. 'Eve, you are a sweet saviour in disguise.'

I feel bad that I don't have a coffee for Jake. I hold out my cup.

'You can have mine if you want?'

He scowls like I've just interrupted an important thought. Then his frown evens out and is replaced with a brilliant white smile. Seeing the offered up cup he shakes his head. 'Nah, I'm good, thanks.'

He certainly is. I mean, if you like the American hipster

type. Born in Los Angeles, he comes from a show business family: his grandparents, his parents, his sister, even the family dog are all actors (that's what it says on his imdb.com profile), except for him. He's the only one that seems to prefer being behind the scenes. It also says he loves skeet shooting. I didn't know what that was so I googled it, and it's basically clay-pigeon shooting. I've added that to my "try something new" list and my "hobby list".

Other than that, that's all I really know about him. We haven't really spoken, but he's certainly not rude like Brian, just keeps to himself, constantly preoccupied. At least he smiles occasionally, and has manners, which is as far away from Brian as Marxism is from Elitism. I'm about to ask him if he's sure he doesn't want my coffee when Brian opens his gutter mouth.

'How about hidden cameras up in the Green Room. We won't let on to the contestants,' Brian claps his hands with sadistic glee. 'Get the real them when they think the camera's not watching.'

I don't hear Jake's response as they all turn and walk over to Brian's desk.

I walk the opposite direction to sit down at my desk, sipping my coffee until it gives that pleasurable shudder – aaah, caffeine. Don't you just love that first thud of coffee of the day!

I open my notebook and start up my computer, whilst digging out post-it notes from my jeans and adding them to my today's to-do list in my overcrowded notebook.

'Eve! Can you go through the arrival schedule? Just make sure I haven't missed out on any of the make-up team's rota and if you have any time can you make sure the stylists are booked. I've lost the confirmation list. I had it somewhere but… oh drat!' Mel's pen splodges all over her fingers and down onto her notebook.

'No probs.' I say, handing her a wet wipe from my desk.

Sometimes I look at Melanie, or Mel as she prefers to be called, and it's a bit like a mirror image. Same height, 5ft4, slim built, but the major difference is that Mel has better hair than me. To be fair a psychotic inmate from a 16th century chain gang would have better hair than me right now. Mel has a blonde layered cascade of glory, whereas, as you know, I have a blonde butchered 'Children of the Damned' hatchet job. And if I were being really picky, my eyes are too small and too close together, and I have a pointy nose and a long face - but otherwise, mirror images.

And like me, Mel is never without her notebook. We both have posh navy A4 notepads with gilt edges of gold and a velvet ribbon. We got them from the stationary cupboard; it's like Aladdin's cave in there, with beautifully-crafted paper goods, gold-trim ballpoint pens, pencils with leads that never run out - even the post-it notes have a gilt edging.

You tend to write more efficiently if you don't want to waste paper. Writing on normal pads makes me doodle too much, whereas extremely posh A4 notepads are definitely the way forward. My writing this week does seem to be getting bigger, or perhaps I just need glasses? Or maybe it's Brian's constant, annoying, non-relevant requests filling up valuable space?

For the next half an hour Mel and I work together in silence with just the tinny sounds of radio four coming out from behind gently swaying window blinds where the little digital radio sits quite happily on the ledge. Brian's is the only voice you can hear, when he talks – or, more precisely, barks – always at a perpetually high volume. It doesn't matter what or whom he's talking to; down the phone, grumbling nosily at his computer, or generally making some sort of noise at everything and everyone. A relentless beat box of grizzles, groans, and vicious undertones.

I block him out and email the hotel where we are filming in a few weeks. I can't wait to go on my first shoot. I'm so excited about it.

We are making a reality TV game show called "*Wedding Wipeout.*" We have five engaged couples competing against each other to win prizes, wedding gifts with all that can entail, designer dresses, floral fantasies, cake creators, gastronomic gourmets, popular photographers, avant-garde arrangers etc. The ultimate prize: £30,000 in cash and a dream honeymoon.

Each couple is given various challenges and have to gain as many points as they can. The couple with the most points wins the money and honeymoon. A simple concept really, and on trend with what's going on in TV. Of course, the challenges have all been meticulously formulated right down to anticipating how each couple will react to one another. Each race and challenge designed to be highly competitive, and they expect couples to cheat, clash, and insult one other.

I wonder if the couples know what they're letting themselves in for?

Bridezilla has nothing on this game especially when partners get involved – let the Blame Games begin, not unlike Hunger Games come to think of it. But I'd prefer to be in Hunger Games than reap the wrath of Miss Kimberley Roberts, soon to be Lady Battenberg, the fallen American star who fell again, this time for a nice but eccentric English aristocrat in rehab, and they've been inseparable ever since. Someone's already seen her lose her temper on the percolator. I haven't met her yet, as

I have been out most of the time being a dogsbody for Brian mainly. Sue called her "a right bunny burner" after witnessing something that she did, where her reaction more or less broke the Geneva Convention, all because she couldn't get almond milk with her coffee! Alastair had to prize it from her hands. We've since replaced the coffee with decaf until she's off site! The tabloids have been having a field day, waiting outside for their precious picture of the fallen starlet. At least the PR side of things is being nudged along. I know she and Lord Battenberg are getting paid generously to lift the profile from the off and hopefully sell the concept internationally. And this is why she's fascinating to watch; you never know what the irrational people are going to do next and that's what makes TV viewing figures and advertising income. All the couples chosen have been cast based on their character traits and out of a few several hundred or so applicants we're down to five.

Couple #1 - Stacy and Brick – She is a Harvard graduate finishing her doctorate. She looks like a bimbo, but isn't at all. I sense cat wars between Stacy and Kimberly. The American civil war re-enacted with a new war paint: mascara! It could be very scary. On the other hand, her fiancé, Brick, is a well natured (a little stupid) super jock American football player.

Couple #2 – Kimberly and Lord Battemberg - the ones we love to hate.

Couple #3 – Sian and Piers – she is a fiery red head English teacher from London, very bossy, but seems genuine enough, and he is a budding politician infamous from his young conservative party antics! People have said his charismatic speeches echo a young Blair or Clinton. Apparently theirs was a whirlwind romance. They're actually my favourite to win.

Couple #4 - Daphne and Patrick – OMG! What can I say

about this couple? They're into, *s&m* (I don't know why I always whisper when I say it). When you see them they look so… normal, even a little dowdy, but looks can be deceiving. I actually caught them mid flagellation in the cleaning cupboard before. So embarrassing.

The door buzzes and in walks couple number five, Gemma and Hamish, a young fashionable London couple, both in publishing I believe. She looks like she would bitch you out the boardroom, where he looks like he would set light to you as you fly out the door. Publishing must be very cut throat. Both have identical black hair colour, hers in a sharp bob, and his is long on top and short round the edges. It's really shiny, odd in some light, and that's comparing against my trusses of treachery. Mel starts explaining the schedule to them and I go make a start on more coffee, the necessary staple of long days.

When I sit back down I have twenty voicemails to catch up on, from the logistics of a crane coming in for the aerial shots down to some special French biscuits for Ms Kimberly Robert's three yappy dogs, which she insisted must stay with her, or rather in her make-up artist's room, all the time. Apparently she doesn't come down to breakfast without twenty layers of war-paint on, she won't let anyone see her until she's caked in the make-up.

Then and only then do I get a chance to sit in with the editor, Stefan.

The edit suite is a fascinating place. Editors are the storytellers; they are in charge of cutting hours upon hours of shots together, creating a cohesive and interesting story (I read that in one of the Stefan's books). It's a real insight into how the footage is put together. As soon as I stepped into the room the first time I was like, 'wow, so this is where the magic happens!'

Sheesh, Ok, give me a break, but honestly, it's like when you find something that completely fascinates you it seems like magic and that's how I feel about the editing process. It also seems less frantic, calming even, almost like lying down on the couch and closing your eyes. No one bothers you in here; the editor is this untouchable force locked hidden away, just coming up for copious coffee and snacks.

Stefan's been showing me how to digitise the tapes into the system and log them into bins (an editing technical term. Trust me). He was the first person who started chatting to me at lunch, and my interest just grew, so he promised to teach me some stuff when I wasn't so busy. He had said "Just come in anytime and I'll talk you through what I'm doing." Thank heavens for Stefan, as at that point Brian was so dismissive of me, it really upset me in the first weeks.

The editing software is a bit mindboggling; Stefan lent me the handbook to start learning, but it's as heavy as the blinking tablet of testimony. I haven't begun reading it yet, too daunting. At the moment he's editing the backgrounds of each couple so we can get a glimpse of them in their homes. This is called the b-roll footage. He said they are interviewing the participants thoroughly so they can "create" a missing scene with interview bites and appropriate b-footage should they need it later on. Clever people these editors.

'The footage from Daphne and Patrick's house needs a lot of editing!' Stefan laughs.

'I hope the camera woman got plenty of the garden then,' I quip.

We giggle and gawp at the screen in unison. I'm turning crimson with embarrassment. Nothing is hidden from view. Jeez, are those hand restraints in a kitchen? Apparently, they had to move house so Patrick could put up the "stuff" on the walls; their humble suburban estate house couldn't take the load. I suppose they are both on the heavier side and tall. Crikey. We're both looking at Patrick with his heavy-duty drill fixing another restraint on the bedroom wall and by the time he's finished both our heads are straining to one side. What an earth do you do with that? It looks more like an animal trap than a device for human pleasure. What do I know? I can barely rip off a plaster by myself. Blondes have more pain receptors according to Daphne.

Gulp... I don't know where to look. The screen is full of their stuff, their home entertainment system, believe me, this doesn't really consist of a flat-screen plus flashy sound system, but I don't want to appear prudish, which I totally know I am, but I know this is so uncool. This combination is impossibly impossible for a prudish prat who can't even talk about "it", let alone watch others discussing "its" habits. I feel an involuntary gag rise up. I try and cough it out, ending up choking.

'You better go and get some water Eve.'

'Hmm, it is very hot, I mean dry in here.'

When I shut the door I hear Daphne talking about mutual thingy. Arghhhh. I'm gonna steer clear of those two; they're more open than a 7/11.

CHAPTER TWO

The rest of the morning flies by. By one o'clock I've managed to do nearly everything on my "Today's To Do" list including one-click purchases on Amazon for the looney parents. What I haven't managed to do is eat, and my stomach makes a loud grumbling protest. Only I don't get a chance because Brian sends me out to pick up his dry-cleaning; then he wants me to dash over to a bakery (which is two tube changes and a bus ride) to get his organic gluten free Italian bread. One can't possibly eat the excellent food around Soho, can one! As if Soho is lacking choice. Oh no, one must put everyone out of sync for one's bloated stomach cravings – that's what one's there for!

When I get back an hour later there's chaos in the office.

'What the fuck, Brian? How could you fail to check Hamish's flimsy story, he's so fucking easy to Google check. He's on Linked-in with a picture that would have helped you put two and two together. He's an undercover journalist if you can call it that, or more like sensationalised bag of bollocks.'

Alastair looks over, seemingly pleased with Jake's English slang, then remembers himself and the severity of the situation.

'Well…I…err.' Brian splutters. He has no answers. He's been caught out and there's no one else to blame.

Jake is pacing the floor, he's unbelievably pissed off, his brows so furrowed that his angular eyebrows are a worthy rival to Jack Nicholsons. 'And Gemma has had her face sprawled all over that tabloid trash site, or should I say J-mi-*Ma "good gossip is bad gossip*." Couldn't have been more obvious if they'd arrived with flashing lights over their god damn heads.' Alastair arms are crossed and there's a look of annoyance on his face that I rarely see. I don't think I've ever seen Brian go quite so red, his fat head slowly swallowing up his beady eyes.

I'm about to scuttle to my desk when Brian says. 'This is Eve's fault.'

My head jerks up and I stop in my tracks.

What!

I whirl round and stare at Brian in confusion, he glares back at me, his beady eyes reappearing cold and calculating.

Everyone is looking at me and I give a guilty blush even though I've done nothing wrong.

'Eve was meant to check through all the applications,' Brian says.

What's he talking about? I had nothing to do with the background checks, even though I begged Brian to let me help.

I walk slowly towards the group, my heart racing and my legs feeling like jelly. 'I didn't do any of the background checks?' My voice cracks a little.

'Precisely.' Brian scathes.

I feel myself go hot. 'No, you never asked me to do any background checks.' I keep my voice steady, but it does a little jump at the end.

'Just admit you screwed up.' Brian gives me a steely glare and even Alastair looks suspicious. 'This is what you get for hiring the inexperienced.'

'I don't know what I'm supposed to have done.' I say, forcing some backbone behind my words. My cheeks are burning and I feel kind of faint. I really should have eaten something.

The entire office goes deathly quietly. Everyone is staring at me and I'm now sweating. God, I hate confrontations.

'Did you do the background checks?' Alastair asks me.

'No. But the point is Brian didn't ask me to.'

Alastair looks at Brian and Brian shakes his head. 'You asked to prove yourself and I said ok, but if you don't take the initiative....' He turns smoothly to Jake. 'I should have double-checked her work.'

'No. That's not what you said...' My voice does not sound nearly as steady as I want it to.

Brian shakes his head. 'Eve it's important to own up to your mistakes.'

'Mel was there.' I whirl round and Mel stares back at me in horror. We are all looking at her, but her eyes quickly dart to Brian and she drops her head.

'I c...c... can't really remember.' She mutters.

My heart sinks. I thought we were friends.

'Now at the eleventh hour I don't care who is at fault.' Alastair finally says. 'Just sort it out. We need another set of contestants pronto.'

I can feel tears sneaking into my eyes so bite into my lip.

'We've got less than a week to find someone.' Jake says, raking a hand through his hair. 'There is no way we are going to do this. We'll have to reschedule.'

'We cannot reschedule.' Alastair voice is final.

'What about Jay and Grant?' Mel pipes up. 'They were our first choice but then Grant had to go in for an operation. He may have recovered now, so I could try and ring them.'

'Or Pippa and Penelope?' I add, trying to trail Mel's logic.

'This is not a friggin' showcase for the LGBT club! Why not Bernard who likes to be called Ballisimo Beauty when on stage. Why not Sarah who wants to play rugby league as a man? Just fix it,' barks Brian. He has a particular hate for gays who want to be someone else, as in change sex – even though he is gay, I think.

I run to the cupboard and grab the box, ripping the failed applicants free from their sleepy suspension file. Mel joins me; I try and ignore her sullen eyes trying to open conversation. I feel betrayed and that doesn't sit lightly with me, but now's not the time to confront Mel.

We start re-ringing couples, leaving messages on voicemails, calling even those that the psychologist notes branded as unsuitable – the situation is imploding. Meanwhile Brian and Jake have retreated to Alastair's office; no doubt Brian is tarnishing my name in the process. An hour later, I want to hurl the telephone out the window – I thought everybody wanted to be on Telly! Some had faked their relationships and when asked seem to have forgotten who they were spending the rest of their lives with; others couldn't get time off work at such short notice; some were even insulted they hadn't passed the initial questionnaire stage and a surprising majority we had to hang up on, religious freaks with a message to the world. I can sense those better than a pig truffle hunting. Mel looks equally beaten. At that point, Alastair's door opens and they all pile out.

They can obviously tell by the look on our faces that we've

had no joy.

'If it's too late to get another set of contestants then we'll just have to go with the four couples we do have,' says Alastair, which I think is a brilliant idea.

'We may have to,' says Brian. 'Unless Eve wants to step in and save the day.' He turns and gives me a snarky smile. 'You're getting married, aren't you Eve?'

'What's this?' Alastair turns and gives me a surprised look.

I might have mentioned to Mel that Adam and I were looking at rings and that he mentioned Paris after his exams. It was Mel who realized what Adam might be hinting at. It seems like Brian had been eavesdropping on our private conversation.

'Are you?' Alastair probes.

'Err…' I feel my face go hot. I hate being the centre of attention.

'Oh Yes, that's right. Adam and Eve were looking at rings the other day.' Mel says forgetting herself. That's it, I'm not telling her anything again.

'Adam and Eve?' says Jake, disbelieving. 'Is your boyfriend really called Adam?'

'Yes.' I nod.

'That's got to be a match made in heaven!'

I give a short fake laugh. Like I haven't heard that before. Although, I think this could possibly be why my parents didn't seem to mind much when I said I was moving in with Adam.

'Do you think you can hurry him along?' Alastair asks.

My mouth flops open. Alastair can't be serious. Even Brian looks shocked.

Jake looks at me. 'How old are you?'

'Twenty-two but I'll be Twenty-three next month.'

'That makes all the difference.' He gives me a tiny half-smile.

I know people will think Adam and I are too young to marry, possibly even my parents, but that's only because Nell made such a balls up with her marriages. Oh yes, she's been married twice already and she's only twenty-six. Anyway, my parents got married when they were twenty so what's the big deal? And I know they can't wait to have a doctor in the family. And besides, if it feels right to us, what does anyone else's opinion have to do with it. Why am I even explaining this? I hate explaining myself umm… to myself.

Jake studies me for a moment. I rub my nose, feeling extremely self-conscious, like I'm under a magnifying glass; Peter Willis and his big fat head torturing all over again.

'Adam hasn't actually proposed, yet.' I tell the room.

'Of course he hasn't. Mythical creatures are hardly in the position to speak. You know fairy-tales aren't real Eve? Come on. You don't really have a boyfriend.' Brian sniggers. No one else laughs.

'I do.' I say, feeling my cheeks go even hotter. 'He's a junior doctor and his finals are this year. After his exams he's taking me to Paris where he'll probably propose.' Ok, he hasn't exactly said those words but as good as.

'Do you think you may be able to hurry things along?' Jake asks.

'I can't do that,' Jake stares at me. I've definitely said the wrong thing.

Alastair tears at his hair, Brian snarls and Mel looks fraught with worry. Shit, shit, shit.

In my mind I search for adequate reasons to make the suggestion to Adam, my job might be on the line here even though I've been wrongly accused of messing the whole show up. We could do with a deposit for the flat I suppose?

I convince myself to fold. Peer and job pressure, a heady mix I can't cope with along with the intense atmosphere flooding the room.

'You have a very enigmatic bone structure Eve, the camera will love you,' is he trying to flatter me into this insane idea? I blush and start to lap it up he has such a convincing way about him.

'Possibly… I mean, I think so… I can't see why not' I mumble, feeling completely under the spotlight and not really know what to say anymore, I want to fix it for Alastair, I don't want to let anyone down. But it's ridiculous.

'Come with me. I'll show you what I mean.' Jake orders, turning away and walking into the side office.

I look at Alastair in disbelief; they can't be serious with this? He ushers me to follow, his face crinkling into a smile. At least he's no longer angry.

Inside the spare office there's a tripod, a camera and a chair.

I stand in the doorway, uncertain.

'Take a seat.'

I walk over to the chair and stumble over a wire on the floor. I look up and, right enough, Jake is watching me.

'Try and relax.' He smiles, showing a perfect row of white teeth. I don't think I've ever met an American who hasn't got lovely teeth, but so do sharks. Well, they have a lot of teeth anyway. Here goes nothing, outmanoeuvred by the masses and into the white jaws of hell then.

I sit down wishing the building to be hit by a tornado, anything to stop this from happening. I wipe my clammy hands on my jeans. When I look up, Jake is still watching me, this time with one hand resting on the camcorder.

'I'm just going to ask you a few questions. He turns on the

camera and my eyes widen with fear. I gulp. Ever since "*the incident*" and my subsequent debut on YouTube, being in front of any recording device sends me into cold sweats and horrid palpitations. How did I end up in this situation!

'You don't seriously want me to be a contestant on the show, do you?'

'Don't you want to be on TV?'

'No.'

'But you want to keep your job, right?'

'Yes, but–'

'Then yes, I think you do need to do this. As you and Mel pointed out, there is no other contestant available at such short notice and I don't know anyone else who is engaged at the moment. Anyhow, we are just assessing whether you could potentially be a good candidate at the moment, and then we'll see.'

Well that told me. I look away and notice a box of jammy donuts on the table, my stomach grumbles.

I really should have eaten.

'Can you tell me your fiancé's name?'

I look into the camera lens. 'Adam.' Ok this might not be so bad. My eyes stray over to the jammy donuts on the desk once again.

'And what do you love about Adam?'

'Um.... well, there's just so much, where do I start?' My eyes stray back to the sugary sweet delights and my stomach lets out a loud grumble.

Jake follows my gaze. 'Do you want one?'

'What! Oh no. I'm fine.'

He picks the box up and my mouth immediately waters, more akin to a greedy dog salivating on sausages, and I wipe some inadvertent dribble. He shakes its stodgy contents. 'Go on, have one.'

'OK.' I reach over and take one with two fingers, mindful of the stickiness, and I ravenously bite into the ball of goo.

'I didn't get a chance for lunch.' I mumble through an oozing bit of jam. Jake stares at the donut devouring, making me painfully aware that the cookie monster dines with more finesse. As I look up I notice the red light is still blinking. Just wonderful!

'So, you were about to tell me what you love about Adam.' He reiterates.

'Oh yes.' I chew quickly, swallowing down hard. 'Well, he's kind and clever. He's a junior doctor.' I think I've answered the question but the light from the camera continues to flash. Jake doesn't look up. I really do feel like I'm under a microscope all over again, all my imperfections inside and out, being studied and assessed. I start gulping, my mouth getting dryer with each attempt.

'And everyone is always telling me how perfect we are together. And…umm… he's a great cook, he always has things like decimated coconut in his cupboard, and the kitchen is full of wonderful garlicky-herby smells when he's cooking. And um, he likes to cook.' I said that already. 'Erm…' My mind goes blank. This is ridiculous. I mean, there's so much that is amazing about Adam, it's just hard when you're put on the spot like this and with a camera monitoring your every twitch – Hal 9000 would be envious. I'd much rather be locked out in space right now. My mind races for something more to say; there must be more to say about the love of my life.

'When I had swine flu he quarantined me in his bedroom and got me antibiotics out of hours.'

Bingo! A great example of "in sickness and in health"!

'I'm so lucky to have him, I really am.' I give my most radiant smile, my face tingling slightly.

'And what about you, tell me about yourself. What makes Eve Poots tick?'

What makes me tick? What kind of question is that? My mind is empty. I reach up and touch my oddly cut hair.

He changes his tone to one that's less Jeremy Paxman and more Holly Willoughby.

'Ok, what's your favourite hobby?'

'I don't have any.'

'No hobbies?'

'Well I have a list of hobbies I want to try.' I say defensively. 'I just haven't got round to trying them yet. I have a list... er. Yeah, a list.'

'A list?'

'A hobby list, you know, cooking, candle-making, calligraphy.'

'Did you only look at hobbies beginning with the letter C?'

Funny. 'No, of course not.' I try to remember what else is on the list. 'I've always wanted to grow mushrooms.'

Jake's head peaks up from behind the camera.

'The gourmet kind.' I add quickly. 'Not, the druggy kind.' I roll my eyes. Honestly. 'I just think it would be fun to grow mushrooms, you know, shiitake, Oyster or Lion's man mushroom. Ooo... especially the hedgehog ones, more for the name than anything else.' I start into a crazed automatic reverie. 'Can you imagine it. Oh here are my hedgehogs I grew earlier!' A gawky laugh erupts from my sugar-caked mouth and the room is deathly silent. Ok, not everyone finds mushroom names as funny as I do.

Then I have what my mother would call an epiphany. Well it used to be my hobby when I was holed up in my bedroom feeling sorry for myself or grounded (which had all too much of a regularity about it, but it didn't bother me as I didn't have to read the bible in there).

'I do have a hobby.' I say feeling inexplicably chuffed with myself. 'I like learning national anthems.'

This time Jake whole body pops up from behind the camera.

'It's a good way to learn a foreign language,' I say defensively. 'And to appreciate the music and erm… lyrical value.'

'Really?'

'Yes, really. You know La Marseillaise, Wilhelmus, Kimigayo, Marcha Real,' I tick off my fingers, 'God Save the Queen… obviously. The Star Spangled Banner…'

'Will you sing one?'

I shift uncomfortable in my seat. 'What now?'

'I think the audience would be… fascinated. I am mystifi… fascinated.'

I can't work out if he's being sarcastic but I did sing "Kimigayo" to our flatmate Ali the other day, and she thought it was marvellous, although we had just polished off a bottle of Sauvignon at the time.

Feeling slightly ridiculous, but wanting to show that I can be interesting when I try, I start singing. The lyrics, in case you're interested are, "koke no musu made, iwao to nari te, sazare ishi no, chiyo ni yachiyo ni, Kimi ga yo wa". Translated it means, "Thousands of years of happy reign be time. Rule on, my lord, till what are pebbles now. By age united to mighty rocks shall grow. Whose venerable sides the moss doth line."

When I'm done there's complete and utter silence.

'I know my accent is pretty terrible.' I feel the blood rushing to my face. 'Did you know they are the world's oldest lyrics in a national anthem, and it's also the shortest one?'

Jake is looking at me, and if I'm not mistaken, trying not to laugh. I stop gabbling and shut my mouth tightly.

'Is there any other music you're interested in besides National Anthems?' He really is taking the piss now. What makes him so high and mighty?

'Oh, anything classical really, Debussy is a favourite and how can you not adore Clair de Lune?' Might as well go for an all out lie, as clearly my own choices are something to ridicule.

Jake's head pops up again. I truly am quoting the life of another and the camera is the Stasi.

'Can't ever get enough of Rachmaninoff.' For God's sake Eve stop now.

'And who are most important people in your life?'

The change of direction startles me, but this is a far easier question to answer. 'My best friend Lucy, my sister Nell, and my parents when they are not being totally unreasonable or delusional.'

A disquieting thought pushes into my head. 'And Adam naturally.' I quickly add. 'I thought you know, you meant other people than "the one".' I try looking unfazed and natural.

'And your proudest achievement?'

Proudest achievement? I think back to Stacy's interview, the Harvard graduate, and even Kimberly in all her fury has been in one of the most popular soaps in America. Well, she may be notorious but she's achieved infamy.

I don't have any proudest achievement, unless you class "*most likely to end up in jail vote*" at graduation day – it was out of hundreds. And I certainly don't feel job satisfaction at the current time; a few hours ago I would have gushed about getting this job, but not now and not like this. My gormless gawp claps up and down, with no audio at all.

'Ok, worst?'

The image of me throwing up pops in my head instantly.

'I'm really quite boring. Are you sure you want me as a contestant?'

He doesn't say anything, which pretty much says that he agrees.

Then he leaps into action, adjusting the light so it's beaming into my eyes, for a moment I can't focus, everything is blindingly white.

'We are trying to encapsulate what makes people want to marry, the biggest commitment that two people are likely to make. Where their mind-set is when they embark on that journey. So I was wondering what you think about your relationship with Adam, only you. You said everyone thinks so. But what do you think?'

I feel wrong-footed. 'I know what you're doing.' I say, lifting my chin defiantly. 'You're trying to trip me up.'

'Trip you up? Interesting.' His eyes narrow and he unnerves me with his stare.

'Yes and you're quite wrong.'

I hear him chuckle, and a small voice inside my head is telling me to stop. But I can't. I have to explain to him how it is.

'Look… I know I'm young, but Adam is the perfect man for me. He's loyal. He's not going to mess me about. I'm just not good in front of a camera and I'm not in the habit of explaining my choices to a stranger.'

'You're telling me there's nothing annoying about Adam at all?'

'That's right.' I say.

OK, sometimes I find it annoying when Adam zones out from morning to night like I don't exist, but he has the most gruelling day out of the two of us. I'd probably do the same if I had to deal with trying to fix people's bodies all day long.

'Every human being out there has annoying traits; it's just how annoying they are to you that counts. Habitual can be misconstrued to some people as annoying, and I like habitual; that means you really know someone and accept everything about them. And when someone's habitual is endearing rather than annoying, you know it's a perfect match.' Finally I manage to say something intelligible.

'OK. That's it, we're done.' he says.

I look back, dazed. 'We are? Right.' I hurry to my feet with the coordination of a drunken squid, tripping over that blasted wire again.

Jake opens the door, and holds it open. 'See, that wasn't so bad.'

I roll my eyes. 'Yeah, a real joy that was.'

He gives me a tiny smile.

I sink into my chair and stare at my computer screen, none of which registers with my eyes. My thoughts bombard its flickering display of unread emails into a distant blur. I feel agitated, as if I really am Dorothy and a tornado has actually swooped me up and plonked me on top of the witch dump, and I'm left sitting there in a pile of festering rubbish.

It's silly. Adam is my boyfriend. He loves me, I love him and we have a future together, and yet... why couldn't I think of the things I love about him? I'm usually so good at lists. Oh, it's just a silly interview. I shouldn't read anything into it. Besides how could I focus properly after Brian's accusations and Mel's betrayal, of course I wasn't in the most loved up frame of mind. The trouble with my fuming is that it pops into my head and never really materialises through my mouth in an orderly manner – no self-preservation tract. My words come out as imposters, jumbled, shaky and without strength. I really need to learn how to be heard. At least I have Adam; he won't let me down.

'Eve.'

I look up and my stomach lurches.

'You look like you've got nothing to do.' Brian throws the application form onto the desk in front of me. 'Try and be useful, and bring it back when you're finish.'

My blood runs cold.

They'll have to run a background check on me. Oh my God! What if they really do find out I was arrested and put in prison?

Well, that's it. I'll be out of a job.

I roll my eyes. Honestly I can be so dramatic. Of course they're not going to fire me if I save the day.

I doubt there's even a record of me being drunk and disorderly on file anymore. Although I was of age to get it on a record. Crikey, one fuck up can really fuck you up.

Another thought springs to my mind – Adam. Oh Christ! Adam! I haven't had a chance to brief him yet. I know we've looked at rings but we haven't really talked about marriage. You can't just throw the word "wedding" in willy-nilly. Although it was Adam who brought it up last time, when he said his parents were our age when they got married. And then there was the ring he let me try on… I feel my spirits lift slightly. Anyway, Adam hardly ever answers his mobile, especially when he's on duty. It'll give me enough time to work out a strategy to drop the bombshell into our everyday conversation.

My head starts to throb, I grab the headache tablets from my bag and it's contents tip all over the floor, only to be followed by my sweaty lunch. The slime oozes out from the forgotten cucumber and overload of egg mayonnaise; my make up bag is decidedly smellier now. The whole office watches me as I scrabble over the mess, the mess of my life unfolding yet again. When did it become a spectator's sport?

I spend the rest of the afternoon trying to work out what I'm going to say to Adam. How can I get him to agree to do this game show, and what if they find out I was arrested?

It's just all too much. When it's time to go home, I'm a nervous wreck.

'Eve!'

I turn and Mel is waiting for me outside.

'Oh -' I look at her coolly.

'I'm sorry about earlier.' She says in a rush. 'I know I should have stuck up for you but…' Her eyes well up, 'Brian is such a…' she pauses. 'Dickhead.'

I stand silent - stunned that she shares the same opinion about Brian as I do.

'I thought you liked him.'

A tear slips down her cheek. 'God no! I didn't want to give him any more reason to be vile. I'm sorry.'

'Have you spoken to Jake or Alastair about it?'

'No. I just want keep my head down and do my job, keep my job.'

'He shouldn't be allowed to get away with it.'

'I know but what can we do?'

'I don't know. But something?'

It's just so silly; here we are, two strong professional women, and yet we can't stand up to him.

I am feeling depressed and miserable when I let myself into the flat. I don't know what to do about Brian and now I have to explain to Adam that I may have involved him in a TV Show. I stand in the hallway for a few minutes gathering morsels of courage. How do I persuade or even promote the idea of an unsuspecting marriage upon an unsuspecting junior doctor?

I walk along the hallway, my pace slowing down as I approach the kitchen, my stomach groaning in hunger and nerves with every step. Then, suddenly, there's a loud clang, like a pan's just dropped on the floor, and my heart leaps out of my skin. I quickly run back along the hallway and into my bedroom, and shut the door.

Leaning my palms against the door I heave out a heavy sigh. This is ridiculous. I just need to tell Adam exactly what happened, he'll understand. I close my eyes and picture the scene, with Adam laughing at the ridiculousness of it, then his eyes burning into mine, telling me he loves me and that he wants to get married. Feeling spurred by the scenario I've painted myself, I stride purposefully into the kitchen and feel a little disappointed when it's just Ali tucking into a bowl of pasta, there's been an escapee, cheese sauce lies splattered on the floor. Ali (optically challenged) is such a mess in the kitchen.

'Where's Adam?'

'He had to work.' She starts blinking and slides the note across the table. I pick it up.

Eve, Sorry. On call. I'll make it up. Dinner. Tomorrow evening. I'll cook. Adam x

I suppose I can always talk to Adam in the morning.

CHAPTER THREE

The only problem is that in the morning Adam is lying there, dead to the world, and it seems a little rude to wake him. So I leave him there, in his dreams of *Tour de France*. I'll definitely talk to him tonight. I arrive at work and somehow manage to convince everyone that Adam has agreed to be a part of the Show. In fact… he can't wait to marry me!

So there. Belief is all you need; my parents' fault really.

The look on Brian's face is priceless, all pinched and glowering, whereas Alastair is beaming. Mel is literally jumping with excitement, and Sue, well Sue remains nose deep in accounting things. Jake's the only one looking at me with an expression I can't read.

'That solves the problem then Eve, you can be the next contestants on the show.' Jake announces.

'What?' I stand with a slack jaw. I didn't think they'd actually cast me. Overnight I was hoping they would have had at least one of the applicants rethink, phone back and agree. Oh crikey, they are serious.

Of course, this now means I definitely have to persuade Adam, otherwise I really am for the chop. I spend the rest of the day keeping my head down working, which is harder than usual because Mel keeps pestering me for details. I didn't realise she was as big a sap as me when it comes to romance and weddings. For the whole day she keeps telling me how happy she is for me, and how she can't wait to see Adam propose, and have I thought about what I'm going to wear. It's a relief when I leave work.

Adam is already cooking when I arrive home. I dump my bag on the chair and put my arms around his waist to kiss the back of his neck. 'Hi.'

'Hey.' he says.

Adam really does love cooking, at least that wasn't a camera-shy fabrication. The kitchen is full of the authentic smell of proper cooking, as opposed to the slightly burning aroma when I attempt. And there's a glass of wine waiting for me on the table. He really is wonderful

'Hiya,' says Ali, coming out of her room and picking up the glass of wine.

'Oh hi Ali.' I begrudgingly pull open the fridge and take out the bottle, pouring myself a new glass. That's when I notice the three placemats on the table and I feel disappointed. I thought Adam meant he was going to cook for a romantic dinner just for us two.

But now's not the time to pull a grump.

I take a sip of wine, pick up the *Evening Standard* and I flick straight to the housing section.

'Ooh a two-bedroom place in Hoxton,' I coo. Ok, it's really pricey, but in a brilliant location. Is that supposed to be the kitchen? Hmm, it looks more like a cupboard.

'Are you two looking at apartments?' Ali's forehead

pinches into a frown.

Adam snorts, 'I can barely afford the rent on this place.'

'But when you become a big clever doctor and have a stable income…'

'I'll be paying off my student loan.'

Oh, I hadn't thought of that. But when we're married…. Stop, I mustn't let myself get carried away. I've got to get Adam to propose first.

'Ooh this one's pretty.' Ali points to a beautiful two-bedroom apartment on the outskirts of Hackney.

I look over. Wow, it is gorgeous. It's got a working fireplace, wooden floors and shutters.

'It's £360,000!'

'Pretty though.' She says.

'You two are living on cloud cuckooland.' Adam pipes in.

'Spoil-sport.' Ali pokes her tongue out at him.

I imagine just for a second that money is no object and we are standing in that kitchen, Adam doing some tasty roast and me sifting through scripts to produce.

Adam comes over and studies the property particulars.

I smile up at him, lovingly.

'It's in bloody Hackney. I'm not moving to the murder mile.'

'You're such a snob,' Ali retorts.

'Actually, it's considered a hotspot.' I say, taking a happy slug of wine and sinking back into my chair.

'Well, if the crime statistics are petering off, it might be worth it.'

'Not long until you start filming *Wedding Wipeout*.' Ali says, changing the subject.

My throat constricts. Ali loves hearing about the TV

Show. She says it helps her escape from the inner city reality. She once played me a tape of the children and, oh my god, there was so much cussing on it no wonder she needs some frivolous fluff now and again. But I can't talk about it for fear I might slip up and blurt out everything. No, I have to be delicate here. I need to speak to Adam alone. I feel bile rising just thinking about it – and that's a real shame because that spaghetti bolognese smells delicious.

After dinner Adam decides a bike ride on a full stomach is just what he needs.

'But you've just eaten!' I say in disbelief.

'Need to stretch the leg muscles.'

'It's nearly ten o'clock.'

'It'll be quiet on the roads. '

Ali slinks off to the living room and I stand there fuming. I'm still standing there, when Adam steps back into the kitchen with all his cycling gear on.

'Are we still seeing your parents on Saturday? He asks, doing up his helmet, oblivious to how annoyed I am.

'Yes.'

'Ok. How about you have a lie-in then, I'll drive us to your parents instead of faffing about on overcrowded Saturday service trains.'

'Ok,' I pout. 'Are you sure you don't want to stay. We could have… erm cuddles, instead?' I try to say in an alluring manner.

'Eve, I'd love to cuddle up with you, but I've been in a stuffy hospital all last night and all day. I need some air.'

'Of course you do… Have a good ride.' I tail off.

I leave him to his bike ride and slope off to bed, struggling to keep my eyes open. Why are emotions so physically draining? Why can't they root themselves firmly in the mind and not interfere with the workings of the body.

I don't hear Adam come in.

CHAPTER FOUR

I wake up the next morning and my first thought is that I've got to tell Adam. I can't go into work again and pretend everything is fine. I get up and shower, potter around in the kitchen, make myself coffee, eat a round of burnt square with marmite slurry, and add 'mayday strategy' to my list. Throughout my morning routine my brain is rattling around for clever ways to work engagement into conversation. Adam just needs some gentle persuasion. It's like when he was buying a road bike and he spent weeks researching, poring over magazines trying to decide on whether to get an alloy, steel or aluminium frame and whether he wanted fourteen, thirty or forty gears. In the end I took him to a bicycle shop and said, 'buy a bike Adam and we're not leaving until you do.' See gentle push.

Pushing marriage, though, is going to be the hardest sell of my life.

Feeling more positive by the cornering technique, I make Adam a coffee and head back into the bedroom. Adam is already sitting up; after getting a bollocking from his supervisor for being late, he's got to be on time today.

'For me?' he says, rubbing his eyes. He looks so adorable

in the morning. That's another thing I love about him. Wish I had remembered that, too.

I pop the coffee down on the bedside cabinet.

'Thanks.'

As I get dressed, I'm aware Adam is watching me, and I do my best to look enticing as I pull on my jeans and T-shirt, this time with the slogan *RELAX* emblazed across the chest. I like my slogan t-shirts and sweatshirts. I've got a whole bunch of them: *LOVE, RELAX, POET, MONSIEUR, CALIFORNIAN NIGHTMARE, GOOD TIMES, SUICIDE BLONDE, GIRL ON FIRE*… I won't continue, it's sounding like a list.

'You never wears skirts anymore.' Adam gives me a smile, but for a moment I'm confused.

'Don't you like me in jeans?' There's crack to my voice.

'You look lovely.' He sips his coffee.

Trying to keep my composure, I start smoothing down my jeans so as not to look at Adam. 'So, um, we need another engaged couple for the TV show, the couple we did have, turned out to be an investigator for the tabloids and Brian blamed me and well… it really wasn't my fault. No one could fill the space in time, Mel and I phoned hundreds of mad… I mean applicants and we couldn't find anyone suitable, not one, they were all you know… it was so stressful, such a pickle and he suggested you and err... I should do it, you know replace them, but only because he doesn't believe I have a boyfriend. And I said I do, I mean I would and that we will be, umm… more like we were sort of getting married anyway… you know eventually speaking, it would help me… um, it's just a speed up nothing serious of course, but I was sort of cornered, but it's not the worst idea really, is it? I thought, doesn't matter when really we… So what do you think?'

I turn round but Adam is tapping into his phone, clearly not listening to what I was saying.

'Adam!'

He looks up. 'Yes, yes I'm getting out of bed?'

'That's not what–' but Adam is already flying around the room searching for clean socks.

'Adam!'

'Have you seen any clean -'

'Bottom drawer, right-hand side,' I reply.'Adam!'

'Have you–'

'Middle drawer left-hand side. Adam!' I try and call him again, following the half-dressed, stressed out man into the bathroom.

'Adam!'

'Eve, cleaning teeth, can't talk, late again.' He sprays all over the mirror, I dutifully wipe it down looking for any opportunity to talk. He whizzes by me after rinsing and I follow him out the door, desperate to spill the truth.

I try and get his attention but time is ticking and we both have to get to work. We're rushing out the door and finally I have the opportunity to talk. The walk to the tube station will be quite sufficient, I think to myself.

Taking a deep breath, 'Adam I have committed us–'

'Shit I've forgotten my staff card. You go on I'll see you later.' He pats my arm, turns and sprints back. Brilliant. Just fantastic. Mission not accomplished.

Noticing the time I quicken my pace, he's made me late now. I shake my head and huff.

With Pharrell Williams "Happy" blasting through my earphones, I feel anything but. What am I going to say to people at work? I'll just have to go on pretending for a little while longer. And anyhow, what could possibly go wrong? I'll talk to Adam on Saturday, when we'll have more time together and I'm sure it will all be fine.

Despite running late I'm actually the first to arrive at work because Alastair has a breakfast meeting with the French producer, François Deville, again. It's all very exciting as François is very well known, and he's a finance magnet when it comes to new ideas. I make myself some office coffee when the phone rings and it's Stefan in a mad panic. He's stuck on the train and he asks me if I can do him a favour and start digitising the tapes. Happy to get a chance to do this on my own and feeling like I am invincible (even if deluded at this point), I head into his room to switch on the machines. While I wait for it all to power up, I go grab my notes and settle down at his desk.

I check the instructions on how to digitise, and when I think I know what I'm doing I pick up the tape which has Daphne and Patrick written on the label. I roll my eyes and slot it into the machine.

'What the hell are you doing in here?' Brian stomps into the room, his face a picture of barely concealed contempt.

Why does he have to be so hateful?

I take a deep breath and speak calmly. 'Stefan is stuck on the train so he's asked me to start digitising.'

'Do you know what you're doing?'

'Yes.'

'Well, don't damage anything.' He stomps back out and I can hear him order Mel to get him coffee.

I turn back to the tape and start logging.

After ten minutes I am gawping at the screen. I can't believe what I am watching or hearing for that matter. Daphne confesses in her interview that she wants to have sex three to four times a day, a couple of times in the morning and a couple of times later. She's clearly got a problem. I mean who does it more than once a week, depending on the week?

As I listen to her talk, a thought slips into my head; when was the last time Adam and I had sex? In fact I can't remember it at all – oh hang on – yes I can it was after Chuck's (Lucy's flatmate-cum-landlord) party; Adam said he was tired and we went home early, but I was just getting into the party and had energy to burn. That was two (or was it three) weeks ago? But sex isn't the 'be all' in a relationship, and it's not something that Adam seems to need too much, and anyhow we lead such busy lives. Most evenings we're just too tired and need sleep. Only, I wouldn't mind having a bit more sex. I feel like we should have more sex and I wouldn't mind feeling the spark everyone witters on about, you know, the true love spark. I let out a gasp. I didn't actually mean that.

I pick up my pen and write on the back of my hand – "6" (I know my lists well) and write "9" next to it. Perhaps Adam and I need to make more effort having sex. We're too young for life to get in the way of, well, you know, what couples in love do, especially young couples.

The weird thing is, Patrick and Daphne don't really look like sexual beings. Patrick isn't exactly desirable, and Daphne would perhaps be more attractive if she tamed her wild hair, which is overgrowing wherever you look – but I can hardly comment with my Nurse Ratched hairstyle. She's more of a Mother Nature type than a Madame, although she has a great speaking voice, warm and husky. Apparently, they met while Patrick was in therapy for sex addiction (of all things!), as he was quite the lothario (hard to imagine) around the office or some such business circles, and Daphne happened to be his sex therapist. I suppose one cliché is paramount: never judge a book by its cover. I'm not sure what their age difference is, but it must be at least fifteen or twenty years. It's not quite the Demi Moore cougar magazine article, but they seem very suited, somehow. Patrick clearly needs a tight leash – literally!

Once I've digitised the tape I group it into its bin and join all the sequences together for Stefan to watch. I play through the sequence, checking I've done it right.

'What I love about Patrick is that I trust him completely,' she says, her mouth curving into a seductive smile for the camera. Ooh, I wouldn't mind perfecting that. I attempt a sexy curl to my lip, flipping my hair like I'm in a Vidal Sassoon ad (I wish!) and mimic her dulcet tone. 'I love it when he ties me to the bed and gags me. When he takes the whip to my legs and bottom. I like showing him how much pain I can take.'

The door of the edit room swing opens and in walks Stefan followed by Jake while I'm leaning forward across the desk with my bum jutting out. I pretend I'm reaching for a pen. The sequence continues to play. 'Sometimes Patrick puts a leash on me while I call him "Sir" and kneel to perform oral sex on him. It was my idea, to teach him the balance of dominance,' her voice resonates loud and proud.

I sink down and write nonsense into my pad, my cheeks burning bright red.

'The first time Patrick hit me with a riding crop it was amazing. I had bruises all across my bum and at the back of my thighs, but it was exhilarating.'

Jake walks over to me, dressed in perfectly fitted black jeans and black T- shirt with a pair of sunglasses attached. Stefan's face seems a little puffed out; I suspect he ran all the way here.

'Oh...Hi,' I say breezily, as if I've only just noticed them arrive.

Amusement tugs at Jake's lips.

Red-faced, I turn back to the monitor.

This is more embarrassing than the time I watched an episode of *Sex and the City* with mum and dad in which they kept referring to a female toy. Needless to say, the channel was zapped.

And the ordeal isn't over... the tape continues playing.

'And then other times it's the other way round. I tie him up and whip his penis and balls, then torture him with candle wax and ice simultaneously. The body is so reactive once it's confused. Free for the primal juices to run.'

The sequence eventually stops running.

For a moment no one says anything, and I can't even bring myself to look at Jake or Stefan.

Stefan clears his throat. 'Super Eve, thanks for that.'

'Sure. It was a... p...pleasure.' I cringe, not looking at either of them.

I make a hasty exit, as I walk past Jake, our eyes meet; he grins and I feel myself blush. As soon as I close the door behind me, I hear Stefan and Jake let out a chuckle.

All morning I can't stop thinking about sex. I even type fellatio instead of aspect ratio on the production notes. Mel kindly points out my error – I was horrified; on the plus side my spelling was accurate, for once. And then I think Alastair has asked me to arrange an orgy? When I ask him to repeat the question, it turns out he wanted me to arrange the orangery. I tell myself to stop thinking about sex. The trouble is, when you tell yourself not to think about something, that's all you can think about, and so when Jake is talking about cinematic climax, I can't help sniggering like a school kid. I have to pop out for some fresh air to try and calm down. Luckily, I manage to get through without any further innuendos. The best bit about the day is having no Brian around. Without him there's a whole different atmosphere in the office, everyone works hard but is far more relaxed, happier.

Before I know it's 6:30pm and I'm heading out the door to collect Lucy.

We arrive at *Cocteau* bar, and while I nab a table, Lucy heads to the bar to order two double gin and tonics. It's Friday, there's already a sprinkling of people at the tables and propping the bar; uber cool Soho types who have that pseudo-creative-rich-interesting persona down to a tee – and good hair.

Lucy arrives with our G&T's and sits down. For a few moments we drink in silence.

'So what's wrong Ducky Doo?' Lucy knows me too well.

Actually, I really want to tell everything to Lucy; it would be good to hear her opinion. So I tell her all about Brian and that Adam and I will be stars of the show. Only she stares at me incredulously, eyes wider than an American highway.

'But they can't force you to do something you don't want to do.'

'It's ok, I said yes.'

'But don't you have to be authentically engaged?' She checks out my ring-less finger and sighs.

I scowl. 'Not yet, I haven't even told him about it.'

Lucy cackles with laughter. 'Oh Eve, that's a relief.'

'But don't you get it, Adam has to propose otherwise I'm

out of a job.'

'They can't sack you. It's unethical.'

'But I want to get married. I want to prove Brian wrong.'

'But why?' She gestures wildly with her hands and a little bit of the gin slops onto the table. 'Besides you hate being in front of the camera.'

'I'll be ok.'

'But why do you want to even get married? Why can't you just live with each other like normal people? You're barely out of the cot!'

'Why can't you just be happy for me Luce?'

'Because I think you're making a mistake.'

I glare at her defiantly.

'You should be having fun not settling for the first guy that doesn't jerk you about.'

'Not everyone needs to shag everything in sight,' I mumble.

'Hey lady, don't be a bitch, it doesn't suit you.'

'No, that's your job.'

Lucy takes a sip of her gin. 'This is all Ben's fault.'

'It's got nothing to do with Ben.'

I know she's anti-marriage; her parent's divorce hit her hard and she's so career-driven men are just toys to pick up and put down. I get that. But just because she doesn't want to settle down doesn't mean we all have to think like her. I've always liked the idea of sharing my life with someone. As annoying as my parents can be, there is no mistake they are made for each other.

Wanting to get off the subject, I start telling her about Daphne and Patrick and their s&m antics and this seems to do the trick. Seeing Lucy grinning is one of the nicest things in life, like putting your cold feet in toasty slippers of love. When she gets a twinkle in her eye it's as though she's devoured the teacher's cookies all over again. Addictions for us both – no wonder we were always in trouble at school.

'I quite like the idea of being chained to the bed and taken by surprise for some rough primal sex,' Lucy says casually, as though we were discussing the weather.

My mouth flops open in surprise. 'But you're a feminist?'

'Being submissive in an intimate relationship is not anti-feminist. One role doesn't necessary mean you're glued to it. Mix it up. I like the idea of a man being a caveman, just taking what he wants in the bedroom.'

'Her fiancé hits her with a riding crop and she says it is amazing,' I say doubtfully.

'The furthest I got was having hot candle wax dripped onto my body.'

I stare at Lucy riveted. 'Did you like it?'

'Not my bag really, not too keen on pain in general, but I could put up with being whipped by pervy Pete's silken drawer of fetishes!' she says with a dismissive shrug.

I feel a tiny lurch in my stomach. Lucy's not even in a relationship and she has more sex than me.

'What else does Daphne like?'

'Nipple clamps.'

'Oo, ouch.'

'They're huge, well she's quite um… and she gets them tugged too.'

'Double ouch.'

'Big Double D ouch!'

Lucy snorts with laughter. 'They sound quite the kinky couple. I think I'll watch the show just to see those two.'

'How much sex do you think you should have in a

relationship?' I ask, casually. 'Like on a weekly scale, once, twice a week?'

Lucy arches a brow at me. 'Well that depends, some people don't need sex as much as others.'

'Daphne says she has to have sex twice to four times a day.'

'Well I'm not sure about twice a day but when I'm in a relationship I can go for days without having sex and then we'll be at it like rabbits all weekend.'

'But it's natural that things slow down, isn't? You know for things to become a bit...' boring, no, I didn't mean boring. I meant... a bit... 'Err... less intense.'

'Oh yeah that's a common problem in long-term relationships,' says Lucy.

But Adam and I have only been together for five months. This can't be good.

'You could try spicing things up. Do you have handcuffs?'

'What do I want with hand... oh' I make a face and get to my feet. 'Another round?'

I have a boring sex life, I think unhappily to myself. Adam and I have never been "at it" like rabbits, and between you and me, I don't much get "it". I mean it just seems so much effort for so little reward. And what's wrong with just having sex, no gimmicks, and no toys, just taking time to touch and caress each other?

As I reach the bar, I recognise the back of a head; it's Jake – oh no just as I thought I left the messy workday behind me. My stomach makes a strange gurgling noise. I haven't really eaten much today and nerves really do go at the stomach lining.

Jake is wearing his black jeans and T-shirt. He's got that macho chiselled look and moody presence a lot of girls go for, all over manly and confident. I've always preferred the sensitive types. The guy next to him is sporting mad hair, one adverse to brushes and hairstyling. I feel I've found a kindred spirit or the only other customer of my mum's hairdresser.

'Two months ago I was off the beaten track, filming a wildlife shoot in Cambodia, the months before that, children in war-torn Uganda, but now I'm filming a fucking reality TV show about weddings,' Jake exclaims.

Mad-hair guy cackles. 'It doesn't seem possible that the man who's the epitome of anti marriage, anti constitution, anti this and anti flipping that… is making a TV show about weddings. You should keep ants as pets mate, you're so friggin antsypantsy!'

'Yeah the joke's on me.' Jake drawls. 'What about you, you always said you drew the line at working on reality TV.'

'Hmm yeah, well my priorities have changed. I have those dreaded blasting commitments now; what do they call them? Oh yeah, responsibilities. Besides, making the jump from Grip to Sound Recordist requires sacrifices. Beggars can't be choosers.'

I duck my head to hide that I am eavesdropping but I kind of want to bring them to task at their arrogant attitudes. Reality TV can actually be really useful, and I think about the marathon run of *Don't Tell The Bride* I watched in preparation for our show and most of the enjoyment derided from the brides hating everything their groom picked out. But I bet shows like *Made in Chelsea* and *The Only Way is Essex* give an insightful glimpse into different cultures? Ahum! Anyhow, I myself prefer the reality shows that are physically challenging. I sit there thinking – I could never be in a kind of show like that, as everything seems scarily high, or the harnesses don't look secure, or who could eat that, it's disgusting. TV Shows like *I'm a Celebrity Get Me Out of Here*, and that island survival thingy. Okay, maybe I'm not a diehard fan of them either.

I suppose I shouldn't be surprised that Jake doesn't like reality TV shows, or maybe it's weddings he doesn't like. No wonder he scoffed at my age and marriage ambitions.

I shake my head and grunt at them under my breath. Unfortunately a secret grunt with alcohol sloshing about in a practically empty stomach apparently is not so secret… they both turn around.

'Hello Eve.'

'Oh hi.' I adopt a tone of surprise as if I've only just noticed them. I turn back to the bar and the bartender looks at me expectantly. I give my order.

Feeling self-conscious, I glance over at Jake and mad hair.

'So, are you ready for your debut?' says Jake.

'Debut? Um… oh that.' I say, immediately feeling stupid.

'Have you met Jet?'

'Not properly, I've seen you around, although you look a bit different.'

'It's the hair, isn't it? Found a lollipop in it this morning. It's in that in-between stage of mayhem and confectionary attacks.'

'Tell me about it,' I relax into a smile.

'Are you here with anyone?' Jake asks.

'Yes a friend, she's over there.' I look over and Lucy is staring, goggle-eyed, at the two handsome men beside me.

'Ok, we'll see you later.'

I walk over to Lucy. She continues to stare beyond me.

'Hot diggity,' she says.

'Lucy, I came here to forget work. Stop and NO! No flipping

way.'

I sit, breathe, and look forward to carrying on our girl's night. I pick up the drink to toast with her…

'How about we join you lovely ladies?' Jet doesn't actually wait for a response.

'Absolutely,' Lucy purrs.

'I'm Jet.' He thrusts his hand.

'I bet you are. What fuel do you take?'

I grimace.

'And I'm Jake, more environmentally-friendly than him.' Jake plonks himself down and Lucy is practically panting. 'You work downstairs?'

'That's right, I'm Lucy. It's acceptable for the gentry to mix with the downstairs now! England's moved on.' She toys with her hair.

I grimace some more. 'Jake is the director on *Wedding Wipeout*,' I inform Lucy, wishing I could pinch her arm from across the table. 'And Jet's the sound recordist.'

'Cool. Pleasure to meet you both. I love a bit of reality TV. The things people are willing to say or do for their chance in the limelight cracks me up,' she flicks her hair. Is this her idea of subtle body language? Enough with people having good hair; if I flicked mine it would sever my forehead just now.

'What sad people do for a shitty bit of fame!'

'Thanks very much,' I say morosely wanting to kick her under the table.

'Well, you my darling will be the exception to the rule.'

'Oh yes, that's right,' says Jet. 'You're going to be a contestant.'

I wince – I didn't mean to.

'You know we're going to be filming your proposal. That's

fucking brave. What a moment to have a camera crew stuck in your face!'

'I'm sure it'll be fine,' I say, swallowing down a scream. 'I hear Kimberly's dogs aren't yet happy with the hotel's facilities.' Moving the conversation away from me.

'Yes, it's difficult getting the right standards for the mutts, let alone her.' Jake quips.

'A train wreck for sure, I hope you're insured.' Lucy rubs her hand in glee.

'She's reformed,' I say. 'And she's found love.'

'Oh how lovely, should be joyful,' Lucy sniggers. 'And who's the one with the Master from Oxford, and so young?'

'That's Stacey. And it's Harvard.' I hunch my shoulders gloomily and sip on my G&T. All the candidates have something interesting to say, but what do I have – a scrapping of a 2.2 degree in theatre and film studies, plus a criminal record for being drunk and disorderly?

'Don't forget online marketing genius,' Jake adds.

'Right up her own arse probably,' Lucy cackles. 'Does she have a Master in that too, or a PHD in 'très irritant'? You wouldn't have a wedding with Stacey, you'd have a debating committee from the H'ordeuvres until you elected the desert.'

Jet laughs. 'You're funny.'

'And you're cute,' she flirts.

I roll my eyes and take another sip.

'My favourite couple has to be Daphne and Patrick, Eve's been informing me all about them.' Lucy gives the table a loaded wink and I choke on my G&T; I snort loudly, which causes liquid to promptly reappear from my left nostril. Classy, Eve.

'Personally, I think people are just jumping on the

bandwagon after that stupid grey book. I mean, if you have to have your grey matter awakened by badly written tripe, you deserve to be whipped and chastised,' Lucy laughs. 'And then, of course, we have lovely, sweet Eve who believes in fairytales and happy ever afters.'

Then, it's as though she can't help herself. 'Rushing headlong into marriage with the first man that comes along.'

I'm not sure what's got into her tonight, but Jet is looking flummoxed, and Jake's brows are knitted in a frown.

I give a short, fake laugh. 'Who doesn't believe in happy ever afters.'

'You don't want Eve to get married?' Jake asks Lucy.

'I don't see why she has to rush into it, no,' she replies.

'It does surprise me someone so young wants to get married,' Jake says.

'Oh, Eve's been wanting to get married since she was five years old.'

They are talking about me as if I'm not even there. 'I have not wanted to get married since I was five years old.' I object.

'You have. You always wanted to play at weddings and you wanted me to dress up as a groom.'

'That's because you looked like a boy,' I retort.

'Now who looks like the boy,' she snaps back.

I subconsciously touch my hair.

'I think it's got a lot to do with your upbringing,' Lucy trills on happily and drunkenly with her let's-attack-Eve-and-her-personal-life-in-front-of-strangers discourse.

There's another pause, where everyone is looking at me and I really don't know what to say. What is this the Blair-Eve-Witch-hunt?

'Eve's parents are evangelicals,' Lucy informs them in

hushed secretive tones. 'Marriage is a sacred vessel in which to conduct a proper union and you know all that bullshit.'

'I'm not marrying Adam to please my parents,' I finally find my voice. 'I'm marrying Adam because he's a great guy, and we have a lot in common.'

'And you love him?' Jake adds.

'Well... obviously,' I snap.

'No you don't,' Lucy says. 'You two couldn't be more different. The thing you've got to know about our Eve is that she has her little lists and she is never happier than when she crosses something off it.'

'What's that got to do with anything?'

'I'm just saying you love lists, and because marriage is on that list, you will not deviate until you've crossed it out. But how can you be sure you're doing it with the right man?'

I blink in shock. I love Lucy dearly, but right now I'm wondering why.

'I'm thinking of asking Andrea to marry me,' Jet suddenly pipes up, dispersing the weird tension between Lucy and me.

The look on Jake's face is priceless, and Lucy has gone a deeper shade of greyish green.

'You're getting married?' Jake seems appalled by the idea.

'I'm thinking about it, yeah.'

'Congratulations,' I say. Finally, a man who believes in marriage and the naysayers can take a running jump.

'She's got a kid,' says Jake.

'Yeah, and he's a great kid too.'

Now Jet is definitely going up in my estimation, whilst Jake is making a steady decline.

'Jake, when you get to my age you will realise that you don't want to be single forever. One day it'll catch up with you and you'll just want to find a nice girl and settle down.'

'Well, I'm not getting married. Period,' says Lucy. I look at her and her eyes are slightly unfocused. Where did she get that wine glass?

'Amen to that,' says Jake, raising his glass in the air.

'Don't you believe in marriage?' I ask.

'It's just a piece of paper.'

'That's what people say when they're frightened of commitment,' Jet and I chorus together. We clink glasses.

'Like I haven't heard that before,' Jake retorts. 'Besides, my life isn't conducive for a serious relationship right now. I'm not interested in settling anywhere.'

'Maybe you just haven't met the right girl yet,' says Lucy, swinging her head to the side and gazing adoringly at him.

I roll my eyes.

'I knew the moment I met Andrea that she was the one for me. It took a while to convince her of that, but I feel happier than I ever thought possible. I am a better man with Andrea and Tom in my life,' Jet says. 'Plus, big bonus here, I actually want to be married to Andrea. She makes me proud to be with her. My very own wonder woman. She's practical, not forgetting the incredible spinning power! Sensible, more gorgeous than a kebab after a keg load, more alive than dodgy fuse-box, spectacularly attractive when pissed off, beautiful, bit nutty, ferociously smart, clever, clever little…' Jet trails off dreamily.

Tears well up in my eyes. 'That's beautiful,' I say. Jet flashes me a smile.

Jake stares at me. It's disconcerting. I look away.

'Many things in life are difficult but that doesn't mean they aren't worth doing. Why should marriage be any different? I'm far happier when Andrea scolds me for making cornflakes sandwiches. Tom, however, thinks it's a smart breakfast; unripe toast and cornflakes in one hit!'

I giggle.

'Do you have a ring?' I ask.

'Well, I was in Cartier the other day…' his pronunciation of Cartier is stressed in all the wrong places, reminds me of Del Boy doing a French accent.

'Me too, I tried on this beautiful solitaire…' I stop. It was in my lunch hour and I was just walking by…

'Well, there was a ring I liked, but then they asked me Andrea ring size and I didn't know. Now I don't know how to get it without asking her, and I don't want to ask because it will spoil the surprise.' Suddenly he looks panicked.

'Ok, does she wear rings?' I say, getting straight to the point.

'Yes?'

'Does she ever take them off?'

'Yes when she is working in the darkroom.'

'Well, then you're going to have to take one. They can get a rough size, then make it fit properly afterwards. Easy peasy.'

Jet nods, looking at me as if I'm some kind of genius. I grin. Even Lucy's heart seems to have mellowed a little, or it could be the other glass of drink she's got in her hand. Honestly, where the hell is she getting all these drinks from? She's really canning it tonight. Oh, there's one for me too.

'Thank you.'

'You're welcome,' says Jake. When did he order drinks?

'You could film Jet and Andrea's proposal instead?' I suggest, in hope.

'No way am I making a tit of myself on camera,' Jet says.

No, leave that job to me.

'Not that you'll make a tit of yourself,' Jet recovers.

'Oh I don't know, Eve has been known to make a bit of a tit of herself on camera.'

I narrow my eyes and glare at her. She better not dare.

'How old are you?' Lucy asks Jake.

'Old enough.'

'What age is that then?' she presses.

'Twenty nine.'

'A proper grown up.'

'Not so grown up,' quips Jet. 'Aren't you thirty in a couple of months?'

Jake groans.

'Ah, my American apprentice. You have much to learn from Obi-thirty two.' We all laugh as Jet does his Alec Guinness. 'The Jedi age will be strong with this traveller. Hair will pop out of unexpected places; this is the work of the dark side! Do not be fooled by the follicle usurpers. Use the force and learn English you yanky skank!'

'What do I have to worry about? Look at all the sense that's bestowed upon one who was so silly in his youth!' Jake holds his hands up as Jet twirls himself into a mini bow.

'Turning thirty isn't so bad. You can't fight it, best embrace it like a tatty rug. Fighting is like a wave running from it's own break, a battle you have no shot of winning. And it's a well-known fact men get better looking with age. I was a dork in my 20s, then I hit my 30s and it was whoa – check me out. Gorgeous packaging or what?'

Lucy and I laugh.

'You're not worried about turning thirty, are you?' I ask Jake.

Jake gazes at me, and I find myself staring back at him, wanting to know more about him, like if he always wanted to be a documentary film-maker, what he thinks of London, of me… I cough at why I should care.

'No, not in the slightest,' but I get the sense he is, just a little. 'Time is as it is, what's there to do about it anyway, not worth any time thinking about.' He smiles wisely.

'Oh to be twenty again,' Jet zones out into his own head. 'It was all about being stupid and having stupid fun. Christ, my mates and I used to… well, as ladies are present, we used to embark upon opportunities as they arose. Do I want to be doing that now? Hell no! Your thirties are just a different fun. Twenties are for rioting!'

'Not married and being tied down.' Lucy snaps.

'I can still do fun things when I'm married, it's not a death sentence.'

'Sentence being the appropriate word.'

I glare at Lucy.

'I have lots of things to do before I'm thirty.'

'I can't remember much of my twenties. What things? Like mountain climbing?' Jet asks innocently.

'Dance on a table in Vegas.'

'You want to dance on a table in Vegas?' Jake is obviously amused by this.

'Why not?' See, I can do fun.

'If it's on *the list*, Eve will do it.'

'Is this like your hobby list?'

'Oh no this one is different. This is called my *Twenty something things to do while I'm twenty-something* list.

'What else is on that list?'

'It's private. I would like to keep it that way. My life is already too much like an open book just now.' I try and shoo the question away, but he keeps staring. Then his gaze falls with interest to my hand and he quirks a brow.

'69,' he reads aloud.

Fuck!

Blood creeps into my face. 'They're just numbers from umm, my list. It really isn't a big deal. It's just a reminder list. It's not as bad as Lucy makes out,' I gulp down my wine, buying time.

Jake gazes at me with an even more amused expression on his face.

'Number six is re-read books from college,' I say. 'You know, the ones that you don't really read, take in properly.'

'Very diligent, I'm sure. And number nine?'

'Erm, learn to spell without auto-correction on.'

'Very worthy goals,' he smiles. 'And there I thought 69 was on your tonight's list.'

I gasp in total embarrassment. I should never have written it on my hand. I begin to try and rub it out. It must have been that dratted permanent marker, an epidermis shortly follows onto the table.

Jake grins.

I roll my eyes at him, but inside I am prickling all over. I look down at my now empty glass, wishing I could have another, but thinking it's probably best I go home, and by the looks of Lucy I should probably, no, most definitely, get her home.

Lucy lays her head groggily on my shoulder, and, as we approach her apartment, a sad look crosses her face.

'I'm so sorry,' she says. 'I didn't mean to be a total bitch tonight.'

'You weren't a total one.'

'It's only because I care. You just can't go through…' She

stops mid sentence, her eyes are drooping; she needs a soft landing surface pronto.

'I know you do,' I smooth her hair back from her face.

I can sense there's something she's not telling me, but now is not the time to probe. I watch as she stumbles up the steps to her flat. She gives me a wave before falling in the door with a thud. I let out a giggle, as Chuck, her flatmate lifts her unceremoniously off the floor. Lucy toodle-pips with her random fingers hanging upside down from Chuck's arms.

CHAPTER FIVE

I wake up on Saturday alone, as Adam has gone cycling – so much for some morning hanky panky. I take a long lazy shower, wax my armpits and legs – hmm, maybe just as well we didn't get it on this morning; I resemble Chewbacca. I lather myself in smelly lotion, pluck my eyebrows, then finish off by trying to brush that dreaded hair. My fringe is less severe now; actually with a little shine serum it doesn't look so bad.

I have just put on a dress, thinking that would be better suited for what I have planned, when the bedroom door flies open and my boyfriend, resembling a bumblebee, hurls himself at me.

'Eww, get off you're all sweaty.'

Ok, perhaps not the response I should be going for when I want my boyfriend to shag me later, but we are going to be late, and he does need to shower.

'You know mum likes everyone to be punctual for lunch.'

We are late, and lunch has already been served, so we hastily sit ourselves down. The bonus of being late is that I didn't have the Spanish inquisition (a favourite pastime of my sanctimonious parents). Proceeding with their line of enquiry before we step a foot through the door surely goes against one of their Christian charitable ways? It's as though you have to pass a test of ample information before you're allowed pass the donkey stone of God's little followers. Thank heaven Nell was early, as she usually has more scandals than me and she throws in a few fake ones for good measure. Her interrogations usually involve yet another examination of her engagement finger ring, and if her name is still the same as her birth certificates. My parent's think that's a clever line of questioning rather than asking directly.

Nell irritates me like any good sister does, but we actually get on well, a relationship of banter and piss-take. She's there for me no matter what. It would have been Nell collecting me from the police cell if it hadn't been for the fact that she was honeymooning at the time. Everyone likes to say how much we look alike, but I can't really see it myself; perhaps when we were younger, but certainly not now. Nell loves dressing up, and today it's a nod to the fifties with a fitted blouse, a full petticoat-type skirt, and her long hair scraped back into a ponytail. She always looks polished and ready for the camera, totally different to me. Some of her past choices have been somewhat questionable, but she's always had that ultra glam thing going on and she is always in a pair of heels even to go to the supermarket.

'Did you hear about the couple selling golden tickets to heaven?'

'What?' I peer at my dad blankly – then recall an article I read about a Florida couple selling golden tickets to heaven. 'They were druggies. Don't tell me you believed it.'

'Eve, what do you think we are? Morons?' Mother scuttles

off to the kitchen. Maybe she didn't want an answer to that one.

Nell leans in. 'Eve, I bet they would have bought them. Shall we retire them to the US? They'd feel more at home there with other nut-jobs... I mean believers, and then our duties as daughters are done. Signed, sealed and delivered. Delivered from our mortal sins at least!'

'Nell, have you still got that roll of poppy paper from your last midnight move? You must have shares in that bubble wrap company by now.'

'Ha bloody ha, just because you and Kildare are so boringly settled doesn't mean the rest of us have to be.'

'What are you two girls whispering about? They were like this as children, always whispering at the table.' Dad unsubtly whispers to Adam.

'Sisters, Mr Poots! Plain chatterboxes talking rubbish.'

'Aren't you a bit spiky today Dr Kildare!' Nell taunts.

'Think you'll find that's Dr McDreamy.'

'Adam, you been at the prescription pad again?'

'No Nell, you been in that time machine again?'

'Yeah, you need to borrow it. When's book club?'

'Children, I mean, please darlings, don't say such…'

'Dad they're only ribbing.' I press his arm in reassurance.

'Ribs, err… no dear I think we're having a joint.' I start laughing.

'So, would you buy the golden tickets after having a joint?' I kick Nell under the table. The thought of my parents having a joint is too funny. I'm on the verge of uncontrollable giggles. Nell is on the brink too.

I don't want to discuss anything remotely adult with my parents - they're just not those sorts of parents. Let them get information via the medium of church meetings and diluted soaps.

'Half the time you girls speak a foreign language, eh Adam?'

'I think Nell's still grappling with the basics of her native tongue.'

Nell pokes her tongue out. 'How's this for native? When's your 55th birthday, next month isn't it Adam? I'll see if the bowls club is open to new members. Might need to spruce up your wardrobe first though. I hear those bowlers are right on trend with corduroys! I fear you might struggle to keep up.'

My dad smiles inanely; he didn't have a clue a minute ago let alone know what they're talking about now, and his hearing is a bit shot at the best of times.

But all I can think about when mum brings out desert is that Adam and I need to do 'it'. Not only the whole proposal thingy, but to do 'it.' It's all part of my two-birds-one-stone masterplan. Once I've eaten cake, I tell myself.

But it's not quite as easy to do either at your parent's house as you might think. I hadn't realised just how many people are in and out of the house, and I now realise that my childhood bedroom has slowly become a shrine for all global publications on Father Murphy, the American galloping priest who can do no wrong even if he is living in a huge mansion house in Beverly hills with old bunny girls among his house staff. Nell's room is pretty much the same as before, so why mine has been sacrificed just puts another stake into their disappointment in me. Anyway there are no flipping locks on any of the door. Not even the bathroom.

But that can just add to the excitement, I tell myself.

Mother comes in with Tabitha and sits down with a packet of smoked salmon in her pocket – my mother is odd at the best of times. Today she's dressed in a head to foot salmon twinset. Camouflage for mothers? Does she now coordinate with the demon cat's titbits? She'd look pretty if she didn't wear a thunder face all day long. Only that wretched creature makes her soft round the edges.

'Eve, I would like you to look for a nicer bed for Tabitha on the net thing.'

'Tabitha already has my bed, why would she…'

'She's not settling, she needs something cosier.'

'Come now Eve. If Tabitha isn't settling.' I glare at Nell.

'I'll keep my–'

'Maybe, red velvet? Nothing cheap looking. I could take it into the kitchen so she always has a place to rest.' Will Dracula's coffin do, Mother dear?

Mother just stares at Tabitha feeding her slivers from her pocket – the smell is gross.

When Tabitha's finished regurgitating, Mother just throws it on the fire. I wish she had swapped hands at that precise moment, and that little Tabs there had got a prompt heat wave. Now we all sit in a stinky den of burning fish and cat sick.

'I'll make a pot of tea.' Mother announces, as she removes the last putrid spill of salmon from her salmon skirt.

'Better take Tabitha with you, don't want her to suffer separation anxiety, do we Eve?'

'Nell's right, Mother.'

Mother dutifully picks up the spoilt beast, who hisses at us from her shoulder. It was a good save on Nell's part, as Tabitha has ruined more of our clothes than we care to mention. Whenever her deluded servant goes out the room she just attacks us with her claws, always has, but Mother won't hear a word against her though.

By five pm, we still haven't done it. Everyone is slumped before the almighty Father Murphy preaching to us the wonders of God's natural selection, and those who are weak and impoverished need to find strength to believe and their predicaments will be answered unto the great and powerful Lord almighty. Tell that to a child born into poverty and suffering, or a girl trying to learn to read and write in a regime that prohibits her learning, getting stoned to death for all her evil longings of wanting an education.

Oh this is ridiculous.

'Hey Adam,' I say in a low, husky voice. 'Fancy a walk?'

'What for?'

'Get some fresh air into our lungs.'

'I've had plenty…' I step on his foot and press down to cut him off before he spouts on about the joys of getting on a bike.

He looks at me confused and frowns.

'After a week in the London grimy air...' I stretch up and feign tiredness.

No one blinks away from Father Murphy's mountain-top rant: Nell is dozing, it's not often she has time off at the weekend.

'Just… be there,' I whisper, feeling the frustration growing.

I hurry down the garden towards the shed wanting out from the mad household of anti-heretics. I hear faint footsteps following. I dart into the bushes.

'Hello there,' I whisper from the leaves

'Er, Hi,' says Adam with a frown. 'Eve, what is this all about?'

I take him by the hand and lead him into the shed. I push the wooden door shut with abandoned gesture and trail my finger down his chest, like a cheap aftershave commercial. 'We never do it spontaneously anymore.'

'What?' Adam just stares at me, now I do feel slightly ridiculous.

'Come on.' I start unbuttoning his shirt with a sultry expression. 'Let's do it. Right here, right now.'

'Are you crazy?' Adam pushes my fingers out of the way and tries hastily to re-button his shirt. 'Your parents are less than thirty feet away.'

'So what?' We're young, we're in love…' I trail a hand even further down and Adam's eyes widen.

'Eve what's got into you?' He hisses. 'Stop it!'

I flinch away. Doesn't he want to have sex with me? A voice cuts through the darkness.

'What are you two up to?' Nell asks with more curiosity than evil Tabitha.

Thank God it is just Nell.

'Oh nothing just needed a break from blaring bullshit disguising itself as God.'

Adam tuts and throws me a dirty look. 'I'm going back inside.' He stomps away and I try not to cry.

'What the hell was that all about?' Nell's green eyes look wide and curious.

'Nothing.'

'Nothing? Looked like a great big nothing.'

'It's just… we were just… it was nothing.' I sigh.

'If there's trouble in paradise you'll have to speak up sooner rather than later. God waits for no man.'

I giggle despite how disappointed I am feeling. 'Would you stop referring to my normal relationship like it was some Barbara Cartland enchantment story.'

'So there is trouble in Paradise?'

'Paradise was where all the trouble started if you don't

remember, child of bibleland!'

Nell grins and puts her arm around me. 'It was all Eve's fault, she was the one who started it; bad apple that one.'

We wander round the garden but I don't confide in her. What can I say? Adam and I aren't having sex but it's ok because I need Adam to propose so that I don't get sacked. I shrug at the feeling of melancholy; I'm sure it will work itself out in the wash. Instead, I question Nell on her *beaus*, she has three on the go at the moment; there's Saturday night man, Mr Wednesday lunchman, and Fun Man Friday. She's not decided yet on any, keeping them on the books until one wins. For that moment, I'm envious of her freedom.

As I get into the car I still feel deflated. I failed on both accounts and now I don't know what to do. I don't even know if Adam wants to be with me. He doesn't seem to want to have sex with me. What if –

I can't even finish my thoughts.

And then I'll have no home, no job. If Adam doesn't really want me, Brian will make sure I get the boot because of it. I'll be back to square one, and that future square could be the dimensions of a cell after I maim Brian.

'Eve, is everything ok?'

'Yes! No!' Who am I trying to kid!

'Look, I'm sorry about earlier, it's not that I didn't want to… you know…'

'Oh I know,' I jump in quickly, blushing like a beetroot. 'Anyway that isn't it.'

'It isn't?'

For a moment we're just silent.

'What is it then?'

It's now or never.

'Here's the thing. We need another engaged couple for the TV show and Alastair wants us to be one of the couples,' I blurt out.

'But we're not engaged.'

'I know. They want you to propose on camera.'

'But that's absurd.'

'Is it?'

I look at Adam and he is looking, well, shell-shocked. Then his eyes return to the road before we veer off into hedgerow.

'If we don't I think I'll be out of a job.'

'They can't make you get engaged,' he says forcefully.

'But it might not be so bad.' There's a slight desperation to my tone.

Adam looks paler than usual and a bit freaked out. 'You're not serious are you?'

I wince. 'Surely being engaged to me isn't that bad.'

'I didn't mean it like that. It's just, we've only been together a while, there's my exams.'

'It's not like they expect us to get married afterwards, we just need to be engaged for the show and there's a £100,000 cash prize to the winning couple. Look, it's silly I should have told them no to start with. They'll just have to find another couple. Forget it,' I say.

'£100,000 you say?'

I feel a glimmer of hope. 'Yes, and the most amazing honeymoon destination.'

'I bet we'd make ideal contestants, me the brains, you the beauty.'

I let that one slide.

'OK, let's do it.'

I stare at him with a mixture of disbelief and relief. 'You really want to do this?'

'Yeah, why not.'

I throw myself at him, giddy as an excited puppy and kiss him loudly on the cheek.

He laughs, as the car takes a swerve. 'I will make you the best wif… I mean fiancée ever.' I promise.

And to top it off, we had sex after we got home. I didn't feel the earth move, but that's ok. I was probably too heated up to relax into it, and at least we did it. Hopefully, the draught season is finally fading. Woohoo!

CHAPTER SIX

I dash to the loo while the film crew is setting up. I feel completely sick with nerves – and where is Adam? He said he was going for a bike ride to clear his head but that was like two hours ago. He has been rather jumpy and nervous yesterday, and we haven't talked much after he agreed to propose, which is why I sent him out to get some fresh air this morning.

I tug at the hem of my leather mini-skirt. It's a bit too short and with the heels I borrowed from Lucy I feel too done up. At least the slogan tee reading *Good Times* tones the look down somewhat. Lucy wanted me to wear a tight-fitting top too, but that would have been a step too far, besides, it would look as if I'd bandaged up a couple of reject dim sums. My best assets are my legs, so I might as well put them on show today.

At least I have finally sorted out my hair, splashing out on a professional hair cut, which was overdue by about fifteen years. To leave home is one thing, to leave the traditional clutches of your mother's whims is another! Any bad haircut you get in Berkshire will have been at some point been backed by my loopy mother. The hair stylist performed a small miracle; she has managed to cut it in longer layers, made the fringe shorter and blunter. I no longer look like a cast member of the village of the damned, and the fringe is now hip not hacked. I also had a professional manicure. My credit card is now seriously maxed out, but this is a special occasion.

That's been one of the perks of knowing he's going to propose, being able to sort out my hair and my nails so I can look the best I can when Adam proposes. And now it's going to be on TV. *I wonder if Ben will see it?*

The random thought takes me by surprise, but as I check myself in the mirror, the thought makes me smile because I have never looked better. I wonder who will see it?

I dab on some lip-gloss and give myself another smile to muster some courage. I wonder if Adam's gone to pick up a ring and that's why he's taking so long? I don't mind if he hasn't bought one because we could always choose it together. Besides I know the production team have brought in a stand-in ring in case he hasn't.

Well, I can't hide in here forever. Squaring my shoulders I take a deep breath and push open the door.

The living room is overrun with cables and lights and I hover uncertain in the doorway not knowing what to do with myself.

'S'cuse me milady,' says Jet, wielding a giant stick.

'Sorry,' I say, jumping out of the way and stumbling into Jake.

Jake's hands grip my arms to steady me. 'Careful, we don't want you breaking a leg.'

My breath catches. 'Aren't you supposed to tell me to break a leg?'

'That would be an awful shame for such legs,' he says.

I try to look disapproving but a smile licks my face. What! I have to take the compliments where I get them.

'Stand there,' Jet commands. 'And don't move. I'll mic you up.'

Jake and I are facing each other and it feels quite intimate standing this close, I can feel my heart thumping against my ribcage. Jet hooks the microphone to the belt of my skirt. The fact that I am sandwiched between two of what Lucy would describe as Hotties has not gone unnoticed by me and my face boils.

'Is this what you normally wear when you're relaxing at home?' His fingers press against my bare arms, causing a tingling sensation all over my body.

'All the time!' I stare back at him, face feeling even hotter. I clear my voice awkwardly.

'All done,' says Jet.

I quickly step out of Jake's grip. 'Did you get the ring?' I turn to Jet and clear my throat again.

'I did. I've got it here.' He pats his jacket.

'You've got a ring?' Jake stares at Jet shell-shocked.

'Can I see it?' I clap my hands with delight.

Jet pulls out the ring and I stare at it. I feel quite faint; it's the most beautiful ring. It's glossy enough to say *wow* and demure enough to wear all the time.

'It's gorgeous,' I whisper in awe.

Jet looks at me proud as punch. Tears well up in my eyes.

'Are you crying?' Jake stares at me.

I sniff them back. 'Of course not!' I turn to Jet. 'When are you going to ask her?'

He shrugs, putting the ring back in his pocket. 'I don't know yet. I want to do it right, make it really romantic, you know, posh grub n'all that fancy gassy grape juice and nothing that you can understand on the menu.'

'In five,' a girl with a natty headset interrupts. 'Is the future groom here, yet?'

With my mic hooked up I walk away from everybody and into the kitchen. I want to get married, of course I do. It's just not exactly how I imagined it. I sort of… would have liked to be surprised, like Jet's plan. I wasn't quite expecting it to be in front of an audience. That's not what's important. Adam is going to propose, that's all that matters, and under these circumstances alone that says a lot about him, conceding to do this to help my career. I open the fridge and pour myself a glass of wine, for some more Dutch courage. Brian comes in and helps himself to a glass - what is he doing here?

He takes a sniff of the wine and wrinkles his nose.

Well don't drink it if it offends your pig nostrils, I think to myself.

He grumbles something like 'cheap plonk' under his breath and I'm just about to retaliate, then think better of it, letting out a puff of air in disgust and walk out.

I'm not hanging out in the kitchen with Brian. I don't know why he's even here. He probably still doesn't believe I have a boyfriend.

Oh come on Adam where are you? No one's going to be happy if you're late.

I reach the edge of the living room while everyone is darting around looking busy. I know we have a lot of crewmembers because I've seen the crew list, but seeing most of them in this cramped apartment is making me feel claustrophobic.

'Ready?' says the girl with the natty headset.

'As I'll ever be.'

But I don't feel ready at all. I follow her over to the sofa, conscious of all the eyes on me. I feel stupidly over… or rather underdressed; oh you know what I mean. Everyone else is in jeans and trainers. I step over the obstacle course made up of electrical cords, trying not to trip or knock anything over. I spent all morning cleaning the apartment, and I have thrown the newly washed throws over the manky sofa underneath. I think the fairy lights are a nice touch, but now all I can see are trampled boots on the carpet and discarded coffee cups all over the place.

'What shall I do with this?' I hold up my glass of wine.

'Just drink it,' she says.

So I do, quickly, and then cough and inadvertently let out a small burp.

'Another?' she asks, looking amused, as I hand over the empty glass.

'Nope, I'm ok, thanks.'

I push the Sunday newspapers to one side and sit down. Jake is messing with the camera and Jet is fiddling with the boom levels. Everyone is busy doing something except me. A wave of self-conscious hits me and my mini skirt. I squeeze my knees together and cross my ankles. I should never have let Lucy convince me to dress like some sort of reality star desperate for exposure. I feel a trickle of sweat snaking down my back and notice my hands are shaking. Why am I so nervous? I need to calm down.

I can feel my confidence about the whole thing waning. I'm no good in front of the camera; I don't even like having my photo taken. I don't know half the people here. Why do I feel so ridiculous, and where the friggin hell is Adam? He should be here by now.

As if on cue I hear the door key go and my stomach swoops.

Oh God, Adam is here! He's finally here! And he's going to propose. I start to fizz and my heart is thumping loudly; I'm surprised Jet hasn't come over to adjust the level. It's weird knowing the camera is watching my every move. I don't know how actors do it.

Adam leans his 6foot2 Hercules frame against the doorway, the image spoilt somewhat by sporting a pointy cycling helmet with a yellow and black striped Lycra top, plus matching shorts. He does resemble a giant bumblebee, a little ridiculous. I hope he changes into um, well, anything else to be frank.

The look on his face is one I don't think I've seen before – guilt-slash-worry.

'Hi.' I smile encouragingly at him, my voice comes out in a squeak.

He stares back not quite meeting my eyes. 'Hi,' he says. 'You look… nice.'

It feels awkward. Of course it's awkward; everyone is watching us like hawks. 'I'm just going to hop into the shower.'

'OK'. I say, trying to sound casual but feeling anything but.

Adam leaves and Jake's camera turns to me. I could really do with another drink.

'Eve, I'm just going to ask you a few questions, ok?'

Oh no. I thought I answered all the questions back in the office.

Breathing out forcefully, I tap my newly painted nails against the armrest. 'Sure,' I smile. 'Go ahead.' My heart thumps, and nerves are making my stomach heave.

'Why do you want to marry Adam?'

Ok I've got this. I've thought about this since he first asked *the* question and caught me off guard. 'I want to marry Adam because he's a wonderful person. He's smart, handsome and kind. He's going to be such a good doctor and he's caring ...' I'm getting misty-eyed. 'He's a good guy and there's not many of those around. He's direct and to the point. You've got to hold onto the good ones.' I meet the camera lens and smile.

'Hold on? You make it sound like a bad boat crossing!' Jake replies.

My smile wavers.

'Do you think your religious upbringing has made you want to marry at such a young age?'

Hey! That's unfair. He can't use information he attained under... under social... conditions, and I'm not too young to marry.

'Religion merely says marriage should not be taken for granted. Plus, it's a public declaration of love and commitment. But even if you're not religious that's got to be a good place to start from, don't you think?' Wow, I've quite impressed myself. 'I've always believed in sharing my life exclusively with one man. I think there's something wonderful about that level of oneness. Scary, sure, but awesome all the same.'

'How long have you been dating?'

'Five months'

'That's not very long.'

'It's long enough to know we have a connection.'

'What was your childhood like?'

My childhood? What's that got to do with anything?

'My parents were... are... devout Christians,' I sigh, wishing Jake would stop this unnecessary intrusion. 'I grew up in a household with no board games, no music except hymns and no books except the bible and pilgrims progress on a Sunday after a long church service. But they've lightened up in their old age. I couldn't name one UK town, but I could have told you about the old testament and parables galore until the cows came home.' I laugh, in aid of making my childhood sound less crazy. 'We were home-schooled until my sister Nell rebelled at seven. Then we went to a regular school and they believe that's when it all went wrong. They thought we went off the rails. They became less rigid, but, that has nothing to do with me wanting to get married at all.'

'But why not just live together?'

'It's not the same. I want to be married knowing we are both committed to sharing our life together.'

'You're very young?'

I'm not on trial here am I? Please change the line of questioning Jake

'Well, I know that marriage is not something you go into and be on autopilot. Don't expect it to work just because you've got married and there's nothing more to prove. You have to nurture it.'

'Do you think he can make you happy?

I gawp at the camera. What kind of question is that? Is he being deliberately obtuse?

I still can't speak. I sit there, dazed.

Finally I find my voice. 'I wouldn't be marrying him if I didn't.'

But will he make me happy? I'm suddenly stricken by this thought. I know I always try to make Adam happy. I always think about things to make his day that little bit easier, nicer. I make him a pack lunch when I can be bothered to make mine, because otherwise he forgets to eat. Okay, granted, they aren't the most appetising of sandwiches, and sometimes the sandwich concept gets forgotten entirely – those are what I call my

Danish open sandwich days (aka sludge in cling film) – but it's the thought that counts. I always let him choose the dinner or the TV channel, but what does Adam do for me? I shake this silly nonsense out of my head, feeling suddenly disloyal and stupid for even thinking this. It's Jake's fault, putting silly doubts into my head.

'I don't think he will make you happy.'

For a moment I am too shocked to respond, is this his intention to mock me in front of everyone? Is he looking for something juicy for the show?

The camera stays trained on me, but I'm still searching for a suitable response, which doesn't involve hitting him or shouting. I lift my chin nobly.

'I am not interested in falling in and out of love. If I can't love someone forever then why love at all?' I can feel the blood rush to my face and tears sneaking beneath my lashes.

'Marriage is a wonderful thing, it's the ultimate gesture of love. It may well be a piece of paper when all's done and said, but it's a symbol of total and utter devotion to another being, another soul, hopefully your soul mate. Why would people continue to get married if they didn't feel that urge, that extraordinary want? Besides from it being its own industry, it is one created from love, and without love there's no hope.'

There's a spontaneous round of applause from one of the crew, I don't know who because I am too busy glaring daggers at Jake. He steps away from the camera and he scowls at me. Why is he scowling? If anyone should be scowling it should be me!

The pretty girl with the headset comes over and starts plumping up the cushion behind me. There are tears in her eyes. 'That was beautifully said.'

'Oh… thank you.'

A few minutes later Adam is back, freshly showered and wearing the clothes I 'might' have put out. He sits down on the sofa and grabs my hand, his fingers squeezing mine. I can tell he is nervous because his hand is a little clammy. I give him an encouraging smile. How dare Jake try and put doubts into my head.

He focuses on me and takes a deep breath. Oh God. He's just going to come straight out and ask me. Lucy is definitely going to be maid of honour and Nell will be bridesmaid. I wonder if I should ask Ali to be a bridesmaid too? I suddenly realise his face is contorting in pain, and as our eyes meet, there's a nervous twitch in the corner of his eye.

'I think it might be best if we had some time apart.'

Gosh he smells good too. That is the Space NK shower-gel I got him at Christmas. Hang on, what did he say?

'I'm not sure how I feel about this anymore.'

I can't speak as my brain tries to make sense of what he is saying.

Is this his idea of a joke? But then I remember he doesn't do jokes. I wait for him to crack a smile but he peers back at me, his face pained.

'I need some space.'

Why isn't he proposing? What is happening?

He continues to look at me with this newly acquired pained expression and I can't help but wonder if he uses this on patients as he delivers the bad news.

'I thought I could go through with this, but I can't.'

Go through with this?

'We're too young to get married.'

Waves of hurt and humiliation race over me. I open my

mouth a couple of times to speak but then I stop. I can't find the words. My brain and mouth have forgotten how to function. All I can think is, *what do I do now? What? What?*

'I think you should pack your things and leave. It's for the best'

His words are like a knife to my chest. Tears are edging past my lashes and I can feel the camera zooming in on me, capturing my reaction. I try to rearrange the devastated expression on my face, but I don't know how too.

'I didn't realize I was getting on your nerves.' I finally say. My throat feels as if it's been squeezed tight.

Adam goes pink. 'You're not. You don't. That's not it.'

He was supposed to be The One. I thought he was The One.

'I'm sorry. You deserve better than me.'

I think I'm going to be sick.

I stand up suddenly, the blood rushing to my head, and I really do feel sick. 'Right…'

I don't know what else there is for me to say.

The camera, the lights, it's all too much. Why did he choose to humiliate me like this - in front of everyone? I have to get out of here. I stagger over cables, rushing for the door, grabbing my bag and not daring to look at anyone. No one tries to stop me.

'Where are you going?'

'What do you care?' I lash out.

'Eve!' he says in alarm. 'Stop! Please!'

I swivel round to confront him one last time but a sea of eyes stare back at me. I can't be here, not with everyone watching, staring. A sob catches me off guard, I turn away, a hand grabs my arm but I shrug it off. My own hands are trembling as I yank open the front door and step out into the cold air, the door slamming shut behind me.

I stand on the doorstep. What the F-uck just happened!

I wrap my arms around my chest to keep warm and to stop myself from shaking like a mental patient, then try and walk down the pathway. If he had doubts, then why didn't he tell me this when we were alone? Why did he wait until we had the entire film crew to witness my embarrassment? Why humiliate me like this? Did I mean nothing to him?

I taste the bile rising in my throat and press my hands to my mouth, swallowing, tears streaming down my face. *This must be a nightmare. I'll wake at any moment.*

'Eve!'

A voice bellows from the front door. Nope I'm awake, this is real.

I turn half-expecting, half-wanting it to be Adam. It's not. Without saying anything I turn on my heels and start running, but wearing these stupid flipping high heels, I misjudge the distance between the pavement and the kerb, and like some stupid damsel in a movie I inevitably tumble over, scraping my knee on the ground. I wail like a three year old.

'Eve!' Jake picks me up, wrapping his arms around me, holding me tightly as I cry into his jumper. All my emotions have smashed to the ground, an overloaded tea tray of delusional dreams; all the hopes gurgling in the spillage, wishing for something to save them, the last mouthful trickling out, dripping off the sides and disappearing down the gutter - forever. I can hardly draw a breath; my chest is so tight with pain. Finally when my eyes can focus and the tears have been absorbed, I look up at Jake's concerned face.

'You must think I'm pathetic.'

'No, I actually think you were very brave.'

A stray tear escapes down my left cheek.

There is silence; Jake lifts my chin gently, checking I'm not going into complete meltdown. His eyes lock onto my face, and his own face looks grim. 'You know we are going to need to film you storming out again.'

I stare at him dumbly. 'But… but we… I didn't get engaged!'

'Think braveheart Eve. We probably won't even use the footage. I will talk to Alastair.'

My stomach contracts, Alastair is going to go ape.

'It's just to cover our tracks.'

Mutely, I nod my head. Of course, my humiliation isn't complete unless a few hundred thousand people have witnessed it. No change there.

I lift my chin and it wobbles slightly. 'Just so you know, this is utter crap.'

'I know,' he says gently. 'God darn reality contracts, they're rigid.'

I slowly follow Jake back to the house and neither of us speak. We both come to a stop at the door.

'You ready? All you need to do is storm out again the way you did before, so we are sure to get it from every angle.' There's a deep frown on his face and I stare back at him blankly. I try out a smile but it doesn't seem right.

'OK, let's do this.'

And then, suddenly, the crew are in front of me once again, and I am going through the motions of storming out the house again, slamming the door behind me, and walking down the pathway. I can't engage with any of it, though. *Wrong word to use.* I'm dazed by it all. I'm aware of the crew but I don't make eye contact. I feel closed to tears, but bite them back. Mel squeezes my arm and says something to me, but I haven't a clue what it is. I just want to get this over with as quickly as possible, then for someone to put me in a sanatorium with a selection of crayons and tranquilisers, and leave me alone for the rest of my life. When Jake calls a wrap and everyone starts packing up all the equipment I look up, and to my dismay, Adam is standing there, and next to him is Brian. Adam looks gloomy, grief stricken. Brian, on the other hand, looks triumphant. I can't face going back to the house, Mel (as if she's read my mind) hands me my coat and bag. I clutch them gratefully to my chest.

'Thanks.'

She hugs me tightly.

'Will you be ok?'

I vaguely nod because tears are welling up in my eyes again. I turn away and walk across the road, aware of all the eyes watching my every step. I need to get as far away from Adam, from everyone as I can, which doesn't seem that far as I reach the corner of the street, and head over to the bench on the small patch of grass that sits in the middle of the square. I sit down and stare silently into the blackness of the sky, searching for… I don't know what. God?

Well God's got a very sadistic streak about my public love life and the humiliation that goes hand in hand with it. What fucking lesson am I meant to be learning from this? How it feels when having my heart ripped out? One minute I was getting engaged and now I'm not. It doesn't make sense. I heave a heavy sigh then pull out my phone. I dial Lucy's number, then Nell's, but both their mobiles are going straight to voicemail. I leave a garbled message on both their phones and call my parents. The phone rings for ages, and just when I'm about to give up. 'Do you know what time it is?' My parents think anything after 8pm is allocated for an emergency. 'You've not been arrested have you?'

'Adam and I have broken up,' I blurt out.

There's silence at the other end and for a minute I think the phones gone dead.

'Mother?'

'But why, what did you do?'

Why did I ever think ringing my parents would be a good idea?

'He wants me to move out.'

'Well you can't move back here, Tabitha is sickly and finally settled in your room. I can't eject one of God's poorly creature.'

'Mother she's a cat. Anyway that's not why I'm ringing…' Actually I have no idea why I'm ringing. Of course I wouldn't get any sympathy here. 'I have somewhere to stay.' Hopefully, Lucy or Nell won't mind me crashing at theirs until I sort something out.

'Is there someone else?'

'No.'

The thought that Adam could be seeing someone else hadn't even crossed my mind. I'm almost certain there isn't, but then I suppose I would be the last to know if there is. But now I come to think about it, he did get a Valentine card this year, a handmade one. At the time, I thought it was amusing. I found it wedged between his cooking books. Adam told me it was nothing. Not being the jealous type I didn't think anything of it.

'What about his flat-mate?'

I roll my eyes. I really don't need to hear this right now. 'Mother I've told you before they're just friends. Men and women can live together and be just friends you know.'

Mother's silence is enough to convey 'yeah right'.

I know my parents think it's strange them living together, but Alison was in the flat way before I moved in, so I could hardly kick her out.

I hang up and call Lucy again, but all I get is the dreaded voicemail. I leave another garbled message, then as soon as I hang up my mobile rings and Nell's name appears on the screen.

'What the fuck is the fucker Kildare playing at?'

A chuckle escapes me, making me feel a tiny bit better. Nell always did have a way of putting things.

'He doesn't know how he feels about me,' I say.

'Do you want to come over?'

'Aren't you working?'

'Yes, so swing by the *Tonto Club* first and I'll give you the keys, or if you want to stay, I finish at midnight.'

'I probably won't stay.'

Nell is one of the six Hurly Burly girls in the *Hurly Burly Show*, a Burlesque extravaganza. Burlesque has become more mainstream since Dita Von Teese, and the show is very mild in comparison, but my parents certainly don't approve mild or otherwise. We don't really mention it around them. But for anyone with an open mind, it's a glamorous night of fun, tongue-in-cheek humor, with great music and fabulous costumes. Nell dances and sings throughout the show. I've seen it a few times. She's amazing, and unlike me, she has no inhibitions about showing off her body, then again if I had a dancer body like hers, and sang like her, I probably would to. Ha. Who am I kidding; Nell is the performer; I prefer to cheer her on from the sidelines. Nell's always had a clear vision of what she wanted to do; she begged Mother to let her do ballet and contemporary dance when she was five, she was always in the school plays and then she got a place at LAMDA (London Academy of Music and Dramatic Arts). It went a bit horribly wrong when she married husband number one, another student who needed more limelight than Southern Electric could manage, and the surge just overloaded the circuit. She divorced him, took off and became a dancer on a cruise ship where she met husband number two, a magician with immorality at the top of the bill, divorced him then came back got a job working on the Dior counter in Selfridges. When she quit that and enrolled at the LAOB (London Academy of Burlesque), I think my parents called in Father Pickles for a serious moral briefing. Which made her more determined than a mountaineer trying to reach the world's only unchartered apex. She auditioned, got the part in the show, wowed her director, and got immediately promoted to lead singer rather than chorus girl.

I get the tube to Leicester square, and I am just rushing up the escalators when my phone vibrates; I must have had it on silent after Mother's reassuring and sympathetic words.

'Eve, thank God. Are you okay? I got your message, where are you? Do you want me to come and get you? I swear I am going to kill Adam, how could he do this to you!'

'I'm in Leicester square. I'm meeting Nell.'

'Are you staying with your sister tonight?'

'Yes.'

'Good. That's good.'

'Luce, can you meet me at *Akarsu's* before work?'

'Of course, how about 7.30, doesn't matter for me how early, it's what you want, need. Then we can talk about this properly.'

'That would be good. Thanks'

'See you tomorrow bright and early. I love you,' she says, making a kissing noise down the phone. 'Don't do anything stupid.'

'I've never done anything stupid in my life.'

There's silence as we both realise this isn't true.

As I slip my phone back in my pocket, I heave a dejected sigh. Adam was supposed to propose. It was all planned. Why didn't he tell me before hand if he was having doubts? Why break up with me in front of everyone and in such a despicable way? Had he planned this all along to humiliate me in public? A searing pain slices through me, and as I walk across Leicester square tears come steam rolling down my face.

When I arrive at the theatre, Nell is waiting for me dressed in a World War II British Officer's uniform with an enviable polished visage, topped with a full red pout. She puts a protective arm round me and ushers me into the back dressing room.

The rest of the Hurly Burly girls look up when I enter the room. I can't help doing a double take; they are all so stunning, which makes me feel even worse.

'Her boyfriend broke up with her. He's a cock-womble,' Nell declares to the group and about eight girls nod in agreement, murmuring things like, 'He so is,' and 'Move on sweetheart, you're too young for that kind of upset,' and 'Tossers, all of them.'

'I thought he was the one,' I give a sob.

Someone hands me a chocolate bar and Nell makes me a cup of tea.

'Give the girl something stronger.'

Nell comes back with a glass of whisky on ice. It burns my throat but it does the trick and numbs the pain.

An hour later, I'm back on the tube again with Nell's spare key (Nell said I should keep a set, which made me into more of an inconsolable blub bag), some bejeweled underwear (goodness knows when I'm going to wear them) and a pair of long silk gloves (I have no idea why).

Nell has a two bedroom flat set over the first floor of a period conversion in a leafy residential street close to the tube. When she first bought it, it was damp and dingy looking, with a shower that didn't work and threadbare carpets, but now it's transformed; it's bright and airy with stripped floorboards, dusty pink walls and a lush shower that feels you're standing in a warm summer storm. I head to the second bedroom, which she uses as a walk-in-wardrobe. She's got a sofa bed in there, so I pull it out and collapse in mental agony. I scrub my face clean using Nell's amazing selection of miracle creams and pull on a pair of her silk-satin pyjamas. My usual nighttime attire is a gingham flannel nightshirt, or one of my slogan T-shirts if I'm feeling lazy and I can't be bothered to change. Nell is never lazy; I look at the selection of beautiful feminine attire. She has everything in here, from cute playsuits to tinie-tiny nightdresses, from sophisticated Kimonos in numerous colours to – oh my god what is that?

It's a purple thingy, a… you know… a toy!

I quickly shut the drawer.

Ok, that's a perfectly normal thing to have in the privacy of your own home, I think. Of course, my sister should or would have one of those.

I jump into bed. I'm just lying here, all by myself, feeling hollow inside, staring at the ceiling, and yet still thinking about the giant purple thingy-me-bob in the drawer, which I guess has distracted me from thinking about Adam.

CHAPTER SEVEN

I sleep better than I probably should have, the extreme tiredness after such a stressful day being my accomplice, but you wouldn't know it looking at me. I stare at my reflection in the mirror and feel a little disappointed that the miracle creams I lathered into my face last night didn't work one tiny miracle on me. My eyes are still bloodshot, and to add insult to injury my face is a shiny red mess. There are pillow creases either side of my cheeks so I look a bit like Heath Ledger's The Joker. I also must have had a reaction to the face cream, red rashes are dotted all over my face – oh god I do hope it was a cream for the face what I used, not for the purple monster that lives in the drawer! *Ew.*

I shower and wash that thought out of my hair, pull on my leather skirt and borrow a black hooded top with the words *Suicidal Blonde* emblazed across it, which I can't ever imagine Nell wearing, so I am not even sure why it's hanging up in her wardrobe, but it's entirely appropriate for my day of reckoning.

I then set about faking happiness onto my face with the help of my magic helpers: mascara, bronzer, blush and lip balm. My lower lip quibbles and my eyes are still slightly red, but the end result is not as bad as this morning's allergic (by an unknown and never to be spoken about or shared) cream remedy. I check my watch. I've still got plenty of time, but rather than sit around I might as well face the music.

True to my word, I dig out my iPod and select Taylor Swift. Swifty certainly knows how to deal with heart break, and maybe her "Shake it Off" will have the desired effect. I listen to it on repeat all the way to work, but I don't feel much different, the same numb feeling sweeping around my system. I still can't work out how I'm feeling; this is new territory on the chart of public embarrassment.

I push open the door to *Akarsu's* and pull the earphones out of my ears.

'Someone's up early?' Mr Akarsu says, as I enter the café.

I give him a watery smile.

'Finest part of the day,' he says in his thick accent, whilst he starts on my coffee.

'I've always been up with the larks,' I say. When he looks at me blankly. 'It's a saying, Mr Akarsu, you know there are Owls and Larks!'

'Yes, yes I know, up with early birds who then catch the… um ppp–'

'Worms, the early bird catches the worm.'

'Maybe I should put worms on the menu?'

I laugh out of politeness, sinking into the seat and blowing into my coffee.

Whilst I am waiting for Lucy to appear, I start thinking that I'm such an annoying Lark, one who doesn't bode well with nest sharing. In fact, I am an evictee species that outstays her welcome and can never read the signals until they're turfed out on their tail feathers. Of course this particular species of lark only has bad things happen to her when there's a camera crew around, maybe next time I should ask to be a runner on an Attenborough production. I hear his dulcet tones in the back of my headspace, which is already strained to the limits.

"And here we have the Eve-Lark a contradictory species. In recent years, the species has become a pestilent to mankind. Moving in and contaminating urban areas, where the only defence is to leave. This particular breed will move on when there is nothing left to damage. Contrary to the national Lark, which goes about its business without making the slightest ripple with the opposite sex. This Eve bird is on route to extinction; the mating rituals are so scary to the best of the males, and they begin to seek solace in the more sublime birds of paradise, whose plumages they find fair and more attractive"

'Why are you crying?'

I look up startled, and brush my hand across my face. Oh God. I've been crying without even realising I was doing so. I close my eyes in hope of turning off the plumbing, only to reopen them to a pair of dazzling green eyes staring down at me.

'My boyfriend dumped me last night,' I say.

'Salak, Ne kadar sersem!'

I have no idea what he's saying but his outrage makes me smile.

'You will be ok. I have sons. One is even productive. One small part of brain even seems to wake in the daylight.'

I laugh. Heartily, too, which is progress. 'Ahmed is fifteen Mr Akarsu.'

He sits his bulky frame down next to mine. 'The man is an idiot.'

'He is,' I say. A rogue tear rolls down my cheek, swiftly followed by another, then the salty avalanche of sadness starts to free-fall. He pulls his arm around my shoulders and I bury my face into his chest. For a moment I just stay there, feeling the security, the fatherliness of the alpha silverback without the threat of other males. Maybe I should start relaying all my life events in an Attenborough-style documentary – they seem to make more sense seen in that way. If only I could see what's happening right in front of my own nose and stop the hideous things before they get out of control. Always an audience and always with complete and utter humiliation; the word privacy has long left my vocabulary and existence.

I pull back and give him a smile. 'Sorry.'

'Never to worry Eve, the human heart is a most strong and unpredictable vessel.'

'I just thought he loved me,' I sniff. 'I thought he wanted to marry me. How did I get it so wrong?'

He pats me gently on the hand. 'Don't think about it like that. You are a young, smart, pretty girl and he's the fool. Sometimes we make wrong decisions in our lives, but we always have a chance to change them. He will realise this or he won't. In the meantime go live your life. Life is a blessing and let no one take that away, not even stupid English boys.'

'How did you know he was English?'

'A Turkish man would never let a good woman go, he would secure her and make her his wife.'

I smile. Maybe I should move to Turkey.

The door to the café pings open and I flick my head upright. I don't know why my thoughts instantly go to Adam, he doesn't even know about this place. And I wish I hadn't moved so fast, I feel a little sick tickle down my throat. It's Lucy, looking great compared to rumple ol' me.

Lucy takes one look at my tear-stained face, Mr Akarsu patting my hand, and takes charge.

'Morning Campers, a double espresso and a chocolate muffin, oh and Teşekkür ederim,' she says.

Since when did Lucy speak Turkish?

'Rica ederim,' says Mr Akarsu, his face beaming, 'I bring Helva, the gift of the morning gods. Capable of bringing sweetness to the most bitter of tastes.'

He immediately starts ranting about where the Helva batch is, clashing about under the counter and storming off to the back. We hear at least three frayed women's voices rise up to exasperation. Lucy and I start to giggle. Men – they can say the right things but when it comes to the practicality of putting it into action, it's like a temporary house of cards in hurricane season.

He reappears at the kitchen door like nothing has happen, standing serene with a silver platter. Lucy and I try not to giggle, then a lettuce comes flying over his head and we burst into laughter.

'You know the way to a woman's heart,' she says.

'Unfortunately not cooks. Woman should compete in Olympic shot-putting, not use produce for weapons!' He says walking across, but clearly loving the attention.

After the Helva tasting and another espresso, Mr Akarsu promptly gets up with the arrival of some delivery van that's parked across his shop front. He's quick on his feet when there is a dispute of territory – the male species behaviour displayed once more in its glory. I'll never understand them.

Lucy turns her attention to me. 'It's going to be ok,' she tells me.

Now I give her a watery smile. 'I honestly thought… you know… he loved me.'

'I know.'

I sip my coffee a few times, staring gloomily at Lucy, trying to resist the urge to cry again. 'It's Ben all over again, the humiliation, the shame...' I exhale sharply, as a searing pain hits like a sledgehammer across my chest. I feel panic, no oxygen.

'Why, did you get wasted and projectile vomit across the room?'

I gasp into breathing again and manage a little giggle. 'No!'

'Did you get arrested?'

'No.'

'Well, how is it similar then?'

'Everyone saw. He broke up with me in front of EVERYONE. It's all on camera and everyone is laughing at me!'

'They are not laughing at you.'

'Brian was…'

'Yes, well, Brian's a prick.'

'I'm probably going to be fired?'

'You won't be fired.'

I hope she's right.

'Do you think I should try and speak to Adam?'

'I wouldn't do anything right now, just go to work and later we'll go pick up some of your stuff.' She gives my hand a squeeze. 'You can stay with me until you're sorted.'

'But won't Chuck freak?'

'That man doesn't know what's going on from morning to night, it'll be fine.'

Tears stream down my face.

'Oh hon.' Lucy envelopes me in a massive hug and kisses the top of my head. 'Adam breaking up with you is not your fault.' The hugs are calming me in the light of day.

'Now,' she says, digging into her bag and pulling out her make up bag. 'Don't take this personally but how about we make you look totally fabulous. That'll show... you know… everyone,' she says sweetly.

There's something soothing about someone doing your makeup. Lucy gently and efficiently prods and brushes my face. I think I even drift off to sleep for a little bit.

'There you go,' she sits back, admiring her handy work.

I batter my eyelashes.

'Now come on, let's go,' she whispers with quiet conviction.

But my bum won't budge from the seat.

'I don't' think I can do it.'

'Yes, you can!' Lucy grabs my hand and pulls me out of my safe seat. 'It'll be fine. You'll see,' she says reassuringly, helping me into my jacket and zipping me up.

'What if they're horrible to me?'

'They won't be horrible to you. They're your friends. Humans can also be nice.'

She turns me towards the door and gives me a gentle push.

'They'll sympathise.'

'Why should they, they're just work colleagues. I will be the deluded naive office girl.'

'Well, if they're horrible to you, come down and get me, I'll sort them out.'

'Ok,' I say, 'I'll do it.' I put on a brave smile, but it wobbles unconvincingly.

We make our way slowly back to the office, Lucy pulling me

as we walk; so this is what a reluctant toddler feels like.

As we reach the corner I stop, blow my nose and take a few deep breaths. The pain in my chest has receded slightly and in its place I have thumping nerves. How am I going to face the office? This is worse than the Ben incident; back then, I never bared my soul, just my personal aka "shitty" sexual side. This is so much worse than being called names.

'Come on, chin up ducky doo.' Lucy gives me a nudge and a reassuring smile, waiting for me to take that first step.

'Ok,' I say, turning back and staring up at the stairs.

Maybe Lucy's right. Maybe everyone at work is already talking about the next candidates, all preoccupied in panic talks to notice jilted Joe here.

I slowly make my way up the stairs and look over my shoulder, satisfied that Lucy let herself into her office.

'The mascara is waterproof pudding. Get in and get on.' She calls out loudly.

I turn back and face the stairs. Suddenly my throat is dry and I can feel sweat beading on my forehead. What if everyone starts laughing at me as soon as I walk into the office?

I shake the nonsense from my head and walk up the remaining steps. I take a deep breath then open the door and step sheepishly inside, trying to look as unconcerned as possible.

Head down, I hide for a moment in the coat stand, then bolt stealthily across the room and sit down at my desk.

The silence in the room is terrifying.

'Eve!' says Brian in sarcastic delight. 'I'm surprised to see you this morning!'

I bite my lip. Tears immediately enter my eyes.

'Leave her be,' Mel says quietly but sternly. I smile at her with astonished gratitude.

‘ I love those fairy-tale endings, they bring a warm feeling to the –’ says Brian.

‘Brian!’ Alastair’s voice makes Brian jump. Alastair walks out of the office, followed by Jake.

‘Eve can I have a word.’

Oh God. This is it. I’m going to be fired.

As I walk past Jake stops me, putting a gently hand on my arm. ‘You’re not are you?’

I look at him blankly following his gaze.

‘Suicidal?’ He points to my hoodie.

I laugh hollowly. ‘I was being ironic.’

He grins. ‘That’s my girl.’

Putting on a brave face, I follow Alastair into his office.

‘Sit down, Eve.’

‘I’m sorry,’ I blurt out, plonking myself into the chair opposite. ‘I had no idea. I really thought… Adam said he wanted to… I just…. It’s just…’ I feel fresh tears prick the back of my eyelids. I suck in my bottom lip and bite down hard, hoping the pain will stop the tears. ‘I just didn’t expect to get dumped.’

Alastair nods, his expression grim. I’m not sure if that’s a good or bad sign.

‘He’s an idiot,’ he finally says. I blink. That certainly is the word du jour, whether in English or Turkish.

‘I’m sorry I wasted your time and resources.’

He clucks at me. ‘That’s hardly your fault. I just wanted to see that you were ok?’

‘Oh, I’ve had better days. ‘ I twist my mouth into a half smile.

‘Falling passionately in love is like having wings,’ Alastair begins, his voice rising slightly. ‘You soar above the clouds but when it ends or it is taken abruptly away from you, it feels like you've been turned to stone. You desperately scramble to grab a hold of something… anything, only to witness your body shatter to a million pieces. It's devastating. Brandy won't heal it but time will. You are independent. You are young. You have your own life, and you don't need him, OK?'

It's an impassioned speech, and he's right of course, but I do notice a flitting pain enter his eyes and the way his Adam's apple bobs up and down. I hate that name now, I will endeavour to call it something else, rename the entire human body. There is pain in Alastair's face, real pain, then as quickly as it came, it's gone. He pops his non-lit cigar in his mouth and smiles.

'The important thing is to get under not over the breakup, because if you're able to shrink the pain, the thoughts of treachery and hurt, your life moves on. You learn to surrender to what is out of your control and focus only on those aspects that are in your control. Do you understand?'

'I think so.' I hope I'm as wise as him when I'm older. 'So um,' I have to ask. 'Jake mentioned you may still use the footage?'

'Brian suggested we use it for DVD extras.'

Of course he did.

'I would prefer it if you didn't.'

'I promise we won't do anything without coming to you first.'

'I appreciate that. Thank you.' I let out a sight of relief. 'So what happens now?'

Alastair sighs. 'It's too late to get another set of contestants. Jake and I have looked at the format again and we are going to work it with just four couples. It may work out better that way.'

That's a relief. 'So um…' it's now or never. 'Do I still have a job?'

Alastair stares at me incredulously. All the blood rushes to my face and I feel faint and sick at the same time.

'Of course you do. Why would…? Oh Eve!'

He stands up and comes over to me. I stand sniffing back the tears as he wraps his arm around my shoulder. 'I can't possibly run my life without you.'

The door opens and in walks Brian. He stares at us both; well, to be more exact, he glares at me, hatred oozing from every pore. I stare back at him, unflinching.

CHAPTER EIGHT

I rummage in my bag for the front door key, deliberately avoiding Lucy's gaze, my hands fumbling over a 'mostly melted' galaxy bar.

'I left a message on Adam's voicemail,' I say. 'I told him I'll be back on Saturday to get the rest of my things and then perhaps he could tell me then what exactly he means by space?'

I think if I say it quickly enough I won't sound so pathetic, but my voice wobbles and I'm fooling no one. 'You think I was stupid to ring him, don't you?'

'I don't think you are stupid at all. It's perfectly reasonable to want to know where you stand,' she says patting my arm gently. 'Just don't do it again. Wait until Saturday then you can both sit down together and talk.' I stare at her in surprise. Lucy grins. 'See I can do soft when I want.'

It feels strange returning to the flat, it's as if I already don't belong, like I'm intruding. Everything still looks the same except there is an ironing board standing in the centre of the living room. I walk around it, stepping over the scattered Sunday newspapers and magazine supplements sprawled across the carpet.

'Got it,' I cry, holding my *Girls* DVD collection triumphantly in my hand. 'Right,' I say brightly. 'I'll be back in a minute. Now don't touch anything,' I warn Lucy.

'Yeah, yeah.' Lucy waves away my concerns.

'I mean it.' I know Lucy and I know if she had her way I'd be cutting up his clothes and putting manure in his shoes.

I leave Lucy and head to the bedroom; a bedroom that, if I'm honest, is far too small for two people to co-habit in complete harmony. I did manage to sustain some kind of order, with my three plastic boxes neatly stacked away in a corner and my red suitcase tucked under Adam's wooden desk. All I had to do was make sure my things made their way back to their rightful places and we were relatively clutter free, in young people terms, that is you could actually walk from door to door without treading on more than three things at a time.

The bed isn't made and I resist the urge to make it now. I sit down and reach for Adam's pillow hugging it to my chest. It smells of him and suddenly I'm crying – again.

I still can't believe it has come to this.

Although that's not strictly true; I mean the whole not having sex in a while should have alerted me that all wasn't right. Oh God, the sex thing has come back to haunt me.

I shake the nonsense out of my head. It doesn't mean that Adam and I weren't right for each other. Or could it be that we were completely wrong for each other from the start?

I shake my head again, that can't be right. And then, without warning, Ben and Tara Mc*Fucking*Auley enter my head and the whole "you're a shitty" lay episode comes back in full force, making me want to hurl as the realisation dawns.

This is my fault.

I lack the sexual skills to keep a man interested.

No wonder Adam was left uninspired.

And Adam only said he needed space, he didn't say he wanted to end our relationship forever. I just need to give him the space he needs, then we can talk and… and maybe we can… I can seduce him.

My heart is racing fast as an ill thought-out plan plants itself in my head. That's what I'll do. I'll seduce him, but how? I don't know the first thing about the subtle art of seduction. I should ask Nell or even the Hurly Burly girls troop. No, it'll be too embarrassing. It needs to be someone I don't know. A Madam. No. A sex therapist! It's a light-bulb moment.

I will be able to showboat my way through, win Adam back using all my wiles and womanly wonders. *Eureka by Jove… I've got it.*

Feeling inspired, I grab the clothes I need for the week and go in search of Lucy, who has suspiciously disappeared. I find her in the hallway bent over Adam's bike.

'What are you doing?' Lucy jumps. 'What? Nothing.'

I don't believe her. She has that old innocent look she used at school, and there's the question of a pair of tweezers in her hands and a slowly deflating tyre.

I let it pass.

'You ready?' Lucy lifts herself off the floor and dusts herself down.

'Yep.'

By the time we've reached Lucy's flat, I've googled Sex Therapist on my phone, and I'm reassured to discover I'm not alone; around 16 per cent of woman can't reach orgasm. Actually, I'm surprised it's not higher! I narrow down a couple of therapists close to work and decide I will call them. I have to call, before I dry up and join a nunnery. Although Dippy Delilah and Jeremiah (aka the parents) would flit in glee with what they would call a calling – a proper career move. A primary objective – marry God not man. What would they think if they found out their second disappointment of a daughter was seeking help for the illusive G-spot? Actually, they'd probably ask where the rest of the alphabet got to! Another godly galoot succumbing to the clan of Christians, they'd be ecstatic; on the plus side hair issues would be gone forever more.

Lucy's apartment is immaculate, like walking into a mini Tate gallery, with modern white open spaces, grand chandeliers hanging from high-ceilings, modern artwork hung on pristine white walls and not much else. She shares it with Chuck, the nickname she's given Charles. Chuck is a city banker and the owner of the apartment. He used to share it with Lucy's brother, Mark – or Scab, as Lucy prefers to call him (Lucy likes her nicknames). Scab is currently working at some merger in Hong Kong, so she took his room in the meantime. Chuck treats Lucy like an annoying little sister, which funnily annoys the hell out of Lucy.

'Are you decorating?' I'm slightly bemused by the plastic sheets and a dust cloth draped over the sofa and armchair.

'Chuck's been climbing over the furniture.' She means Chuck Junior the cat, and not Chuck Senior. She called the cat Chuck to 'annoy back' Charles. This cat is adorable, though, unlike my parent's evil bag of claws and fur. I lug my bag behind Lucy's pert backside, and follow her into the spare bedroom, which is smaller than Adam's, but I'm not complaining.

'Chuck's mother is coming over tomorrow.'

'She is. Why?'

She shrugs. 'Don't know, Chuck said she invited herself. Said she's got something important to discuss with him.'

'Sounds interesting.'

'I know, right.'

'Do we need to make ourselves scarce?'

'Oh no. I want to know what she wants.'

I drag my case to the centre of the room with a portion of difficulty.

'So what do you fancy to eat?'

'Oh, I'm not hungry.'

Maybe the loss of appetite will see me drop a dress size. Of course only a girl can be giddy with happiness at this thought. Silver linings from the depths of despair.

'You have to eat something.' Lucy hands me the photo album, which I discover contains only takeaway menus and business cards of restaurants labelled from A-Z.

'Wow this is organized.'

'Oh that wasn't me. That was Chuck.'

I'm impressed, a fellow glazo.

'Where is Chuck?'

'Out with his girlfriend.'

'Chuck has a girlfriend?'

Lucy shrugs. 'If you can call her a girl, more like a…' she stops herself saying more, as though her brain is battling the bitch thought. She's in a funny mood again. I look at her nails and notice she's bitten the skin raw around her right thumb. Not like Lucy to show signs of agitation, or nerves.

'Are you ok?'

'Me? Yes. It's you my poppet who needs looking after.'

I let it go, but for good reason. Lucy isn't good at sharing her feelings; until whatever is bothering her is well and truly over only then she reveals what's been bugging her, and usually she makes a big fat joke about it with her usual sarcastic finesse.

'Right, time now for some vino.'

'Ok, just give me a second.'

Lucy totters off to the kitchen and I slump against the shut door, staring at my new base. It's stuffed with ski equipment and overloaded books in the futon library, aka my bed. Hmm maybe I'll be taking up skiing in my sleep. Nell said I could stay with her, but Lucy's is far closer to work. Besides Nell and I under the same roof is a brief happiness only to be experienced temporarily. Maybe we'd be more cohesive now we're older, but I think this is a better short-term plan with Nell's hours.

It could be worse. I could be curled up in a cardboard box under Vauxhall Bridge for all Adam cared. I check my phone for the millionth time, but there's still no text from him.

I drag myself into the kitchen.

Chuck ruffles Lucy's hair and she pushes him away. 'Do you know how irritating you are?' She says flattening her hair.

He goes to ruffles it again but Lucy picks up a spatula. 'Don't you dare!'

Chuck grins. 'That's better. Irritation complete.'

Although he's a city banker, Chuck could easily be the perfect rugby poster boy. He's tall, six foot three, with broad shoulders and dirty blonde hair. He still has a boyish imp look, the sign of mischief; you can't imagine him in a professional high-powered world at all.

They both turn as I walk into the room.

'I thought you were out with your girlfriend,' I say.

'We broke up,' he says matter-of-factly.

'Oh God, I'm so sorry.' What is the world coming to, when

even the divinely handsome are broken up with.

'Oh it wasn't anything serious,' He grins. 'All well that ends well.'

I stare at him aghast. Lucy elbows him.

'How long were you going out with her?' I ask him.

'Long enough for her to start getting ideas.'

Lucy shoots him a shut-the-fuck-up look but Chuck continues. 'It was only ever a casual relationship, but you know, she wanted to settle down, get married.'

'Chuck can't commit to anything but a rugby match.' Lucy says, hurriedly. 'Men! They're not worth it.' She tuts and eyeballs Chuck, as tears begin to roll down my face.

Chuck looks at Lucy with a helpless shrug and a 'what did I do' expression.

'How about you get Eve a drink,' Lucy suggests.

'Good idea,' he says, popping his head in the fridge.

'Chuck is commitment-phobic, so anything he says is tainted, a trollop of twaddle.'

'He hasn't texted me back.' I show Lucy my mobile.

'Oh. S…' I can see her brain curbing her mouth. 'And… um… how does that make you feel?' She says, adopting a counselling-like voice. Chuck raises a brow.

Lucy ignores him and puts a hand on my shoulder.

'He was the best thing to happen to me.'

'No. You were the best thing to happen to him.'

I grimace.

'Eve I'm serious. He was lucky to have you.' My chin wobbles again. Lucy retracts the past-tense faux pas. 'Lucky to have you… you're smart, full of creativity, and when the hair lets you, positively gorgeous. You don't want someone dulling your senses at… '

'My tender young age.' I say spitefully.

'Erm… well, yes. For Christ's sake, yes. You're too young to be worrying about someone else's life constantly. Living through him, ignoring your own life.' She grabs the bottle of wine out of a perturbed Chuck's hand.

'Ladies, ladies seems to be a subject best left alone. Drop it Lucy, let Eve just be.' His eyes widen as we give it contemplation. Lucy and I give each other the "D" look, then glare at the half-petrified Chuck. We do our secret nod and launch, pretending to catfight just like school – our way to get out of classes we didn't want to be in. We figured a detention together was better than being at our childhood homes most evenings.

Chuck tries to break us apart; we can't hold the pretence and burst out laughing.

'Very mature girls. Right funny pair, aren't you! You're lucky you didn't get a slapped cheek. Lucy is anyway. I'm on your side Eve!'

He pushes us onto the sprawling L-shaped sofa. We laugh a lot that evening, reminiscing our school tales to Chuck, him taking the piss out of us in return. Feels good to be with familiar people, to be back in your own history.

I clear my throat. 'Well, I think I should head off to bed.'

'But I've ordered Chinese, plus we've got a nice bottle of Sancerre to get through.'

'I'm just not hungry.'

'Don't text Adam,' she warns me.

'I won't.'

I take my glass and walk to my room.

'You sure?'

'Positive, and thanks.'

'Stay up for a while longer, just for one little prawn cracker?'

'Leave Eve alone you lunatic,' says Chuck replacing Lucy's wine glass with a glass of water.

'Sleep well Eve, if you hear rhinoceros's snore in the night, it's only Chuck having yet again fallen asleep out here.'

Lucy waves over enthusiastically. As I turn to slide the Japanese doors, Chuck gets some cushions to stabilise her swaying frame, and I suddenly realise how lonely I've been in the last half of the year. Those small touches of someone's gentle care I've never been privy to when I was with Adam. I plonk myself on the hard futon and sob into a pair of salopettes.

CHAPTER NINE

I bolt awake in the morning to the beep-beep of a text message, nearly knocking myself out in the process with a stray ski. Finally, I find my phone under a leg warmer. My heart leaps; it might be a heart-felt apology full of regret and all those caring sentiments that have been lacking.

It's not; I ignore the sinking in my stomach and park my feeble hopes.

Nell:

Pecker up?

I reply:

I'm not a bird!

Nell immediately writes back:

With silicon, even guys are birds, what's your problem?

I smile and type:

Allergic to big tits anyway!

Nell:

That's what I heard, how about a Captain Sparrow then?

Me:

I am not going to your pirate party tonight and that's that.

Nell:

Shiver me timbers then, I'll just have to find another themed night of sin. Don't think you're getting out of getting out x

I clasp my phone to my chest and smile; best friends and a sister, that's what every girl needs. Even when life turns to shit they have a way of cheering you up. She's right. I just need to refocus on something new, something positive. Start living it up a little.

Feeling energised I get out of bed, pull my hobby list from my bag and climb back into the puffy Egyptian cotton duvet. Chuck has really nice stuff.

Today is the day I start a new hobby. It'll take my mind off things. But as I flick through my hobby list, it all sounds pretty lame. What am I trying to aspire to, a throwback at feminism?

1. Sewing.

Because I've always wanted to make a cushion and maybe a pretty skirt.

2. Learn to cook.

Now that I'm on my own it's even more essential. I won't be able to live on burnt toast every day.

3. Grow mushrooms.
4. Learn to iron.
5. Learn to bake cakes.

I tear the list from my pad and start again. My list needs a dramatic overhaul, a new direction.

1. Start a course of intensive training and get super-fit.
2. Take up martial arts or any kind of self-defence.
3. I still want to grow mushrooms.
4. Run some sort of 10k race or maybe 5k to start with.

I used to run a lot at university, and then I hurt my Achilles heel, plus my pride, and I stopped.

5. Take up boxing, and get kick ass biceps.
6. Learn to shoot like Angelina Jolie. Maybe start with skeet shooting.
7. Get a tattoo.

Adam hates tattoos

8. Learn magic.

I've always wanted to know how to do a sleight of hand.

Well, that's a start. I don't want to be overwhelmed too soon.

By the time I've showered, blow-dried my hair, put on some war paint, pulled on my grey jersey sweatpants and teamed them up with a bold Camouflage-print sweatshirt. I feel ready for the day ahead.

I push open the door at the same time Chuck steps out of his bedroom.

'Morning,' he says. He's wearing a furry onesie, and yet somehow manages to pull the look off without the slightest air of embarrassment.

'Nice outfit,' I say, grinning. Actually, it looks quite cosy, I might get myself one.

Chuck strikes a pose. He looks utterly ridiculous, and I start to giggle.

'I'm only wearing it to wind Lucy up.'

We walk downstairs together and head into the kitchen. To our surprise, Lucy is in front of the oven, scrubbing it clean.

'What are you doing?' Chuck says, incredulity in his voice.

'What does it look like?'

'But why?'

'You're mother's coming over.'

'She's not going to be inspecting the oven.'

'I want the place to look nice.'

I've never seen Lucy like this before. I know she's super efficient and tidy, but cleaning? Domesticity isn't something that sits easy with Lucy. She has a mother who basically ironed her socks, and an over bearing father that could have come from the fifties. She rebelled against it all ages ago, not wanting to end up like her mother. Because of an unplanned pregnancy, she succumbed to a chauvinistic (not altogether bad) pig of a man, who wouldn't have his wife working for a living. Before that, her Mum had been a brilliant art teacher and was heading for her first exhibition. MEN! That wasn't the exhibition's theme by the way, just an expletive.

'And what have you got on?' She scowls at Chuck.

'Cassandra bought it for me.'

He prances around the kitchen, and because he's a large rugger type, he looks like a giant Forrest Gump.

'You look like a twat.'

'I love your breakfast compliments, makes me feel all fluffy inside.' Chuck mimics a halfwit. Lucy throws a tea towel at him along with a scowl, and then resumes her oven scrubbing. I feel like I ought to help, but I'm really hoping she says not to bother.

'Do you want me to do anything?'

'No. I've got it all under control.'

'Of course you do,' mutters Chuck.

It seems I've walked into some vague domestic tug of war?

I busy myself with the kettle and make a pot of tea. Tea is the answer to all the world's problems.

'I'll have a coffee if you're making,' says Chuck.

'Me too,' says Lucy.

And coffee – the Robin to Batman's tea!

Chuck and I sit at the kitchen table quietly; we're trying to behave whilst Mrs Hubbard there is hell bent on giving steel molecules a new patina.

'Luce.'

'Yes.'

'You're not due for another week.'

'What?'

'You know how you get freaky OCD with your PMT.'

'Eve, what are you… LOL.' She then throws a tea towel at me, which flies over my head and lands in Chuck's massive coffee cup, splashing his onesie all over with Nicaraguan nectar.

'Brilliant Luce, I was going to wear this for Mama. Now what my Mama gonna think?' I burst out laughing when Lucy's face contorts to horror; Chuck really does know how to wind her up. Why is she so concerned about what he looks like anyway for when his own mother arrives? As far as I remember, he's always a bit dishevelled in that rugged way, mostly merry, and decidedly doesn't give a flying hoot apart from when he walks out the door on a Monday morning looking pristine, polished and professional. Dr Jekyll and Mr Hyde, except that he's constantly in a good mood.

'Shall I go shopping for blob-a-thon then?' Chuck teases. 'Ten kilos of chocolate and stringy white marshmallows?'

'I'm ignoring both of you, before I get to the Japanese knives there.' She takes a look at herself and starts laughing. 'Chick, oh I mean Chuck; difficult to tell when you walk around in an indiscriminate bag. Make some proper coffee.'

Chuck's mouth falls open and he presses a button on his iPhone; "You sexy thing" by Hot Chocolate blares out of the surround-sound system. This massive man in a stained fluffy onesie dancing provocatively round the kitchen is too much, and we're holding our stitches when he starts smearing Nutella all over his face

'Chuck, *Chuck*, the floor.' This provokes him to add crushed almonds to his chocolate attire.

Lucy gives up and pushes his face into some icing sugar on the counter. *Why is there icing sugar out so early in the morning?* I run out nearly wetting myself with laughter. He certainly doesn't let Lucy boss him around. That is no mean feat, it's easier to agree and go with the flow with Ms Sassy Pants.

With less than an hour until Chuck's mother arrives I want to make myself scarce, feeling decidedly more bouncy about tomorrows, besides Lucy turning into 'Cleanzilla.'

Oh no, another idea for a Reality Show? Get a load of OCD's together, the filthiest kitchen in Britain, and be judged by my mother; throw in an Evangelical hotline, and I think you've got the first fusion of Christian Clean.

I pull on my battered Converse. A good walk should brush out the cobwebs.

Lucy has changed too; she's wearing a pretty printed wrap

dress, very demure and feminine. What's going on? She whips the dustsheets off the sofas. She obviously wants to impress Chuck's mum, but why?

'Is Charles's Mum a Windsor or something?'

Lucy scowls at me.

'Bit overboard isn't one?'

She gives me a double scowl.

'Royal roulette on the menu?'

'Eve what are you talking about?'

'Because if you've been baking, it will be more like Russian roulette for teeth.'

Lucy stops in her obsessive tracks, swings round and chases me out with the vacuum cleaner; the uncharacteristic warm-cake's smell follows me. She's turned into a Stepford wife overnight.

I'm beginning to wonder… perhaps… maybe… no, definitely, Lucy fancies Chuck. She's always socialised with him, and their dynamic is very much matey-mates, and it has been like that for years – what has changed?

I'll have to catch her on second cocktail and see if I can worm anything out of her.

Unwittingly, the next time I look around, the river Thames is all around me; I must have walked for miles, and how come I'm in Greenwich? I remember lazily following a Spanish tourist group just to see where they were taken to and how they got a short insight into London, and I inadvertently must have stepped on the boat at Westminster, after the traditional Big Ben and houses of parliament picture opportunities. I haven't gone with the flow for ages, definitely not down river either! I feel quite excited – it's like my little unplanned adventure. The sun is out and I feel peaceful, sleepy. I wait patiently in queue to buy a BLT at the deli, and wander out into the park. After exhaustively watching the visiting groups come and go, I have a rare afternoon nap, feet sloping downwards under a small tree. A small trickling of bobbing heads are still coming and going when I wake up a couple of hours later. I head back in hope that Cleanzilla has zilled herself out; I need to be fresh and on the ball for Monday morning.

CHAPTER TEN

The office is completely empty when I get in, which gives me some blissful quiet time to type up my thoughts about the script I read last night. I've taken it upon myself to sort through the pile of scripts that have made their way onto an even bigger pile next to Alastair's desk, precariously close to the bin. All these people with their big dreams, having sent their precious work in the hope to spark an interest. I know Alastair is far too busy, but I think someone should at least read them. For this, the writer gets my naïve but heartfelt opinion on the strengths and weaknesses of their script, advice as to what I think they need to do to make it better. I've been reading a script a night whilst curling up with a cup of hot chocolate, a much safer thing than curling up with a cretin who will break your heart.

Alastair mentioned he wants to produce a TV comedy series next, and I really think I might have found a potential amongst the pile. It's called *Comatosed*. It's about a guy in a coma who talks to us from his coma state, while he tries to investigate what happened to him. Was it an accident or was there something more sinister at play? It's really funny while being totally compelling. I spent ages writing my comments, highlighting the strengths and weaknesses of the concept, premise, plot and subplots. I've broken down the story and given my assessment of its suitability for production.

When I'm done, I leave the pile on Alastair's desk with the note '*Start with Comatosed!*'

There's another reason I'm really enjoying work at the moment. We have a new runner called Pete, so now Brian has someone else to order about and I can get on with more important things: pinning note cards to bulletin boards, distributing camera notes, cast and crew lists, shooting schedules, etc. ... They've cast contestants who hopefully will get the British public engaged. You've got to be really competitive and I'm not that competitive, so I'm actually kind of relieved Adam and I are not taking part. Am I meant to stop saying Adam and I? When's the cut off for that?

All the games are contrived to provoke action and conflict. Brian came up with the '*Lie, Tie or Bye*' concept. It forces one of the contestants to conceal one of their deepest secrets for points; each contestant has a piece of history the other one didn't know. Now I'm really glad Adam and I are not taking part. It's all been thoroughly researched and accounted, but the catch is they pitch their partner against them; their job is to get the truth out – there's mighty big points to be had, and regardless to that prize, you'll have two unhappy bunnies at the end of that one.

When I'm not helping out Mel or dealing with Alastair's diary, I'm spending time with Stefan in the cutting room, digitising (relatively competently) and going through the hours of footage. Stefan said I didn't have to help him if I found it too painful – you know, because they're engaged and I'm not. But I don't mind. It's only made me more determined to give Adam the space he needs. I know what he did was pretty unforgivable, but I did sort of push him into a corner with the whole engagement thing. He could be regretting the whole break up and is genuinely sorry for humiliating me like that, but I won't know this until we meet up. I'm trying not to think about Saturday, which is why I've been preoccupying myself with lots of work, and plus things are a bit tense between Lucy and Chuck so it's been good to keep out of their way. I've tried talking to Lucy, but she just keeps clamming up. All I know is that Chuck's mother wants Chuck to settle down and has a nice girl in mind, a Huntingdon-Parker or something. Lucy said his mother was really scary, and for Lucy to say that, she must be formidable. Lucy's not even scared of my mother.

But the big news about today, well tonight, is that I'm – actually I need to whisper this to you in confidence – I'm meeting a sex therapist. I just think it's time I did something about my insecurities, you know, speak to someone who actually knows a few things about sex and can pass on their pearls of wisdom to an untutored student.

On the dot of six pm I stop typing, close my computer down, grab my bag and immediately find myself prickly with self-consciousness. I don't know why I'm being so paranoid, it's not as if anyone knows where I'm going. But all day I've been thinking someone is going to ask me what I'm doing tonight and I'm going to blurt it out.

'Bye,' I say casually, pulling on my jacket and tucking the script under my arm. 'See you tomorrow.'

Brian looks up and gives me a dirty look; the others in the office don't even raise their heads, but Jake flashes me a grin and Mel's smile is warm.

'Ooh doing anything nice?' she asks.

'What!' I say, rooted to the spot, my heart thumping quickly.

'Nope. Nothing at all, just taking this script to bed.' Why did I mention bed? The guilt rushes to my cheeks. I hold the script up in front of me, my fingers clutching it tightly, as though the activity needs a mime for anyone to understand. *Over-stating, Eve – get a grip.* 'Erm, reading at home, in bed… or wherever, not necessarily in bed. I mean… I just get comfy. I mean the bed is the most comfortable place to read. I'm going to read this at home, not in any particular room. Maybe I'll fall asleep um… just need to get through this one. Very interesting script… to read, you know, wherever you are.'

Why am I still talking? Shut up Eve.

'Er, ok,' Mel says, giving me a bemused look.

Jake's mouth twitches into another smile, and I rush out the door.

That's me, cool and collected.

I sit nervously on the tube; it's only one stop to Marylebone.

'This train will be terminating here. There are electrical problems on the line. London underground apologises for the inconvenience as well as Boris Johnson's hair.'

More often than not you do get a witty announcer on the tube; they're used to giving out the dreaded traffic news, so they have to amuse themselves and calm the masses, it's more human when a big personality booms onto the stuffy air.

I laugh then realise the implications, I'll be late. Surely this is a sign, I don't think I can go through with it. Who was I trying to kid?

As people stream off the carriage, I sit patiently, not wanting to make a move, or more precisely a decision. On the other hand, I'm quite curious to see an office in Marylebone; that's one fancy address. Plus, I need to go somewhere soon as the inspectors are edging down the platform and I'll be thrown off in a minute. I decide to stomp up the escalators and quickly march through the back roads to Marylebone, avoiding Oxford Street, which is a necessary skill if you live here. Not more than fifteen minutes later, I'm standing on Wimpole Street. Yes Wimpole Street. I know what you're thinking.

Gudrun's office is situated on the first floor of a grand Georgian building. I climb the five steps up to the glossy black door looming underneath the white columned porch. The bell sits on a freshly-polished brass plaque with perfect miniature rose bushes either side growing in some rather symbolic pots, looking a bit like voluptuous boobs. Her bell just has the word Gudrun on, nothing titled or medical. I get buzzed in and reluctantly climb the marble steps; the runner carpet is a deep plush dark grey and it's heavenly putting your feet on it. If I didn't know what lay upstairs I would imagine I was viewing Coco Chanel's haute couture collection by appointment only. The double doors at the top of the twisting staircase make my deliberation worsen… there's still time to turn around and run back down the stairs.

'Eve, please come in, vel-kommen. Make yourself at home, I'll be with you in a minute.' A soft, low voice trickles down to my stair, was that a German accent? I'm not sure. Definitely European-ish, but I can't quite place it. My pulse is racing; shit I'll have to go in now, she knows I'm here. I cautiously peer round the open door, and to my surprise, there is no reception, just a beautiful, magnificent, apartment. She must do very well at this, or is a clever fraudster, indeed. The hall is in a dark burgundy, with candles scattered all over the place. On the walls there are dark metal antique candleholders, and on the hall table next to a very phallic pot plant, even floating ones in the small water feature you step past on the threshold. The wall candles cast their light on pictures of Victorian woman, in not so Victorian poses, and I avert my eyes and walk towards the main room; surely a few of them look like they are giving birth, but I guess that could be my prudishness blowing through the copious candlelit anatomy. Deep colours hit my eyes as I tiptoe into the… drawing room? I don't know the correct terminology I just know grand places have different room names than the rest of us use. The two tall windows are framed by deep red velvet drapes, heavy, sumptuous and beautiful. The furniture is in dark wood, there are several emerald green lamps and a floor-to-ceiling bookcase with its very own ladder stretching across the whole right wall. The titles on the shelves make me blush, even though I notice that most of them aren't even in my language, but I'm sure their contents behold something I can't cope with.

'Eve, please sit and make yourself comfortable. I will be with you so soon my dear. Pour yourself a drink, some port perhaps?' The voice oozes from the double doors on the left-hand side, also ajar. She sounds weirdly foreign, like a Transylvanian countess. I sit down on the chaise lounge, which I presume is for therapy; or is that just a cliché? I eye up the decanter and think that could be drugged. The decanter's facets reflect the candlelight and it tricks my eyes; I follow the colours change when they bounce off the side and into the port, mesmerised. I've never drunk port, believe it or not, as I've always put it down to an old fogey drink, but here it seems like the height of sophistication. I peer at her desk, which is by the window, set into a corner, it's French form ornate, and it's surface is in green leather; there is no computer just books, a notepad to die for and a proper fountain pen with an inbuilt ink well; now, that's lush.

'Most Vel-kommen, Eve.'

I bolt upright from my reverie and stand, nearly taking the decanter on parade with me.

'Iz natural to be nervous. Sit, sit. Please.'

Gudrun is tiny, not even five feet. Her voice sounded as if it was coming from a huge body, a tall woman… I'm confused. The depth alone made me expect someone a lot bigger than myself. She has short bobbed hair, black, straight and very glossy. Her dress suit is like a Chanel style, or actually I think it must be a Chanel; it certainly has all the signs of tweed godliness. The perfectly pressed silken cream blouse underneath reveals nothing with its high neck. I'm relieved she is dressed well and she is not some hippy letting it all hang out with no underwear. Her black shoes are perfectly polished on her tiny feet; it's safe to say she is not what I expected at all.

'Now Eve, you vont help. Correct?' Her tone is succinct and direct, coarse but soft with its deepness, the accent I still can't place.

'Err… yes, I don't think you'd find my problem that interesting.' I say backpedalling with nerves.

'Oh yes and why is zhat?'

'Don't you… I mean don't you need to be interested in it '

'Interested in *it*… vhat an interesting choice… No Eve, not it, it has a name. No?'

'I suppose…'

'Interesting indeed, I think we start. Okay?'

'Er.' Not knowing what's going on. 'Er.. Yea.–'

'Good, now you tell Gudrun why look for Gudrun?'

I'm just digesting the last exchange; she speaks fast and with that funny accent I have to recap what she could have meant.

'Oh.. umm.' I've got it. 'I have, or have been told…'

'Now vat is it, you've been told or you yourself Eve has told yourself.'

Again I play the sentence back in my head.

'Both.'

'Which first?'

'What?'

'Told or come to own conclusion?'

'Told.' I'm getting good at this.

'I see.' She stands back.

'Ve have many things that are told to us, do we believe all?'

'Er..'

'No Eve, we do not, do you believe all what the television tells you, all that the British newspapers say?'

'Well, I…'

'No Eve ve don't, and people they can behave in newspapers' fashion, yes?'

'Um… I ..'

'Yes or no?'

'Yes.'

'Ve have to find one who is like BBC, trustworthy. Othervise wars happen don't they?'

'Yeaa..'

'You see, people can give misinformation, too. No one is bad at sex. It is about chemistry. Sex is bad when no chemistry. Sex is natural and instinctual.'

'Err…'

'Please now you take some port, I have some too. Ve don't

want you thinking I'm a small pot-crack.'

'Crackpot.' I giggle, unsure of the reception; Gudrun smiles wisely. She has taken down the barrier without doing anything remotely embarrassing. I look at her one more time, and think to myself that she must be in her late sixties.

'Precisely. Pot crack. Your English slang is most amusing. One still can't master it after twenty years; nearly as old as you, I've lived here my dear!'

'I'm 22.' I relax into a smile.

'Oh, 22, vell you have a wise head with young shoulders. Very clever Eve, very clever indeed.'

I feel a rush of pride. I still don't know what's going on, but you should take compliments where you get them.

'For one to relax one must trust implicitly, I feel this is the case here. No problem Eve, just retraining ze brain a little.'

We clink the tiny port glasses and Gudrun studies me.

I wouldn't say I'm finding it any easier now, just less scary than I thought.

'Zis is my home Eve. I've velkommen a stranger into my home. It is the same for me as for you. You see?'

'Er. I suppose I do, yes.'

'Zis is good start Eve. Now for ze clitoris…'

Gulp, she never gave me a chance to bail. Clever, clever Gudrun.

New Dawn, that's what Gudrun calls it. I have to take a chance and go with my sexual desire in the next six weeks. Identify it and act on it. Everyone has at least one apparently. I have to encompass my true sexual being, take control, and unleash the beast, so to speak. Crikey, what if I don't have one? Not everyone is overtly sexual, are they? What if my beast is more of a domesticated budgie grateful for a few seeds and a new piece of sandpaper? The Nunnery is looking the more attractive option right now. I don't think I can do the practical therapy.

But I'm not about to give up. Not yet. She made me write a list, and you know how much I love lists, so we're going to do the following:

1. Fiddle a bit (I can't bring myself to say what she actually said to do) in front of a mirror.
2. Find G Spot.
3. Do that at least five times before I return.
4. Buy a girls' toy and not the type from Hamley's!

The man opposite me on the tube is bulked up like a superhero, wearing a white t-shirt tucked into grey jogging pants, solid and manly and not altogether unattractive - Alpha male. Gudrun says I should fantasize more about having sex; think of it as often as I can. I'll try, but I have never done it in the past, so it feels wholly alien. I'm trying to imagine him naked, all his muscles pumped and glistening in oil. I'm staring and staring at him – a huge no-no in London. When my gaze finally reaches his face, the man is glaring straight at me, a dirty look plastered all over his face.

I stare back, shocked and horrified. Shit. That's not how I'm meant to react. I try a flirty smile, but it ends up being my goofy smile I usually reserve for family put-downs.

Glad that the next stop is mine, I practically leap out of the chair and throw myself onto the platform.

When I get back home, Lucy and Chuck are bickering about

the mess he made in the kitchen earlier and whose turn it is to take out the rubbish. They sound like a middle-aged married couple. I slide past them and go to my bedroom, gladly shutting the door.

I take out the list I wrote in Gudrun's office. No. 1. Fiddle a bit in front of a mirror.

"Ven you explore vith the mirror Eve, please make it normal mirror. Shaving mirror makes ze clitoris look like giant pimento stuffed red olive, not appetising for martini night. Too much magnification, okay! But you must make the stuffing pop out, iz right reacton. Swelling vith colour, a most beautiful state."

I stare at the words on my list until they start swimming in front of my eyes; it's a Homer Simpson's moment, reading 'stuffed red olive' is just making me hungry.

I look at my reflection and have the urge to giggle. Honestly, you can be so juvenile, I tell my reflection sternly. Come on, if I get number one out the way the next three won't be so bad.

I un-tuck the t-shirt from my jeans and undo the top buttons of my jeans. I slide my hand under my t-shirt and inside my bra, cupping my breast, playing with my nipple. With my other hand I push it inside my jeans and slide my fingers inside my knickers and then I…I…

FREEZE. What if Lucy barges in, or Chuck for that matter? What if I don't know how to do it properly, and what's this going to achieve anyway… I can't do it. I stare at my reflection; I look flustered, not aroused. I can't do it. I pull my hands out of my jeans and button myself up.

I know Gudrun says I need to get to know myself, but somehow I just feel… stupid. I am stupid. I can't even say pussy inside my own head, let alone write it down. Can't even acknowledge it exists. How lame is that.

'YOU'RE SUCH A MORON!' I hear Lucy shouting, before hearing a door slam.

I poke my head outside my room and Chuck is standing outside Lucy's room. He rakes a hand through his hair. He looks angry and confused.

I quietly step back into my room and close the door. I really need to speak to Lucy about what is going on between Chuck and her.

It's going to be pyjamas and a script for me tonight, not… ahum, whatever Gudrun put on the menu.

CHAPTER ELEVEN

Lucy said I could borrow a car, and I got excited because I thought she was talking about Scab's BMW Z4. I quite fancied pulling up outside Adam's place in a flash convertible; let him see how well I was doing without him. What I actually get is Chuck's rusty brown Volvo spluttering and wheezing its way along Lambeth Road. The guy earns a mint and he drives around in a rust bucket, but that's Chuck; he doesn't really care what people think.

Not quite as impressive though!

Lucy offered to come with me for moral support, said she'd sit quietly in a café while Adam and I talked it through, totally unobtrusive. Nell also offered but I didn't fancy scraping Adam's brains off the gutter.

Anyway, it's important I do this on my own.

I park the car and it shudders to a stop making a gurgling noise long after I've pull out the ignition key. I give the door a firm shove and it jerks open on my fourth attempt. Moments later I'm standing on Adam's doorstep with my finger poised over the intercom button.

I can't bring myself to ring it.

I have a key but it doesn't feel right to use it.

Suddenly my heart is thumping hard and I look down at my palms and they're sweating. Come on get a grip, its only Adam. Everything's going to be fine. What is it Lucy said? We've got to sit down and talk it through like mature adults. Communication is the key.

Ok deep breathes in out in out in - Oh sod it! I press down on the buzzer and wait for the familiar gruff voice to answer.

'Adam?' I lean in. 'Adam. It's me.' Then add, 'Eve.' The buzzer clicks and I push open the door, stepping into the hallway. Adam is standing at the internal door; he gives me an awkward smile. 'Hi.'

'Hi,' I say back, my smile equally awkward and there's an uncomfortable silence building while we both look at each other but neither say anything. Then we both speak at once 'How are you?' 'You ok?'

We both genuinely smile, and I realise it's going to be ok.

Adam gestures for me to speak first.

'Fine,' I say. 'Great… actually.' Ok, that's stretching the truth a bit. 'You?'

'Tired. Work's stressing me out.'

No surprise there.

We come to another halt.

I've been rehearsing in my head what to say, but now I'm here I've forgotten. It's weird, but as I look at Adam I find myself really looking at him, like I did the first time we met. He wouldn't be everyone's cup of tea; most people can't get passed the ginger hair, but he's tall, which I've always liked, broad shouldered, a strong jaw line, straight nose and beautiful hazel-eyes that droop down at the side. If he does have a fault, and it's only a minor one, hardly noticeable, but if I was to pick a *something* then it's his smile. Considering his dad is a dentist you would think his teeth would be in a better condition, but they're not. They're all jagged; they remind me of the caves in Majorca that my parents took me to when I was a kid. Personally, I like the all-American-white-smile. Like Jake's, Jake has a great smile, great teeth. Why am I thinking about Jake?

Mine aren't too bad thanks to the brace I endured as a teenager. Fathead (aka Peter Willis) used to taunt me with *'what's the news on long wave today metal mouth?'*

'You coming in?'

Ok he's peeved because I'm a little late but it really isn't my fault the car could barely do twenty without rattling, and every time I went over a speed bump it took a good thirty seconds for the car to follow gravity again. I had to drive all the way from West London to Vauxhall under twenty miles an hour, and that was when traffic actually moved.

I squeeze past the three bikes blocking the hallway and knock my leg against a pedal, only managing not to swear by ramming my fist in my mouth. I notice they've had a tidy up in my absence it seems different but the same. They've even managed to put away the ironing board, which usually stands in the middle of the living room for days on end, but… my nose starts to wrinkle, what's that smell? It hits me as soon as I enter the living room.

'Hi Eve.'

'Oh, hi Ali.' I notice she's holding an aerosol can.

'How are you?' She asks me gently.

I casually put my sleeve to my nose. 'So-so' I say, trying not to choke on the fumes.

'That's good. Well I'll leave you to it,' she edges out of the room 'If you need me,' she gives me and Adam a sympathetic smile. 'I'll be... I'll be in my room.' Can't she find something to do outside the perimeters of this apartment? You'd think she would have scarpered before I got here; it's a delicate situation. I wouldn't want to be here if I didn't have to be.

'Shall we go to *Começo*?' Adam asks, 'We can talk there.'

'Yep,' I say backing out of the room. It's not until we're halfway down the road that I take my hand away from my nose.

'Did you deface my photo?'

'What?' I look at Adam with genuine puzzlement.

'My graduation photo,' he says. 'The one with me and my parents.'

Shit! I told Lucy not to touch anything. 'I thought you took loads that day.'

'That's hardly the point.'

'Well it wasn't me.' He doesn't believe me.

'Who else could it have been?'

'Lucy came with me to pick up my stuff.'

'I suppose she hates me.'

I shrug my shoulders.

'What did you tell her?'

Typical Adam, always worried what everybody else will think. 'Let's just say you're not her favourite person.'

He winces. 'Do your parents know?'

'Yeah, why, haven't you told yours?'

'No, they'll be devastated.'

'Didn't see the reason to hide anything, we're all grown ups.'

'Jesus, Eve, I can't believe you told your parents.'

'Well, what did you expect? You dumped me and you waited to do it in front of a camera crew.'

'I haven't dumped you. We're… we're… having time apart.'

Maybe this space really is just a temporary thing. My heart lifts. Lucy and Nell have got it wrong.

'How's work? I ask.

'Shit,' he gives me a lopsided smile.

'No change there then.' I attempt a smile. Same conversation different day, I hide my disappointment.

'I had to tell a patient's husband that his wife's cancer had spread and she only has a few months to live.'

My smile drops. How can I possibly understand the pressure Adam is up against? The biggest trauma I have to deal with is that the toner in the photocopier needs changing. Although, I suppose Brian makes up for it with his consistent vileness.

There was a time when all Adam had to do was read lots of medical books, enough to get a fairly good idea of how things in the body should work. Now he's in at the deep end, dealing with real people with real sicknesses, who expect him to make them better, and usually at three am in the morning, when the only person around with half a clue is him.

'What happened?' I ask.

Adam sticks his hands deep in his pockets. 'He saw me coming and ran the other way.'

I want to hug Adam, to comfort him, but I keep my hands by my sides.

'She has two children, a boy of nine and a girl of seven.'

Tears form in my eyes. That poor, poor family; I still don't know what to say. I never did… do.

Adam starts walking away from me quickly and I have trouble keeping up. I'm five-foot-five, but I'm wearing three-inch-heeled knee-length boots and a skirt that is far too tight for movement, so rather than walk I bob up and down – a demented jack-in-the-box on heels.

Começo is a Portuguese cafe on the corner of South Lambeth Road and has been a favourite of ours for as long as I've been living here, but as I sit here cradling the menu I wonder if this will be the last time I come here.

Adam thrusts out his hands. 'I've got the shakes.'

I raise an eyebrow. He always gets the shakes when he's hungry. 'I'm sure your omelette and chips won't be long.'

'Hope not. I'm starving.'

We sit there for a moment not saying anything and I can't remember the last time I felt this awkward. 'Did you get the Thomies job?' I ask, desperate for something to say.

But this just furthers the awkwardness.

'No, I didn't.'

'But I thought it was in the bag?'

'I never said that. Getting on the team with a world-renowned Professor isn't easy. '

'Oh well, I'm sure something will come up.'

'Expert in Oncology now?'

I resist the temptation to snap back. 'Of course something will come up, it's not like it's a dying trade.' I immediately regret the phrasing.

'Yeah, but I don't want some crappy position. It's three years of my life. You know you didn't have to move out straightaway.'

The abrupt change in conversation catches me by surprise and I wait for him to elaborate, but then the waiter arrives with coffee.

For a moment, we just sit staring into our coffees. I take a sip but it's too hot. I'm looking at him but he keeps staring down at his damn cup and won't return my gaze.

'Do you actually care where I've been all week?' I can't help asking brusquely.

'What sort of silly question is that?'

A part of me wants to scream at him, hit him; anything to get him to tell me what is really going on here.

'Adam?' I say, and before I bottle it. 'What is really going on?'

He rakes his hand through his hair and gives me a tormented look.

'Work is driving me crazy at the moment I just need to be on my own, to figure stuff out.' Before I can ask him what *stuff,* his omelette and chips arrive.

'You can have some chips if you want?'

I shake my head. 'No. Not hungry.'

Adam, on the other hand, tucks in with relish but he's always did have a gigantic appetite. His whole day centres round food, what to have for breakfast, what to have for lunch, what to have for dinner. The night before he'll be thinking, planning what to eat.

'You should eat,' he tells me through a mouthful. 'You look thin.'

And if I have my way I'll be slinking my way into a pair of skinny jeans before you can say Victoria Beckham.

'I'm in no position to be marrying anyone,' He suddenly says.

'I know.'

'I'm up to my eyeballs in debt.'

I didn't know that.

'I haven't even got my job sorted yet.'

Adam stares into space for a bit then gives a heavy sigh.

'I just don't want to wake-up two years from now and think we've made a terrible mistake, you understand? We could both use the time to figure out what we want?'

'Is there someone else?'

He gives me a look.

'What?' I had to ask, that blessed mother of mine first conclusion.

'No.'

Oddly enough I believe him. I'm not sure how it makes me feel, he'd still rather be alone than with me but I'm glad there's no one else.

'I care about you a lot,' he mumbles, 'I just need some time to think.'

'Right.' I answer unenthusiastically this conversation is going nowhere.

He smiles, and it's the familiar lopsided smile I know and love.

'How much time do you need?'

'I don't know.'

I don't know. I don't know. I thought he knew everything.

'Aren't you filming for six weeks?' he asks.

So he does listen to some things.

'Yes.'

'Ok, well let's meet after that.'

I nearly say deal but I don't feel in a jokey mood.

'Well that's everything,' I slam the car boot shut.

'At least you've got your wardrobe space back.' I'm surprised at how upbeat and jolly I'm sounding.

Adam attempts to smile but he doesn't quite pull it off and for the first time I sense that he might be reluctant to see me go.

'Well I'll see you in six weeks.'

He nods. 'Take care of yourself.'

We gaze at each other and he looks like he's about to say something then changes his mind.

'Right then,' I say springing into action, jumping into the driving seat and tugging the door shut. The engine takes several attempts before starting.

Adam knocks on the window and I wind it down. 'Is it safe?'

'Not really,' my heart gives a lurch when I see the panic in his face. 'I'll be fine.'

'I really do care about you.'

I nod and busy myself by revving up the engine. He really didn't give the excuse a lot of thought. No effort again even when he has the opportunity to explain. I feel myself getting angry and rev it up again. He's not going to get off feeling innocent here.

'Drive safely,' he says, his voice cracking a little.

'Mm.' I say unengaged. I can't be bothered to do the expected pleasantries now.

'Bye.'

With nothing more to say, I snap the window up (which did nearly snap) and drive away.

There is no reason for me to go back to the flat again. And it feels so final and yet it's anything but.

I watch Adam in the rear view mirror, shoulders hunched and a weary face like he has the weight of the whole world on his shoulder, looking like someone much older than his years. And a small part of me brightens. I'm glad he feels a tiny bit shite.

CHAPTER TWELVE

'Nell what are you doing here?'

I'm back at Lucy's with my entire pitiful life stuffed in the boot of a car to find Nell casually sitting in the kitchen as if it's the most natural thing in the world.

Nell jumps up from the chair and envelops me in a hug. 'Hello little sis.'

I disentangle myself from Nell's arms and inch away. 'Checking up on me?'

'No. I came round to give you these?' She points to a pair of green wellington boots, which she borrowed, must be two Christmases ago. Crafty sod.

'Really?' I say, quirking a brow to show it won't wash, which Nell expertly ignores and plonks herself back down in the chair.

'Isn't it great about Nell's new role?' Lucy blurts out.

'It's not official yet,' Nell holds crossed fingers up in the air. 'But I'm down to the last two. West End here I come.'

'You should get it,' I say, 'you're a brilliant actress.'

Nell seems genuinely taken back. 'Ah thanks.'

Have I never told my sister how good she is?

'It would be a brilliant opportunity to showcase the larynx and my natural flair for melodrama!'

It's great seeing Nell get excited about a new role.

'I've been reading scripts at work and there's one I really want to show Alastair. It's really intriguing and there's a role in it that would be perfect for you.'

'See it's not what you know but who you know in this business.'

'So how are you really?' Nell asks, eyeing me up and down.

I pause because I'm not sure. On the drive back from Adam's I've been trying to put into words how I feel but the only word I can come up with is, betrayal.

'Better now that Adam and I have talked.' I'm amazed at how adult and mature I sound.

'That's good,' Lucy hands me a cup of tea.

'Thanks.'

'I must say you look remarkably well. I like the skirt and boots combo.' Nell remarks.

'Lucy let me raid her wardrobe.'

'And your hair looks better.'

'Thanks,' I beam.

'So go on, tell us what happened then?' Nell says. Ah the true purpose of her visit couldn't even wait for tea.

I shrug, 'Not much to tell. Adam's been under a lot of pressure at work and just needs to get his head down figure out what he's going to do next.'

'So he still wants space?' Lucy's brow furrows.

'Yes… but we're going to meet in six weeks time.' I say. 'And there isn't anyone else,' I add, giving Nell a so there face.

'Don't worry Lucy I'll buy Loot tomorrow.'

'Don't talk daft you can stay as long as you like.'

'Really? Thanks.'

'You know you can always move in with me?' Nell offers.

I laugh. 'We'd end up killing each other.'

Nell gives me a fake hurt look.

'Anyway, Adam and I could be back together by then.' But even I don't sound convinced.

Nell and Lucy exchange a look.

'I saw that.'

Nell looks like she's about to say something but changes her mind.

'Go on spit it out.'

'What?'

'Whatever it is you want to say.'

'When a guy wants space it usually means it's over.'

I look at Lucy waiting for her to disagree but she is staring down at her cup and won't meet my eyes.

'It's my fault. I've be on at him about getting married, buying a flat together and it's just got too much. He's still in the middle of his exams. He just needs to concentrate on those things, get the registrar job then we… I mean he can think about other things.'

'And that's what you really want? And think woman.' Nell asks.

'Err?'

'Do you really want to get back together after what he did?' She trails off. They both look at me. This isn't the cosy chat I was expecting.

'Because sometimes a relationship has just run its course,' Nell adds.

'Well you would know all about that,' I snap. Nell doesn't batter an eyelid.

'How many divorces?' I ask

'Two.' She recounts something in her head. 'Nearly three, but that's a story for another day. So I know what I'm talking about.'

It's hard to believe that Nell has been married and divorced twice, engaged numerous times and she's only twenty-six. *Hang on, nearly three?*

'I don't think you should just make do, is all I'm saying.' Nell gurgles over the top of her cup.

'I think you should sleep with other men,' Lucy pipes up.

My mouth drops open.

'Adam and I have decided to take a temporary break and you're… you're suggesting I sleep with other men. That's hardly going to patch things up.' But like a flashlight my treacherous "*in therapy*" mind thinks having sex with another man might be exciting.

'A break is a break you can sleep with whoever you want.'

'I'm not about to go sleeping with a man while I am still with Adam.'

'But you're on a break.'

'A temporary break,' I say.

'Anyway I have a bone to pick with you,' I say, jabbing a finger at Lucy and changing the subject. 'You drew a moustache on Adam's graduation picture.'

Lucy recoils from my finger but she doesn't deny it.

'Did you?' Nell laughs.

Lucy nods and Nell gives her a high-five.

'I think he should be thankful that's the worst that happened,' Nell says.

Lucy exchange glances with Nell and I get the impression there's something she's not telling me.

'What have you done?'

'Nothing,' Lucy says, but she's got that guilty look on her face. I'll press her later.

'We're not saying find the first man to shag but if someone…'

'Takes your fancy,' Lucy adds.

'Then it's worth considering,' Nell finishes.

I'm so glad I never told Lucy about the sex therapist. They'd have a field day now.

'Look,' I say flitting my gaze from one to the other. 'Can we just drop the subject?'

'I will, if you remember to drop your drawers!' Nell jokes. 'Just promise me you'll think about what you really want.'

'OK,' I say, shuffling to my feet.

'Where you going?' Nell asks.

'For a walk.'

'But I've come to take you out for lunch?'

'I'm not hungry.'

'Oh, well, I'll come walking with you.'

I look pointedly at Nell's footwear. 'In those?'

'Can I borrow your wellies?'

'No!' I say, slipping out of my boots and putting on my trainers. 'Look I just want to be alone. We can meet for lunch next week. I'll text you.'

'OK Greta Garbo. Fine. Have it your way.'

I wave my hand and head for the door. I know they're going to talk about me as soon as I'm out of earshot, but I really don't care. Then I hear the muffled words,

"Prawns… radiator… stench…"

Lucy Fraser you are awful, but my heart glows. It's good to have a 'prawns revenge' loyal friend.

CHAPTER THIRTEEN

Tonight I have another meeting with Gudrun, and she has asked me to bring a vibrator with me this time. I can't think what she wants me to do with it aside from the obvious, but no way am I doing anything in front of her. Anyway, I've had 'buy V' on the top of my 'to do' list all week, but it's been so busy at work that I still haven't ventured into one of 'those' shops, and now I've run out of time so I'm going to have to do it this lunchtime.

The office today is like Piccadilly Circus, it's as if the entire crew have descended all at once. I've given up on my fruit names as a memory ploy, simply ran out of fruits. I thought about using vegetables but really I'm just over-complicating things best to just learn everyone's name instead. I wait in line to make myself a coffee then squeeze past a group of burly technicians to find Jake perched on the corner of my desk. I take a moment to run my eyes over his long, lean body. I don't know if it's down to Gudrun's instructions about fantasizing more about sex, but I am becoming fixated on Jake. I want to run my hands over his body, to kiss his faintly stubble chin. I feel a surge of longing as I'm imagining his lips on mine, his hands ripping off my clothes…

Oh God he's reading my kindle!

Fuck! I bought the Kama Sutra on my kindle this morning. The book's been around for years so I figured it must still be relevant. No. He can't! He doesn't know my PIN.

'You can't pick up someone's kindle; it's like… going through their diary.'

I take it from him and put it in my drawer.

'I'm waiting for Jet.'

'Still doesn't give you the excuse to rifle through my things.'

'Anyone would think you've got something to hide?' His eyes twinkle at me.

'Still not allowed.' There's a small silence as he watches me. I can feel my breathing start to quicken as I maintain eye contact and sip on my coffee. I suppose he thinks it's fun to wind me up. His eyes don't move from mine and it feels like an eternity.

'Good morning chickadees.' Jet slaps Jake on the back and leans in to sip my coffee.

'Get your own.'

'Have you seen the queue?' Jet grumbles.

'Yes. I was waiting in it for ten minutes. Now, haven't you got something to tell me?'

'Tell you?' Jet says, suddenly looking confused. 'Oh shit I wasn't meant to prepare something?'

'No, silly, have you proposed?'

'Oh that. No.'

'No! But why not?'

He shrugs, 'She might say no?'

'For the love…' I put my coffee down and fix my eyes intently on Jet. 'But what if she says, YES. Don't let what happened to me put you off. You know what you want definitively.'

I feel myself burning with an important message that I need to share. 'Jet, listen to your true emotive self, if it feels right to you grab it with both hands, otherwise you'll be forever wondering "what if." Do not let fear steal your chance. Without chances there is no opportunity and you'll miss life passing you by without so much as a ripple lapping over your toes.'

Jake and Jet are silenced by my sudden soapbox speech. Actually the entire office has become silent.

'You've got to seize the moment,' I say, lowering my voice a little. 'Carpe Diem.' I turn to Jet and grab him by the arms. 'Do it now. Go to her studio and ask her right now.'

'What now?'

'Yes now.'

Jet looks at Jake for permission.

'Go!' says Jake, 'We can catch up later when your sanity returns.'

'That long eh?'

Jet starts to laugh nervously. 'Ok, I'm gonna do it. I'm gonna do it now.'

I whoop with glee.

'To the firing squad troops,' he quips buoyantly and skips to the door, and if a bear could skip that's exactly what he'd look like.

Jet pulls open the door. 'Wish me luck everyone.'

The entire office erupts into whoops of cheers and cries of good luck. When I turn to Jake he's not looking at Jet but staring at me, his expression unreadable.

'What?' I proceed warily.

'You still really believe in happy ever afters even though?'

I smile. 'What you mean even though mine didn't happen?

It doesn't mean it won't.'

'Disney's missing out on their biggest advocate to date.'

'I would rather promulgate the Beatles "*All You Need Is Love*" than a clichéd animated film but thank you all the same.'

His face flickers with amusement. 'You've got gumption I'll give you that. Stoic little miss aren't you.'

I'm not sure if that's a compliment or not.

I'm incredibly busy for the next few hours and it's only when my stomach starts grumbling that I stand up with the realisation I need to do two things.

1. To feed myself.
2. To buy a, you know, a certain piece of equipment.

It's all very well telling other people to be brave; to seize the moment and face their fears but it's very difficult when it's your own fears. I bide time and treat myself to Eggs Benedict in *Balans* on Old Compton Street, because I still need to work up the courage, but instead my embarrassment is growing by the minute. I wish I hadn't woofed down the lunch quite so fast, then I could of bailed with the "where did the time go" argument. But then again, Gudrun said if I didn't get one there was no point in continuing. Her gentle forcefulness is covertly Jedi. I would feel like a naughty child if I didn't produce my homework.

"Eve, next session you bring ze vibrator and we take it and talk to it. Vi vill become friends vith it. It is an exercise that sounds pot-crack but you vil see. Ze penis is not your enemy, it is to make good friends vith. One you can laugh and play with."

Arghhh!

It is such a small thing to do; although I hope that it's not quite so small, and not too big either – just right, as Goldilocks would say. I chuckle and cough on my muffin. Gudrun's right, though, if I know what I like, then instinctively my partner will catch on because I won't be afraid to express it or encourage them towards my needs. But what if I don't really have needs? I may be naturally low in the libido aspect of life. I'm sure I'm trying to force something that isn't really there. I mean, people are different and we're allowed to be different.

I check the time on my phone and I've got half-an-hour before I have to get back to the office, so it's now or never. Dropping the bill with a beautiful man and his perfectly sculpted eyebrows, I walk out with purpose.

It takes me less than two minutes to get to where I need to go. The sense of purpose immediately evaporates the moment I step inside and I falter.

'I haven't got all day lady?'

An impatient man pushes past me, knocking me off balance and through the red tacky beads, onto a huge display of whips, ticklers and something very industrial-looking. They topple over like a dirty kerplunk tower.

'Aren't you a keen one, sugar.' A very camp Asian man announces down his shiny black shirt. I look up from beneath the pile and realise the blow up display dolls crotch is in my face, tasselled thong n' all, worse still it's stuffed undercarriage is now sitting on my shoulder, a pair of glued ping pong balls.

'I'm s….s…so sorry.' I don't know where to look. Nowhere in here is going to give me the solace that this humiliation deserves.

'Looks like you've already got a bollocking!' he gives me a brief smile. 'Don't worry darling, happens to us all.'

I unstick the ping-pongs from my shoulder and try to rectify the damage by stuffing them back in the thong when a huge great rubber snake thing drops out.

I let out a scream. 'Aghhhh!'

What is wrong with me! My hands are frantic as I helplessly try and stuff everything back into its rightful place. Oh, sink-hole, please appear now.

'Edward! Hans! Don't worry sugar I'll get the boys to sort it out. Needed a revamp anyway. Old droppy drawers here is getting a bit slack!'

There is nothing remotely droopy about him though; he towers over me, lean, trim and strong as he pulls me up onto my feet. I stare at him, my face flushed and blood pounding through my ears.

'Let me guess, first time?'

'Is it that obvious?' I say, clearing my husky throat. I want to retreat back to my conservative world and yet this towering Asian man and his black shiny shirt has me transfixed.

'I'm here to shop,' I say.

'That's good; we are a shop.'

'I'm here for err a thing.'

'Goooood… we have things to sell.'

I let out a giggle.

'We do individual things as well as bulk!' He laughs and winks. 'But trust me, you'll love a bit of bulk.'

He grabs a double-ended thingy. 'See!' My eyes nearly pop out my head, he cackles.

After five minutes I've found my new best friend, gay as a princess on marshmallow-scented rainbow heels. He is totally uninhibited. I suppose owning a shop like this you'd have to be. We wander into the aisle of coloured latex electrics… see I still can't say it.

'This is the stalwart of all women this side of the hemisphere.'

I look at it and my jaw drops.

'When someone introduces you to the world of sensual oneness, do you always gawp like a fish out of water?'

'I am out of water!' I gasp.

'Luckily the bunny is a ground lover.'

'So this is the...'

'... Oh yes, the new improved Rampant Rabbit, guaranteed to keep listening until you reach the heights of your private conversation.' He laughs as he turns it on.

'Blimey that's quite an action.'

'All the colours, to suit every taste. Shall I wrap one up for you Miss –?'

'Poots.'

'Well Miss Poots, this doesn't hoot or shoot!'

'Glad to hear it.'

'Staying in has it's plus side, Miss Poots.'

Realising the time, I opt for neon pink and say goodbye to more money than I can afford right now, and skip out the store with my head held high, feeling rather proud of myself. I did it. I seized the moment and it really wasn't so bad.

'Hello, Eve.'

Shocked to hear my name, I swing round and there, standing in front of me, are Jake and Mel. Oh just splendid, the one time in my life I actually do this type of thing and I meet people I know. I blush.

Of course I blush. I am standing outside a sex shop in Soho.

'Oh Hi!' I say, trying to sound nonchalant. 'Fancy bumping into you two.'

Jake eyes the shop's ominous black frontage and the plain black shiny bag I am holding and raises an eyebrow. My blush deepens as if he knows what I've been up to, which is ridiculous, of course he can't possibly know. But guessing can't be difficult at this location.

'Ooh have you been shopping?' Mel asks innocently enough, 'Did you buy anything nice?'

Trying not to freak out I shake my head. 'Oh nothing exciting.' I glance over at Jake and he smiles knowingly.

'Right, well. Don't let me keep you. See you back at the ranch!' I dash off, waving as if surrounded by angry wasps (is there any other kind!).

When I get back to the office, I'm so flustered and sweaty that I need a distraction and somewhere to hide. I decide to sort out Alastair's filing cabinet. I'm still placing everything in alphabetical order when I hear Jake and Mel return from their lunch an hour later.

Jake suddenly pops his head around the door and my heart jolts with fright and something else, something far more alarming, I drop the files, scattering all the papers across the floor.

'So this is where you're hiding?' He says as his face crinkles into a smile.

'I'm not hiding,' I say defiantly but I know I must look flustered. I gather up the loose bits of paper.

'I'm looking for Alastair.'

'He's not here.' Obviously.

But instead of leaving, Jakes walks into the room and closes the door. He is ridiculously handsome; violet eyes, high cheekbones, a straight flaring nose that draws the eyes down to his full lips. I take an inward gasp. Oh my God! I fancy him.

No, you don't, I argue with myself. He's too cocky and sure of himself. The word cock makes me think about the black bag locked away in my desk's drawer.

'Do you know when he might be back?'

'He said around four.'

I return to the file in my hand when I still feel his presence. I turn to him. 'Is there anything else?'

The spark of amusement returns to his eyes, and I feel a flush. 'Nope, just thinking.'

'Right, and this where you come to think?' I blurt out loud with nerves.

'Today, this is the perfect place to think.'

At that moment, someone shouts his name from the main office and he leaves me in peace.

'Vel-kommen Eve. I zee you have been to shops. Very good.'

I immediately take a slug of port.

'Will you show me?'

I hold out the bag expecting Gudrun to take it from me.

'Why don't *you* take it out and show me.'

My cheeks burn as I reach inside the bag and pull out the big black box. A pink 'R' and the words 'RAMPANT RABBIT The Neon One' glare at us. I hold up the box.

'Vel done.' Gudrun hands me a pair of scissors. Oh crikey she wants me to take it out of the box too. I snip at the seal, slide it open and there, centred in a pile of black tissues, is a large pink neon vibrator. Why did I think pink neon would be a good idea? In Gudrun's candlelight room it actually glows.

'Vell, up vith it.' Dear God she wants me to do it in front of her.

'Up, up vith ze box. Let us look.' Thank goodness, small cardiac arrest now over.

I hold the box upright.

'Now take it out of ze box for me.'

Oh crikey. I gingerly pick it up between my fingers and hold it up from the battery end.

'Zis is a good size for a beginner, not too big.'

How can she tell?

'Now don't be frightened, it iz just a toy. A rightful pleasure.' She clocks the fear in my eyes. 'So vhat ve wait for?' She stands and despite her tiny stature she seems like a giant.

What! She doesn't actually want me to do it here. I gulp repeatedly.

'You have batteries, yes?'

I nod, still too choked and embarrassed to speak.

'Ok, vell pop zem in. Let's hear it.'

I fumble with the battery holder and insert the batteries, holding it up to listen. It's not working. It must be broken.

'Eve darling, how do you expect to be turned on, if your little friend isn't!'

We both laugh. Now it's become a technical puzzle.

I search for the on button and it press down. A light comes on. Eureka.

'Familiarise yourself with the toy, give it a firm grip, hold it up, don't be so afwaid. It von't bite!'

I hold it in front of me and weld it around like a neon Star Wars Lightsaber at first, unsure what to expect, literally getting to grips with it. My confidence grows, so I then switch another button on and the whole thing starts to move like a giant wobbling sword. I burst out laughing. 'So ve have a working rabbit. Vunderfull. Ze good technique you start slow. Take your time with it. I suggest you warm up ze erogenous zones.'

I must look as blank as I feel.

'Vith your own little digits first.'

What?

'Fingers Eve, your nimble fingers. Familiarise you vith your own wonders. Ze clitoris is von very essential part of ze woman's nerve centre. Map out your vulva lips, explore ze vagenie vell. Yes? Then you move onto intense setting and ze socks vil fall off. It vill help you find ze climax, you vill orgasm, yes?'

'Right,' I say, unsure I'll ever take it out of the package again.

'You've been ignoring ze key of all female gratification and that particular bit needs your attention. Think of zis as making a cup of tea. Vhen kettle boils, ze sveat of excitement. Not over think ze things. No monotone, no?'

'I don't think…'

'Yes, don't think,' Gudrun says. 'Grasp a moment in time rather than plan every detail. Be spontaneous.'

I pull a face without meaning to.

'Vhat wrong? Vhy you hide imagination? Do you have it? Vhat you wait for? A man to show you how you function?'

All right, Gudrun, steady on, feeling my rage rising.

'Ze pussy and the bunny go to sea now. Auf Wiedersehen Eve,' she practically shoos me out of the door, but not before setting out homework for the next six weeks. She calls it an exploratory period of enlightenment to my… my well… first things first, is to find and watch the enlightenment in a mirror, then implement my newly found mechanical man piece with its own tickle stick when I know what bits should be introduced and tickled. After she said I've been ignoring the key of all female gratification and that particular bit needs all my attention, I thought I never really did do self…um… self-pleasure… oh you know the M word, when I was growing up in the house of godliness gone gaga. In my vast (choke) sexual experience, I just let the man get on with what he wants and never what I liked. I don't really know what I like; too aware of disappointing whomever I'm with. I've become a slave to my own inadequacies, which in turn has cemented them into my further failings. I've lost sight to what really should be good, fun and above all very, very pleasurably – so they say. I must see this through and really determine if my libido is truly tainted or waiting to be ignited by this self-knowledge.

I am restless that night, tossing and turning, dreaming of giant vibrators and what may lay beneath Jake's blinding teeth and crisp trousers. Surprisingly, when I wake up I do not feel tired. I jump out of bed, ready to seize the day.

CHAPTER FOURTEEN

I haul my suitcase up the flights of stairs and into the office. Sue from accounts is in already, and so is Alastair.

'Want a coffee Sue?'

'Would love one.' I don't need to ask Alastair, he doesn't ever turn down a coffee.

I hop, skip and jump down the steps and cross the road to Akarsu's, feeling unusually buoyant and happy.

'Günaydın, günaydın.' Mr Akarsu sing songs in Turkish.

'And a good morning, good morning to you too,' I say, beaming at him. Proud I know what that means after seven months of hearing it! Mr Akarsu hands me an espresso while I wait.

'Teşekkür ederiz.' *(Hmm, maybe, I can strike second language off hobby list?).*

'Someone's chirpy this morning.' My heart slams into my mouth as I slowly turn and stare at Jake.

'Oh hi.'

'A sneaky coffee why you wait, eh?'

'Turkish coffee just sorts you out sometimes.'

'It does, indeed.'

'She drink for free, you have to pay.' Mr Akarsu's paternal protectiveness rears its gruff Turkish head.

'Could I try a Turkish coffee then Sir, I mean if it's that ok?'

'Put your money away, you try and then say.' Jake politely takes the coffee from Mr Akarsu and winks at me.

'That's a damn fine cup of morning splendour right there.' Jake says, over-exaggerating his soft American accent with Southern twangs.

'How about you Peggy Sue, you want another?'

'Sure would,' I say, trying out a hillbilly accent. Jake smiles at my effort. We take our coffees; I balance four while Jake carries the other two.

'He likes you.'

'I'm a regular. Now can you get the door? I've run out of appendages!'

'Luckily us men have one more.'

I blush crimson, scampering across the road.

When we get back to the office, Alastair pokes his head round the door.

'You read my mind?'

'Kinetics!'

'Actually Eve, can I have a word.'

'Sure,' I say, tucking pen and paper into my jeans and carrying in our coffees.

The second I sit down I notice the scripts I left for him. I can see he's scribbled some notes of his own.

'Why is this one your favourite?'

'Have you read it?'

'Yes. But I want to hear what you think.'

And then, I hear my voice in my head, and it's very loud

and clear, saying "*grab opportunities when they arise*" (number 23 on my to-do list).

I take a deep breath.

'Because it's bold and original, you have no idea where, or on which… how it's going to unfold. You're not even sure of the story yet, that's what I like, and yeah the story unfolds only at the time of each word. No predictability at all. "Peep show" peppered with Cluedo meets black comedy at its best.' The words tumble out of my mouth. I pause to clear my throat and calm down. Alastair is looking at me and – surprisingly – is still actually listening.

'I'm not sure it'll be easy to get commissioned but -'

He likes it. He likes it. My face lights up.

'I think the back story still needs work,' I brighten. 'And the boss character needs his own back story.'

'I tell you what,' Alastair says. 'Contact the writer and suggest the changes you have in mind.'

My mouth swings open and I stare at Alastair. 'That would be… super,' I say.

Alastair smiles at me. 'And when you have a second draft ready let me take another look.'

He goes on to explain everything. He likes the script but agrees with me that there are areas that need developing. He also has concerns about the ending and he wants me to work on this. I realise he is as enthusiastic as I am; trusting me with this is major for me. This is a very big deal, a very big deal indeed. It could be the making of my career as a producer.

There is a knock at the door and Brian appears. He looks at Alastair and I as thick as thieves and I know he's just dying to know what we are talking about.

'The cars are waiting.'

'Ok, we've finished up here.' He gives me a wink.

I stand up. 'Thanks again, Alastair.' I clutch the script to my chest.

'No thank you, if you hadn't shown the initiative to go through the scripts we might never have come across this quirky gem.'

I flush with pride.

I walk past Brian. His eyes run dismissively over me. I give him a cheery smile in return because I'm not bothered. I'm really not bothered what he thinks of me. Wow. For the first time since starting this job, I really don't care. Alastair likes what I have to say and that's all that matters.

I sit back at my desk with a huge, goofy smile on my face. I am so going to be able to cross no.1 off my list.

Immediately I start drafting up an email to the writers of *Comatosed* when Mel comes over to me in a fluster. 'I can't find the reference for the hotel.'

'Mel it'll be in your notebook. Everything is in your notebook,' I say, standing up and walking over to her desk. I pick up her pad and starting flicking through her pages. Wow, it is so neat. Everything is either in red, green, blue or yellow.

'Why are these written in red and these in green.'

'Oh it's colour co-ordinated for levels of importance.'

'Wow!' Clever?

For the next fifteen minutes I help Mel sort through the last minute details.

'Where's Brian?' I ask, climbing into my seat on the minibus, settling at the back.

'Riding in the other car with Alastair and Jake.'

'That's a relief.'

'I heard him call Sue a hopeless glorified paper-pusher the other day.'

'No!' The man's a sexist pig.

'Sue said, "Good I hear there's a lot of glorious paperwork in a tribunal."'

I laugh. 'I can't even imagine Sue ever saying that. Actually I can. She might be quiet but she's totally switched on.'

Mel nods her head, about to say something else, when her mobile starts pinging erratically.

'Better check if these are urgent.' She buries her head; strained eyed at the downloading list.

I slump into the seat pulling on my earphones, the sound of London Grammar filling my ears. I watch as the blocks of flats and offices give way to the flat motorway.

Leaving London is always strange nowadays. I glance over at Mel, who is nose deep writing in her notebook. It's as though her head is leaking with important stuff that she just has to get down on paper. I daren't disturb her.

I stare out the window and my mind wonders to Adam. I haven't really given him much thought, work and other stuff have kept me occupied I guess. I must have given him the air of psycho bunny boiler and that's why he wanted numerous witnesses because I can't think why else he would want to publicly humiliate me like he did. He should have turned up with the anti-marriage proposal song, a musical video with all friends and family included then I could have had another YouTube hit, along the lines of…

Eve you might get peeved,
I'm not going to marry you,
Instead I'll leave you in front of a camera crew.

Witnesses will be present,
When I turn on you and feel you've been run over like a pheasant.
For all to watch and jeer,
And I'll just go on with nothing to fear,
Because I shan't marry you,
I'll just break your crumbling heart in two.
How we will dance and sing,
To see your heart jittering,
For just at that moment when you think love is true,
I'll act like a gigantic poo,
A coward is I,
So no need to cry.
I'm just a massive ginger shit
Who's become the ultimate tit.
Humiliating you in public view,
Just so your work colleagues can have a go at you too."

I giggle. That is rather good.

Bring back the Gladiators - that's what I need. A bit of fighting, then home to their woman and off again. Super simple. Rules as easy as baking from packets (excluding Lucy on the baking bit).

Because the way modern men shit on you from above, they're a plague of sky rats.

But what do I want? This is the question that keeps going round and round in my head. Nell and Lucy are right I can have sex with anyone I want to. What is it Gudrun said? I need to be spontaneous and not over think things so much that they become monotone, unnatural, and not alluring to any species. Actually, I thought that was a bit harsh but she's the expert. I have to at least try and take it on board, keep an open mind. The thing is I did all this so I could seduce Adam and now I've realised it isn't about Adam at all. It's about me.

Part of me wants to hear Adam say he's made a terrible mistake and he wants me back, but that's only so I can tell him to fuck off. I realise right at this moment that I have finally made up my mind. I don't want Adam. I don't love Adam. Because I've tried to look at this space as a positive thing for both of us, a chance for us to take stock to see just how good we are together, but to be honest I just feel… let down. ARGHHHH! Why is everything so hard?

Well – maybe not everything, especially in Adam's case!

I laugh to myself, that's pretty funny. Soon I'm laughing so much I have to take huge gulps of air, tears dripping down my face. I've been so obsessed with getting married that I lost focus on the rest of my list and I need to refocus otherwise I won't accomplish anything and then panic sets in.

'Eve! Are you ok?'

I try to speak but nothing comes out. Mel is gaping at me with a look of worry. I stare back suddenly unable to breathe and my heart is pounding out of my chest.

'Eve, speak to me?'

'I haven't learnt Spanish,' I say, clutching Mel's arm in despair.

'What!'

'Or French,' I say. 'It's on my list. Get married. Buy a flat. I can't even do a proper one-handed cartwheel. Dance on a table in Vegas. Learn to spell without auto-correction on. Become a Producer. It's all on my list.' I double over, clutching my chest. I think I'm going to have a heart attack.

'Eve, breathe into this.'

She empties the contents of her brown paper bag, the sandwich and apple juice falling to the floor and thrusts the empty bag into my hands.

I take the bag and breathe into it. Mel is busy stroking and patting my back, making some sort of cooing reassurance sounds.

I haven't done half the things on my list. I know some of them are a bit daft, but I still want to do them. A sob rakes through my body.

No, no, stop. I can't let myself think like this. Ok deep breathes.

'Sorry.' I give Mel a tiny smile

'You ok?'

I nod but she peers at me doubtfully.

'It's just, I thought I knew exactly what I wanted to do. I realise I haven't got a clue,' I shrug and try another smile.

'Who really knows what we are doing?'

'I feel as though I can't trust myself anymore.'

'Oh, sweetie,' she pats my back again. 'You're super. You're fun. You're smart. You take everything in your stride.'

'Me?'

'And you don't have to marry to be qualified as a woman.'

I blow my nose and push myself up.

'And you can still do the other things on your list. What's it you want to do, master a one-handed cartwheel? Well I can help you there. I used to do gymnastics when I was younger.'

I stare at Mel with surprise. 'No way!'

'Way. I competed on county level for a couple of years. When we get to the hotel I'll teach you.'

This perks me up. 'Really?' Wow, swings and roundabouts.

'And Alastair has asked me to assist on *Comatosed*,' I tell her, shyly.

Mel beams. 'As Assistant Producer?'

I nod.

'Wow, that's great. See. You've got lots of great things happening and we have our own Short. We make a great team.'

'We do.'

Men! Who needs them!

I feel better already. Honestly, I can be so over-dramatic sometimes. And I should be proud of how I've handled the whole humiliating episode, it wasn't the prison cell all over again, I didn't spiral like I did with Ben. I must be maturing.

'How do I look?' I ask.

Mel delves into her tote pulling out a compact mirror and make-up. My face is blotchy and red along with dripping mascara.

'Here, let me.' Mel digs in her makeup bag and helps with repair and renewal.

The sign for the town nearest the hotel comes into view and the driver pulls off the motorway, we pass an old market town then turn onto a small country road. This goes on for a few miles and I can count the houses we've passed on one hand. We drive through a tiny village with a fairy-tale allure even I can't resist, then down a narrow track towards another hamlet, the light dimming as the overhead trees form a dense tunnel. We both stare out the window, small stone cottages flank the road and in the distance across a rolling green field, the peak of an elegant manor house rises. I'm not one for twee countryside villages, but this place isn't twee, it's bloody good enough for an Austen novel.

We pull into a gravel track, the minibus struggles with the

steep twists and turns of the track, then and an extraordinary country hotel comes into view.

The photos in the brochure don't do it justice. This place is beautiful.

I notice the other mini bus pull up. I strain to see inside but I can't make out anything through the smoky windows. The car door opens and jean-clad legs with scuffed sneakers appear. My heart does a little skip. It's Jake. Followed by Alastair and the malodorous Brian.

CHAPTER FIFTEEN

Mel and I are sharing a room. Mel's already changed and heading for the bar but I want to make a phone call first.

'You go ahead. I'll follow you down.'

Mel is wearing a sixties trapeze dress with an embellished collar and looks elegantly elfin. I decide I'll wear my "it'll be all white on the night" prom dress. It's not as bad as it sounds, it has a cute bow at the waist but I have teamed it with my sky high Jimmy Choo pumps, what is it that Marilyn Monroe said, *"Give a girl the right shoes and she can conquer the world."* They were an obscene amount of money and technically I am too poor to spend this sort of money but I threw caution to the wind plus I get to tick off 14 on my list. That was worth a splurge on the credit card. Figured that's break even because of the free therapy… okay maybe that was fitting circumstances to the impetuous splurge, but classics costs.

'I'm here! I'm here! Sorry.' I cry breathlessly throwing myself into the chair. Mel peers at me curiously. She pushes a mojito in my direction and a bowl of sweet potato chips.

'I figured you'd want a drink and I got us nibbles. Should

still be warm.'

'You read my mind.' I pop a chip into my mouth, reaching for my mojito and taking a much-needed greedy slurp.

'I had to ring Adam and finish it once and for all.' I say, involving myself in obsessive dipping at the DD's chipotle sauce, which in turn ignites my mouth like some miniature smoky furnace, yum. There's silence. When I look up to check Mel heard me, her mouth is gaping. I check my cheeks haven't caught light and see she's actually agog with shock.

'I asked Adam if he wanted to be with me, and he said that he couldn't believe I was asking him this over the phone, and I said that it's a simple enough question. So he asked if we could talk about this another time and I said "No, not really."'

Mel stares at me totally agog.

'So I said I can't hang around waiting for him to make up his mind whether he wants to be with me or not. People wildly in love with each other do not need to take time apart. It's bullshit. And this is a bullshit way to treat someone you claim to care about. I don't love Adam. I don't think I ever did. So I told him it's over, and I put the phone down.'

Mel continues to stare at me open mouth, and then she grins. 'Are you OK?'

'I am, as it happens.'

She leans back in her chair. 'Wow!'

'I feel relieved, like a massive weight has been lifted off me. I needed some sort of closure. Specific is terrific!'

'I told you, you're super.'

We both take a sip of our drinks. It makes me feel quite heady.

And I do feel fine. Ok, I'm not jumping up and down in happiness, but I feel like my life hasn't crumpled and I haven't been banished for eternity into the realms of utter loveless despair. I've taken the decision and I am moving on with my life.

'You two look like you're discussing the finer details of life.'

Mel and I both bristle.

'Huh? Err… Brian,' Mel smiles sardonically.

'Carry on,' he says, looking at us both with contempt, before walking away victoriously for no reason.

'He makes my skin crawl to the point of fungal infection,' Mel whispers from behind her hand.

I giggle. 'Bacteria has more appeal.'

'Wouldn't it then be in competition with itself?'

We cackle into our glasses.

'You know, for what it's worth I think you've done the right thing.'

'I know I have.'

I look around the room. This is the first time that all crew have been together in one place, and there's a party atmosphere. My eyes immediately stray towards Jake, as they have so often been doing in this past period. I like looking at him. He just seems so sure about – well, everything. I take a moment to appreciate his tight behind. Physically he's more than appealing, and he's also a bit mysterious and powerful. I've never leered over a man, but the very thought makes my pimento stuffed olive quiver with longing. This must be what lust feels like. I give a tiny inward gasp as the idea sinks in. It must be the Mojito talking. My brave detachment has just gone loopy, that's all.

As if sensing me watching him, Jake looks over, and for a moment our eyes meet. I find myself unable to look away, and my heart starts racing.

No, no, not my type. But then again, he is sort of my type, you know, the 'spineless treacherous' type hasn't been exactly effective so far, and perhaps a stab into the unknown could be the ticket.

'Maybe men should come in canapés, on a platter, so you can taste a few before ordering a main meal, let alone a weekly shop.'

Mel laughs.

Gudrun would be proud though if I actually put that one into practice. Now I feel guilty for not doing my little homework. When am I going to get a chance now that I'm sharing a room with Mel? I've left the thingy stick stuffed in a pair of ski socks hidden in my suitcase. I'm not sure what to do with it anyway. I was hoping for an Ikea instruction booklet plus Allen key. How does it even stay in place, and won't it be like having an affair with a robot?

Too weird for my blood.

And as for the mirror exploratory stuff I can't very well hog the bathroom searching for pimento's popping out of olives.

The policy of girls sharing is that a bathroom is only locked when doing number twos, otherwise it's access all areas; make-up application, hair-styling and general outfit checking can't wait for all and sundries bladders. And no… the mirror in the hall hasn't got the right light! Women do incessantly pee when they know they have to be doing something for the next few hours, it's as if our bladders won't let us out of the room before a triple check and trickle has been completed and signed off by the brain!

'It's a cliché but time really does heal,' Mel says.

'What heals?' Jet comes springing into frame and joins us at the table.

'Battered egos,' I joke. Composing myself. 'Hi Jet.'

'I wanted to come over and thank you Eve.'

'You do?'

Jet beams at me. 'Marisa said yes,' he looks like he can't quite believe it.

I jump up and give him a hug. 'Wow, that's amazing news.'

'Congratulations,' Mel says.

'I'm really happy for you.'

'So you still believe in marriage?' Jake's warm, deep voice creeps up behind me and my heart gives a little swoop. 'Even though you were about to marry the wrong guy.'

'Well, I better make sure it's the right guy next time,' I reply politely.

Jake smiles, his eyes boring down on mine, and I tingle.

'It will happen,' says Jet. 'You will meet someone you prefer to everyone else in the world. You'll never know when, or how, or why, come to think of it.' He looks mystified, shocked and elated, as if it's only just dawned on him how truly in love he is and that she said yes. 'Don't worry mate it will happen to you too.'

Jake scoffs.

'Mark my words. And when it does I'm going to mock every loved up word that comes out of your soppy American mouth.'

'That would be good to get on camera.' says Mel.

'Yeah, from scorn to forlorn in one foul swoop if she says no!' I add a little too zealously.

'Funny,' says Jake. 'I'm intrigued, so what does this man you're going to marry have to be like?'

You! The thought pops into my head out of nowhere and I stare at Jake in shock.

'Oh, I don't know.' I shrug. 'Someone who makes me laugh, is kind, thoughtful… erm… um… a monogamist.'

My answer is laced with clichés, making me sound more deluded than sexist fairy tales (although women got more lead roles in those!) But I don't know what it must be like to really be in love, like Jet. I definitely haven't experienced it yet and that is painfully crystal clear now.

'I think the essence might be someone you cherish spending time with and they feel exactly the same. You're always happy to see each other. No, you're always excited, ecstatic to see them. They light you up even if you're in your darkest moments. You feel what they feel. You are one being, well almost one. You feel complete, I know that sounds clichéd but it must exist, otherwise why does anyone get married?'

My audience is awed and I swear Jet is tearing up. He coughs in embarrassment. But I meant every word.

'Most people get married because of time clauses.' Jake says in a sarcastic tone. 'Time served! Time lapsed nothing better to do and too lazy to move on, financially or otherwise. Men are categorically apathetic if their world is organised for them, love has nothing to do with it - convenience does.'

'That's so cynical.' I pick up my glass and take a large sip.

'The truth has a habit of dashing dreams.'

'Why on earth invent something that wasn't wanted, what people chose to be the ultimate gesture of Love.'

'Marriage was invented when the lifespan wasn't more than thirty years. You're full of optimism at twenty,' he says but I detect a wry smile behind his prophet of doom.

I glance over at Mel and Jet and they are watching us like it's some kind of tennis match. Actually, it does feel a bit like a tennis match, but who's winning and who swapped the Barley water for rum?

'Let me put it another way,' Jake continues. 'The rise and success of dowries in marriage, dowries are still very much in existence. At the end of the day, it's an arrangement, financial or otherwise; love has nothing to do with it. Convenience definitely has.'

Ok, now he's just being annoying.

'Only in barbaric or archaic cultures,' I say. 'Even the Babylonian's custom was just a way of dealing with inheritance issues and women's rights were non-existent. That's hardly the case these days.'

Maybe Jake's just had his heart broken and now he's bitter and twisted. Plus, he's a man, so why expect any different; by his own admittance men are lazy callous creatures.

'Basically, the good old days were no more than a cattle market; women couldn't experience the world and when the man got bored, tired and too old to play the field he settled for a wife. Thought you'd be an Austen fan by default.'

I glare at him defiantly. 'Well Mr America if you knew anything about her literature you'd know her heroines marry for love and with full wits intact.'

He laughs, which makes me want to hit him. This topic has gone on far too long, and it's too bleak, too depressing.

'You two should agree to disagree and order more pretty green drinks!' Jet slaps his drink down on the table making me jump. Mel scuttles off to the bar, relieved to get away, I guess.

'At least the playing field's a little more even now,' I say. 'We can now vote. Fancy that. And we wear pantaloons on Tuesdays! ' I pick up my mojito and take another large gulp.

Jake stares at me across the table, while Jet whitters on about various pantaloons he's worn to parties. I avoid eye contact with Mr Doom and Gloom and decide to take in the room around me.

It's very classy, all dark wooden panels on the walls and ceiling, plush leather Chesterfields beckoning tired bottoms. The green antique lights hanging discreetly above the panels and the candelabras on the tables cast all their mysterious light around the room. There's a huge inglenook fireplace roaring away on the far side of the room, three elderly men sit inside the grand space sharing a bottle of port and smoking cigars sneakily up the chimney, the management must turn a blind eye as the smoke goes straight up the chimney, you can't even smell it in the room, also I think they might be lords, perhaps Earls or something Austen gentry style. They have that air, and inaudible vowel pronunciation going on.

The light flickers as someone rushes through the double doors into the bar snug, aptly named the Nook. Jake reminds me of two-face from Batman, all dark and moody on one side and the illumination of a highly disagreeable cheekbone on the other. Mel interrupts my thoughts as an odd looking waiter carrying a bumper silver tray of drinks and olives follows her to the table.

'Hi folks, Steve Carressle is right on time.' A strange mahogany polished man swoops down and grabs my fresh icy tumbler of minty revitaliser.

'Caressle by name, caresser by nature.' He winks at Mel and I, sitting straight down with my Mojito. He wrinkles his ultra tanned nose, his slick black hair doesn't move, it just glistens in the light. I'm just about to steal my own drink back when…

'Careful, the candles.' I hold my arm between his flying hair and the naked flame.

'My heroine, Tobias the toupee is eternally grateful.' We all laugh heartedly; our cheesy TV host certainly isn't as vain as first impressions.

'Steve, darling how are you?' Brian runs up and hugs the drink thief with air kisses galore.

'So you've met everyone?'

'No darling, hardly had time to pick up a drink.' Steve winks at me. He grins widely showing his immaculate façades.

'This fine filly gave up her drink for me, what a gesture. I'm going to like this shoot.' Brian is put out and snarls a half smile.

'And what was your name fair maiden?'

'Hi Steve.' I hold out my hand, 'Eve.'

'Please call me Franc.'

Confused but shaking Steve, aka Franc's hand, I succumb to his gall.

Brian leaves and everyone relaxes, Steve does a quick turnabout after chatting with the beautiful stylists, they all giggle coyly and I think what on earth they find endearing.

'Shall we formally introduce ourselves then?'

'Jake,' says shooting his hand across the table, 'I'll be directing and splicing this slice of wedding heaven.'

'Good to meet you Jake, now just say what you will. I'll work on my shy nature!'

Jet springs up and shakes his hand vigorously, 'Jet, your expert handyman of sound.'

'Good to meet a human aircraft at last.' Everyone laughs. Steve certainly possesses a quick cheesy charm. It's funny. I'm warming to him.

'Mel.' She holds her hand out to shake.

'Oh Mon Cherie.' Steve takes her hand in the manner of a matador with a cape, kissing it in the air. Mel giggles like a schoolgirl.

'Mel for the melody of merry love?' Steve continues his romantic onslaught; she gets bashful with all the attention.

'I already know you, health and safety rep?'

'Eve pleased to meet you,' I hold my hand our like a man. 'I take it you're in front of the camera then?'

'How did you guess my dear… oops is it alright to call you that?'

'I'll live, George Hamilton!' Everyone laughs.

'Why thank you kindly, Eve deary. I get the finest bronze polish flown in from Paris weekly. He's my tanning idol!'

Thank goodness he's able to take the piss out of himself.

'So I'm your cheese fondant showman, the host if you haven't already guessed with my obsessional OTT bronzing. Hope we're all up for some fun during the shoot?' Steve exaggerates a cheeky look at Mel. 'If you weren't before you will be by day three, when you're ready to kill at least one of the contestants!' We all cheers to that.

Alastair and Brian wander over.

'Right gang, shall we just go over the morning schedule?' Alastair says cheerily.

We all settle around the table, Steve politely pulls up a couple of chairs.

'Make sure all trades have arrived, especially the crane for the aerial shots, then after everything is checked we'll meet in our temp green room, which weirdly enough is called the green room. Make sure all the contestants are in the hall after arrival. We have all the pre show footage to take and we can't capture that after they've begun like other reality programs.

This one has to different, edgier and revolutionary.'

'Tall orders from you then Mr Alas-starry!' Steve jokes.

'Good to have you on board Steve, you're going to make this historic.'

'Don't think the noble peace prizes go to reality show-hosts Alastair, unless a category's opened up that I haven't been privy to. And Alastair stop trying to sell the sausage, sell the sizzle!' Steve's exuberant jazz-hands complete his point. Alastair begins to chuckle then raises his glass to all of us.

There's a good feeling around the table that we'll be making something that causes headlines, in whatever way that will be.

CHAPTER SIXTEEN

This morning I wake up smiling and it isn't forced either. I can hear Mel humming along to the radio in the bathroom.

Steve certainly put everyone in the topper of moods last night. I've come to the conclusion he's not only a good showman, but also a very skilled people's person, there is more to him than meets the mahogany paint brush so to speak.

I swing open the wardrobe and fling the following onto the bed, blue ripped jeans, a white tank and my Brian Lichtenberg "Feline" hoodie all the while dancing and singing to Rihanna's "Bitch Better Have My Money"

'Very smooth' Mel grins, walking out of the bathroom and catching me with my hairbrush microphone, gyrating to the music.

She throws her straighteners on the bed and joins me. We look totally ridiculous, me in my unicorn onesie and Mel with a towel ensemble, towel on body and towel on head thrusting and gyrating but definitely giving RiRi a run for her money.

We enter the grand reception room thirty minutes later, suitably dressed and ready for business although I can still hear the music in my head and I might have done a sneaky twerk when no one was looking.

The reception has three floor-to-ceiling paned old French doors and I can't quite believe this elaborate space is going to be the production office. We immediately set to work, getting the place ready. We have a couple of runners who are at our disposal and between the four of us we get the place up and running in no time at all.

Stefan the editor has been set up in the Siam suite next to us. Next we visit the green room, which as you might recall is conveniently called The Green Room, where unbeknown to the contestants hidden cameras and microphones have been set up. Leading from this room just separated by double doors is the grand hall, where we holding the first task,

"The Trade Off"

The hall is all set up for the task and is relatively empty. Mel drops the unit list on the table. The others are having lunch but Mel insists I follow her.

'Right, stand there and watch me,' she says briskly.

'What for?'

'I'm going to teach you how to do a one-handed cartwheel.'

Mel spins three perfect one-handed cartwheels in a row and finishes off with a perfect back flip.

'OMG!' I say, applauding. 'That was amazing.'

Mel grins. 'I wasn't sure if I could still do that.'

'No question there.'

'Now it's your time.'

I guffaw.

'Let's start with a basic cartwheel first.'

I take a deep breath, preparing myself, give a light hop and a skip, and launch into what I can only describe as a tumbling turd. I spin myself awkwardly around, limbs practically detached, head down and posterior bruised.

Oof!

I start laughing through my weaning pride. 'Told you.'

Mel chuckles but refuses to be defeated. 'Ok let's start again. This time straighten up and keep straight before you launch.' She hauls me to my feet.

We spend the next fifteen minutes trying to get me to straighten up. Once I've mastered the cartwheel Mel shows me the one handed cartwheel and the trick to this is to take off with a bit more spring and then, guess what, I get it. After the billionth time and even though my arms are aching I throw myself lightly over and perform a perfect cartwheel. I can't actually believe I did it.

Mel claps her hand wildly. 'You did it.'

Unbelieving, I try it again, bursting with happiness as I complete the second one handed cartwheel of my entire life.

'By Jove! I think she's got it!'

I grin as Mel rushes over and hugs me. 'Oh Mel thank you.'

There's no stopping me now. I do a series of cartwheels across the hall feeling all lithe and athletic. I can't help giggling.

There's a loud round of applause, I turn round to find Jake and Alastair have entered the hall.

'Darling Eve you were like a floral windmill.'

Jake looks over at me, and grins. 'Yes, very energetic.'

I give them a dorky thumbs-up and pick up a box of walkie-talkies.

I am elated inside; I have mastered a one-handed cartwheel, another tick for the list.

What else does this day have in store?

Mel's phone is pressed to her ear. 'Shit.'

I look up. 'What is it?'

'No signal here.'

She walks over to Jake and they have an animated conversation.

'Ok here's what we do. How many walkie talkies do you have?'

Mel rushes over to where I'm recovering from the impromptu gymnastic performance.

'There are only two fully charged.'

'Ok Eve, I need you to stand at the gate and stop the limos from arriving at the same time, you're to send them up one by one so we can get true footage.' Jake says hurriedly.

'The contestants can't meet yet, we need to build the tension up for tomorrow, capture those candid first looks of competitiveness.'

'Ok.'

'Try and time fifteen to twenty minutes between each one and that should keep the energy flowing, we'll be mastering pre-occupation when they arrive.'

I start walking to the front gate and that takes nearly five minutes even at a brisk pace.

The first Limo arrives with a mass of red wavy hair flowing out the window and a guy face down in his phone. The girl tries to get his attention as she sees the magnificent hotel for the first time; he pushes her hand away quite rudely if you ask me. He doesn't look like a lot of fun. Self-important type.

Must be Sian and Piers.

I pick the walkie-talkie up and press the button to warn the film crew, it doesn't make a sound.

'Hello, can you hear me?'

'Eve over.'

I wait a second and try again.

'Sian and Piers arriving in a minute.'

Damn it, either I can't work one of the simpler forms of communication or the batteries just died.

'Hello, anyone?'

'Hi Eve, sorry about that must have been on the wrong frequency or something.'

'Is that you Jet?'

'The one and only.'

'Why have you got the… oh never mind, can you tell them Sian and Piers will arrive in seconds!'

'Righto big gate chief! Out and over and over and out.'

'Quick Jet otherwise they won't be able to pan the drive in!'

The walkie-talkie goes dead and another black limo comes crunching up the gravel in the distance.

I stand in the middle of the gates with a hand up signalling halt. The back windows are steamed up so I can't see its passengers. Gradually, the driver's window buzzes down.

'Ow long do I 'ave to wait 'ere?'

'I'm just waiting for the cue.'

'I didn't sign up for–'

'I said I'm waiting for a c…' The walkie-talkie is making a crackling sound and I can hear faint voices, but nothing clearly.

'They're animals, I've had to put the screen up. Vulgar, distasteful…'

I have no idea what the driver is on about.

'Look can you just wait like you've been asked?' I wish he would shut up, I can barely hear what's going on up there.

The back window rolls down, and quite a large woman pokes her head out; her long mousy hair stuck all over her sweaty forehead.

'Hi there, why have we stopped?'

'Er… Hi we're just waiting for the cue.'

'I'm Daphne.' She holds her hand out for a shake.

'I wouldn't touch that love, not where it's been on the journey down.' The driver pipes in.

'You bigot.'

'Listen love, I didn't ask for a show.'

'I wasn't giving you a show, you were supposed to have your eyes on the…'

'Right, would everyone calm down, I can't hear the walkie-talkie! I'm Eve, by the way. We spoke…' The radio starts to crackle and I use this as the perfect excuse not to touch the hand, giving a short wave in place, then busying myself with the walkie-talkie, the driver has more than a valid point.

A small skinny moustachioed man appears from Daphne's neck, he looks like a pathetic snake erupting from her medusa long fuzzy hair. Urghhh I feel nauseous and I'm not even good with my imagination!

'Patrick sit back, I didn't give you permission to move did I?' Crikey Daphne's a schizo.

'No Madame, sorry Madame.' The moustachioed snake coils back into the darkness of the limo's tinted windows.

I think I'm going to hurl, this is too far at the other end of the sexual spectrum for my stomach to handle.

'What's the time dear?'

'What?' Daphne's voice resumes a perfectly normal chatty tone.

'The time.'

Confused I look down at my watch. 'Oh it's just before three.'

'Patrick, you only have a few minutes left of obedience. So sit there quietly and button up.'

'Yes Madame.'

I plead for the walkie-talkie to crackle with the green light to go, so that I can rise from this sea of filth. Put that one in your pipe and smoke it Gudrun. No one said I had to relinquish taste in order to join sexual therapy! The very thought of Patrick sliming over Daphne's rather large frame repulses me and to think he would probably be in a garden that hadn't seen hedge cutters for some time!

That's the second catty lewd joke I've laughed at without feeling like a lobster being invited into bisque.

'Ready Eve.'

Thank goodness, I was just pondering over a life of abstinence, purely to get any image of "it" out of my head in this moment of time.

Barf, I'm making myself gag.

Off they go with half the gravel drive spinning off the back wheels, the driver eager to deliver his load. Arghhh! I'm in a sexual innuendo nightmare.

After about forty minutes two executive cars arrive together. The second car comes screeching to a halt. A scarf-clad woman bolts out the back of the first car and tries to stomp off with three yappy fluff balls behind her. The towering red stiletto's sink into the gravel, the more she tries to stomp with shoes that are wider than her inhuman spindly legs, the more she sinks. A spider in drag springs to mind.

'Umm, can you come back here please'? I shout.

She stops dead in her 'not so fast' tracks, turns round slowly and pulls her oversized sunglasses half way up, eyes full of venom.

'Could you come back to the car please'? I stand my ground, which is far more than moody britches can do at the moment as one heel sinks even deeper into the stones.

'Jumping Junipers moons, for Christ's sake get back here Kimberley.' A plummy, slightly slurred voice booms from the back of the car.

At this precise moment, if she had a spiders web handy both of us would be spun and devoured imminently. The look is one of anger or madness, the face red; is the kettle about to blow? Half of me considers getting a camera down here, this should be on the dailies, and the other half is suspended in dread.

'Kimberley Roberts get back here this instance.' A bear of a man gets out the car; cravat dishevelling as he assembles himself onto the brogue clad feet. He's enormous, must be way over six feet tall with the build of a rugby player. He mumbles something at me and I then realise he's not drunk but frightfully, I mean, ridiculously posh. The two can get confused in the very English of English language.

'Sorry, I didn't–'

'Bloody young fillies, never know when they're going to buck.' He lights a pipe, leans back and admires the hotel's grounds as if he were contemplating where to put the new lodge, totally unaware that he's even on a reality show let alone in the modern day. I feel like saying *"listen Downton Abbey, would you get your filly a bit before she starts biting,"* but don't as fear he wouldn't understand anyway, obviously not the type to watch pedestrian TV or be bothered by dreary reality in the first place, must be such a nuisance in those circles. Think I'm going to like him, the casting crew must be salivating at the thought of Lord Battenberg's very first words on film, jaded with archaic un-pc comments and the golden nuggets that will jump out from the colourful family crest.

If I remember rightly he's stuffed most of the family estate up his nose; that and backing crackpot business ventures conjured up by his barking mad friends and now he does (or must do) anything for cash. Think one of the ventures went along the lines of *"Safari's for your most beloveds, your loyal Pets"* – can't think what went wrong there! Can you imagine pitching that one to *Dragons' Den*, first question from the dragons?

*"It's not so much as a holiday for pets, it's called bait you moron! ARE YOU TAKING THE P***"*

Can't wait for the reveal of his chequered past (no pun intended), you have to admit it's a bit of a funny name. Maybe his family made their money in marzipan? Okay Eve. Stop right there. Not that funny. Don't give up the day job just yet. Come to think of it I heard there's a loose connection to the current royals.

'Kim-ber-LAY "IMPOSSIBLY INTRACTABLE" Roberts!'

The driver and I jump, he shouts louder than a sonic bugle on a foxhunt. Standing rigid and with hands on hip of his tweeds, pipe eloquently balanced. He doesn't move an inch. Surprisingly she does an about turn, (well tries to in the sky-scraping heels or potential murder weapons!). She skulks back into the limo huffing and puffing as she goes, small dogs yapping at the towering heels. The Pekingese leading the other two puffballs with legs, one promptly poops on the gravel and the other pees up the tyre followed by a massive tuba sounding fart, you wouldn't think that could come out of something so small, and unrecognisable as a creature in general, the two other yappy creatures are intent on inspecting the tyre whilst the weird looking flat faced ball of hair jumps in the back of the car. I'm not sure what these dogs are, even if they are dogs.

'Oh Tula you stinkypoopoodidums.'

'You've got more sentiment towards disgusting hairballs than you do the human race dear. Quite curious really. You do look rather splendid in a rage though ol' gal!' Lord Battenberg bellows. Kimberley to my surprise, giggles like a Japanese schoolgirl.

And with that, the car door slams and the driver restarts the engine, pipe smoke spiralling out the window with wisps of 'eau de dog.' I must say all the drivers so far have looked beyond distraught. I signal for him to go, I figured the jumbled crackling noise from the other end must have meant as much.

I root around in my pocket and take out a crumbled tissue. I pick up the poop, grateful that it's tiny. Now what?

There isn't a bin around, so I pop it back down on the floor still wrapped in tissue as the second car pulls up. Squeaky noise pollution just erupts out the slow lowering window.

I can't understand anything this girl is jabbering about, it's a high-pitched talk-a-thon gone wrong. Quick talking is an understatement, it's as though Disney have made a princess machine gun.

'What?' I snap out of exasperation.

Noise; eternal noise; screeching noise; inaudible tone; tinny nasally din; for goodness sake slow down woman and take a breath for the love the ear canal.

Jet's going to have a field day with this one. She continues and for the lack of interest and the health of my eardrums, I turn and ignore her, pretending to listen to the radio.

'Hey!' Ouch, there goes my upper frequencies. 'HEY!'

'I'm sorry, are you talking to a human?'

'What?'

'Can you hear dogs barking?' I've never been so bravely cutting. Must be standing out here in the cold for hours on end.

'I don't understand.' Then it turns into an inaudible mess again… a crazed woman in a helium balloon fest.

I signal the driver to roll up the window and drive on. I don't care if they're not bloody ready, she has to go now before I do something I will most definitely regret. A car door thuds from afar and a tanned chisel hunk charges at me. Oh my god is he going to…

'Sorry bout that Ma'am. She yabbles when she's nervous, the pitch just keeps getting higher. We haven't had thirty seconds to think straight and we've been on the road for over two hours.' I smile in sympathy; his voice is as soft as it is simple; a truly, wonderful American Southern twang. My minds flits to *Of Mice and Men*, the noise capsule in the car being the mouse in this case!

'I couldn't understand a word she was saying, sorry. Had to listen hard as the radio is having trouble picking up–'

'That's Stacey Ma'am. Her brain works so fast her mouth has trouble keeping up with it. She's real smart you see.'

I laugh as he holds his hand out sincerely.

'I'm sorry if she caused you distraction, what with you having important things to look after Ma'am. She don't mean anything by it.' His sincerity and protection over her touches me, what a gentle soul considering how much of a brick he is.

'I's Brick Ma'am, Brick Small.' I smile to myself. Figures, as big as a house and what were the odds his surname would be as in the Steinbeck novel, one book I actually did read at college.

I shake his square of a hand and watch the blood flow trickle back to my fingers.

So this is the football player and the Harvard protégée. Interesting, very interesting.

I radio in, but it's gone totally dead. I keep the car waiting with Ms Robert's arrival there's bound to be a kerfuffle. I've been told the crew are under strict instructions not to reshoot anything or show her any footage at anytime, apparently she is obsessive on how she looks on camera, she fired a lighting crew because she said they kept using her bad profile (I think the recent rhinoplasty botch is a tad sensitive). She's also been hounding the office day and night about what lights we're using and the tones, they had to vet calls and let the voicemail takeover for two weeks. She launches the phrase control freak into the outer hemisphere, an entirely new category.

'Eve. Come in Eve.'

'Jet?'

'Keep the car there, a hairball has attacked the booms, we're just getting set up again in the Lobby.'

'Okay, was it the one that looks like it's been hit by a frying pan?'

'Yeah how did you know?'

'Looked like the Emperor of the hairballs on legs. The notorious four-legged hairy gang!'

'Eve!' Jet sounds as excited as a (normal) puppy dog!

'Jet!' I equal with wryness.

'You've got to look at some of the footage when you get back, Battenberg mistook Alastair for the concierge, his face is priceless when he stuffs a tenner in his top pocket, you know the one with the pocket watch. Then he gave his cane and hat to Jake. This guy's more oblivious than oblivion itself.

I'm not sure he's even aware he's in a show, let alone not in the 17th Century. Called Pete the cameraman an overzealous paparazzi picture-mongerer on steroids. Then waffled on about knowing his great grandfather who was a gentleman of the highest command. It was freaking hilarious. Psychedelic show time. Far out man. We've not only got a hum dinger of a reality show, we've got Back to the Future, Downton Abbey, Julian Fellowes and pop trash rolled into one.'

'That's great Jet, but are you ready now. It's freezing out here.'

'I'll get back to you Eve. Jet out.' The radio crackles and I hear a barrage of high-pitched yaps. It sounds like pan-faced furry pandemonium up there.

It's forty minutes or so until I get the all clear. I am officially in my own ice age by then.

Coordinating flipping car arrivals has taken hours, and it's dusk.

Holding the poop out in front of me I start walking up the winding drive. It feels much longer than on the way down.

The lobby is deserted by the time I get back, no sign of the crew or any paraphernalia of filming – and no bin anywhere. Spooky. Have I just gone into the twilight zone? With my cerebral homemade trepidation I walk in, still unable to feel my fingers or toes, but happy to finally feel the hotel's warmth coursing through my veins. I'm about to ask the receptionist where to dispose of the poop when I notice Jake standing there. Maybe I'll wait until he's gone. I turn and walk to the open fire, it's less grand than the one in the Nook but adequately grand for any manor house on earth. Its warmth acts as sirens to my homing cold tootsies. I slump gratefully into the big plush velvet armchair and stretch out my legs, the fire instantly warming up my feet, while the slow pop of the logs and the heat of the fire make me drowsy. My eyes start to feel heavy. It's so goddamn cosy - mm-hmm.

Just as I'm being lulled to sleep something bites my arm.

'Eve!'

I open one eye and squint at the shadowy figure. It's Jake. His beautiful face stares down at me, violet eyes sparkling from the flames. He really is gorgeous to look at. He smells pretty damn good too. My olfactory senses piqued by the smell of leather and orange, and the hotel soap.... I lean forward, reaching out towards the smell, wanting to inhale it, cuddle it... I wonder if he tastes as good as he smells -

'Eve?'

My eyes snap right open and I drop my arms away from the shadowy neck, pathetically fizz into a flailing effervescent. For just one day, ONE DAY out of three hundred and sixty five could I have a non-embarrassing moment?

'Sorry?'

He shrugs it off. 'You've been dead to the world for about twenty minutes.'

'Have you been watching me?'

'As it happens, yes.'

My heart experiences a tiny flip.

'Are you fully rested now?' He asks.

'Yes, very rested, was thawing out a bit... thanks,' I reply, coughing out the sleep.

Momentarily trapped by his gaze, I feel warmth radiating through me and it's not from the fire. Jakes doesn't falter his gaze as he examines my face almost robotically. I must look awful, weather beaten and spaced out. My eyes are out of focus, running from the smoke backdraft from a popping log.

Must have panda eyes or the look of a Dickens chimney sweep by now.

'I had trouble with the Kimberley's, I mean the radios.'

'Ah, yes we're five sound booms down. Pesky, yappy, and spoilt–'

'Yes, she is,' I say.

'The dogs,' he says.

'Oh yes… the dogs,' I say quickly. Jake just stares at me, inadvertently I start smoothing down my fringe, which has stuck to my sweaty 'fireplace' brow. Then realising I'm holding the poop wrapped in tissue to my face.

Eurgh!

'Although you could tar them with the same brush, God knows how we're going to work around that creature.'

My laugh comes out like a whale calling for pizza. I try and cough it out with the rest of my dozy state.

Jake sniffs the air. 'There's a funny smell around here.'

'Oh, sorry, that would be me.'

'Come again?'

I hold up the poop wrapped in tissue. 'I didn't know where to dispose of it.'

Jake takes it from me and throws it in the fire.

Typical. My first day on location and that woolly jumper has a habit of unravelling in front of an audience. Never in private, oh no that would be too dull, my mistakes come with a legal requirement – everything must be made in public view. I wonder if my body made a deal when I went out with the tequila that fateful night! Traitorous being it's been so far.

I get up from the chair. 'Actually I think I'll freshen up. Can't really turn up like a raffle prize for rambling dogs.'

He looks bemused, and I realise that didn't make any sense

at all.

I need to establish a more professional atmosphere.

'I'll wait for you,' he says.

'Oh, that's not necessarily.'

'Oh, but I think it is.' He raises his eyebrows. 'I wouldn't want you to be forgotten again. Besides I'm waiting for a call from reception.'

The gesture almost has a romantic ring to it.

'See you in five minutes,' he says.

Five minutes? Does he think I'm superwoman? I rush up to the room, which has all the evidence of *"previous woman getting ready in a rush"* strewn about the place and add to it's mayhem. Mel must have been caught short too, that Roberts' woman has a lot to answer for and we haven't filmed a full day yet.

I grab my black leather mini skirt and grey silk blouse, then swap it for my belted, black georgette dress and black pointy ankle boots. All the coat hangers are free to roam the room now! Mel's bed is also covered in liberated wooden hangers. We have set the whole hanger-nation free. One smudge check in the mirror, wipe off a bit of green debris from my cheek, spray some perfume, walk into it and I'm off. Five minutes… FIVE MINUTES, who ever says that to a woman getting ready for dinner!

I rush down the panelled corridor, checking my armpits don't whiff, swooping down the low-lit staircase, slow up when I reach the last five steps, take a breath and walk into the lobby unhurried with a fake relaxed look plastered over my quite naked face, Jake is in deep thought or mesmerised by the flames of the fire.

'Ready.'

Jake bolts up and looks at his watch. 'Impressive.'

'I aim to please.'

He raises his eyebrows and I hide my blush by staring at my boots.

It's weird walking into the dining room with Jake, I'm somewhat heightened. I feel the press of his hand on the base of my back as he leads me through the double-doors into the dining area. The crew are already inside merrily swigging cocktails and ale. None of the contestants are allowed to sit next to one another as we want for them to meet the first time tomorrow but I can already see them checking each other out. Trying to work out which of the diners are contestants or not. But no one can ignore Kimberley and her Aristocratic misfit. She's such a vivacious character, I would say brash, crying out for any or all attention. Everyone is staring at her.

'Where have you been?' Mel pats the empty chair next to her.

'Waiting for the all clear outside! Didn't want to interrupt any golden shots. Radio must have gone dead.' I hiss in her ear.

'Oh shit! Sorry hon.'

'Sshhh. I don't need everyone to know what an idiot I've been.'

Mel stiffles her giggles into her wine glass. I scowl at her.

'We were all delayed because of that witch.' We both turn to look at the brash trashy noise across the way trying to be discreet, which tends to end up with the opposite desired effect.

'I literally had to throw something on, we've had no break at all.' Mel whispers.

We both scowl in her general direction, and start giggling.

A tall man with a tuxedo comes over, bows at the table and beckons us with an open palm.

'Your dining room is ready for you. Ladies and Gentlemen.'

The food here is mouth-watering even though we just had a hot buffet in our own cordoned off gala room. The Hotel has one of those Michelin starred Chefs or something. We have the run of half the hotel as they couldn't let down their regular (very rich) guests, it would be financial madness. Mel heard the starting price per room is over eight hundred pounds, the hotel is so exclusive it has no website or prices anywhere. With dinner over, I really need to soak in the bath after being on my feet all day. The wind and rain has tired me. I slip away while everyone is enjoying an after-dinner drink. There were a fair few bottles on the table. But I'm in no mood to be social. I'm kaput. As soon as I reach the foyer I pelt it to the elevator around the corner so I'm not dragged back in. I can't be bothered to climb up all those grand stairs.

OH NO! Daphne and Patrick are waiting and standing next to them is an older 'incredibly proper' couple in full evening regalia. I can't back out now they've all seen me.

A moment later, it pings in front of us, and the doors open.

The doors close, and we begin to travel upwards but instead of silence, which is normal protocol in these situations, Daphne and Patrick are discussing the advantages of latex and water-based lubricants.

'Then how would I know my performance hasn't produced the ideal conditions?'

'It can always be heard dear.'

'But I like all indicators on. You know what I'm like in the car if I get a warning flash.'

'I know dear, I know.'

I purposely try to look busy checking my unconnected phone to hide the fact that I'm crimson faced,

'It's like an acceleration of pleasure,' explains Daphne, 'but it is so nice. It's a monthly weather cycle, as you know, some days wetter than others. Sometimes a little oiling of the parts helps. Cuts to the hard penetration and you know how hard I like to go.'

'But I pride myself…'

'Dear it enhances what's already going on.'

'Your love juices are all I need.'

'I know dear, I know you are my stallion of hardness. Your voice is enough to make me flow and when I see that hardness all wrapped up, fighting against it's tight latex prison it makes me want to jump straight on and suction it all down with my yearning love garden.'

Patrick's eyes widen and I swear there's movement in those badly fitted chinos.

She purrs at him and without reservation says with the most vampy purr.

'Willy Wampire must be hungry?'

'My sausage meat stick is too dry for my liking.'

Seriously! Do they really need to talk like that! I feel like I'm trapped in a low budget adult movie.

They start getting very touchy feely, I smile awkwardly at the old couple, wishing I was elsewhere. Talk about a Peter Sellers lift moment, only this is the porn version!

As soon as the doors ping open for the old couple I follow in quickstep even though this is not my floor. I can't possible listen to anymore and I certainly don't want to be the third person alone in there. They might suggest a soothing three-some with Patrick's appetite… Ew.

Talking about sex is bad enough, but listening to others talk about it is even worse.

I listen for the elevator to ping from the stairwell and after a thud, which I presume is them getting fruity, I peg it down the hall and up the flight of stairs to my room. Swinging the door shut I flop facedown on the bed, groaning. I am such a priss!

Why get embarrassed about a conversation that at best is comical out of context and a great anecdote. Some people find it easier to orate, discuss, seduce, get passionate and know what they want in a fly by of a moment, just because I can't openly behave like that. Honestly, I have the backbone of a frigid Victorian spinster. Maybe the sex therapy isn't helping, I seem to be getting even more self-conscious than before.

I'm as alluring as filing paper or rearranging the garage. One thing I do know, I've never been myself with anyone in that department, and that's because I don't know who I'm supposed to be and that's not my department at all!

I look around the high-ceilinged room with its grand stucco, the Greek key pattern hypnotising in the low light spilling from the gothic black lamps. I haven't had a chance to breathe in my surroundings at all; it's ages since I've had a space to myself, and by the looks of Mel earlier she won't be up in the room anytime soon. I thought she was getting rather friendly with Jake at the bar. What's not to like, he's good-looking even if he knows it. I wonder if they'll end up getting together? Mel is demure, lovely and probably has a normal take on sex. I actually think I send out bad signals, maybe like frigid signals because deep down I really am.

Sighing at that sobering little thought I feel myself deflating. I run a bath, lay in it for five minutes then feel even hotter and sweatier than before. I jump out feeling giddy, pull the hotel robe on, and then give a big yawn. I decide to make a hot drink and chill on the balcony. Our room (or should I say our vast suite) has a little turret alcove which has a beautifully ornate iron railed terrace, its full of seasonal oversized plant pots, a strange mixture of Evil princess and Miami chic. I can just imagine a writer penning their novel in such a setting.

With a steaming cup of real chocolaty heaven I nestle down into the imposing iron throne of a chair, gently sipping it whilst watching the night's clouds reveal the stars one by one, and I feel my eyes start to roll and zzz…

BANG!

A noise from a nearby balcony jolts me out of my doze. I feel my heart race out of its ribs.

'Fuuuuuuck!' I curse, jumping up and despairing at my newly decorated robe, a chocolate Pollock on white fluffy canvas. I peer over the railings, squinting as I look below. I can't see anything moving and wonder if I dreamt the noise. I look between the grand oak trees with their uplighters and the night's air is still. Maybe it is Mel returning, I walk back inside and I'm still alone. I return to the balcony washed down and with a second cup of hot chocolate, sipping it until sleep beckons.

I head to bed.

CHAPTER SEVENTEEN

Breakfast time is an odd affair. All the contestants are instructed to sit at specific tables, none within listening distance to one another. I suppose they're trying to encourage the competitive spirit and psyche them into rivalry, even before hair and make up!

The host Steve goes round each table and spends a few minutes in what seems like casual chitchat. I watch from the top of my coffee cup, mildly amused when fake smiles aerate as he walks over to each table, the only ones who behave naturally are Daphne and Patrick. Piers's is fussing over his blazer; he spilt orange juice on it while trying to domineer the conversation with our larger than life host. Swiss Franc (aka Steve), which is how he's now been nicknamed, for getting the best out of people, or what is really required for top viewer ratings. I knew I detected a slight accent when he introduced himself; maybe a second language isn't such a bad idea.

They call him Swiss Franc because:

1) He's Swiss

2) His name is actually Franc!

No one on this shoot is about to let that comedic opportunity slip past. He's a curious character, I swear he should recruit people into a sect or top-secret vetting. When he talks to you without the showbiz factor, his accent or rather his pattern of speech just make you half glaze over with a smile, you never know when he's about to finish or start the next sentence, so you're held under his spell while trying to figure it out. His syntax possesses a melody that never quite ends, knowing when to interject is painful, it inevitably overlaps and one of his eyes peers at you, the slightly rounder one. I swear he's from the past and that eye had a monocle stuck to it during wartime interrogations. I do like him though; he's made his multi-cultural schizophrenia a working asset.

I heard Jet rib him early, yet he manages to retort so quickly in English you wonder if there's a super computer running "witty Google translate" behind his perfectly dressed façade. I end up looking for signs of electrical enhancement on the back of his head as he strides over to Kimberly and Lord Battenberg. Battenberg stands up, nearly saluting Swiss Franc's coffee cup into orbit. That was bloody funny. Perhaps they're both from another era.

When the waiters and waitresses come in to clear the room, it's our cue to get everyone out. I lead the bubbling group down to the hall in to the Green Room.

This is supposedly the room where the contestants get to relax before they step in front of the camera to participate in the games, they don't know about the hidden cameras. I do feel a little like we're being dishonest with the contestants, but I know why we are doing it; people behave differently when they think camera's not on them, their real personality shines through, which means they are likely to say or do something unexpected, the more dramatic or unkind the better for the show. Anyway it wasn't my idea. This was Brian's contribution to the show and, begrudgingly, it's a good one.

Mel comes in with Daphne and Patrick looking flushed. I wonder what conversation preceded that little walk. If it was anything like the elevators, her stomach will be regurgitating the omelette.

Next is Stacy and Brick, efficiently finding their place and sitting woodenly straight as if waiting for an award. Stacey jots down something on a pad for Brick to look at. I wonder if that's allowed? Mind you, I understand the desire for lists. Maybe she's one for the 'to do' lists as well. I know there is a monitor picking up all the action happening outside, so Mel and I make ourselves scarce.

Lord Battenberg holds the door open for us and we slip past, Kimberly barely raises a smile as she sweeps by, nose in the air and a look of contempt on her face.

Mel and I enter the room next door. The rest of the crew are in there, most of them behind Jake crouching in front of a monitor, which is split into several screens, he has headphones clamped on his ears. Brian is next to him and though I can't hear what is being said I can tell by Kimberly's actions what she is thinking.

Her eyes zip up and down at each woman in the room, taking in every detail of their appearance, pricing their hair, their clothes, their shoes no doubt. Then a slither of a smirk lifts the corner of her mouth and she turns away, visibly relaxing with an attitude that says all too clearly that no one is any competition for her. Lord Battenberg sits next to Sian. She says something quietly to him, and he smiles.

I wonder if Jet picked up on the sound. I look across and he's chuckling.

I'm definitely going to pay a visit to the editing suite later.

Swiss Franc walks into the room and greets everyone with a loud booming voice. He sets out the rules. Not the most scintillating television watching, but necessary. Stacy and Brick faces are focused, concentrating on every word. Daphne and Patrick are looking around, Sian and Piers look like they're at a conference, but Kimberly wins the prize for oddest appearance. She has a face so frozen, so heavily made up (far too theatrical for even the most dramatic of theatre productions) it resembles a bad cartoon. In one light she is a fuzzy with powder and in another outlined by a light marker pen. I know a little something about contouring, but you could colour by numbers with such make-up application. Lord Battenberg keeps fidgeting with his inside blazer pocket and bending under the table as if he's lost something, swiping at imaginary flies then blowing his nose in a monogrammed hanky.

'Now we're acquainted with the rules Ladies and Gentlemen. Well, at this very moment you're all Ladies and Gentlemen, but who knows after round one!' Swiss Franc raises a sardonic brow. 'Let the games commence, and you won't have to actually kill one another, let me make that clear. No hunger games tactics even if you are a bit peckish!'

There is a huge round of applause as he leaves and the room erupts in talking.

Stefan is going to have his work cut out luckily he's now got an assistant editor helping him cipher through the hours of material.

I watch as Jet and Swiss Franc battle it out for the first to be out the door. Jet heaves the camera to his shoulder and Swiss Franc grabs the ragged booms.

Sian and Daphne muffle laughing at Jet trying to put the

ragged dog bitten booms back on microphones. The new ones should arrive from London soon.

CRASH

Jet recoils ambling over a box and some wires, the booms aren't filtering anything and Swiss Franc's thunderous voice must have been recorded on the wrong volume. Jake looks over at me and I burst out laughing, then Mel, then Alastair. Jet is in hysterics at this point even Brian manages a chortle. The whole room is in the throws of mirth, apart from Kimberley who just watches the camera's every move as though they were highly trained snipers.

With a reset, Swiss Franc is off again.

'Will you be today's fact finders or pact punchers? After all, matrimony is the most sacred of pacts. Do you have what it takes to float in the others' moat?' Sian giggles and is very quickly joined by Lord Battenberg. Swiss Franc frowns at them, good-humouredly though. He waits for the camera to zoom in and capture it all.

'Laugh now my little contenders, for after you may well be found out as the biggest pretenders. This is eternity teaming, don't let your mind wander over to scheming.'

He should really have the biggest market stall in London with all those adlibbed corny rhyming gems.

GAME ONE

Our location, the Hall in the Hill hotel is famous for the much-loved children's book by 18th Century author Mr Pickett. An infamous tale of Magical Mayhem, a children's classic written and set within the grounds of this unusual hotel. If the contestants were even slightly alert or switched on they would have recognised the Hall from the long winding driveway on the car journey up. The driveway and Hotel are indented on most people's childhood memories.

The contestants, if they were paying attention would have already come across many pictures and works of art in homage to the book and its author, along with scattered dedications all over the hotel.

'Your first challenge will be one of mental agility and physical mobility. Are you ready to problem solve? Will you unravel the key to your imminent travels? Cryptic clues have been placed around the grounds much like a treasure hunt, each clue leads you to the next clue, the aim is to find the key that opens the iron grate of the wine cellar.' Swiss Franc lowers his head and whispers to the camera. 'Secret tunnels run out from the cellar all over this magnificent house's grounds.'

What he doesn't tell them is that the tunnels have been rigged with haunted figures and blood chilling sound effects.

He turns to his avid audience again. 'Your task when you unlock the inner sanctuary of grape heaven is to pick the most expensive wine that you would like for your wedding breakfast. Here's your first clue…'

It's a poem taken from Mr Pickett's book when Chancey meets a grumpy fairy.

Swiss Franc mimics Richard Burton's Welsh voice; we're all stifling a laugh. We have our very own European Rob Brydon on the set.

'If one had wings to beat where would they land.
Far away from this magical clan,
They sing and laugh all day,

But I'd like to bury my head in the deepest clay.
Where sound can bother me no more,
I look beneath the tower's ball.'

The clue is a clear reference to the bell tower set in the westerly corner of the vast gardens. It's where the grumpy fairy takes solace in the book. The Bell tower is featured all around the place with its grumpy mythical creature. There's a huge mural behind reception depicting it; you would have to be unconscious not to have spotted it. Even the crockery for afternoon tea has the grumpy fairy engraved inside the rims plus the tower itself is on the daily newsletter that gets left on your bed by the turndown service.

Swiss Franc pauses for dramatic effect.

'You can ask only one question, if you meet anyone along your path. Remember one question or forever hold your tongue.' He wiggles his eyebrows and stands in front of the doors, raising his arms and gesturing like a matador to begin.

'Ready, steady. Lets go heading for the ultimate wedding.'

And off they go Stacey and Brick leading the pack.

We all gather round the monitors to watch the game unfold and I get jostled from behind and nearly fall onto Jake's lap.

'Sorry!' I squeak, my cheeks flaming. Jake acknowledges me with a smile then turns back to the screen. I quickly sit down and do the same but I can't really focus on what is happening, my vision is fuzzy. Jake crosses his leg and as it casually brushes against mine, my body starts to tingle and fizz.

Suddenly Jake leans forward and the connection is lost. I force myself to concentrate.

Honestly, you would think I would have learnt my lesson by now. Relationships have caused me nothing but misery and embarrassment. Not once have I had the upper hand, ok upper hand isn't what you want in a relationship unless you're Daphne and Patrick, but always being on tenterhooks isn't exactly relaxing either. First, with Mr Cheat and then with, Mr I Need Space.

With everyone running around like headless chickens, it's almost like watching a spoof film. Lord Battenberg just walks a little more briskly with his cane, trying to trail Kimberly who's extending her legs and gesturing her arms like a loony - unnatural and really hammy dramatics. She should just live in an American daytime soap, seems to be all she knows.

'What is that woman doing? She looks like a daddy longlegs being electrocuted!' Jake says.

I snort with laughter and then cover it with a cough just in time to see Swiss Franc running.

'I need an inhaler and oxygen tent to keep up with Fit Brick here. Hey Brick, slow down you're running in pixels!' he yells.

Poor guy sounds like he's going to die.

As I continue to watch the action unfold in front of me I am also deeply aware each time Jake moves; when his body turns towards my chair, when his foot is on top of mine.

I tell myself to be cool.

Besides he's probably totally unaware of me, too busy concentrating if the camera angles are right. Not me though, adrenalin pumps its way around my body and my breathing becomes laboured, and – Oh God, there's something moist happening downstairs. Flustered, I move forward in my chair. Right Eve, concentrate. Concentrate on the footage.

Swiss Franc runs towards the bell tower, the first couple are about to discover where the first clue is hidden. Piers and Sian are arguing about the literature reference, Sian just wants to push on but Piers is insisting on sounding clever, looking for the camera that is trailing him.

Daphne and Patrick are bobbling along; Daphne can only bobble with an impossible to support breast size.

'It's like watching two melting blancmanges take battle stance,' says Jet. 'My money's on leftie!'

All the guys giggle and the girls laugh behind their hands, they are rather large and swinging, gravity is not their friend but a bra would be!

Kimberly is running over the lawn, manhandling flowers like she's in some merchant ivory film and Lord Battenberg is lighting his pipe (again), no urgency at all. Brick forces open the creaky door and helps Stacy up the turret's crumbling stone spiral staircase; gallantly he climbs up behind her. You would feel safe with him, he may not be the brightest star in the sky but he is the nicest. Mel, I and in fact all the ladies and stylists automatically lean forward watching his arms bulge with muscle as he hangs onto the rickety rope rails in case his lady tumbles, the camera views tight on his derriere. I see Jake's eyes glance at me.

'So we have some eye candy to appeal to the Ladies?'

Mel and I spring right back in our chairs.

'I'd say so, look at that body. It's perfection. Naturally bronzed, taught, and he hardly needed any corrector on his skin,' says Jody, the make-up artist.

'Oh yeah, his skin is dewy, nearly perfect. The light bounces off it.'

'He's a make-up artist's dream.'

'Low maintenance, high buttocks.' The girls giggle.

'Wouldn't mind doing a full body make up on him. Are there any swimming challenges Jake?' One of them jokes. 'Bet you wouldn't mind one of those, would you Brian?'

I cough in my coffee cup. Those girls are funny. How she had the gall to say that to him of all people I'll have to find out. Or maybe I'm just being timid and he only acts like Emperor Nero when he's in he's own kingdom.

Jake eyes flick to me, flashing into my periphery. His leg pressed against mine. I gaze down my cup studying my cold coffee and readjust my space. Sitting isn't a contact sport.

'Ladies you're so spoilt, you've got Adonis in the room.' Jet jokes.

No doubt the camera loves Brick. Filming stops when everyone has found the clue. Daphne and Patrick beat Kimberly and Battenberg by miles, and that's saying something. The crew will need to reset for the tunnel finding part, which will be difficult. It's hidden away under fake vegetation, and a fallen tree trunk. The key has a puzzle on it and they haven't been able to open it, it's sealed with wax. They must all lay the clue out in front of them when they get back, no cheating. Clue in foreground with worried, peeved, excited, and benevolent faces behind it.

The time they've beaten the other couples with will be their head start.

So it will be Stacey and Brick, Sian and Piers, Daphne and Patrick then Kimberly and Batty Battenberg. Jet is taking bets!

The next few days are a blur of long hours and long damage control i.e. Kimberly and her four-legged friends. The new booms have arrived just as Kimberly came down to walk the fluff balls; they associated it with the previous enemy and attacked the lot along with the box. Jet now walks around with masking tape attached to his belt and pieces of foam stuck in all his pockets. Despite the havoc and their destructive nature I think the dogs might get their own spin-off show. They are rather cute, unpredictable small demons in fluff.

Filming got cut short one afternoon down the tunnels because Daphne and Patrick thought they were off grid and apparently they found some shackles, so we've (or rather Jake) has had to read the riot act of no nudity or nude activity when filming. Daphne's reaction was memorable, she said, 'when would you like to see us then Jake, we don't mind cameras, we thought the shackles were just for us. Why don't you join us for a nightcap.'

I couldn't stop laughing. Jake politely declined and Swiss Franc jumped in at the end, well not in with them… not for the nightcap, not in their room… I mean at the end of the conversation.

'Now there's a practical wife, utilizing her surroundings, you must consider yourself very lucky Patrick?'

'Oh, I do Franc. I do.' Patrick answered, totally straight-laced to Swiss Franc's tongue-in-cheek remarks.

'The garden shed must have realms of possibilities for your Daphne. What that woman can't do with a trug and a hose isn't worth knowing, now is it, Patrick?'

'She's quite good with vegetable netting too.'

'Keeping off the pests, eh? For the fruits to ripen.'

Jake's face was quite ruddy at this point. The maze game victors were Sian and Piers, and surprisingly the obstacle course was won by Daphne and Patrick. Daphne's extra ballasts served her well on the lake balancing challenge. It's head to head for the three couples, Battenberg is still entertainingly unaware that anything out of the ordinary is going on and Kimberly is getting more furious by the day, she's taken to falling over like an Italian footballer for attention. She literally fainted on Jet the other day because he was standing with Paul the camera guy. Batty Battenberg still thinks Piers is a butler or something and he invited Sian for afternoon tea right under his nose.

'You can bring your man if you want a chaperone.'

'Err…'

'That's settled then, tea at three.'

Piers just stood and looked, he's in awe of gentry, peerage and past like a good conservative politician from the 18th century. He smiled and treated it like his own invitation. I'm not keen on Piers, something of the oily oik about him, but Sian is incredibly sweet in comparison.

It certainly has been a colourful shoot so far and I haven't seen Stefan come up for air in days. I'm left trying to work out if Jake touches me whenever he can, or simply, and more probably, the first night he was just being gallant, and in the green room preoccupied.

CHAPTER EIGHTEEN

Today ends like every day so far; me rushing around for Mel, handing out call-sheets, and herding the contestants back to their rooms. This time Daphne and Patrick tell me that mutual "M" word is better than doing it alone. When I do eventually get back to the room Mel is already changed for dinner, in a beautiful little pink shirt and white jeans.

'I thought we could ask K-TV for the funding of *Beautiful* and I've got the copyright agreed for the use of Macavity the Cat in the film, but only if it's been shown on demo. If it's shown at a Festival publicly or television, we'll have to pay for it.'

The woman is like a walking organising machine.

'Are there like two of you? How do you manage to be downstairs dishing out, and the next minute already changed and looking so fresh?'

Mel laughs. 'See you downstairs, slow coach.'

I shower and pull on a pair of clean pale blue jeans and a white t-shirt with *Stoked* emblazon across the front. I do like my slogans. I can't be bothered to wear a dress but I pull on some pink ballet flats, comb through my damp hair and tackle my blatantly annoying eyebrows. One of them is having a growth spurt all by itself. Lots of mascara, a little bit of bronzer and blush to fake good health, a smudge of lipbalm and I'm ready. I wish you could just have a make up bucket that you could just stick your head in, one dunk and done!

On the walk to dinner I see Alastair at the reception, I walk with him into the dining hall. I spot Mel with her ever-present notepad taking notes from Kimberly. Mel looks up with a look of 'help me' on her face and another of 'what's going on.'

I give her an apologetic face as I sit down with Alastair. It feels as if I've been upgraded to the grown up table.

I gesture that I'll tell her later.

She frowns, as Kimberly points a fake nail at her notepad.

'Eve, have you contacted the writers of *Comatosed*?'

'Yes,' I say, returning my attention to Alastair. 'In fact, I was talking to Clare, one of the writers, last night. They'll have a new draft by the end of next week.'

'Very good. I had lunch with Harold Hunter at Channel 4 yesterday and he is very keen on the concept. When we get back you should set up a meeting.'

'So the Assistant Producer role is real?' I ask

He smiles. 'Of course, it is.'

I'm speechless. For a second or two my mouth swings open and just hangs there.

'Wow,' I grin. 'That's awesome.' Ok, note to self, try sounding less like an American teen. 'I mean, I really believe in it too! Phil Spencer, a young man locked in his own body turns detective as he tries to figure out who put him there,' I enthuse.

Alastair nods. 'A comedy whodunit.'

'Exactly.'

'They'll be a lot to do before we pitch to Harold properly. Get me a copy of the redraft as soon as possible.'

'Deffo. I mean definitely.'

'You also need to get them to rework the outline.'

'Done.'

'It is?'

'Yes.' The outline job is to summarise what the show is about and how each episode will develop but it was coming across too formal and a little boring. I knew they could do a better job with some guidance.

'I've been talking with the writers and I think you'll agree their new outline reads so much better. They don't enjoy the synopsis and background stuff, but I told them to write it like they write scripts, the same energy and style. Made it much easier for them.'

His expression is delightful. 'Can you send it to me?'

'Consider it done.' I pull out my mobile and forward the email to him. Wi-Fi works in here.

When I look at Alastair he is watching me.

I give him a winning smile. 'I won't let you down, I promise.'

'Oh, I don't doubt it. The little hard worker you are, a joyfully motivated Eve.'

'Gosh, thanks.'

'And everyone has only nice things to say about you.'

I quirk a brow, 'Everyone?'

Alastair laughs. 'Is there going to be a problem?'

'Not from me,' I reassure Alastair. I'm not going to let a weasel like Brian spoil it for me. But I have to ask.

'Will Brian be working on the project?'

Alastair laughs then shakes his head. 'No, I think he's got his work cut out on other projects. He isn't what you think, one day you might…' He trails off and like a reboot button catches himself mid-thought.

As I look around me I see Brian staring at me from the other side of the room with open disdain.

'And what's this about a Short you and Mel are producing?' asks Alastair.

'It won't interfere with my full-time job I can assure you.'

'I'm not reprimanding you,' he chuckles. 'Shorts are a good calling card, it'll add to your body of work, you'll also find out what type of work you are interested in and what area you want to pursue. You and Mel work well together.'

'We do.'

'She'll be busy with the show when we get commissioned to do the other 12 episodes.'

'Do you think we will get commissioned?'

'Have you got any doubts?'

'No,' I say with absolute conviction. 'The stations will be fools not to want it and I know Mel has already shortlisted the next round's contestants. When do you think you'll film the rest of the series?' I ask

'Jim is turning up at the end of the week to see how it's going, to get a broad idea, and look at the cut right now. See if it has the makings for prime time TV.'

A little worry swims into Alastair's tired kindly face, and he adjusts his dickie bow.

'So what's the Short about?' He wants to talk about something else.

'It's called *Beautiful* and it's about a young boy, Troy, who's nine years old and has leukaemia. It's about the effect this has on his mother Juliette and his sister Dana.

The piece is very poignant. It's about loss and how we cope.

Loss for the parent, having a childhood stolen, it's dignified.' Tears start to prick my eyes I wipe them away. 'Hence the title, it's just beautiful.'

'What's beautiful?' asks Jake.

You are, the voice in my head pops up. Stop it! I give myself a telling off. I'm getting far too aware of Jake's presence.

'It's the short Mel and I are producing,' I say.

'Have you got a director?'

'Not yet, would you be interested?

'Might if the price is right,' he winks at me.

'No money I'm afraid.'

'Amazing what some people do for attention.' Brian interrupts, scraping back a chair and sitting down. I glance quickly from him to Alastair and Jake. Brian doesn't look at me but he's holding a package in his hand (stop sniggering in the back, it's not that kind of package. Yuk, nothing would repulse me more!) Brian looks mighty chuffed with himself.

'That's what Reality Shows do best. Was it Kimberly or Daphne this time?' says Jake.

'Oh I'm not talking about those little show offs.' Brian looks at me, smug contempt oozing from his eyes. I return his gaze. It's not that hard after all, I swear my spine grows one more vertebrae.

'Being drunk is so regrettable, especially on camera.'

'I've checked Lord Battenberg's hip flask. It's only very weak, dubbonet or something you English drink.' Jake adds.

No one knows what Brian is twittering on about.

'Sad and pathetic.'

'Oh I don't think it's the crime of the century. Sometimes it can be quite funny to get drunk, just don't get out your mobile!' says Alastair.

'Golden rule!' says Jake.

That night I can't sleep. I'm sufficiently shattered but my mind is whirling like a ghoul's carousal. There's nothing for it. I climb out of bed and boil the kettle, Mel doesn't even stir, lucky her. I make myself a hot chocolate, promptly spill a bit of it down the white robe (again!) and sit on the balcony. The chamber maid must think what carnage to their *oh so fluffily* white robes. Mel is lightly snoring in the background.

A waft of smoke trickles over the huge plant pot it smells like a cigar. I stand up to look for the source.

Clatter.

That's two brown splodges.

I peer over the iron railings and there, just a floor down to the right, is Jake in his tight boxer shorts having a brandy and smoking a cigar. His torso is better than Bricks. I hide behind the plant pot, guilt reaping havoc with my insides. I'm turning into a voyeur. He adjusts himself, and I wish I could see what his hand did.

I go to bed, feeling a little happier, thinking of Jake's body.

I can't help myself. I wonder if he might be … um. If he might be… you know… well endowed. Gudrun said my previous encounters sound a little on the inadequate size for gulp… female satisfaction. She might have well drawn the conclusion from the fact that I never knew if they were in or out. I think she's a bit of an idealist though, I mean what man can keep it firm all the way, I mean rigid. Anyway she thinks they all had that dysfunction whatnot going on, and no wonder I had low confidence in doing anything at all. There was me thinking it was a couple of minute's window and that's that. I don't have a black book to compare, pages of encounters, and I never talk about it with my friends, far too prudish, aren't I? Anything depicted in article or film I put down to sheer social exaggeration on the size front. Now I'm not so sure after seeing the adjusted bulge that shadowed Jake's leg. Maybe balcony lanterns just magnify things.

CHAPTER NINETEEN

Today's filming is *"Who's coming to Luncheon?"* the etiquette challenge. They all have to have dinner with another's partner and see if they can behave platonically, respectfully and with decorum. Sounds easy but the contestants must rile the other into divulging information or behaviour about their betrothed. Could be their weaknesses, hates or the worst… getting them to flirt or be suggestive with you. Each dining couple will get their own objective, i.e. information, weaknesses or *'make a play'*. They get points for each hit for their team. They're given three cards to choose from but the cards are rigged according to what the psychologist's has suggested.

We are all really tired. You can see dark circles forming under everyone's eyes apart from our make up girls and Brick. Whenever Stacey is out the way, they rush to touch up his makeup, which if you remember he didn't need according to their professional opinions. They certainly are forthright. I wish I were a bit sassier like they all are. They have fun with it too, not taking anything seriously.

Mel and I have no feeling in our feet anymore and even Jet looks weary with his canine problem. Every time they see him they yap, growl and show their teeth.

I really hope we get commissioned after all this, and the footage is unlike any reality show I've ever seen, it's compelling on a totally different level. You root but don't entirely fall for anyone's victory, your support wavers from minute to minute, the ones you think you'll like you end up doing 180 degree turnaround within the next shot or minor reveal. It's riveting watching. I really hope that Alastair gets the deal. Over the last day the anxiety has built up with Alastair, he takes the majority of the financial burden, what investors expect for a return and all that business stuff. Must be terribly fraying on the nerves.

Mel and I have been up since early doors, me at 4:30am, topped with hardly any sleep at all, so my eyes feel like they are filled with sawdust. Mel got up just before 5:30am in a panic that she didn't have time to wash, dry and straighten her hair now it's on the sliding side of limp. She opted for tieback and dry shampoo spray. We're both in need of a caffeine sugary boost. Work today, starts at 6am, helping set up the dining room, hiding Jet's tattered booms, making sure the background works with the lights etc. We're using antique Chinese screens to evoke intimacy; each screen has a hidden camera to get the smallest of facial gestures, how the eyes flick when trying to deceive or get someone to reveal something… that's what one of the quacks was saying. The contestants think it's all about revealing what they found out afterwards, they have no idea it's all being filmed (yep that's what they signed up for - legally and willingly). They must realise to some extent that's what is going on. But with our nutty bunch I think they're so psyched up, unaware or delusional it wouldn't matter if you revealed it or not.

The first for the lunch date is Kimberly and Brick. Kimberly's face lights up when she sees who her dinner date is. She flirts outrageously and that wasn't even her task, her task was to find out Stacey's weaknesses. Brick is just plain hungry after finishing two hours in the gym, and wolfs down the lunch nodding politely. That's how he stays so beefed up. I don't think Brick gets two words in, Kimberly rattles on about how tiresome it is being the object to everyman's desire, she needs more of a bodyguard than a husband to keep the wolves at bay. Brick refills her water glass as she rejigs her stuffed up bra. Ironically Brick pays more attention to the breadbasket than the basket case in front of him and her under duress boobs! He manages without effort to get all her wedding dress idea's out which was his task... the sacred dress. He only asked, *"what would you like to look like on your big day then Ma'am?"* and she didn't pause for twenty minutes. Already the first lunch has overrun on schedule. Kimberly and a camera is all you need for chaos. We reset the room and reset it again after Kimberly's yap-bags rush at Jet as soon as the doors were opened. Like magic we get back to the adjoining room and elevenses are on the table. Pastries, coffees and shortbread light up the table along with Grumpy fairy cups and plates, so elegantly laid out, the staff here could make mud and crickets look divine. I wonder where they learn to make it so perfect? It must be a posh hotel school; it's a skill that has always eluded me I can't get a pre-cut scone to look appetizing on a plate.

The room just needs some technical adjustments so we have some time to drink, scoff and revamp. Mel gets summoned by Brian mid coffee pour, so I quickly grab a cup, crunch up a pastry in my fist removing myself from his vicinity. I slope off and sit in the corner for a momentary minute of solace.

Gazing out the window I spy Batty Battenberg swiping at some bushes with his cane. You'd think he was doing a spot of beating for an old fashioned shoot, ruffling out the partridges, pheasants and ducks. He does have plus fours and a deer-stalker on; I suppose that's the usual luncheon attire for him on his impoverished estate. It's a welcome distraction from Brian's vibes, our own period wardrobe in sight. One of the dogs runs at him and starts biting his cane; he tries to fling it off. I start laughing to myself.

'What's funny?'

I look up and it's Jake, his gaze unwavering. I point out the window at the ever-increasingly infuriated Lord Batty.

'The man's a complete buffoon. Isn't that what you English say?'

'Oh I don't know, I think he has a certain charm.'

I stifle a yawn; maybe sitting down wasn't such a good idea.

'So that's what you women find charming.' Jake raises his eyebrows at me. I then remember last night's brandy boxer shorts show and my cheeks warm. He sits down next to me with his coffee and my temperature steadily rises.

'He's entertaining in an inadvertent way.' I couldn't say that twice!

'So you like oblivious detachment?'

'I didn't say that.'

'Okay, archetypal sexism?'

'I'm sure you'd want me to agree with that if you were an archetypal sexist.'

'Touché. Touché. I think our Lord B will be the most interesting in the next game.'

'Yep, he doesn't beat about the bush.'

'Well, evidently he does.' Jake nods at the window and

Battenberg is beating his cane with the dog still attached into a mulberry bush. We both laugh.

'Would you like a plate for your crumbs?' He asks, looking at my palm cradling a squashed pastry.

'Hmm I think that might be a good idea. And erm... while you're there, you couldn't get me another could you? Maybe a fully formed one?'

'I quite fancy a bit of pastry myself, naturally fully formed.' He leaves with a devilish smirk. I feel my heart pound as I watch the confident and masculine American stride over and take what he wants. I try and discard the remnants of pulverised pastry into the paper bin.

He returns seconds later with a plate piled high with apple puffs, cream doughnuts and a traditional Chelsea bun with a cherry on top. I opt for the sticky bun.

Jake sits back down next to me. I straighten my back and correct my lazy slouch, trying to look composed while eating. I can smell his aftershave mixed together with the pastry. I push my fringe off my face with the back of my hand, one or two strands refusing to comply.

'You've got crumbs on your face.' Great! I can sit up straight, but I'm still a messy eater.

'Never could keep myself–' I swallow the next word, as he leans forward and brushes his finger lightly across my nose. Our eyes lock and I don't dare breathe.

I even feel a little faint.

He smiles and I smile back, my heart wanting to explode.

There are no two ways about it, being this close to Jake is making me feel really, really good, quite giddy, an energy I have never felt by merely sitting next to someone.

'Good, aren't they?'

I nod. I daren't speak with a mouth full of bun. We sit in silence watching Batty, banqueting on cake contently, both of us enjoying the solace.

It is interesting and slightly disconcerting how differently couples behave away from their partner. On the one hand it's reassuring to know that loyalty is still important to some, at least it is to Daphne and Patrick. On the other hand it's slightly worrisome just how phoney, slimy and downright disloyal some others behave. I can't fathom why they say or act the way they do. But I suppose this is Reality TV at its best or worst (take your pick).

Stacey is merciless in her interrogation of Patrick, but Patrick holds his own. After all we know he likes the dominating woman at times much to Stacey's growing frustrations. Piers (as Kimberly before) spends the whole time talking about himself to Daphne. I can see Daphne's mind ticking over. She also does an impressive eye roll when Piers said, 'to have power of one's destiny, the country's destiny is what makes me wake up in the morning.' To which she replied, 'start with trying to have a power of a real man boy, then run a country!' This made me giggle helplessly. I missed the other lunch dates but I just make it in time to see the last one of today. The lunch date with Lord Battenberg and Sian. This I'm looking forward to seeing.

Lord Battenberg looks like he's stepped out of an Evelyn Waugh story, those plus fours are underscored with chequered brogues, and hilarious stocking socks with tassels. How didn't I notice those? I've never seen anyone wear things like that in real life. He actually looks pretty cool unintentionally, eccentricity aloud one might say.

Sian clears her throat, 'Hello again. You've dressed for lunch, how nice.'

'You look very appetising yourself my dear.'

Sian face glows pink.

He inclines his head slightly. 'So, Sian, would you like to meet up with me after the show?'

Sian claps her hand over her mouth in shock. 'Ooo um… I don't think that's allowed.'

'We know I am not going to marry Kimberly.'

'You're not?'

I catch Jake's eyes and he is gripped. Indeed a fortuitous moment in filmmaking when you catch something monumental. Their eyes lock.

'Of course my dear what an absurd idea that would be. She's quite a happy sausage about it, has some old flame burning in the back of her mind. We simply have a jolly old time. She was coming to England, I said I was English and there we were sharing the same plane. Well one doesn't want to be discourteous if one has a guest in one's country. She said this type of break would be fun. You know how simple the Americans can be, fun and games, popcorn and fizzy drinks. Rather endearing in a childlike fantasy.' By all accounts, especially Lord Battys tumbling ones, the estate has someone who takes care of the money, by court order, so he is pretty oblivious to this whole concept of what is actually going on around him. Sian is speechless.

'And we all know you won't be marrying that fellow with the ill-fitting blazer. Shocking tailoring.'

He slips that in at the end and Sian is blinking uncontrollably.

'What makes you say that?'

'Why would one marry beneath one's station? You should always marry for social gain my dear. Marrying the help really! This isn't some bad rendition of Lady's Chatterly's lover. What will the family make of it?'

Sian is completely gobsmacked. We all are. 'Well I don't see that's any of your business.'

'Your Irish Estate must be out in hands of trust for future generations. One shouldn't dilute good stock. They might want to be business people or something tawdry. I mean have you seen that commoner Trump. Dear dear me, what a spectacle of bad barbering. Once saw him at a polo match. He doesn't even speak the Queen's English, such a loud, vulgar chap. That is what business does for the character. That is not the pinnacle of a society member. No, no, no. More incorrect than a poodle on a foxhunt.'

'Err, I don't come from… my family doesn't have an estate.'

'Not another word on the subject my dear.'

He holds his wine glass close to his lips, a gleaming grin on his face.

After almost a minute of silence Sian pushes the wine glass away and stands up.

'Of course, the time, how forgetful of me. I expect one as beautiful must have her afternoon rest before the evening's delights.' Battenberg stands up, moves her chair and grabs her hands before she can do anything remotely stompy. He shakes her hands with vigour, thinking she is of the exact same opinion about him. You couldn't script this better.

Sian turns a brighter shade of red and it looks like Batty is going to kiss her left hand, he just plants his face down as she whisks away. It's another Peter Sellers moment all right; Batty is left kissing the air, mid-faltering on brogues, as the camera sweeps in for the dancing socks' shot. Brilliant.

I'm captured, I'm sure the UK will be, he's our own un-pc posh prat. When I turn away from the monitors Jake is looking at me. His gaze is unwavering and I wonder if I've forgotten something. Realising I'm holding all the call-sheets for tomorrow I thrust one at him.

He stands up abruptly. I'm not sure if that was a small sign of impatience? He's difficult to read at times; sometimes he is friendly and other times indifferent and preoccupied. I suppose he has just as much riding on this as Alastair.

CHAPTER TWENTY

Tonight I'm going straight to bed, no supper as I had enough cake, pastry and buns to last a year, any more food and I'll explode.

There's a cool breeze as I walk past the huge conifers aligning the west garden path. I immediately notice Daphne and Patrick and I'm about to say hi when I realise he is pulling at the hem of her skirt – strike that, he is pulling it up, bunching it at the waist. Good God, what is he doing?

I jerk backwards, eyes looking away, and then again on them just to check I'm not seeing things.

Oh no. No. No. She's… she's unzipping his trousers, oh Jesus! There they go toppling to the ground… argh he's not wearing… he's flipping commando. Oh no, I think I'm going to be sick. For a moment I am rooted to the spot. Do I turn back and try not to make a sound on the gravel beneath me? I don't want them to think I am watching them. My insides retreat into my panicked stomach. Why would they… I mean they're thoroughly out in the open. Anyone can walk by, like I just did.

This is ugly and brazen. The slow penny drops… This is half

the fun for them.

I can't watch anymore, I turn hurriedly away and walking towards me is Jake.

He is smoking.

'Oh, hi,' I say, dazedly. 'I didn't know you smoked?'

'I don't.' He drops it on the floor. 'Trying to give up.'

There's a short silence. His face is only a few inches from mine: a prominent chin, that strong nose… swallowing hard I drop my eyes to the non-performing ground and stare at the dying embers of his cigarette.

'What's got you all hot and bothered.'

'I'm not hot –' my cheeks rev up to full flame.

He starts to step towards the bushes and I grab his arm.

'I wouldn't go that way,' my hand is on his arm and for a moment I stare at it.

When I look up he is staring at me, his face alight with intrigue. 'Why not that way?'

My face roasts further. 'Daphne and… um well they are… they are… um, that is they're… having a moment.'

He laughs. 'Not again, nowhere seems to be safe from the potency of Patrick!'

He moves towards the bushes again and I stare at him anxiously. 'You're not going to look are you?'

'It's a public space.'

'Isn't there a channel you can subscribe to for that sort of thing?'

He shoots me an amused grin. 'The look on your face!'

'Whatever turns you on,' I sniff, walking off in the other direction. Jake chuckles and catches up with me. There's a short silence as we walk together. I feel stiff, awkward and very much aware of his presence. I glance at Jake and he seems totally the opposite, easy strides and staring ahead with his usual impenetrable stare. As if he senses me gazing at him, he looks at me. I quickly look away.

'So what's the story with you and Adam?' He suddenly asks.

My heart is in my mouth. 'You were there, you saw what happened.'

'And you're not hoping to get back together?'

My heart plops back into my chest and starts beating that little bit faster.

'That would be the worst mistake of my life,' I reply.

'Good,' he says.

Good? I look at him and there's a small smile on his lips.

'Because… that is….' He stops and plants himself in front of me. In my ballet pumps, I come up to the top of his chest but it's what I see in his expression that makes my insides squidgy. I think he wants to kiss me, and I realize my breathing isn't quite so even, in fact my ribcage is rising and falling erratically, like a lung machine short-circuiting. No, surely I must be imagining it.

'I like you Eve.'

'You do?'

'Very much so.'

'That's good to know,' I say, my head is whirling and I try to make sense of what is happening, but I can't, I can only feel what I want… that is… I want him, have wanted him for some time. 'I like you, too.'

His mouth twitches into a smile. 'You know, I saw you watching me the other night.'

I'm flummoxed for a response.

I shrug. 'I couldn't sleep.'

'I actually was hoping you might have come down. Said

hello and joined me for a night cap.'

My heart hammers in my chest. Oh my God. Oh my God.

He steps closer, brushing my hair away from cheeks. My eyes feel like they're about to pop out.

All of a sudden my breathing becomes deeper, I stand silent, unprepared. My whole body stirs. His hand falls to my waist and draws me close. His eyes dance over mine, his pupils widen as he studies all my features. I feel his fingers slide down my neck. The grip tightens, we're magnetised to one another and the lust is boiling. He presses his full, firm lips to mine, his stubble rasping my face. The quickness of his move makes me gasp. His lips smell like cigarettes and mint and that's about my last coherent thought because the kiss is explosive.

His fingers are strong against my skin as his kiss deepens. His scratchy stubble ignites all of me. I lean in wrapping my arms around his neck and grabbing at his short hair, kissing him back until I forget to breathe. He slides his hands under my t-shirt, along my spine, hands lingering on my bare skin. His skin feels so hot on my body. I pull him even closer to me, winding myself tighter against him. I have no control, just desire. His tongue devours me. I can't breath. I don't care. I pant, his tongue licks the top of my lip and I stand breathless. Our air mingled. He ravages my neck and I nearly faint, my body flops in the surcharge of feelings I cannot identify. He holds onto me, strong and in control, tilts the back of my head up for more. This ignites a feverish frenzy and I kiss him back, not wanting to miss any of his face. He groans for more. I bit his ear, kissing all around his neck. I feel a hard mass prodding my stomach, I go to move the phone in his pocket aside, but it grows even more. This sends me into overdrive. I pull at the top of his shirt, beckoning his lips to my neck; he pulls the small of my back in. I can feel him, his excitement. Our hands frantically search, grabbing anything they can get hold of. My mind is on fire.

This is weird, just around the corner Daphne and Patrick are probably, no definitely, having it off, and here I am snogging Jake with a need more essential than breathing. A ravishing appetite has awoken, my hot temperature makes me swoon, I'm breathless. He breaks away, trying to hold my pounding body upright. 'Let's go.'

I can't answer. I simply nod as my heart starts hammering again. Jake takes my hand in his and pulls me towards the hotel. It feels warm, masculine and tight. As we get closer he lets go and we walk side-by-side into the lobby. For the sake of anyone watching we're just two colleagues walking together and not heading anywhere in particular. I'm not sure what the plan is but I daren't utter a sound. Our pace quickens as we go unnoticed, we practically march up the stairs, neither of us saying a word. The intensity is rising with every step. The electricity between us is a strong stealthy hum, and our aim is not to encounter anyone, nothing to blight the connection that grows with each flavoursome second. Somehow, we make it to his room without seeing any other guest. Jake produces a key and rams the door open. And we're in. The room is very grand. My eyes sweep over its decoration, dark, exotic, and for a moment I'm terrified.

But that all dissipates when the door slams shut and we lock eyes again. My confidence starts to wane. This is a real man, and I'm not a real woman. I try and think of Gudrun's confidence mantras…

'Now where were we?' Oops too late for those mantras to

surface.

He steps towards me unbuttoning his shirt, his eyes never leaving mine. I keep my eyes locked on his, I have no choice, it's as though he has me in a holding beam. His torso is pumped and I can almost see his heart beating fast. I hold up my palm and place it on his chest stopping him in his tracks. My palm strokes his chest, keeping him at arms length. I have no idea where this is coming from but it feels right, natural.

Jake continues to undress, shirt off, next his trainers, and as he bends down to remove them, the muscles in his broad back move deliciously underneath his skin. All that is left is his belt, his jeans and whatever underneath.

Is it my time now?

I unzip my hoody, my small tight vest straining against my breathing. I'm sweating underneath. He takes a finger, trails it over the top of my breasts and licks it afterwards slowly. Oh my word, I never knew sweat could be so darn hot. OK, I know you are hot when you sweat, but you know what I mean. My body is in overdrive so much so I can hear my heartbeat in my ears, head, chest and down below.

He steps closer and pulls the zip of the hoody, forcing me to move forward into his chest. His rock hard broad chest. This is so cavemen… a tiny giggle erupts from me, I muzzle the noise, pressing my lips and nose to his chest, loving every ridge of it, revelling in his body. Then he takes my face, pulls it up and kisses me hard. It is like nothing I've ever known, the feeling of his skin burning against mine, sliding against mine, one hand caught in my hair, the other tracing the curve of my spine. He toys with the top of my jeans, edging to loosen them. Each stroke makes me want to devour every part of him. I'm feeling out of myself. Who is this person? I want to strip, but his touch is driving me to distraction, I don't know what I'm doing as my hoody drops to the floor. I push his hand down my jeans, slowly. I groan in his ear and bite it when he gets near to my… erm… my clitoris… there I said it! The yearning controlling me is far beyond my hang-ups about it. The fact is, I've never been turned on, hence I've never known what to do. I'm not an automate, but you have to switch on the machine by all accounts – the sex machine. Thank the Lord! And I thought there was something wrong with me! There… it's said, out in the open. I now know what. *Ooooh…* he toys with the lace trim of my knickers, I want him to delve right in but he's teasing me. He undoes my jeans, and discards them from the foot, slowly kissing my legs on the way up. He stops at the edge of my knickers and starts to lick slightly inside. I can't contain myself, I push his head into me. He responds by biting them. He takes me up in his arms and throws me on the bed. I'm lying there with a vest and very wet knickers. He discards his jeans and the sight is tremendous.

His erection is a massive, whooping proper erection scrambling for freedom. I'm going to send flowers to Gudrun, she was absolutely right. So that's what a real hard on looks like. By gum madame it is magical. I feel my knickers getting moist, everything is flowing… this is amazing. He looks intently at me, my pupils must be moonlike. He climbs on top of me, his penis sticking out of the top of his white boxers, and it's spectacularly large and moist, getting harder as he sees me look at it with pleasure. He pulls my arms over my head and removes my vest. My bra is half undone already, he unhooks it completely from behind with the power of a gladiator, and there I am topless, with nipples so erect you could stack CD's on them. He groans with the sight of them and rubs his erection against my wet panties, probing the material, and my pussy is so ready. (I said the word! Gudrun would be thrilled, but not as much as I am right now). He stops himself and starts kissing my neck, his fingers gently circling my clitoris, I arch up in response nothing in my mind but sheer pleasure. Jake knows his way round better than Google Maps! He pulls my knickers down and kisses where he's playing, his tongue joining in. My body is in a loop of spasms, as he licks me, long swipes of his tongue making my hips buck and jerk upwards. I am moaning. I don't recognise the sound but it comes from deep within and I can't stop even if I wanted to. I have never had a man licking and sucking between my legs before. Why not? Ooo.... ooo...

I buck and bounce against Jake's mouth; the throbbing heat intensifies. I moan for more, my body yearns every touch, and he gently starts stroking again. He moves his palm down so I'm fully held by his hand, he inserts a finger and I feel a gushing, what was that? This makes him groan in my ear with animal breathlessness.

'You are the most responsive woman I've ever met,' Jake husks as his lips move back up my body. Can't say I've ever responded like this before.

'Now, now,' I manage to breath as I bite his lobe. This is a new side of me; I'm desperate to have him. My hands grab at his boxers fervently. I slide them down releasing all of him. The heat of his throb sends me giddy with excitement. He groans as I slide my fingers down and cup his tight balls pulling them towards me. He stands up. My breathing is manic. I want all of it now. I sit up and play with him, legs akimbo, so he can watch me. His breathing deepens and he grabs for the bedside drawer. He stands looking at me while he pulls on a rubber (glad one of us is thinking). It looks as if his penis is about to burst. I lick my lips. He leaps onto the bed, and then, with one quick thrust, he's inside me. My eyes roll to the back of my head and I scream with delight and exquisite pain. His mouth closes down on mine devouring my every pant as I move into him. His erection is rock hard and I feel the shaft thicken as he looks at me with lust.

And there's really only one goal in mind after that. Jake sets the pace, pumping hard and fast, me grinding and groaning with each deepening thrust. The pumping and bucking intensifies as we race towards the same goal. I orgasm again and again, Jake revels in it, riding me faster and faster each time, keeping me on this new plateau of pleasure. This surely is the Tibetan heights of climaxing. The hot, sweet confusion, lost in him, lost in time, alive from my toe tips up to the magnificent awe of it all. I'm alight with all the passion I've ever dreamed of. It's simply wonderful. My arms are flailing around, I am travelling out of my own body, it's core on fire, combusting, I'm exploding inside and Jake is trying to hold back, his eyes are intense with a potent urgency.

'I'm going to have to.... need to...' I groan deeply in hearing those words with that sexy voice, it makes me come again with that and he yells out as he thrusts in long and hard, his eyes roll into the back of his head, his mouth open with total and utter satisfaction. Oh my word, he looks so darn sexy, I've never seen a man in abandonment, unequivocally and completely in the moment.

His body shudders and collapses on top of me, heavy and contented. We lie in silence.

Then he slides himself out and flops onto his back pulling me into the crook of his arm.

'You…' He manages to say grabbing my bum and pushing me into him.

I feel like a proper sex kitten. I hold him tightly and he pulls me even closer, our bodies coiling like electromagnets on charge. He strokes the side of my breast tenderly and kisses my forehead. I have no words. I'm so high with the sensations running around my body. We lay in a supreme state of serenity, both of our hearts still pounding up and down, breathing almost as one. We drift off into sleep, our bodies so in tune they mimic one another.

CHAPTER TWENTY-ONE

My bladder wakes me up, and I have every intention of getting up, but first I carefully roll onto my side; Jake is quietly snoring with a half smile fixed on his lips. It's really cute and makes me giddy with glee. My eyes drift and I notice the bedside clock… 4am. SHIT! I don't want anyone to know about my private life. What if Mel wakes up and I'm not there. I just don't want questions. I couldn't lie or act myself out of a puppet convention where I'm the puppeteer, let alone answer questions about my whereabouts last night. I take one longing last look at Jake's naked body peeping out behind the white sheet. He's definitely all man, just watching him makes my 'down below bits' fizz with excitement again. I could wake him up, see if he fancies another shag! Shocked that I'm actually up for a *shag* this early in the morning I take one last lingering look, slip out of bed, follow the trail of destruction, pulling on my knickers, jeans, t-shirt and hoodie, and creep out as quietly as I can.

Mel is out with the fairies she doesn't even so much as stir when I bump into the chair, which happens to be doubling as our between door - wardrobe - mirror clotheshorse.

'Yikes.' This has caused rapid dislodgement to the expertly held bladder, and it's now about to burst, so I catapult onto the loo louder than a herd of incontinent bison, collapse on cue and the Niagara Falls of all pee splashes everywhere.

Thankfully Mel is out for the count, thank goodness for that, otherwise it could have been awkward to explain why I am dressed and on the loo doing a piss a horse would shy away from.

I slip out of my clothes, grab a T-shirt from the chair, slink into bed, and within seconds I'm out for the count. Physical exercise does wonders for quality sleep. And that was quite a work out. My dreams burn into sexy images on reply.

The alarm shrieks at me, and while Mel sprints out of bed like a nuclear war has been declared I pull the duvet over my head and go back to sleep. Mel might be feeling bright-eyed and bushy-tailed, but I'm fried, my head is floating. Well what did I expect? You don't get to have hot, hard, hanky-panky all night, less than two hours of sleep, and bounce out of bed like Zebedee on speed. The adrenalin rush isn't so fervent this morning, bet it would be if I'd woken up besides Mr Humpy-Pumpy. Well at least I'm making jokes! My words might not be as lewd as last nights, but they have sexual reference and that's self improvement right there. Stick that on your rubber toys Gudrun and smoke it, or more fittingly, rub it!

My eyes remain shut even through the dubious crashing emanating from the bathroom.

Zzzz...

Mel comes skipping out of the bathroom all too soon.

'Bathroom free.' she trills far too loudly for my morning ears. I grumble from under the duvet.

'Eve, time to get up.'

'Yes, yes.' I reply quickly, pulling the covers down from my face.

'I think there might be bits of porcelain on the floor from the soap dish. I'm sure I got all of it, but be careful where you tread in case. I didn't have my contacts in.'

I never knew Mel wore contacts. Now it makes sense why she studies things more closely, especially at night. I thought she was just being seriously efficient with concentration. I drag my feet towards the crash scene. The shower manages to power a little bit of life into me, but what I need is about a zillion cups of coffee or to go back to bed for several hours. How am I going to survive the day on less than two hours sleep, plus the previous night of insomnia?

I pause in front of the large mirror and look at myself.

I have humongous bags under my eyes and my wonky eyebrow has decided to veer off road. Other than that I look, well, like me. I don't look like I've been shagged senseless. I feel sort of disappointed. How does one look after that? On closer inspection of the wreck that is my sleep-deprived face, my eyes are definitely twinkling, nope… they are actually sparkling. Glitter overload or what, they look so different, even the colour seems brighter. I look closer still, in between the patches of blotchy red 'the shower was way too hot' skin, I spy a plump glow. This could merely be circulation but my face is alive with life. I do believe I have a glint in my eye, the one that men are always supposed to have. Now if I start having a spring in my step, does that make me a male stereotype?

Frankly, and I mean it, last night was pretty fucking perfect (which, by itself, is an impossible statement to make for someone like me). Excuse the expletive but if ever there was a time for one it's now. I comb through my damp hair. It was the best sex I have ever had and we didn't do it just once, we did it twice, the second time for even longer, with a lot of slow caressing and attention towards me. Yep twice in one long, lusty night, and we didn't get going until later. No one has taken the time to lavish me with that kind of attention, he was tending my needs before his own, and not once, but continuously. Ok I'm never going to compete against the likes of Daphne and Patrick's eight-times-in-one-day marathon, but two times is a sex feast for me. I realise now that the meagre selfish attempts with the others before Jake weren't sex at all; they might as well have had a ripe melon to pathetically pump, fail, and fall limp into. Going from anything relating to last night, they never even managed to create a ripe environment, not dewy at all, those boys were useless at it… not me. Okay, okay, I'm back to my old habits of avoiding the real descriptive, but at least I'm metaphor-ing it and not avoiding it altogether. Melons are a good choice, in this case I mean the inside flesh and not the voluptuous shape, but it wasn't just the sex, it was the feel of the night, the passionate energy between us. It was that illusive spark. The sexual chemistry was the missing link that has finally introduced itself.

So pleased to meet you.

I dress in my jeans and pull on my 'Happy' T-shirt. Yep that describes me perfectly today. I stretch out my over-exercised stiff hips, which haven't seen that much action since Lucy bought a zumba DVD.

Mel pads into the room holding her notepad and showing her wild side in ripped jeans and leopard print sweater.

'I totally zonked out when my head hit the pillow last night.'

'Me too.' I say, my face tingling with the half-truth. Of

course, I'm blushing, but she can't tell under my newly-found rosy exterior, besides Mel's too busy scribbling away to notice the finer nuances of my skin tones.

'You ok?'

'Suu-re.' I stutter, picking up the call-sheet from the dressing table.

'So we need to check the obstacle course, check the Health and Safety guy has crossed off all his copious forms. Make sure they all have the right footwear. Kimberley's trying to pull a fast one with sponsorship of some stupid friend of hers who thinks she's a shoe designer. Oooh, the jelly balls will arrive soon.' She rambles off in swift monotone, handing me the new list robotically.

'The jelly balls?' I repeat while searching for them on the list.

'Oh some last minute idea from Swiss Franc. Jake thought it would be funny too. Men, they always do that. You organise everything and then…' She trails off.

'What are they…?' I stop mid sentence, Mel is totally preoccupied, checking off and mumbling to herself. I'm a little weary now, so I order coffee to the room. I feel very grown up but not terribly with it.

Ding-a-ling. The tray of critical morning-starts is here.

All I can do is focus on pouring that first cup; just the smell wakes my brain cells into perpetual motion. Mel is just a muffled sound until I sip the first mouthful. Then I'm back in the room.

'Last game,' I say, with renewed alert. 'Can you believe it?'

We sit in silence for a few minutes, perched on the edge of the bed, sipping our coffees, gazing at the to-do list, psyching ourselves up for the next eight, twelve or however many more hours. Who knows how long when you've got Kimberly to film!

I'm also nervous about seeing Jake again. What are we going to say to each other? What if he ignores me? So we had sex and that's it, we both wanted it, all very civilised and mature. No more than a bit of fun at the end of a work project, although I wouldn't mind having some more civilised interludes. Who wouldn't after a performance so hot and with that much pleasure?

After spending an hour checking and double-checking the odious obstacle course and ensuring that the dogs didn't poo in the mud tunnel, I am just returning for my zillionth coffee when I see Jake and Jet standing in front of the catering truck. I can't rely on my voice to stay calm so I just nod at them both and order my coffee.

'Saw you wrestling with the yapballs,' says Jake, his eyes dancing at me.

My cheeks flame.

'Jake mate why didn't you say,' interrupts Jet. 'I could have trapped them in there for the day. Perfect solutions don't present themselves that easily.'

'More's the pity,' I say. 'I could have done without trailing down there with my mobile torch thinking at any moment my knees were going to be squirming in fluff faeces! I could have definitely done without that exercise this morning. I'm shattered.'

'Oh yeah what did you get up to last night?' Jet jests, his eyes twinkling.

For a minute neither Jake or I speak, but I know I'm blushing. Jet doesn't seem to notice.

'Ah for fuck's sake.' Jet bellows. 'Get those dogs away from the camera wires.' We all look over and they're having a pee scent competition.

'I'm gonna murder those rats, canine hooligans.' Jet rushes over, does an about turn running away with them, all in flight chasing after him; he forgot the scraggy boom sticking out of his jacket. It's quite a spectacle; the camera guy quickly starts recording, zooming in, as he gets near the lake, bloody funny. We laugh when he trips over and the small things just kamikaze him; no one goes to help, everyone is filming (either professionally or not). All watch in glee. Finally when I've stopped giggling I realise I'm standing with Jake out of crew earshot.

Our eyes meet.

'So,' he says.

'So,' I say, taking a deep slug of coffee.

'Last night was...' He pauses for what seems like forever, 'Delicious,' he smiles. 'I would very much like a repeat,' he says in his smooth American voice.

I've never been known to interest a man by that pursuit. The thought jolts me sideways; you know what I was expecting. *Thanks, it was fun but...*

Jake... delicious... delicious Jake... wants to do it again. I flash him a smile, my mind roams into dirty realms.

'Repeat! How about a brand new episode?' I say brazenly, a new, naughty Eve surfacing. Jake's face is a picture. I bite my lip, suddenly feeling less sure.

He takes a step closer. 'Can't wait,' he husks in my ear. His tone excites me far too much for nine in the morning. I think my mind just cracked, fried and burnt in the thought. What a turn on, a wonderful new sensation to have with someone, a mere suggestion sending my body into overload. I wish later was now. What I wouldn't do to jump his bones right this minute.

Jake goes to Jet's rescue and I watch as he patiently unravels Jet from dogs, wires and foliage. I'm lost in the world of sex, day-dreaming what he's going to do to me next.

I gulp down the rest of my coffee, dribbling a good portion down my right shoulder, under the delusion that those thoughts are written all over my face.

'EVE!' Mel rushes towards me, but she is beyond stressed to notice my odd behaviour, and is thankfully unaware of my uselessness so far. 'Do you have time to meet the jelly ball people, they're late and Brian has given me too much to check, which of course wasn't on the original plan. I'm going to murder someone or something soon.'

'Mel, just hand me what you can't do and I'll get on it.'

'You're one in a million.'

'If it's not perfect, Brian only has himself to blame.'

'Yeah, yeah you're right.' She says grabbing my coffee and finishing it off.

Poor Mel, I must get my arse into gear and stop fantasising about it being on another gear stick entirely.

All the contestants have been rounded up, Battenberg and Kimberly are no better than wayward sheep; him with Sian and her with Brick plus cameras plus fame, plus her friends glittering trainers and the blessed make up cart. Hence the dogs are running riot more than usual. Swiss Franc takes the matter in hand, grabs the megaphone and takes control, of course making sure the cameras are rolling. He rubs his teeth, flicks his hair or someone's former hair. I think it's a piece, but I wouldn't ask directly – I must think of a clever comeback if I do get up the nerve to ask.

'People, people…PEE –POLE. Now hear this and adhere to this.' He raises a perfectly plucked and dyed eyebrow at the camera. He's the king of ham, just brilliantly expressive, and the camera loves him and his many caricatures.

'I want you all to line up. You know we said we're going to do a Mr and Mrs type of Q&A, but this Mr and Mrs comes with a tiny twist. What can it be? I hear you fret, is that your brain fretting away Miss Roberts? Well, we can rule out a few of you, can't we?' The crew bursts out laughing; Swiss Franc's last comment was just to the camera as the contestants didn't hear a thing. He picks up the megaphone again.

'Each time you fail a question, you fail your partner,' Swiss Fran does an all cloaks and daggers action down the lens, and the camera crew slowly pan all the contestant's understandably worried faces.

They and the audience don't know what the forfeits are. They stand in a set-out circle, which is basically a massively oversized paddling pool that will protect the hotel's garden. In the middle there is an opaque, ominous black cube, and that's where the forfeits happens, inside, in darkness, filmed with an infrared… just to add to the fear. I wouldn't want to be in their shoes, particularly Kimberley's OTT footwear, which is causing a reflective nightmare for the lighting guys.

When the first person cocks up and the type of forfeit gets revealed, it will generate instant tension between the contestants, so there is pressure to get it right for your loved one. Onset panic and more wrong answers are likely under the duress, their partner's seething growing when they'll know what is at stake. That's how the behavioural psychologist put it, an element of the forceful confessional. Although in my opinion it is slighted towards the spite, frustration and resentfulness that can brew only too well underneath a weak relationship (don't I know it). Sometimes the ego just thrives in the close proximity of audience, but the audience is ignored; two people can exist side by side without knowing each other at all. It's more common than you think according to the psychobabble team, and funnily Gudrun said the same thing but about the bedroom activities.

So there's the black box but there's also the black tunnel of turmoil. You have to crawl though it to get the point back, not knowing what you're going to encounter and with no vision again. That's for the playoff, if there's a drawer in this game. I think they've come up with hideous things that feel like creepy crawlies, horrible evil eyes and slimy creatures (loosely based on the Japanese Endurance game). Britain's top horror team has created the effects, the ones who do the films. I hope it's them. I haven't seen any tanks, aquariums or animal handlers on set. I know the sound effects guys from Hammerhouse have been working with Jet this morning, wiring up triggers and whatnot. Bit too technical for me on this bright morning.

My phone goes off, the jelly ball people have finally arrived. I dash up to the hotel, spot the van and usher them to come quickly. They follow with some strange containers. I get them to Brian and promptly leave them to it, ignoring Brian's arrogant skyward-pointing finger, which basically means you have to stay until it dismisses you with an insulting gesture.

I don't want to interact with that poisonous toad today if I can help it, so I run off before he has time to chastise me.

Breathless on my return I stand next to Mel.

'Look's like you've got a stitch.'

'I'm fine.' I pant, holding my side. I swear I might have

pulled a muscle last night.

'Just in time, Swiss Franc's ready to start the questions. I've been looking forward to this.'

'Secretly, so have I...ehrr…ow…' My stitch violently stabs me, a pyrrhic victory to the hips.

Swiss Franc, our genius host, takes up a curious stance and the sergeant major of the mic begins. First up is Sian and Piers.

'What perfume does Sian use?'

'Umm… An evening musk? Umm…'

'I must hurry you for a final answer.' You can see the clock ticking in Swiss Franc's head and he wants him to get it wrong. We all do, Piers is a smarmy ass. Not that we want Sian to suffer, but she could definitely do better.

'Cherries, it has cherries in it. No, it's musk. I can't think of the name.'

'Evidently, Piers! I must have your final answer.'

'Oh, um, er... Flowers of the garden.'

'Incorrect.' Swiss Franc booms in an over the top, deep announcer voice.

Lord Battenberg pipes up out of nowhere. 'Umm… hint of green, floral overtones. Citrus I would hasten a guess at Christalle Eau Verte.'

'Batty…I mean Lord Battenberg, it is not open season. The question is for Piers only. Only Piers can answer it. But that happens to be the correct answer.'

Sian looks at Batty with astonishment, her mouth in disbelief, then she turns her attention on Piers, and the look is quite different. How could he even get the basics wrong of her everyday smell?

'Cherries? Musk? Do you even have nostrils?' If she had a bludgeon at hand she would use it vigorously.

Piers's is all too aware of the camera and stifles his reaction to her cold insult.

'I've never been good with smells, you know that darling. Couldn't get on at the wine club at college either.'

'I'm not a bouquet. I'm your fiancée.'

Once again we're all riveted, we know this will make great television.

'You're obviously missing the point.'

'Precisely, we're missing the points entirely. That is the point of the game. POINTS! Simple concept really.'

'Darling don't fret. A mere oversight of love, insignificant to what love is,' Piers thinks he's winning imaginary points from a non-existent public audience, performing the right clichés for the camera.

Another precious moment caught on camera. They are staring at each other as aliens would across time travel.

Gripping stuff.

'Sian, please, follow me to the box.' Swiss Franc's tone is eerily serious. Sian's skin flares up to red alert; as a redhead, she looks super angry. All the contestants look on in fear. No one knows what's in there.

We don't see the interior monitors from outside; Stefan and the crew have them set up in the hotel conference room with Alastair and a few others. The team has been split today. Jake is bouncing between the two, not that I'm watching him!

'Arghhhh, you're an utter rat Piers. I'm going to throw up. I can't do it anymore. Let me out.'

Sian's scream is blood curdling, what the hell is in there?

'To regain the point you must hold it for one minute.' Swiss Franc's voiceover sends shivers down all of our spines.

'Oh… No. Take me out. I can't. Take me out. I'm going to

be… *Get me out now!*' We all hear the gagging and shivering.

'Sian, think about what's at stake. Yes you can.'

Our stomachs drop, it sounds like real torture.

'C'mon Sian. It's not like touching Simon Cowell!' The crew crack up at Swiss Franc's non-wavering snipes. He knows what's going on in there, so I tell myself it can't actually be proper torture. Where's Mel gone? I look all over for her, and then see a dotty leopard print bouncing towards me.

'Eve.' She pants.

'Where have you been Mel?' I whisper.

'Oh my god Eve. It's revolting.'

'What is?'

'What Sian is holding.'

'Mel you're being even more cryptic than Swiss Franc.'

'It's called a hagfish, the most disgusting thing I've ever seen.'

I retch, I know what a hagfish is. I always watch QI when I can't sleep. *Yuk, yuk and hurl.*

'That's what the jelly ball people are. They've got loads of them.'

'Slime pus producer is more apt. I bet they're going to put the slime into the tunnel.' Both of us shudder.

'Poor Sian, her phobia is eel-like creatures and she's scared of even swimming in the sea because of them.'

Sian steps out. She did it, her face is traumatised and at the other end of the colour spectrum, ashen and pale.

Swiss Franc gets her back in the circle, his arm round her shoulders practically holding her up.

'Sian, are you ready for your question about Piers?' Sian's eyes pierce Piers with intent only reserved for pure vengeance. Piers is visibly sweating, loosening the collar on his stuffy chequered shirt. He approaches Sian in trepidation. She steps back into Swiss Franc's arm; you can hear her inner hissing. Piers backs away speechless and fakes a smile. I have a feeling that even if Sian knows the answer she'll waiver it for revenge.

Love, eh? The building blocks are unstable at the best of times.

The crew are edging in to see what she does.

'Sian, your question about your fiancé, the love of your life, your ultimate partner, the man of your dreams,' he is goading the rift well.

'Your question is…' he creates even more drama by stilting the timing. 'To get back in the game… The question is…'

Sian just glares at Piers. Her eyes haven't left him since getting back in the ring.

'If Piers had the choice of backing a bill about gay adoption, which way would he vote?'

Sian regains colour and her evil twin takes over. She knows, she definitely knows.

'Sian I need your answer.'

'That's a no-brainer Swiss Franc.'

'That might be so Sian. But would it be a yes vote or a no vote?'

'Well being the well-loved politician that he is, of course he is a humanist.' Piers is sweating, his tie is a mess, he's still trying to loosen a collar that won't get any looser.

'He would vote YES!' Piers physically shakes. He tries to remain cool, but Sian's smile vanquishes revenge. I look around; the psychologists are muttering to one another and the pipe, beardy man (Mel and I can never remember his name, bit odd…Tarquin, Tolken, Tolstoy?) nods his head. They're a bit like Bond villains seeing a plan hatch.

Brian is smiling. Jet looks perturbed, when he's not inflicted with the love-bug he's inflicted with the pugs! Can't tell which it is at the moment.

Swiss Franc steps dramatically towards Piers.

'Is that the correct answer Piers?' He knows it's not, he's seeing if Piers will lie.

Piers's eyes flicker, for a moment. 'Yes, that is correct.'

Sian would blow steam if she could.

'You liar... He's lying!' Sian shrieks.

'Piers is that true?' Swiss Franc asks with fake earnestness.

'Is what true? What she said or I?'

'The truth,' he commands, knowing he's confused.

'Yes,' Piers replies meekly.

'Yes, that you would vote yes? Or yes that Sian was correct?'

All the crew are confused, the contestants even more, it's bloody funny at the same time as being stomach wrenching.

'Yes that you lied, or yes to gay rights?' We're all aware of Pier's repugnant attitude to gay people. It was part of the initial interview process when they questioned him, as at that point we had our lovely gay couple in line to compete. Piers went mad when he heard he might be competing with a same-sex couple. The man deserves whatever he gets now.

His lips purse, and through his teeth he hisses. 'Yes to gay rights.'

One of the psychologists is whispering to Sian off-screen.

Swiss Franc stands fixed with the microphone under Piers's chin. You could cut the atmosphere with a blunt machete. He waits, just staring at Piers and his accumulating sweat. Of course Piers's punishment was admitting to that on camera, far more hurtful to him than any forfeit in the black box.

'Well of course it is. Sian and Piers have regained some

points, next up are Kimberly and Batty…Lord Batten…' Kimberly springs into the close-up camera and Swiss Franc has to pull her out the way, as she's blocking it entirely. Battenberg is watching an old propeller plane in the distance.

'Err… Lord Battenberg would you mind?'

We all laugh.

'Bloody Bristol that was.'

'Fascinating as that may be Lord Battenberg...' Swiss Franc is revelling in his eccentricity.

'Haven't seen one of those since I was a boy with Father.' Batty chomps down on his pipe still looking dreamily at the distance. Swiss Franc gestures down the camera with mad quizzical eyebrows.

'Quite.'

'Marvellous… just marvellous, where were we old chap?'

'Kimberly is just about to answer a question about you.' The crew are in stitches and Swiss Franc is actually having a hard time trying not to laugh.

'Questions? That gal couldn't answer a questionnaire on herself,' Batty scoffs.

'Battenberg, you tease,' Kimberly feigns affection.

'My dear, you couldn't answer one of *The Times*'s crossword questions the other day.'

'Not cryptic questions, Lord Battenberg, a personal question,' Swiss Franc patronises, trying to reel him back into reality; well our reality program, so is that reality? A question for another day I think.

'Personal question?'

'Yes Lord Battenberg.'

'But that by the very merit of the description - personal. No, no, no… you shouldn't be asking those sorts of questions on camera. This is a movie camera isn't it?' Batty says prodding the camera with his cane. Mel and I are giggling like school-girls. You would think this would be the easier of the games… not when Batty's about.

'I shan't answer if I deem it off the mark old chap.'

'Right, Lord Batty-berg. Just stand there and listen to Kimberly,' Swiss Franc roots him to a spot; he's still looking for the Bristol.

'Kimberly are you ready?'

'Sure Swiss Franc, I was born ready,' We all cringe; she is truly abhorrent.

'For the point, what has Lord Battenberg's family crest got in the centre of it?'

'Well that's not personal, that's public knowledge, historically documented. Go on gal, that's far easier than a crossword.' Batty mumbles on still, not fully grasping the rules. Swiss Franc grabs his arm, whispers to him to 'shhhh.' By the look on Kimberly's face I expect this question doesn't bode well, for her or the viewers, unless she's faking it? Nah… she's not that good an actress. Mel looks at me and we both stare at Kimberly; she's definitely making the most of being in the spotlight. After five hair flicks, two giggles and seven pouts, Swiss Franc's had enough.

'I must rush you now for your answer Kimberly, and may I remind you the controller has switched the forfeit receiver for this round.'

'What the****?' Swiss Franc manages to drown out her profanities by stepping in front of her.

'Come on dear, easier than shooting guinea fowl.'

'I must ask you to remain silent Lord Battenberg,' Swiss Franc squeezes his arm.

'Frightfully sorry old boy.'

'Less of the old!'

'Can't pull the wool over these old eyes. I've stuffed bears with better hair than that.' Wooah, we're all waiting with bated breath Swiss Franc's retort.

'Hanging on a wall since colonial times. The Rise and Demise of the Raj was exactly what I was going for!'

Batty chuffs out an old buzzard laugh. 'Touché old bean, touché.'

In the meantime, Kimberly is trying to see if Battenberg is wearing his ring, which of course has been removed from his left pinkie.

'Now, Kimberly, your answer, please.'

'Guinea pigs.'

'You fool! It's guinea fowl not pigs. No wonder we sent you lot overseas. Bloody disgrace to the empire.' Battenberg is shaking his head.

'Thank you Lord Batty…berg, your commentary has been sufficient.'

Battenberg couldn't care less but Kimberly is fuming.

'I won't go in there.'

'Rules of engagement Miss Roberts.' Swiss Franc voices for the camera, pleased with his play on words.

Forcefully, he takes her arm and leads her to the box, a spoilt brat in a tantrum springs to mind.

Mel and I run towards the green room. We can't wait to see her suffer, if we're being honest. Well she's hardly the endearing type, what would you expect? The others, whether you like them or not, have shown some signs of humility, but her and Piers are stomach-turning in their self-promotion.

We hear the final "Steve" shove and slam of the door before

we reach the hotel.

The grand double-door down the hallway has a sign on it saying "no entry"; Mel and I slip in hardly opening it, and no one notices as they are all glued to the monitor.

We sit on a table at the back just so we can see over the many heads that have gathered round. Jake turns; I pretend not to see him.

'I'm not doing it, I'll stay in here until you all get bored.' Kimberly is still kicking up.

'Kimberly you will be taken off the shoot, all footage removed and made to pay the penalty of $20.000.' Swiss Franc is very stern in his delivery you *would* do anything he asked. The guy can pull anything out of the hat at any given moment. What a skill to possess.

'I'll answer one more question. Then I'll do it if I get the next one wrong.'

'Kimberly there is no negotiation. Either do it or pay the penalty.'

My eyes try to work out what's inside the box. I can only make out a table with a bowl on it. What's in the bowl? Oh god this is exciting stuff, Mel is gripped; well, we're all gripped to see what it is.

Kimberly continues to huff and puff for a further five minutes; luckily this isn't live.

'You have five minutes left to complete your forfeit Kimberly.' He starts a clock on the outside.

'Don't know what the filly is making such a fuss about, it's only…–'

'Yes, thank you Lord Batty-berg. You have to shhh here too and remain shhhh.' For some reason Batty responds to Swiss Franc's shhh and squeeze technique, so the secret is still safe.

The television company would be stupid not to commission this; if the crew are on the edge of their seats with half of them in the know, how will the home audience be riveted. There will be silence sweeping across the UK at 9pm.

'I won't do it.'

'Better get your cheque book out then Ms Roberts.'

We see Kimberly grab something on the table and throw it in the bowl; we can hear a faint murmur, a wobbly top lip perhaps?

We bend forward trying to see what Kimberly has to douse on her face. 'I'm going to have to start counting you down Kimberly,' Swiss Franc turns up the volume of the ticking clock. We see Kimberly rub at her face, either fake crying or actually crying; it's difficult to know what's real with her.

'Your time is up Ms Roberts, please exit the box.' Mel and I are still unsure what she had to do in it.

Kimberly moves towards the door tussling with her hair. Swiss Franc opens the door slowly; she's just about to run when he grabs her arm. The crew, contestants and us all gasp in unison.

'Happy, now?' Kimberly stomps off, pushing people out her way as she goes; Batty doesn't bat an eyelid, and shifts his feet towards Sian.

Mel and I stare at each other in disbelief. So that's how Kimberly looks with no make-up on. If you hadn't guessed it already, Kimberly was made to take off all her face gunk. Her sad spiralling journey is evident on her bare face, from the excessive partying, the drug abuse, the bodged nose job, all of it has wrecked her youth and now she is left with a bloated face and unnatural expression. Why oh why did she get fillers in her cheeks? And the lip injections make her lips look too puffy for her face; even her eyebrows have been plucked out of existence (I feel quite protective over my own wayward eyebrow now).

That's it, I am never going to get my lips injected or have cheek fillers, EVER!

Vanity has its price and that price is high. But the reaction is perfect and Stefan has acres of footage to play around with.

I feel a pang of sympathy for Kimberly as she's never been seen like that, unguarded and natural, all remnants of what was once natural now gone, and all that's left behind are the bad choices she's made. If she was a nice person, I would want to go over and give her a hug, but she's not. Maybe there's some truth in the fact that those people who are insecure are often mean spirited to solely make themselves feel better. I can't figure out why else you would lose your temper over something so minor. Perhaps she might change her ways? The game has done its job too, making us think and discuss. Alastair looks as pleased as punch.

Mel and I return outside as the crew set up the next box forfeit. We notice the contestants are quiet, still in shock. The drama is high.

Swiss Franc is getting powdered by his gaggle of girls and Batty is watching with keen interest; he hasn't had a make up brush near him the whole time, wafting the make up team away every time they ever dared to go near him. I do like Batty, he's honest with his treachery. Swiss Franc and Batty are talking about some old war and Batty's in his element. What an unlikely camaraderie to spring from an odd situation.

Everything is ready for the next couple, Stacy and Brick. They both look serious, but I think Brick is just copying Stacy.

'Stacy what was Brick's first major football injury?' We all expect Stacy and Brick to breeze this one. So Mel and I decide to get a soda from the tent, all this excitement makes you thirsty. We move out from the back quietly, tiptoeing out of camera shot, then a sweeping sense of self-consciousness stops us both in our mouse steps. There is a deathly silence, and Mel and I look at one another thinking we've somehow trashed the shot. Our heads slowly peer back; relieved we haven't got an audience of a thousand eyes staring across the garden at us, and we remain still to see what's going on. Crikey, Stacy hasn't answered yet and she is sweating profusely. Wow. Physically you can see she's been affected by previous results, she's blanking. There's no way Stacy wouldn't know everything.

"Stacy's frozen." I can hear the crew from the tent. Mel and I creep back in to watch what is going on.

Brick tries to look reassuring but she's having a panic attack. Her breathing is irregular.

Swiss Franc, instead of making a quip, goes and puts his arm round her, looking her straight in the face and whispering something. She takes a huge breath, but chokes on a cough. He gets water, sits her down on the ground until she breaths evenly again. The medic is on hand.

'Fuck, who would have thought Stacy would crumble?' Mel looks shocked.

'I think the psychologists have planned this down to the tee. Stacy would never have frozen if they were first up.'

'You're right Eve,' Mel looks concerned.

'Terribly clever really, drama on top of drama.'

'Feels cruel,' Mel says.

'Mel, no one forced them to play.'

'I know, just feels a bit…'

'I know what you mean, but isn't that the point of reality

TV? See what comes out in the wash?'

'Yeah. This game is good isn't it?'

'Bloodyhell, yeah!'

With Stacy recovered, filming resumes. Of course now they have to change the question.

Much discussion is going on inside the tent; Alastair, Jake and Brian have come out.

'Brick doesn't have any big phobias or secrets. Basically Brick is an open book. We only had an endurance thing for him. We'll have to swap them around now.' Jake says all matter of fact.

'I don't think we can put Stacy through anything stressful at the minute. The medic is concerned.' Alastair adds.

'So what the hell are we supposed to do?' Brian snaps.

'Why don't you let Daphne and Patrick go instead, then Stacy will be calmer and maybe there will be no need to swap,' my thoughts just spring out even though I'm not in the discussion.

'That's an idea Eve,' Alastair beams at me. Jake nods his head in contemplation, very professionally I might add. Maybe it won't be so difficult to work around the sex god after all.

'I know the psycho team planned it down to the detail but at least you'd get all the game shot. To be fair you've got the dramatic ones already. Daphne and Patrick will be off the wall but will know the answers on each other more than any of them. Stacy will feel far more relaxed by then,' I continue with my thought.

'What's the point of paying psychologists is you're not going to follow their instructions?' Brian scowls out of spite. If I said black, he'd say blue.

'So you'd rather not complete? Lose more footage. It's just a tiny adjustment. But not much point filming at all if it actually causes harm Brian, is there?' I snap back, Mel takes a sharp breath in and I see a few eyes widen in the crew.

'Precisely,' Jake backs me up.

'Right lets get on with Eve's plan people,' Alastair rallies everyone back to his or her posts.

The rest of the filming is calm, Swiss Franc has a lot of tongue-in-cheek comments about Daphne and Patrick, and Stacy even giggles at him. She starts to relax and we complete shooting the game. Daphne and Patrick are the winners, Brick couldn't answer what Stacy's favourite philosopher was… well, he did answer, but mispronounced the name completely. Brick takes the forfeit instead of Stacy (on recommendation from the medics) and the make-up girls are happy to see strength and sweat in action. Because there is no tie, the tunnels aren't used, and because of the delays, Jake decides to call it a day. By the time we finish it's past nine. It only takes me five minutes to reach my room and I flop back on the bed in exhaustion.

I must have fallen asleep because when I wake up, Mel is dressed for bed and snuggling under her duvet. 'Sorry, did I wake you?'

'What time is it?' I say.

'Ten I think.'

I sit up, my stomach grumbling. Remembering I put a banana and a packet of cheese and onion crisps in my bag, I get out of bed.

'Shall I turn off the light?'

'Don't worry I'm going to be out like a light as soon as this head hits the pillow,' Mel replies.

Nonetheless, I turn off the main light and switch on the

bedside lamp, grab the crisps and banana, devour both almost simultaneously and check my phone. No text from Jake, but then he did have the meeting with the guy from the BBC this evening. I flick onto Facebook, scrolling aimlessly down my news feed, when something pricks my interest. There's a photo of Lucy and Chuck dressed up in Star Wars costumes, his Obi-Wan cloaked arm around her Princess Leia tunic, their faces filled with laughter. They look ridiculously happy. I stare at it for a while longer; do they not realise how right they are for each other?

I comment on the photo, "The real stellar of Love, Obi-Wan's deepest guarded secret coming in Star Wars 8" and I press "Like". Lucy will have a comment to say about that for sure. But I know what I'm actually doing. I'm pretending not to be waiting for Jake to call.

I give myself a mental slap and go brush my teeth.

He's not going to call, it's far too late and the day has been torturously long. I need to shut off and get back to sleep.

I scoop up a handful of water in a vague attempt to remove the grime of the day and rub a towel roughly across the dripping fatigued-bitten face. Picking up a fat tub of cream, I splodge on far too much moisturiser that will take at least a week to absorb.

I change into my PJs and climb back into bed, lying there with a face heavily laden with gunk. I can't turn otherwise I'll stick to the pillow and therefore I won't be able to sleep. Tired as I am, the restlessness is starting to irritate me and I don't want to disturb Mel's sleep. She needs a good night sleep after Brian gave her so much unnecessary stress today. I sit up and pick up *Lord of the Flies* from my bedside table.

A buzzing sound flits in my ear; some insect must have got

in via the balcony doors. *Buzz...* I swat the air, roll over, then realise that page 237 is stuck to my face. Oh bugger, I've fallen asleep.

Buzz...buzz...buzz...zzzz...buzzz.....

My eyes snap open, my phone is lit up with one missed call and two messages containing question marks.

Barely breathing, I look across at Mel; she hasn't stirred at all, thank goodness. A booty call or a booty text, the two are interchangeable if you ask me.

What to do?

It really is late and I'm in my PJs, I've taken my make up off, my face now replaced by a slimy mask dotted with ink print, and I've got to get up early in the morning. My eyes focus on the first message,

You up?

Should I reply, "I can be if you are?" And by up I mean... you know.

I *Umm* and *Ahh* for a few minutes, my hand sticking to different parts of my face with different adhesive strengths. It's tempting but I'm far from attractive and too close to being cream-crackered. I try ignoring my phone but -

Who am I kidding! Of course I'm going.

I slip quietly out of bed and pad to the bathroom, closing the door carefully and switching on the bathroom light.

I sit on the loo and read the second message.

Jake again:

Hope you're awake. It would be nice to see you for another night. Probably too late☹"

A booty message it may be, but the newly-awakened Eve doesn't care; domesticity and regularity have only given her grief, this is far more satisfying.

I reply:

See you in five minutes.

A Cheshire-cat grin spreads over my face and then I frown at that unprepared reflection. Oh dear, my hair is a mess and my face is slick of goo. I start washing the copious layers off and set about reapplying my make up, subtlety, so not to look like I have tried too hard, but what to wear? A dilemma that womankind will ponder about even in space-time travel for eons to come. Even if modern civilisation is uniformed and homogenous, women will find something to fret over on appearance, even if it is cyber glasses, arm shapes or lens colours! They'll probably rotate their social diary depending on the moon's luminosity, in tune to the reflective quality of their space skin tone… ok stop procrastinating.

I have an idea.

Only now as I knock on Jake's door I'm kind of half-hoping he's not going to be there. Why oh why did I think this was a good idea?

I didn't realise how naked I would feel under my coat. Perhaps because I am naked!

At least I haven't bumped into anyone I know. How would I have explained the rain mac and spikey heels indoors? Or for that matter, why I am knocking on the Jake's door?

Before I can bottle it, the door opens and I'm ushered in like a wanted criminal.

His eyes rake over what I am wearing and his eyebrows rise.

I give him what I hope is a sexy smile. His hair is messy, his eyes bright but a little bloodshot.

'Hello Mr Richards,' I say, feeling rather stupid now and aware that my cheeks are burning.

'Good evening Miss Poots.' he replies.

I step into the centre of the room. Jake closes the door behind him, when he turns to me I let my coat slip off.

Jake gives me a wickedly hungry grin and I feel less like an idiot. I strike a pose, adding a sexy come-hither hip jut. My effort, or somewhat lack of it, has the desired effect.

Jake gazes at my nakedness (well, except for the bejewelled sparkly knickers from the Hurly Burly girls – who would have known they'd come in handy so soon!) His gaze is so intent that desire pools in those glitzy knickers.

He walks towards me and I stand where I am, trying to be confident, and sexy, only my heart is pounding really hard, even more than last night's asthmatic attack.

He stops in front of me. In my high heels I'm almost eye-level with him. I brush my mouth against his, pulling him closer to kiss him roughly. He grabs me round the waist and shifts his thigh between my legs, pressing up against me. I can feel his erection so big and hard that I moan into his mouth. Wow, this feels good.

At first I am on top of him, wrestling with his belt buckle and zip, then somehow I am on my back being overpowered. How did he get his jeans and pants off so quickly? He pulls my knickers down, the sequins scratch my legs and I don't care. He takes one look and slowly runs his hands over the scratches, easing up to my throbbing *CLITORIS* (there I said it!) The sensation of his fingers on my naked damp skin is so intense that I scream in delight when they enter me, as he continues to kiss me hard.

My God, I think dizzily. Here we go again, it's even more intense than last night. My body shudders violently. Ahhh-ggg…Bliss, no wonder all the poetry.

Jake pulls on a condom and then he is back, lifting me up

and pulling me down on top of him, as he thrusts deep inside me, and all I can do is cling on, damp faced against his damp shoulder, his cock hitting the right spot every single time, his power rubbing on my ecstasy. We are both utterly concentrated. It takes barely a few minutes for me to reach orgasm, and Jake is right there with me, again and again as we both twitch and spasm.

We collapse against each other.

'Gosh,' I mumble into his skin, breathing in the heady mixture of leather, orange, and hotel soap.... And yes he does taste as good as he smells, I think to myself.

Will I orgasm like that every time I am with him?

I make a small protesting noise as he slides out of me. We lay back down on the bed, breathing hard, facing each other. He pulls off the condom and wipes himself with the sheet, hardly taking his eyes off my face through the whole process.

'Sorry, I don't know what came over me,' he says.

'Well, theoretically you came over yourself.'

He bursts out laughing.

'I need to touch you,' he whispers as his fingers wander over my swollen lady bit. Slowly he starts to circle around it and, within seconds I'm arching in the horny ecstasy again. He keeps going until I pounce up and pin him to the bed; by that time he's ready for second helpings, I grab another condom from the bedside table and work it on.

I ride him hard, my only aim is to reach that higher plateau, nothing in my mind apart from feeling the pleasure intensify with every thrust. I lean forward prohibiting his movement and he just groans in delight. He pulls my head down and says, 'stop I'm going to...' Too late, his body shudders uncontrollably and I feel empowered, my body's senses electrified on full power.

'I'm buzzing all over,' I say, resting my head against his warm chest.

'Well if you're buzzing, I've just blown all my fuses!'

His eyes crease up, that's a man who is truly satisfied. I'm still in awe of the look.

Two very happy faces sharing a look, glistening in sweat. I must look like the Cheshire cat who owns the entire dairy.

Why is it that a man I barely know can make me lose all sense about myself? I am too busy revelling in the sensation of his touch and the intention behind his every move to worry whether or not he thinks I should have bigger boobs or any of the other hang-ups I usually suffer with. He makes me feel desired. He holds the key to a room I've never ventured in. I know it's just sex, and yet… if we're this sexually compatible then what's to stop us continuing this when we get back home? It works out well on that level, and the fact that he makes my inner workings work, then it could all work, and we could work.

We lay in each other's arms, stroking and caressing each other until we're both dozing. I'm sure I just heard a morning call from the birds. I drift off with possibly the world's biggest smile. The birdsong gets louder, and one eye reluctantly flicks open.

CHAPTER TWENTY-THREE

I pick up another pile of lever-arch folders and place them in the box, sticking a label on it, then start on another box.

I leave Mel's desk alone, but everything else that's not fixed down or hotel property I box and label. I'm missing out on today's filming, but the runner Pete has been begging for a chance to get on set, so I sent him off. I'm actually relieved that I have something mundane to do. I need distracting, and if I was on set I wouldn't be able to keep my eyes or hands off Jake and then everyone would know our secret.

Last night, well the sex was mind-blowing, obviously, and we had quite a giggle messing about in the water so to speak. I left his room in the last minutes of the morning, and due to that fact the bags under my eyes feel like they're holding a kilo of potatoes, but it's been totally worth it. I don't feel silly around Jake, well maybe a little awkward at times, but as soon as I'm alone with him that dissipates quicker than butter on a hot griddle. One thing that has come of this is that I'm not afraid of sex anymore; quite the contrary, I'm ravenous for more.

To stop my thoughts from wandering into dangerous

territory I put pen to paper and scribble down all the things I need to do for the short Mel and I are going to produce. My thoughts are beautiful, how fitting that my first independent project is called *Beautiful*. I sit there day dreaming about it all when my phone rings.

It's my mother.

She never rings me, unless it's to tell me about other's triumphs, outright successes, forthcoming marriages, tell me off about my otherwise perfect behaviour, or she wants me to buy something for her over the Internet.

'I'm working.'

'That's good…' I'm used to my mother ignoring anything I say, so with a tried-and-tested learnt discipline, in bad daughter fashion, I lay the phone down, put it on loudspeaker and continue what I was doing.

'You have to wear something a little more um…' as with any conversation with my mother, it starts mid conversation. 'More sophisticated, something with grace not emblems, emblems are for achievement not wayward decoration.'

'Have you just phoned to give me a fashion lesson Mother?' My voice is terse (as all you daughters know, you're not being disrespectful and it doesn't insult them, just makes them more eager to say the same point fifty ways over!)

'Oh you know what I mean, if you were in a society, a fold, you'd have purpose, a belonging, and then you could wear a slogan that others shared. I don't know what half your wardrobe means.'

'It's not supposed to mean anything to you, you're old.'

'Eve, that's a rather rotten way of explaining yourself.'

'That's my point.'

'What is?'

'Because you're not twenty you don't know what they mean.'

'So all twenty-year-olds know what you're about by some meaningless print on a T-short?'

'It's T-shirt mother.'

'Yours are all too short…' I turn down the volume and grunt every so often to make her think I'm agreeing or listening. It's not really essential trying to explain the finer lines in life to my mother.

Just as I've managed to zone her out, her voice changes and zones me the hell back in.

'So I've signed you up and your duties–'

'What?' I stutter. 'What have you done?'

'Really, Eve, your concentration is shocking, have you been taking the medicine I sent you?'

'Mother I'm not about to take some dodgy pills from an American charlatan.'

'Really Eve, he has a following of thousands.'

'Read that on his own website did you?'

'He's a most reputable man of God. He wrote a lovely letter back when I said you'd lost your way and mind.'

'You did what?'

'One does have one's own crosses to bear.'

'So now I'm a cross?'

'Metaphorically speaking, I suppose you are.'

'I thought you didn't agree with metaphors, emblems and throwaway symbols! And how much did you pay for my saviour with pilgrim pills?'

'Eve don't get caught up in the small stuff.'

'That much, eh?'

'They've been blessed in the holy water of Ziah.'

'And what the fff… flipping heck is Ziah when it's at home.'

I stop, I've got to hear this one. *Is Ziah flipping Zod's BFF?*

'Ziah channels God's thoughts.'

'Does it now?'

'Yes she does.'

'Oooo equal opportunities happening in heaven now?'

'You're being purposely blasphemous.'

'How come Ziah isn't in the holy book then mother?'

'Eve, God must find his soldiers now on earth too.'

'Interesting use of words mother! Did you know all wars are mostly caused by fictional beliefs?'

'Eve are you having a bad day? Shall I phone in an hour?' Her usual default when you start pointing out real fact.

'Actually, mother, I was having a pretty fantastic day until I was interrupted with madness.'

'Those television people are godless and quite mad, poor you. You should find a place and pray in peace for five minutes.'

'How ironic you find TV people godless, that's where your idols make their money mother dear.'

'Well, well… Sunday is for the cleansing.'

'What? What are you on about now?'

'Really Eve, write things down, Sunday's your expulsion of the devil's work. We'll do it by the river at Pastor Pickles house.'

'And who's idea was this? Ziah's?'

'Oh you did listen, good.'

'Mother.'

'Got to go now, got things to organise.'

'MOTHER!'

'Eve you've been on this phone far too long, that's why you never keep a job.'

'This is my first proper job!'

'Two o'clock. Sunday. On the dot. Don't be late and wear something floral or feminine for a change.'

'MOTHER!'

'What is it dear, I really must go.'

'Number one,' I keep my voice steady and low. 'I am not coming and being part of this circus…'

'Now now…'

'NUMBER TWO, I do NOT and have NOT believed in GOD since I was seven, and even at five it was a push, a secret struggle because I had reason. Thought, deduction and a logical mind! Anything that causes so much pain and misery in the world is not the organisation for me. DO I MAKE MYSELF CLEAR?' Silence, I hear a weird breathy whimper from the receiver.

'We all have bad days Eve, but we don't shout like a banshee just because of it.'

'NO, NO… NO MORE. I will not indulge in the make-believe world that is your life, just blow any inheritance we're gonna get on Ziah. See how the return on investment is when you need groceries, doctors and someone to play bridge with because you're too darn old to cope! See how Ziah sits with you and makes your twilight years more comfortable or talk at him through your cheque book because that's all they're interested in!'

She hangs up, my skin's tingling in anger. It was about time, ok it was rough, but I've put up with it all my life and I can't take anymore, being roped into the biggest scam on earth. I return to my beloved boxing up, something that makes sense. No more than fifteen minutes goes past and I get a text from Nell.

'Whatever you said has caused panic with the pious!!'

Trinngggg, another message. My phone is quite the hotspot at the moment.

'Eve it's Dad… Is it all right if we support our parish with a token donation for the spire and new bell? We've decided to concentrate our efforts with those around us. Your mother's had a flight of doubt with these evangelists and she is asking for her money back.'

I wonder how that happened?

Good grief, finally some reasonable Christian behaviour. How on earth… my Dad is a bit of an 'anything for a peaceful life of goodness and charity' type.

'Sounds sensible Dad. Nell and I will help you to get out of the monthly payments. I'm sure none of it is legal in this country and the contract is suitably confusing.'

'Seems like they've been taking double of what we said.'

'I know a lawyer. Get all the papers ready.'

'Good girl Eve… oh and thank you.'

'Gotta go Dad last day and very busy.'

'☺ luck. Cannot wait 2 hear all about it.' I love it when my dad attempts text speak.

Wow what a difference a rant makes!

With everything said and done, knowing that my parents are back on the road to a sliver of sanity, I make Stefan a coffee and beg him into show me a clip from *Wedding Wipeout.*

He shows me a B-clips when Kimberley tries to touch up Brick, and Piers keeps badgering Batty for an endorsement into a London gentleman's club for contacts of money, and I can't help wonder what sort of monster we've created. The liars, the cheaters and their amazing ability to justify their behaviour; it's unthinkable, and yet addictively watchable.

Just seeing it edited and a little bit polished I know we're onto a winner.

Being engaged should be amazing; you should know the partner so well and yet I doubt any of them, except for Daphne and Patrick, will actually get married.

'What are you doing in here?' comes a flat male voice.

I jump in my skin.

'So this is where you're hiding.'

'I wasn't hiding,' I reply.

'I asked Eve's opinion on a clip,' says Stefan, coming to my rescue.

'It may have escaped your notice but we're shooting and you need to get your effing arse out there and deal with stuff,' he sneers.

I bite my lips, as tears sneak into my eyes. I hold them back. I refuse to cry in front of him.

'No time like the present,' he says more or less directing me out the room. I look at Stefan, and when Brian isn't looking he gives me a wink.

I follow Brian out into the large anteroom (stroke) office, and walk back to my desk.

At times like this, I wish I could tell him what I really think of him, but I can't risk it, not with *Beautiful* and *Comatosed* on the horizon.

That weasel will not get the better of me.

'And while you're actually doing something for a change, man the phones, and you can read this and write up a report.'

It's a script. I stare at him in surprise.

'You're giving me a script?

'Well done Sherlock. Sharp aren't you.'

Maybe he is coming around and actually listening to the

opinions of others after all.

'Alastair and I are in agreement it's got a lot of potential. I just need you to write up a report, any suggestions for polishing.'

'You've read it?'

'Of course I have. But I haven't got time to write up a report. So you can do that.'

'Er okay...er...thanks... I mean thank you.' My words fumble out like a bluebottle trying to get out of a window.

'Hop to it then!' he says forcing it to sound like a snipe.

Brian leaves me alone for the rest of the day as I read the script, and then read it again trying to work out where the brilliant part of it is. Did Alastair really think this was good? It's not all bad but it's like it's been written in haste. I decide to be true to my own voice and write a script report. I'm just re-reading the report when Mel wanders in with sauce all down her top.

'What are you doing?'

'I'm manning the phones.'

'Eh, why?'

'Brian told me to.'

'But I've got all calls diverted to my mobile with the hotspot coverage.'

'No wonder the phone hasn't been ringing.'

'He also asked me to do the report for this.'

I put my report and script onto Brian's desk.

'Did you know you've got sauce down your top?'

'What? Oh that's erm, must have been the pickle. Anyway I've got some fabulous news. The show's been commissioned.'

I jump up and start leaping about the room with Mel. 'Though don't say anything. I mean it's not official yet. I think they'll announce it at the wrap party. Roger was delighted with the footage he saw yesterday.'

'So I'm staying with you for another six months.'

'Yay!' We both do a jiggy dance around the room.

I wonder if Jake will do any more? I know it's not really his thing but maybe he'll do another episode. My mind starts going through sexy scenarios in the workplace. I have to stop myself fantasizing and get back to reality; a bit of slap and tickle on set is probably all he wanted. I'm just a distraction at best. And he's a pleasant one, too. Leave it alone Eve - it will all go wrong if you start having expectations.

'And Alastair has said that I will have the assistant producer's role. Just one snag.'

'Brian.' We chorus.

We then spend another hour getting the wrap party set up. Mel and Jet have already done most of it, organised the music, lighting, and the bigger-than-life-sized photographs of the contestants arrived this morning. Hanging up a giant Kimberly and Piers is scary, Batty sort of fits the setting though.

When we've finished, the room is transformed. The small stage has been set up with a microphone stand. On either side of the room are two long bars. It's just up to the caterers to dress the trestle tables and lay out the food. Everything looks beautiful when we leave it. With only forty minutes to get ready for the party, Mel and I rush back to our rooms to set about the arduous task of glamming our tired selves up.

Halfway through undressing, Mel steps into the room with a sneaky gin and tonic.

'Thank you darling… maybe a little appetiser for Dutch courage.'

'Why would you need Dutch courage?'

'Isn't that a good excuse for a drink?' I say. 'Wowser, that is strong.' One of my eyeballs has literally rolled back into my head.

'Flip, isn't it just.' Mel says.

The next forty minutes are spent dutifully shaving my legs, showering, blow-drying my hair (and gin-splashed clothes) then slurping down the remaining gin, and finally putting on some makeup. I am eternally grateful to the inventor of concealer; makeup hides a multiple of sins, and mine are plenty this week in more ways than one. I slip on the powder blue silk-satin mini dress I bought from *Topshop Unique*. Short but not too short, it's off the shoulders and nipped in at the waist.

'You look very pretty.'

'Thanks, so do you.'

Her halter neck black dress with it's back slash perfectly fits her gymnastic frame.

I sit down and pull on my bootie-heels, then sashay across the room, feeling happy.

I so love dressing up, it makes me feel ready for anything.

CHAPTER 24

The orangery is twinkling in an array of coloured fairy lights; the grand candelabras illuminate the buffet and bar. The high-arched windows look magical in all the flickering light. This is a proper old orangery dating back to when the hotel was built I guess, not a decorative conservatory like I thought it was when the hotel manager suggested it.

"*How are we going to fit all the people, cast and crew in a conservatory,*" I asked myself, but had enough sense not to voice it at the time; would have made myself look pig ignorant and unsophisticated, not an image I want to continue throughout life.

There's a huge terrace outside, down some grand stone steps. The gardeners in this place are sheer genius, every pot hedge is a different animal. I hadn't even seen this part of the garden before. It has a walled bit at the end and a maze. Although I do remember that the maze would be used for another game if we got commissioned. The terrace has been lined with open-flamed torches, and I feel like I've stepped into the setting of a masquerade ball. Imagine what went on here, especially in the roaring 1920's. It's impressive. A fake stone fountain has been placed at the end of one bar, Pimm's flowing down its tiers, surrounded by sliced delights of citrus fruits and cucumber. Bunches of mint have been made into a lollypop tree; it's a great idea, a brilliant one for a wedding reception!

The wrap party is just getting underway when Mel and I enter the room.

It's packed and Jake (takes me a nanosecond to locate him) is standing on the far side talking to Jet, he really is an eyeful of gorgeousness. As if sensing my presence he looks over. He smiles and I wink in return then Jet says something and his attention is drawn back to the conversation.

Alastair is in conference with Roger as Brian snakes in on them, sliming his way forward. But my eyes stray back to Jake, I can't help myself. He is wearing a suit. I've never seen him in a suit before. He looks suave, really manly, a proper man, his stubble is growing through and the few grey hair makes him look mature and drastically handsome. I realise now that if you want good sex you should go for a man not a boy. I will take that advice and spout it when I see Gudrun next, if I do indeed need to see her again. Maybe it's not necessary anymore after my discovery of what should really happen in bed. But I do owe her for getting me over the hump, so to speak!

'Just the person I'm after,' says Alastair. 'Brian showed me the report you did for Carousal?'

'Oh right.'

'And you didn't like it?'

'Well I didn't say that exactly...'

'Brian on the other hand thought it was a brilliant idea.'

'Yes the idea is good but the script needs a lot of work.'

Brian sniggers. I look at him, getting the feeling that

something is off. Brian stares back, his face is smug and snarky.

'I thought the premise was good,' I say. 'And while the idea is fully formed, the script isn't, it's not very good, you know not tight, it's as if it's been written in haste?'

'Well I did write it many moons ago.'

I gulp. 'You wrote it?'

'I thought it would make a good movie.'

I'm going to kill Brian.

'That's what I mean,' I say backpedalling. 'The premise, the idea, it's all there but the script uh…'

'Is a pile of pants. I think you said in your report.'

Why the fuck did I write that? I need to explain. I also want to throttle the life out of Brian's skinny neck.

'I also said, that if the script was re-worked with someone that, oh god, actually knew how to write, then it could be really good.'

Alastair does something unexpected he starts to roar with laughter.

I stare at him in slight shock. Brian seems just as shell-shocked.

'Thank you, for your honesty Eve!' he exclaims.

'You're not angry?'

'Not at all. Why don't you get those *Comatosed* writers to take a look at it and maybe they can sort out the mess.'

'I think that's a super idea,' I say, my chest leaping with relief. From the corner of my eye I can see a mighty perplexed Brian.

Alastair and Brian are whisked up on stage. I stand back watching. I can't help feeling that I may have caused some trouble for myself. On the one hand, Alastair does seem genuinely ok that I thought his writing was crap, but Brian just hates me, possibly more so now. My head spins in confusion. So I do the only logical thing, take a sip of my drink, trying to remain in a state of confusion.

Alastair coughs and taps the mic. 'This seems like a good time to say a few words.' A spotlight appears from nowhere and lights him up. The crowd go respectfully silent.

'I would first like to say an enormous thank you to Jake and Stefan for their endless energy and hard work. To the amazing team behind this project, from the make-up artists, to the cameramen, from the caterers, to the whole crew, every one of you. I am so extremely grateful for everyone's very hard work in the past few weeks. Thank you also to Mel, Eve and Jet for putting this bash together so beautifully.'

Everyone claps politely. Daphne whoops and Patrick gives a very supportive fist pump, which looks weird on someone who better suits an anorak teamed with train-spotting book.

'As you know this has been a huge project for a pilot game show. One of the biggest. All of you who have participated in making this project come to life have done really rather well. Did I say well, I meant awesome!' The crowd cheers and whoops at Alastair's attempts at a teen American accent, Jake laughs, Kimberly just looks down her nose as her eyebrows can't actually move anymore to show disdain.

'Let's not forget to mention that…' he pauses. 'Without such vibrant, diverse and occasionally unpredictable outcomes, our first and most wonderful contestants this project wouldn't have had such amazing results.' The crowd goes wild, I take a moment and look at everyone's happy faces; Batty comes into my peripheral view, he's studying where the Pimm's might be coming from, like a colonial colonel's first steps in the tropics. I laugh to myself, he is undoubtedly one of the funniest characters I've ever met and I've met quite a few in the house of Mummy and Daddy Jeremiah!

'I really want to thank every single one of you personally,' Alastair pauses dramatically, eyes are boring on him. 'Because without you all doing what you do best we would never have got commissioned!' He throws his arms out in gratitude and the room erupts in frenzied happiness. The high-fiving and clinking of glasses goes on and on. Mel hands me a gigantic Pimm's and we nearly slosh them all over ourselves in glee, just saving ourselves from a true Leslie Nielsen moment in *Airplane*!

The room bubbles into life with more clapping. Jake mounts the stage. I wish it was me!

'Now some of you who knew me before know what a task-master I can be, but the ones who didn't will certainly know it by now.' His humour is dry, and now that they all know he is actually joking people start to laugh.

'I'm sure Alastair has suffered his fair share of grumbling and artistic spats from me not doing what I usually do in this business.' The room is silent, Jake from day one has held a certain gravitas, people are a little in awe of him, when he's directing he means business not endless discussion, and it took a while for the crew and contestants to get used to his directness.

'But I can truly say this project has been a joy, an unexpected joy on top of that. I had some surprisingly tender moments with some extremely surprising people. Not my usual stance on a set as you might guess,' everyone laughs.

'So cheers to you all, especially the surprising ones!' I wonder if those words are directed to me? He raises his glass to a big applause with the backdrop of clinking and crashing glasses again. Amongst the adrenalin and the Pimm's, people are a little bit squiffy now. Much jubilance fills the air and everyone is in high spirits. People are nattering about the next game, if they'll be involved etc. etc. I zone out a little, the alcohol has temporarily sedated my lack of sleep. Mel is jabbering on about the jelly ball people to some of the crew and how she nearly puked up when she saw one, Jet is enjoying (not flirting, I might add) the attention of some of the make-up girls, Alastair and Jake are talking incessantly about something or other, Brian is nowhere to be seen. I just stand and listen to snippets of many other conversations blurring in and out of my sub-consciousness.

I hear someone calling my name.

I wheel round and stare incredulously at the familiar figure striding towards me.

'Adam!' I blink rapidly, my eyelids almost spasm. 'What are you doing here?'

'Wow, Eve, you look incredible.'

I can't breath. I can't move. I can only stare.

'I know I've been an idiot and I know it's going to be hard for you to forgive me, but I miss you.'

I look around the room and I can see Jake watching us but he's too far away.

'I need to speak to you. I've come to ask you something.'

There's gasping nearby, the room is falling quiet, Adam is already down on one knee and I can feel everyone watching, a few people start nudging each other.

I stare at him in astonishment.

'What are you doing?' I whisper through gritted teeth.

'Isn't it obvious?'

'Get up!' I command lowly, my face boiling like a furnace.

But he's not listening.

'I know I fucked up. And not just by what I did but also by not realizing how truly amazing you are. You are incredible and I need you in my life… erw, ow.'

I drag Adam by the arm and lead him out into the corridor. I can't bear anymore of this performance, my skin is bubbling with anger.

'Adam you shouldn't be here? In fact how did you know where to find me?'

'Lucy gave me this address after I pleaded.'

'You should have rang first.'

'Oh, I thought you'd appreciate a romantic gesture in public,' he shrugs.

'Yeah I'm all for public humiliation as you well know!' I'm fuming beyond words, not sure if I'm going to boil over at any moment. He just looks at me as if I'm the mad one.

I take a huge calming breath, 'What was your thought process behind this grand, misguided gesture? Was it… no…' I hold my hand up for him to shut up or be slapped. 'Was it something along the unimaginative lines of "lets just pick up where we left off?" Are you bored of shirts not being washed by themselves?'

'I miss you,' he says meekly.

'You said you weren't sure how you feel about me. You said you need to concentrate on your career.'

'I made a mistake.'

'Yes you did.'

He gives me a half-smile.

'I love you. I want to marry you.'

He looks as if he's going to go down on bended knee again and I stop him.

'No, Adam. Don't.'

'Too soon?'

'No, rather too late!'

'I love you. I love the way you try and organise me, and the way you look when your hair goes funny in the mornings, and the way you always burn your toast but nimble round the edges anyway. I just like the way you make me feel. I want to be around you, I've neglected everything wonderful around me, and that everything was you Eve.'

Flipping heck that's pretty romantic. I'm suddenly not sure how to respond to such a heart bleed; this isn't the Adam I left.

He gazes lovingly at me, and just for a moment I am moved, but then my body prickles and I need him to understand.

'Adam, you humiliated me on camera and in front of the people I work with. How can someone who's so enamoured by me do such a treacherous thing to someone they love?' 'What can I say? I…I wasn't thinking straight.'

I'm silent for a minute while I get my words in order. 'You were right to do it. Not in front of everyone, that I could have done without,' I say finally. 'But the space helped me figure out a few things. I don't love you. I told you on the phone that it was over.'

Adam looks bewildered. 'I thought you were just angry.'

'I was. I am.'

'I don't understand. You said I'm "The One".'

'Yes, well, I was wrong.' I shrug. 'It must have been the hormones kicking in or sheer madness. Momentary lunacy!' I know this will irritate him. He hates it when women blame hormones for emotional revelations or reactions. 'I don't love you Adam. We were never meant to be forever,' I am being kinder than he was to me.

'You really mean that?'

'Yes. I do.'

'Is it because of the money?'

My body tenses and I stare back at him.

'I only took it because my parents refused to loan me anymore and I couldn't get the overdraft.'

'Money? Money for what?' My voice sounds strangled.

'£5,000 to break up with you on camera.'

'You took £5,000 to break up with me?'

Adam's face goes bright red.

'We were going through a rough patch. I needed the space. I was feeling smothered. I thought you knew!'

'Adam, who gave you the money?'

'That man with the big belly.'

'Brian?'

'That's the one.'

'I think you should go.'

'But what will I do without you?'

'I'm sure you'll survive. Go for a bike ride, clear your head, with five thousand pounds in your pocket I don't really care.'

I plaster a smile on my face as I push open the door and return to the wrap party. Inside I am beyond rage, I am beyond my own control, I feel murderous.

Jake is still talking with Alastair and yet as soon as I step into the room his attention focuses on me. My head is whirling with this new information. Who knew about the transaction, this filthy deal? Did Jake know?

'Hey! Was that Adam proposing?' Mel whispers in my ear.

'Yes.'

'I hope you told him where to go?'

'I did,' my voice rising in distress.

'Is that why you look like you want to murder something or someone?'

I know I have to confide in someone otherwise I'll burst at the seams.

'Do you want me to get you a drink?' She says intuitively.

My face must look scarily thunderous (thank you Mother for that gene) because Mel runs off sharply as my breathing becomes odder. I wonder if I'm going to do a Stacey and just fall to the floor. My mind spins, my thoughts are broken, nothing makes sense. Well it all makes sense.

I was used – by everyone.

How can people you trust act so vile, how can they play with your emotions as though you are nothing more than paid entertainment?

Mel returns with two large glasses of wine. I down mine in one go.

'Apparently Brian paid Adam £5k to dump me?'

Mel jaw hangs to the floor. 'That's impossible. Only the contestants get a fee. Nothing was paid to your ex.'

'That's where your wrong. Adam just told me.'

Mel's face changes expression. 'I'll be right back,' she takes my empty glass and thrusts her full one into my sweaty hand.

Everyone breaks into a round of applause but I have no idea why. I clap along politely and try to look interested when I spot Brian stepping to the mike.

'Darlings, darlings, my wonderful fellow beings of joy.' What a phoney creature he is. He makes me sick to my gut.

'The entertainment isn't over yet.' He holds his arms out for effect until everyone stops talking. 'Hang on a little while more, the bar's open all night. I just wanted to share something with you.'

'Haven't you had enough fanfare Brian, get on with it, anyone would think you wanted to be in front of the camera!' Alastair heckles, wobbling slightly.

'Quite Alastair, though not me, I'm soundly content with a few solitary sliding moments on stage, but some of us, well, some of us we like to perform don't we?' He waits for a universal crowd "*YEAH!*"

Now he's got the crowd riled up, he walks to the front of the stage and reveals something in his hand. 'I've just been handed this wonderful clip from a time before. Not so shy as they seem, some people in the background crew that is.'

My body goes cold, my face filling with horror as I see myself appear larger than life on screen.

Mel has returned and I can feel her curious eyes on me as she looks at the screen then at me.

How did he… How could he? My entire body clenches in horror.

All I can do is watch myself, in all my re-run "*Ri-ri*" un-glory, mouth open, and utterly soul destroyed. Time bends, all voices are dull. I can't tear myself away from the screen. Everyone is in hysterics holding their sides, pointing then staring at me.

'You go girl.' someone shouts from the front.

'You getting sexy back.' Another voice shouts from the fast-blending crowd.

The audience is a mass of commentary, I feel nauseous. They start merging at the edges, a sea of hair melding into one. I think I'm going to keel over any second.

'That girl is fly.' I hear one of the cameramen shout. My eyes are wide open with humiliation. I can't even close them even if I tried, shock has disintegrated any bodily function. I'm numb. My humiliation knows no depths; its fathoms keep revealing themselves winning each time, strengthening their grip on me. I cannot fight the dark forces around me. Maybe mother is right, join a group and disappear into the bible, spouting shite to others. Absolve all responsibility of your own thoughts, actions and succumb to a scapegoat of chosen lobotomies.

But I know what's coming next, as the crescendo of my performance is on the cusp of pure horror. There's an almighty gasp as the tsunami surfaces on screen, my curtain call, and my moment of film fame. I hear a huge roar of laughter and I bury my face in my hands. I would run but I am paralysed with shock.

I think I am going to be sick, well it's about time for a sequel. As I look up I see Jake looking at the screen then at me. I have no idea what he thinks, but Alastair looks livid.

When the clip finishes, everyone stares at me as though they're expecting me to do something. Most faces are enjoying the spectacle, though some faces are sympathetic. I'm too dazed to think of anything, paralysed with the shame yet again.

'It was the Tequila, ok.' I manage, as everyone continues to gawp at me.

Mel is not laughing, she's looking at me with an expression that says "I'm glad I'm not you."

'Laugh,' she says.

Dazedly I try, but feel like I might hurl too.

I didn't think people could be this cruel.

'And drink this.'

She hands me Swiss Franc's glass and I take one swift gulp, some weird European schnapps disguising itself as whiskey. Bleurgh.

'Isn't that what people drink when they're in shock?' She asks me.

'Is it? Yuk.'

'Enough of the speeches, lets get on and party,' says Alastair swiping the mike away.

Everyone is still laughing, huddling together and making a wild stab in the dark – talking about me. The room seems to be getting smaller, people are approaching, shit what do I do? I'm surrounded. Where's that flipping sinkhole hiding? Then a most peculiar thing happens, men start winking in my direction and women start cheering me then the whole crowd bursts into a song.

"For she's jolly good fellow, for she's a jolly good fellow, for she's a jolly good F-e-l-LOW and thanks for making us laugh!" My stomach settles down, perhaps my little policed incident isn't such a big deal anymore, but I still feel tainted, tarred and terrible.

Gut-wrenchingly embarrassed.

'Do you want to get out of here?' Mel whispers in my ear.

I nod. Mel grabs hold of my arm and we walk out the room together. I'm slightly unsteady on my spindly heels already, but that's not the only reason I stare at the floor. I just don't want to look at anyone. I don't want to know what they're thinking. Unfortunately the gods are conspiring against me. Brian is lurking in the foyer, presumably pre-empting my escape route and positioning himself for one last gloat.

'Leaving so soon?' He's so sickeningly pleased with himself.

I look him straight in the eye. I have to ask. 'Why did you do it?'

'What? Can't take a joke!' he says.

Suddenly I don't feel intimidated by him, I have nothing

more to lose or hide.

'You're not a very nice person,' actually I can do better than that. 'I'm curious, what sort of pleasure do you derive from making everyone around you hate your guts?'

Mel gives me a "way to go" grin! Brian looks like he's about to burst an eye socket. 'Does it make you feel better about yourself?'

'Much better now that a little upstart has been put in her place,' he shrugs.

'You know what, Brian? Alastair deserves better than you.'

'I quite agree,' a new voice interrupts from behind.

My stomach churns as we all whip round to see Alastair standing there.

'Brian you've gone too far this time,' he says wearily.

'Oh it was just a joke,' laughs Brian.

'Yes, I can see Eve is really enjoying the "joke."'

Brian shrugs. He couldn't care less about my feelings, or anyone's feelings for that matter. I look Brian straight in the eye and keep my gaze there, unflinching. 'I should have you up at a tribunal for bullying.'

'Me too,' blurts out Mel.

'Oh pipe down girls!' groans Brian. 'Have you both had a humour bypass? Is it the time of the month?'

I exhale sharply. 'You are the most abhorrent person I have ever met.'

'And your breathe smells of pickling vinegar,' Mel says, then claps a hand to her mouth, as if she can't believe she said that out loud.

'Amateurs. Idiots. Fucking women…' Brian streams off a whole list of profanities laced with insults personal and to the general population.

'ENOUGH Brian!' Alastair's voice bellows a shout and we all jump. 'Why do I even bother!' He shakes his head as if realising something for the first time. 'I thought you might apologise for your behaviour, but instead you hurl insults. How about you call it a night and we will talk about this tomorrow.'

'You're taking sides with inconsequential nobodies?'

'Oh do shut up Brian.'

There's a long, tense pause when Brian stares at Alastair furiously.

'Brian we've known each other for a long time but you will never change. You will always be the spiteful, vindictive thirteen year old I met at school blaming everyone else but yourself. You are a bitter, twisted individual and I've let you pollute my life, my business, for far too long.'

'Screw you… you pathetic old man,' Brian shouts. He takes a swing at Alastair, but Alastair is quicker and punches him straight on the nose. Brian's face is one of disbelief as he stumbles backwards, tripping over a rug and falling onto the floor, blood dripping from his nose. He looks at me from behind his fingers and I see pure hatred in his eyes as if this is somehow my fault.

'You haven't heard the last from me,' he says, picking himself up off the floor, clutching his bleeding nose.

'I'm counting on it,' Alastair snarls.

We watch him leave, routed to the spot trying to get our heads around what just happened.

'I'm sorry I got arrested,' I sigh. 'I'm sorry I didn't like your script and… well thank you for everything. You've been a fantastic boss and I'm sorry.' Alastair regards me for a second, his face unreadable and my world starts sinking within my digestive tract, and I feel like I want to be sick.

'That's good because you're pretty fantastic yourself, really quite extraordinary. Besides, I've done far worse in my days. Once I blew up a cop's car and got sent to the slammer for a week!'

'You never did!' I exclaim, all feeling of sickness gone.

'Brian used something from my past and I was too weak to stand up to him at that time, he preyed on my nervous breakdown, my parents would have disowned me if they found out I was gay. I won't stand for it now. Even though it didn't matter, I kept him on staff because I was a bit of a naughty boy, well I was a fruity fruitcake let us leave it at that. We might not have had mobile phones but cine-film is also damning. I truly sympathise Eve.'

Mel and I are open-mouthed.

'I looked terrible with leather hot-pants and antlers! Always had a podgy tum, antlers do nothing for podgy cheeks either.'

I cough a giggle at the thought of Alastair as a kinky starlet. Alastair pulls us in for a hug.

'Those Antlers in your office?' I manage to pipe up.

'Yes the very same. He hung them there. The sight of them was daily torture. A sadistic reminder.'

I lean over and give Alastair a hug. Mel hugs him too and the three of us stand there hugging.

'Please don't start calling me Rudolph!'

We laugh.

'Thank you Eve. Thank you Mel, I'm sorry it was bad for so long.' He shakes his head and clears his throat. 'Why don't you both forget this… unpleasantness and go and enjoy yourselves, it is a party after all. Be young for heaven's sake!'

But I don't' really feel like celebrating. I can't bear to face

Jake. I just need to lick my wounds in private.

'You go and celebrate. I'm just going back to our room for a bit.' I say to both of them.

'Look I'm sure everyone's forgotten about the clip, besides they're too busy laughing at Jet's attempts to be the Pimm's fountain,' he says.

'It's not that,' I lie. 'Maybe I'll come down in a little while.' They both look like they're going to try and convince me otherwise so I plaster a smile on my face and quickly walk away.

CHAPTER TWENTY-FIVE

I let myself into my room, kick off my shoes and flop down onto the bed. I stare into space for a bit then sit up, feeling a surge of irritation. How dare Brian spoil my night, I should just go back downstairs and party with everyone. And what about Adam? In the daze of all that has happened I almost forgot that he proposed tonight!

I raid the minibar and pick out a mineral water, and morosely pour it into a glass I then pull out my mobile and go through my missed messages. There's a voicemail from mum, asking for legal terms to use in her letter to Zaido or whatever his or her name was. I'll deal with that later. There's also a text from Nell.

Can't wait for your schedule to lighten up. The olds are driving me potty.

I reply:

Now you know what it's like to be the close-proximity daughter of doom!

The other text is from Lucy.

Are you still alive? Haven't bought a stich for the funeral, but be that on your own head if you still have one. I mean, an ancient French ghost could have severed you with a guillotine but how would I know? Call me. Luv u xxx

I glance at my watch. It's nearly midnight but I know she won't mind; it's Saturday and she's never in bed until late. I pick up my mobile and dial, only Chuck picks up?

'Er, Chuck, sorry I thought I was dialling Lucy's...' I stare at the mobile blankly.

'One second.'

'Hiya, what's up,' Lucy's voice giggles down the phone.

'What's up? I think I should be asking you what's up. Why is Chuck picking up your phone?'

'Oh he's erm fixing my… my computer,' she giggles. Lucy isn't much of a giggler and I'm onto her.

'On a Saturday night at flipping midnight!'

'Oh is it?' She clears her throat and reins in her voice. 'Anyway, why are you calling this late?'

'Oh no you don't, you don't get to wriggle out of this one. I smell horse…'

'It must be important otherwise you wouldn't call me so late,' she interrupts.

Well if she won't share, I will. So I begin to tell her about tonight's debacle and she is outraged on my behalf. I knew it was a good idea to ring. I'm just finishing off telling her about Brian storming off when – I pull the phone from my ear and stare at it in shock.

Lucy and Chuck are either playing vigorous tennis or gobbling food down like gluttonous vultures –

'I can hear you!' I shout down the phone. 'I'll phone you when you're both less occupied with COMPUTERS!'

I hang up, stare at my phone and start laughing. Oh it feels good to laugh.

So Lucy and Chuck. Well that was so meant to happen? I wonder how it happened?

I take out my pen and write in my notebook "question Lucy about Chuck". My handwriting is a swirly mess. I sip my Gin & Tonic calmly. Just thinking about Lucy and Chuck together makes me smile, although I would have rather not heard them. My mind turns to Jake and how happy he made me feel, then quickly remind myself not to think about him. Oh God, I can't believe he saw my *YouTube* debacle. Hang on. Was that the door? I listen intently. Another knock, this time louder.

My heart pinballs round my ribcage. It must be Jake. Who else could it be? Mel's got her own key. I pinch my cheeks, run a hand through my hair - not too bad for a broken woman. I hurry to the door -

'Adam! Not you again!'

I go to shut the door, but he stops it with his hand.

'Eve. We need to talk.'

'We've said all we need to say.'

'Please, I beg.'

Ooh, begging, that sounds like something I'd like to see. I open the door and step out into the corridor. 'Ok. You have one minute.' I fold my arms.

'I should never have done that to you.'

'What, splitting up with me or taking £5000 to do just that?'

'Both. I should have kept… I mean married you when I had the chance. I'm sorry.'

For a moment, I'm silent. 'Are you for real? Look, how else can I say this, I don't love you.'

'You don't really mean that. We're good together. Adam and Eve, we're meant to be together. We can pick up where we left off and put all this silliness behind us.' He leans in to kiss me and I pull away.

'Silliness. Public humiliation is just silly to you, isn't it?' He looks confused as I push him away with my fist. 'Yeah, let's get back together. I miss all the ignoring, self-centred bullshit. '

'But if we don't get back together would I have to give the money back?'

I'm thunderstruck. 'Unfuckingbelievable!'

'What?' He looks at me with his stupid droopy pale eyelashes and I think I might actually kill him.

'You should go now Adam.'

'It's a lot of money –'

'Just fuck off will you,' I say, unable to stand it any longer.

'No need to get nasty –'

'How about you prescribe yourself some blue pills and try and fuck your way out of a paper bag. Don't advertise yourself as a man, it's against trading standards. I've had more fun picking scabs than being with you,' the anger whirlwinds in me.

He raises his hand. 'Why do you–'

'Eve.'

I wheel round and see Jake steaming down the corridor.

'Jake!' I yelp.

'Is everything ok?' Jake eyeballs Adam mafia style.

'This is personal business, butt out!' Adam snaps indignantly.

But Jake ignores Adam and looks straight at me, his eyes burning intensely that I feel I might go up in flames.

'Eve wants you to leave.'

'Who are you to tell me what to do?'

Jake flexes his muscles, grabs Adam by the scruff of his collar and pins him to the wall.

He contemplates for a moment as Adam's eyes nearly drop out of his head.

'I'm someone who actually cares for Eve. Now go before you regret it.'

Jake steps forward and Adam retreats like a bad smell, huffing and puffing down the corridor. He looks to retaliate, and then runs as Jake actually growls at him.

Wow. I'm flabbergasted. He looks so completely and utterly macho that I feel quite faint.

'Are you okay? Did he hurt you?'

'I'm fine,' I say in a wobbly voice. Adrenalin disperses from my body and I begin to shake. Jake steadies me.

For a moment we stand there, Jake gazing at me, and me staring back at him – my whole body aching for his touch.

'Why did you rush off like that?'

I don't really know what to say. 'The video thing put a dampener on things.' I give a shaky laugh.

'Making a fool of yourself at least once is a rite of passage.'

'That's what I tell myself, but everyone has now seen my bum,' I whisper in horror.

'And a very fine bum it is.'

I giggle. Even in this dark hour he manages to cheer me up.

'If it makes you feel better, when I was at university I drank a bottle of Jack, got stark naked except from a bowler hat, threw up in the sacred library and passed out on my professor whilst he was in full throws of reprimanding. I still have that bowler hat!'

'Did it appear on *YouTube*?'

'No but there's a photo of it somewhere in a year book.'

I gaze at him, happier now that he's here.

'So what now?'

'How about we retire to my room?'

'Retire?' I can't help giggling. 'It sounds so quaint.'

I cannot believe that with all that's happened tonight, all I can think about right now is Jake's naked, glorious body on top of mine.

Jake smacks my bottom while practically carrying me up the stairs caveman style into the room and throwing me on the bed.

Then we are kissing, first tenderly then fervently in passion. We can't keep our hands off each other, our hair is getting very ruffled and this kiss seems even more passionate than the ones preceding our naughty nights. It's hot and we're getting hotter.

Jake is like floating on a flotilla of pleasure bombs - more get planted each time I explode in ecstasy.

We lie down next to each other, stroking each other's bodies and talking about everything and anything. He tells me about growing up in LA, his parents being actors and how he spent his childhood on the movie sets. How he's always known he wanted to do hard-hitting documentaries but his parents thought he was mad, especially because he had the opportunities to make lavish films with all their contacts. They took him to a shrink because it wasn't right for a ten year old to be so serious and intent. It was devastatingly (his mother's words) unnatural and simply not magazine-feature worthy. He made his first documentary aged ten about Biff the Beetle who lived behind the barbecue in their garden.

It is great to finally have someone to speak to about the lunacy of parents. I tell him my parents would probably fit into America more than rural Berkshire. He concludes that parents should really learn that encouraging the opposite might get them what they want from the prodigies, but they're so hell bent on making mini me's to do that. I really laugh my socks off; well I would if I hadn't been stark naked. I divulge that "The Royal Tenenbaums" is my favourite film and I gush about my love for German director Wim Wenders.

We talk and talk and talk until sleep drifts into the conversation. My head buried in his chest, his hand stroking my hair until a small snore stops its conforming motion. I am on cloud nine. *That's my next slogan to wear*, I think to myself. My dreams are peaceful. I am truly peaceful.

CHAPTER TWENTY-SIX

Mel doesn't look the least bit surprised when I waltz into the room the following morning to grab a shower and some fresh clothes. Actually, on closer inspection, she's not doing or saying anything at all. She is fully dressed while lying very still on top of her bed.

'Mel, are you ok?'

She makes a whimpering mewing sound.

'My scalp hurts,' she finally croaks.

I let out a giggle. 'Would you like some water?'

'Yes please,' she whimpers.

I grab a bottle from the fridge and help Mel sit up.

'Oh God!' She groans, after taking a sip. 'I did cartwheels on the dance floor.'

'You're good at cartwheels.'

'But everyone would have seen my bum!'

'Welcome to my world! I'm sure they were too merry to notice.'

'I even did the splits.'

I'm impressed. 'You can do the splits?'

Mel groans miserably and puts her head in her hands. 'It

was Jet's fault, he brought out the tequila.'

Now I'm really glad I didn't stick around. Then I notice her face go really pale.

'Mel are you going to be sick?'

'I kissed Pete,' she whispers.

'The runner?'

Her moan turns into a loud squeal of anguish and she flops back down onto the bed, staring at the ceiling.

I giggle again, I can't help it. 'Oh honey, that's not so bad. It's not like you slept with him?' I look at her. 'You didn't, did you?'

'God no!' She pauses, as if she's double-checking with her hazy memory. 'Anyway where did you get to last night? Like we all don't know!'

My face splits into a wide grin. 'Come on let's get some breakfast. You'll feel better after you've eaten something.'

'I can't go down there, everyone will laugh at me.'

I giggle.

'I'm glad my mortification is amusing you.'

'Oh, like I know nothing about mortification?' I raise a brow.

'Oh yes, I forgot.' Suddenly, Mel perks up. 'Ok maybe some breakfast will do me good.'

There's hardly anyone down for breakfast so Mel and I are spared from any finger pointing.

After breakfast, we rush to finish the last of the packing and Mel seems a little bit better now that she's eaten. Well, she doesn't look like she's about to throw up anymore at least, just winces every time something is dropped. When Pete walks into the room she goes deathly pale, but manages to coolly order him to help the camera and lighting crew pack up their vans.

No one has mentioned my *YouTube* performance, but that might be because everyone is too busy dealing with their own hangovers. I take great pleasure in throwing out the copied DVD of me. Alastair thought I would be the best person to dispose of it.

'Dar da da dah, da dat de dar…' sings Mel.

I look up and Mel has put on a wedding gown. 'What are you doing?'

'It was Stacy's wedding dress, wardrobe forgot to pack it.'

'So you thought you'd try it on?'

'When in Rome and with so much romance in the air!'

I can't help giggling. It's a beautiful dress. I love the ruffles that cascade from the lower back to the floor and it has a swaying skirt. Mel does a cartwheel. 'Showoff.'

But when she is the right way up, I notice she's gone a deathly grey. She puts her hand to her mouth.

'Mel?'

'I shouldn't have done that. Quick!' she mumbles.

I scrabble for the zip and help Mel out of the dress, the next second she is bolting for the door.

Nothing worse than a tequila hangover.

I hold the dress up. It's quite light for a lot of dress. I love how the silk-satin feels against my fingers.

Slightly possessed, and without giving it another thought I step into the wedding dress, breathing in as I pull the slightly too small gown up over my waist. It's supremely feminine and figure flattering even if I'm a little scared to breathe too deeply and can't zip it up all the way. I love it. I feel like a princess. Just how I felt when I was a little girl trying on my mum's too big wedding dress. Goosebumps spring up on my arms.

There's a veil on Mel's desk so I pull that on too. I do a little twirl. Now if I could just do up the zip.

'That's pretty fancy attire for the office?'

'Jake!' I clutch at the veil but it slips out of my hand and onto the floor. 'I erm… I was… we were… just messing about.'

'You know it's bad luck to see the bride in her wedding dress,' Mel titters, walking in from behind. She looks decid-edly cheerier now that's she had a good vomit.

For a moment Jake gazes at me and I blush furiously. Oh God, I hope he's not weirded out by the wedding dress.

'Mel wore it first,' I say, giving her the evil eyes.

Slowly he walks towards me, an unreadable smile on his lips.

'I was just taking it off,' I say, reaching for the back of my dress as he stops right in front of me.

I look up and meet his eyes, feeling quite breathless doing so.

'What to do with an incurable romantic?' he says. There's a waiting silence and I can hear my heart thudding in my chest.

'Give them a remedy not a cure?' I hear myself say.

An odd expression comes to his face and I'm completely transfixed. I'm unable to tear my gaze away. I know his views on marriage and the last thing I should be thinking about is marrying, and yet – no! Stop. It's enough that I have met some-one who makes me feel at ease and that should be enough for a twenty-something and yet – stop it! I give Jake a big smile, before I say something stupid. Suddenly Jake grabs my waist and swings me around.

'What are you doing?' I yelp.

'Dancing.'

'You two aren't going to be unbearable to be around are

you?' Mel says, picking up the veil before one of us trample on it.

'Probably sickening Mel,' Jake replies, as he waltzes me around the room, careful to avoid the stacked boxes. I've always wanted to waltz.

'Oh right then, I'll grab some carrier bags for the journey back then,' she quips.

Jake sweeps me round the room like a pro and I try not to giggle or trip over my own feet. It's all very surreal, and I do feel a bit like a Disney princess but it does feel incredibly romantic.

Epilogue

As if I'd leave it there. Love is definitely in the air. Nell chose Mr Wednesday lunchman in the end because he's far hotter than Mr Friday even though Mr Friday's wallet was bigger. His name is Ron, Ron Burgundy, I kid you not. It's his actual real name. He's not a bit like the film character though, but still odd to think he shares the name. Nell is finally getting the break she deserves, Jake put her in touch with a really cool casting agent and she's got a part in an upcoming indie flick, plus we've cast her in our Short, so onwards and upwards.

Lucy and Chuck are officially an item and I've never seen her so starry-eyed and happy, and noticeably less spikey about marriage and love these days.

Mum and Dad have recently removed themselves from charlatan TV, unsubscribed from Sky and enrolled in a "safe" computer course. They're focusing on the parish and their own community. The cat is still causing carnage, Dippy Delilah was looking after Pastor Pickle's budgie for a couple of weeks and the poor creature lost all its feathers from the stress of being swiped at by claws every minute of the day.

And me -

Well it's been quite a year, hasn't it! I feel like a totally different person to the messy 'Prozac' bait I was at the beginning of the year. Just goes to show that as long as you are true to yourself everything will work out in the end. At least you owe it to yourself to give it a shot.

As for what's in store for this New Year, for Jake and I? Well, I take each day as it comes, and there's Paris. Yes. Paris. Jake and I are seeing the New Year in the most romantic city in the world. We're actually at the airport. Jake is queuing up for lattes and I run an appreciative letch over him. I'm always doing this but he really is good to leer at. Judging by the appreciative glances I'm not the only female (or male) to think so. As if sensing me watching him he turns around and rolls his eyes ruefully. The queue is taking so long.

So long in fact that I've managed to complete another list. I've been reading an issue in a magazine, "100 Things I Love About My partner". It should be easy to just keep naming things until you hit 100. Because when you're in a relationship that is real and solid, even the tiniest things should get noticed. Well you know how much I love a list and I thought I'd give it a go.

The Things I Love About My Partner.

1. I love that you smell of Orange Musk.
2. The fact that you have a favourite colour, and it's green.
3. How often you tell me that I am beautiful.
4. How you keep the same grip on my hand whether we are alone or in public.
5. Your smile.
6. The way you place your hand on the base of my

spine.

7. Your generosity.
8. Your honesty.
9. How funny you think I am (even when I'm not trying to be.)
10. All the nicknames you make up for me. Like Madame Pootiff and Lady Lush.
11. That you're a good listener.
12. How you make me tingle all over.
13. Your kisses.
14. How well you get along with Lucy and Nell.
15. How well you get on with my parents (even though they thought and addressed you as the American Lawyer for two months, asking how they could get their money back from Ziah!)
16. How athletic you are and yet you never go to the gym.
17. Your body... yum yum yum.
18. Your sexiness.
19. How you get mad when I'm late, yet you're always late.
20. When you're tired and can't be bothered to shave.
21. How you look perfect by my side.
22. The way you walk.
23. How you bend over with laughter at some of my Berkshire colloquialisms.
24. The way you wake up in the morning and the first thing you do is hug me.
25. How at ease you are in declaring your love every-day.
26. How easily you can make me laugh.

27. The way you surprise me with little things, like this weekend away.
28. Your lips.
29. The contents of your pants.
30. That the picture on your phone is you and I kissing.
31. How tight you hold me when you kiss me, so I can never escape.
32. Your encouragement.
33. The way you text me just to say hey and see how my day is going.
34. That you don't snore loudly.
35. That you don't own a bike.
36. How confident you are in yourself, without being vain.
37. Your dress sense.
38. That you enjoy your space and give me mine.
39. That you get involved with real people's problems and try to make a difference. (making documentaries out of your own money to highlight real issues.)
40. How you love it when I wear heels.
41. The way you get carried away in your story-telling.
42. Your intelligence.
43. How you're passionate about the things you do.
44. How you suck at skeet shooting (Ditto... see No. 27.)
45. How good you are at everything you do (except skeet shooting.)
46. The fact that you're as competitive as I am,

without having the necessary skills to be that competitive. You don't mind making an arse of yourself for fun.

47. How adorable you are when you iron your clothes.
48. The fact that you love anything that makes me happy, even my music tastes, which are flitting and random.
49. How your eyes squint when you smile too hard.
50. How well you remember little things.
51. How easily you turn me on.
52. How hot you look.
53. ...

'What are you writing?'

I slam my notepad shut. 'Nothing!'

Jake grins, putting our lattes on the table.

'Another list?'

He knows me so well.

I suppose you might be wondering about the original list, the one that got me started. Well it's changed.

1. Become a successful film producer

As you know I'm producing a short film and we're start filming in two weeks. I'm also got assistant producer credit on my next job. So nearly there but not quite.

2. Always wear matching bra and knickers in case of unforeseen circumstances, whether that is A&E or a lucky night out!

Well the A&E propelled me into life again in a convoluted kind of way.

3. Learn Spanish or French.

I have been brushing up my French GCSE for this trip.

4. ~~Move out of parents house. Pronto~~
5. ~~Conveniently loose family cat to a farm needing a willing murderer for vermin.~~

I think I have finally come to accept that the family cat is here to stay.

6. ~~Have lots of sex.~~

Yes, Jake and I are creatively active on that front.

7. ~~Re-read books from college.~~

I've striked this off this list because I now have an independent reading list and I've completed my first read, *Lord of the Flies*. At first I thought it was really boring, but I'm glad I stuck with it. Next on my reading list is *Of Mice and Men*, although I haven't bought it with me. I don't plan on doing any reading this weekend.

8. ~~Sleep under the stars.~~

Jake and some of our closest friends took off to Wales and we all slept outside on a clear night with hats on, watching shooting stars.

9. ~~Have lots of good sex.~~

I don't think I could ever go back to how it was before. Not with Jake anyway. The sex is amazing. It should always be amazing.

10. Go to Vegas and have a moment "what goes on in Vegas stays in Vegas."

Pending.

11. ~~Drink responsibly on nights out. (Try to). Perhaps have the right intentions pre third cocktail at least!~~

What it should say is. Don't drink Tequila.

12. Kiss on top of the Eiffel Tower.

Hopefully I will get to do this on this trip. We're boarding soon!

13. ~~Master a one-handed cartwheel.~~

14. ~~Own a pair of Jimmy Choos or Manolos.~~

15. ~~Girls only holiday clubbing in Ibiza.~~

One week in August all booked.

16. Take a road trip without planning every detail.

Pending!

17. Learn to bake (ok cook in general).

I made Jake an apple pie the other day and burnt most of it. He ate a mouthful from the middle, bless him, but I've still got a way to go before Masterchef comes knocking.

18. Learn to spell without auto-correction on.

Not a frekkin chance!

19. ~~Treat my sister to a session at a recording studio.~~

Thanks to her film debut she's recording and getting paid to sing from some famous Jazz producer.

20. Learn how to fold clothes nicely so everything doesn't look like it's made out of crepe paper.

Still hopeless.

21. Marry.

Not sure that's going to happen for while or at all.

22. Buy an apartment.

Well the current government have a *Help to Buy ISA* and every £200 you put in they give you an extra £50. I've put in £200, so I've currently saved £250.00!

23. ~~Learn to take opportunities when they arise, listen to your own voice and don't cower to people (refers to big A-hole Brian).~~

No one has heard or seen Brian since he left and the office has become a happier, positive environment as a result.

24. ~~Get brave and tell my parents I'm an atheist.~~

Thank heavens I did it otherwise they'd be penniless!

25. ~~Get a hobby.~~ (Refer to independent hobby list.)

Jake bought me a mushroom kit for my birthday. I've already ruined it – over watering.

26. Remember unlisted things and save time by not writing so many lists, it's getting a bit OCD.

Cough. It's how I function.

27. Take Rampant Rabbit for a spin.

I still haven't taken it for a spin. Jake has been keeping me more than satisfied, but I'm glad it's there, tucked away in my knickers drawer should the time come when I want to have a go. I think women should have as many orgasm-inducing options at their disposal as possible.

28. Read Kama Sutra.
Top of my reading list!

29. Try something new
Well I'm thinking of letting Jake film me doing a striptease. Risqué but it's something new…

'Eve. We're boarding.' Jake kisses the nape of my neck and I feel an instant bolt of lust. Yes, I am *totally* going to striptease for him tonight.

I brush my lips against his mouth

'What was that for?'

'Just happy,' I sigh.

'Me too,' He says and we kiss again. We don't come up for air for some time so much so that we have to make a dash for our gate.

I have something new to add to my list.

30. Join the mile high club?
Pending!

The End

Acknowledgements

Firstly we would like to say a colossal hearty pirate thank you to Stephanie Reed for wanting to publish our book. It's phenomenal to work with you. To the team at So Vain Books for taking care of everything else and making the whole process a delight, and so much more velvety than even the best chocolate.

Thank you to our family and friends who have promised to buy the book. Yes we will be checking!

And of course, to our fantastic readers who've stuck with us through the proof and the non proofread phase, you're inspirational and that's why we do it. Big hugs to you all for reading our books, for your enthusiasm and kind reviews (even if there were commas flying out at you in odd places). It's what keeps us going, that and those copious cups of tea that keep promising to turn into bubbles when the next few chapters are written!